TIME
OFF
FROM
GOOD
BEHAVIOR

Also by Susan Sussman

The Dieter

Published by POCKET BOOKS

TIME
OFF
FROM
GOOD
BEHAVIOR

SUSAN SUSSMAN

POCKET BOOKS

New York   London   Toronto   Sydney   Tokyo   Singapore

POCKET BOOKS, a division of Simon & Schuster Inc.
1230 Avenue of the Americas, New York, NY 10020

Sussman, Susan.
   Time off from good behavior / Susan Sussman.
      p.   cm.
      ISBN: 0-671-68516-3 : $20.00
      I. Title.
   PS3569.U814T56   1991
   813'.54—dc20   91-18586
                                             CIP

First Pocket Books hardcover printing October 1991

10 9 8 7 6 5 4 3 2 1

For my beloved mother, Edie Rissman, née Ida Leavitt, 1912–1990, whose courageous battle against illness this past year played painful counterpoint to the writing of this book.

Acknowledgments

To the many wonderful people I have called, written, and otherwise imposed upon in search of primary source material, thank you for sharing memories and knowledge and allowing me to invade your respective worlds. Please forgive the places where I have molded your facts to fit my fiction.

Costumers: Elizabeth Passman, Mickey Antonetti, Jennifer Jobst, Marcia Fink, Sue Saltmarsh; Illinois Film Bureau; "Father Jim" Production Company; the Campbell Soup Company, Napoleon, Ohio; Rabbi Arnold Rachlis; Storytellers Robin Goldberg and Hon. Emanuel A. Rissman; Lyric Opera Publicist Danny Newman; Attorneys Arthur Rissman and Kenneth H. Denberg; computer wizard Aaron Sussman; Yiddish translator Anita E. Abraham; Actress Sarajane Avidon; theater maven Sy Sussman; Auld Reekies expert Steven Rissman; designers Barbara Munic and Vivian Maroff; Reanne Berman, author *How to Survive Your Aging Parents;* Kaye and Joe Rotskoff. I am also indebted to my agent Jane Jordan Browne and editor Jane Chelius for their gentle humor and constant support. And, as always, my special love to Barry, who unselfishly offered to research Asher's Time Off. Nice try.

TIME
OFF
FROM
GOOD
BEHAVIOR

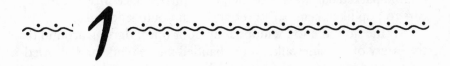

1

A miracle! A day of miracles!

Careful, Sarah. Good luck spits if you look in its face.

Still, I remembered to have Asher's suit cleaned and ready for his meeting. Then, the Nabisco people approved my costumes for the Krispy Korn commercial. *Then,* Fanny was actually dressed and waiting in her lobby when I came to pick her up. And, most miraculous of all, a car pulled away from in front of Miller's Meat Market the exact moment Fanny and I pulled up.

Careful.

I folded my station wagon into the compact's space. Fanny unknotted her diamond-studded head scarf and patted her stiffly sprayed hair, searching for strays. Please God, let me finish shopping with Fanny, feed her, take her home by one-thirty, two the absolute latest, and I will never ever ask you for another favor. Marko Fazio, I'm talkin' 'bout *the* Marko Fazio, invited me for an interview at three o'clock. Please.

Fanny struggled with her seat belt.

"Mom, why don't you wait in the car while I get the meats?" Hey, Sarah! Great idea!

"I am still able to pick out my own meats, thank you." She yanked the belt violently.

"Ma, I didn't mean—" I reached over and released her buckle. "I just meant there's no place for you to sit down in Miller's."

"And why should I sit? I'm buying meat, not paying a social call."

Fanny pulled out her compact. Alert! Alert! Full battle gear; there are men on the horizon. She patted powder on her powdered face, drew lipstick on her painted mouth. I gripped the door handle, waiting for a break in the Devon Avenue traffic. Careful. It would be a pity to be killed on such an important day.

All around me, cars meandered over double yellow lines, traveled east in the westbound, stopped mid-street to drop off and pick up passengers. In this one-mile strip between California and Western avenues, in this crossroad linking Israel, India, Mexico, China, Pakistan, and Eastern Europe, all rules of the civilized road were suspended. Vienna Beef trucks double-parked across from double-parked Sari World trucks, clogging the aged artery, forcing cars to pop like aneurysms over curbs and onto sidewalks.

Traffic slowed and I whipped my door open, darting around to the safety of the sidewalk. Fanny handed me her cane and allowed me to help her out of the car. Hardly any weight to her anymore. Shouldn't she be gaining it back by now? I'd call Dr. Fishman tomorrow.

Fanny walked through Miller's' door, leaning heavily on the cane. She had walked from her lobby to my car without using it once. Ah, the elixir of a rising curtain to an aging actress. She stopped just inside the door, waiting. Chin up, shoulders back, regal yet benevolent. No one noticed. No matter, she would wait. Me too. The daughter of an actress knows better than to rush an entrance.

Women shopping for the Sabbath meal jostled for position through the three narrow aisles. Fanny didn't move from the door. Another nervous flip of my stomach.

"Mom, maybe I should get in the meat line and . . ."

"Just [beat] a moment." She held up one hand, slowly pulling off her glove, finger by finger. Please let her be doing Queen Victoria. Miller's wasn't ready for a seventy-eight-year-old Gypsy Rose Lee. She finished the left glove and started the right. My stomach pains shuffled into double time. I had to play this carefully. If I rushed, she might draw out the performance. Ruven waved from behind the meat counter.

"Helloooo, Mrs. Feldman!" A blush deepened Fanny's rouge and ten years melted away. To be heralded by Ruven himself, across this particular crowded room, was like headlining at the Douglas Park Theatre. She took her first brave-but-weak step into the crowd. Ruven, I could kiss you.

I left Fanny at the meat counter and darted up and down the narrow aisles, loading my arms with the other items on her list.

On my way back, I picked up a jar of pickled herring. A little treat for Asher. Should I yes or should I no? So much salt. And the heartburn. Still, it's not every day a man sells his business. One little treat wasn't going to kill him. By the time I rejoined Fanny she'd captured center stage, neatly combining cane, chutzpah, and charm to go to the head of the line.

"So, Sarahlah?" Ruven winked.

"How're you doing, Ruven?"

"With such beauties in my store, how could I be doing? I'll just go get your lovely mother a fresh chicken from the back." He disappeared into the cavernous freezer, bypassing the sad sampling of plastic-wrapped meats in the display case. At Miller's, the regulars always bought "fresh from the back." And if it took a while for Ruven to emerge from the freezer, it meant he was taking time to look for the best. Time I didn't have. Not today.

"Is this your daughter?" The woman in line behind Fanny smiled at me. "Such a pretty girl."

"Thank you," I said. Fanny looked into the display case and became engrossed in a package of giblets.

"You're lucky to have such a nice daughter," continued the woman. Sorrowful head shake. Deep sigh ending with a faint "Oy." My mother wasn't the only actress on the premises. "My Francine lives two blocks from me. It might as well be two thousand blocks for all the good it does." Does who? Her? Me? Us? Come on outta the freezer, Ruven, I've got a life to live.

The woman, sensing a wider audience, played to the rest of the line. "My daughter has a full-time job. Leaves her two gorgeous babies with a sitter doesn't even talk English. If I didn't bring food, God knows what those angels would eat." An undercurrent of murmurs swelled like a Greek chorus.

Fanny, who had little use for other women, their problems, and especially their children, flashed her Helen Hayes grandmother smile and gripped my surprised arm.

"My Sarah works full-time, too. But [beat—sigh] some things are still important to her."

If I were Catholic, I'd be up for sainthood. The woman touched the sleeve of my coat and, blinking back tears, said, "God should only bless you for being so good to your mother." Not a dry eye in the house. I patted her hand comfortingly.

Ah, the joy of self-employment. How I longed for a Scrooge of a boss to shackle me to my desk until I put in a twelve-hour day.

Being self-employed meant never having to say "I can't come just now, Mother." Ruven brought two chickens, Fanny picked the cutest, and we said our good-byes. The seas parted as we paid our bill and walked out. A successful visit by anyone's standards. Even Fanny's.

I'd budgeted twenty minutes for Miller's. We'd run a few minutes over. So far so good. Next stop, Fashion Shoe Shoppe to return the same pair of shoes a third time. I really dreaded this one. Last week Mr. Seid warned Fanny that he absolutely, positively, without the *slightest* chance of changing his mind in this lifetime would not let her return *this* pair of shoes again. "Final sale," he said. "If you buy 'em, you eat 'em, pure and simple. Done. Finished. Kaput." It was the sort of challenge Fanny lived for. But my day of miracles held.

"Mr. Seid," explained the salesman, "has been called away on a family matter and will not be in."

"I hope it's nothing serious," said Fanny. "He's such a dear man." She sighed, opening the box. "I'd like to return these."

"Do you have your receipt?" *The* receipt whereupon Mr. Seid scrawled "DO NOT TAKE THESE BACK!!!!"? The receipt marked "FINAL SALE!!!!" in ink the color of blood? The receipt kept like a trophy in Fanny's wallet?

"Receipt? Oh, dear no. You see, these shoes were a gift from my son. He means well but he really doesn't know the first thing about women's fashion. These are an old lady's shoes. Hardly the sort of thing one would expect me to wear. Surely you can see that." She flattered, fawned, and finagled, swishing a hip here, touching a hand there. There were lessons to be learned at Fanny's knee. The man counted the refund into her gloved hand. Her skin, sallow as dish water when I picked her up, glowed vibrantly. Granted, the triumph would have been sweeter had she dealt with Mr. Seid himself. Fanny did leave him a little note of thanks. God forbid her victory went unnoticed.

I thought it kinder not to mention to the nice salesman that my mother had no son. In fact, if he had looked at me more closely, studied the slight twitch starting under my left eye, listened for the muted grinding of clenched teeth, he would have seen quite clearly that I, Sarah Rose, was Fanny Feldman's only child.

2

"You're not eating." The smell of spilled dill pickle juice, aging meat, and rotting veggies rolled out from her refrigerator. I tossed last week's cottage cheese, whitefish, hamburger meat, hard rolls, sweet rolls, and other barely touched groceries, and stocked in a fresh supply.

"I'm eating. I'm eating." Fanny sat on the edge of a kitchen chair, watching me work, pretending she could see what I was doing.

"Mom, you're not—"

"Sha! I eat when I'm hungry."

"I'm putting the other half of your sandwich in here." I held up the giant tuna on a kaiser roll left from our lunch at The Bagel. She had eaten only half of a half.

Why should a broken hip make her lose her appetite? Before the accident—"So I slipped in the shower. It happens"—Fanny ate like a construction worker, fueling up for her daily jaunts downtown. She'd check in with the casting companies, read for parts, go on cattle calls, take work as movie extras. Not a hell of a lot of jobs for a seventy-eight-year-old actress, even one who only admitted to seventy.

Everything changed with the accident. The fall broke something more than her hip. A couple of weeks in the hospital followed by a slow recuperative period in my home left a mark on her psyche that wouldn't heal. Seven months had passed since the fall, and too many things still weren't back to normal. I had never seen Fanny not bounce back. It frightened me.

Two o'clock. The refrigerator begged to be washed but my meeting with Marko was an hour away. I had no time. Five cups of lunch coffee hit my bladder and I went into Fanny's bathroom. She forgot to flush. In the sink, Clairoled hairs curved like blond cracks in the dirty bowl. The tub area was clean. When had she last bathed? What was going on here? Fanny was the world's most meticulous housekeeper. Was. I scrubbed the sink and gave the toilet a quick once-over. Dust balls shifted in the corners. This place needed more than a lick and a promise. Dynamite, for a start.

"All right, Mom," I said, pulling on my coat, turning on "General Hospital." "I've got to go." I kissed her cheek and sniffed. Musty but passable. "Next week I'll bring Marisha, give this place a good cleaning."

"You think I can't keep up my own apartment?"

"Of course you can." Think fast. "I just don't want you to have to. There's too much here that needs doing."

"Like?" Like flushing your toilet and wiping out the sink.

"Like your curtains have to be taken down and cleaned, the windows need washing way up where you can't reach, and the cabinets need scrubbing. Why should you do it?" Meaning why should I do it.

"I don't want someone digging around in my things."

"It's not 'someone,' Ma, it's Marisha. Tell you what. I'll drop her off when I pick you up. By the time we get back from lunch, she'll have the whole place cleaned." Bravo! Bravo! Let's hear it for the world's greatest daughter. Fanny did not return my smile.

"I am not leaving someone alone in my apartment. You want a job done, you got to work right alongside them every minute."

"Ma, Marisha's cleaned for me for—"

"I don't want her!" Fanny's voice, trained in the days before stage microphones, rose like thunder from her diaphragm. When I was a kid, the volume knocked me over. I was older now, had more substance. I could almost stand up to it.

"I'm bringing Marisha next week and you can watch her all you want."

"I will *not* have her see my apartment in this condition." She slapped her hand on the table, pushed herself up, and walked without limp or cane to her television chair. Sometimes, Sarah, you have the sensitivity of sandpaper. So maybe Fanny's eyes couldn't focus on the dirt. She sensed it, and she was ashamed to have anyone besides me bear witness.

Two-oh-five. I tore off my coat and dove into the fridge, pulling out the things I'd just put in, running hot soapy water into the sink. Had to remember to bring a box of baking soda next time. The sound of housework brought Fanny like a call to arms. She watched, supervised, forgave.

"You need a haircut," she said, by way of making peace.

"Been too busy."

"How's Asher?" Asher! I'd call him as soon as I got to my studio. It wasn't every day a man became a twenty-millionaire.

"Fine, Ma. Busy. You know." I'd wait a decade or two to break the news. The idea of Asher selling his business terrified her. I was her only security and I damned well better be married to a man who left the house every morning to go earn a living.

I finished, repacked the fridge, wiped out the sink, and settled Fanny into her TV chair. A garden variety soap opera vamp in a lacy teddy ground her hipbones into a handsome man forty years her senior. I suspected she wasn't his wife. Fanny nodded at the seduction.

"You keep yourself nice for Asher," she said. "Too many women let themselves go. I always kept myself nice for your father, he should rest in peace. A lot of men still look."

"Good-bye, Ma." I put on my coat for real this time and hugged her. Less and less to hold on to. And I didn't like her color. I would definitely call Dr. Fishman. "See you next Tuesday."

"Yeah," she said, already moving into the world of "General Hospital." "Be careful how you drive."

3

The three-piece Suit across the desk from me uncapped a gold Cross pen.

"Ready, Asher?" he asked. I forced a smile.

All eyes in the small room locked on the pen as it hovered like a vulture, circled a few times, then dove to the thick stack of contracts. I held my breath. My heart stopped altogether. There was still time to back out. A deal wasn't done until a deal was done.

Martha stood behind me, digging her bony fingers into my shoulders. My-sister-the-attorney was also not breathing, although with Martha you couldn't always tell. I shifted in my chair. I could use a drink of water. She pinned me in place. The survivor of two previously aborted sales, Martha knew what I was thinking. Her finger-digging foray into my bursal sacs was a sisterly reminder for me to behave.

I tried to look relaxed, as if selling a business for twenty million was a regular event in my life. Sweat dripped down the back of my neck, wilting the cotton shirt and silk tie Sarah bought for the occasion. How did the three-piece Suit stay so cool and unwrinkled? My suit, which carbon dated to my eighteen-year-old nephew's bar mitzvah, dug into my waist and strangled my balls. The wool sucked up sweat. I smelled like a wet sheep.

"Maybe you could open that door behind you?" I said to one of the five Pinstripes accompanying the Suit. The man hesitated, then turned the doorknob with the tips of his thumb and forefinger. So maybe the office needed a cleaning. Rosie's Soup Company was clean enough where the food was, where it mattered. The other men shifted around so the door could open.

The cool air brought a rush of beef barley. Ambrosia! I inhaled greedily. The Suit kept signing dotted line after dotted line. How could I turn my life's work over to a man who didn't stop to smell the beef barley? Martha's fingers dug deeper. She bent to my ear. "Asher, no. Not this time."

"I'm surprised Mr. Hochman isn't here." I said, prying Martha's fingers from the most painful spots. "He has such a nice feel for our company."

"Didn't I tell you?" The Suit didn't look up. "Mr. Hochman was needed to troubleshoot a company for us in North Carolina."

"No." Surprise, surprise. "You know, in all the time I met with him, he never once indicated he might not be here." The Suit shrugged.

"These things happen."

"Yes," I said. "And at the most interesting times." Hochman had been quick to smile, easy to talk to. Half the success of Rosie's was its happy employees. Hochman, bright, personable, compassionate, would know how to create happy employees. One of the reasons I let this deal go this far was my good feeling about Hochman. "Who will replace him?"

"Mr. Kimball." One of the Pinstripes stepped forward. "Mr. Rose, I'd like you to meet Kirk Kimball. MBA from Northwestern. Graduated second in his class."

"You couldn't get me first?"

"Engineering and computer undergrad. He's been with us three years and I can't think of a better man to take over management of Rosie's."

I took stock of Kirk Kimball, MBA. The spit-shined pisher felt all wrong. Salon-styled hair, manicured nails, custom-tailored suit, gold tie pin, French cuffs. This refugee from *GQ*, this hard-bodied, unsmiling piece of arrogance, wouldn't know matzo balls from kreplekh. Why should I let his two-hundred-dollar Italian shoes climb the corporate ladder on the backs of my soup cans? He'd better keep his nose to the computer and his hands out of Rosie's kitchen.

"I look forward to working with you during the transition period, Mr. Rose." I tried to picture myself spending the next five years with Kimball.

"You know, Mr. Kimball," I said, "a lot of the people working here grew up with me."

"Quite a few of them are relatives, I believe."

"By blood or by proxy. They've worked here most of their lives. Where we grew up, soup was more than food. It was the great healer of the body and the spirit. When someone got sick, a chicken died." Kimball didn't smile. Animal sacrifices were not in his ancestry. "No matter what the outside world did to us, coming home to the smell of soup simmering on the stove set everything right."

"Ah," said Kimball, a light of understanding in his eyes. "Sort of like those Jimmy Stewart Campbell commercials." The last bit of air left the room.

"Yeah. Like that." Martha's grip tightened. I rocked back suddenly, ramming the chair mid-diaphragm.

"Ooomphhh!" she said. Her fingers loosened.

"If you'll excuse me a moment." I pushed up out of the chair, squeezed through the group, and strode out onto the metal catwalk that ringed the plant. Martha's sensible shoes thudded after me.

"Asher! You stop right now." I picked up speed. Anger energized me, set me off in unpredictable directions. Martha kept up.

"Goddamn bait and switch," I said. "Bunch of snake oil salesmen. I knew Hochman was too good to be true. They should at least have left him here until I signed. Stupid. Blew their little soup-buying deal all to hell. No one to blame but themselves."

We rounded the far end of the catwalk. Impossible to breathe. I yanked open my tie and tore off the suit jacket, clutching the wet wool.

"Asher Rose, you stop this!" Martha grabbed my arm. I yanked it away.

"This time it's not my fault," I said.

"Of course it's not your fault. It's the fates, your Karma, the lunar alignment. Would you *please* slow down? I'm dying back here."

I stopped and she crashed into me; shtick left over from childhood walks home from school. On the plant floor below us, thousands of tons of equipment belched and boiled, cooking the best soups in America, maybe the world. There wasn't a piece of machinery I couldn't operate, not a person working that floor I didn't know by name. Well, maybe a few of the new people. But time was I knew them all. I leaned on the railing, looking down over the empire I'd created. Martha slipped a comforting arm around my shoulder.

"Asher, I know how hard this is for you."

"You can't."

"I can."

"You just want the sale."

"Of course I want the sale. For you as much as for me."

"Ha."

"You've backed out twice before. I'm too old to take much more of this."

"You know what your problem is, Martha?"

"Having a rock-head brother for a client?"

"Your problem is you've always counted your chickens before the eggs were laid."

"Twenty million dollars buys a hell of an omelet." The muscles across my back tightened. I rolled my head, trying to untie the knots. Martha ignored me. "Asher, I'm not backing down this time. It's not like I haven't been here since the beginning. Remember me? The curly-haired pest always begging you to make beef barley." She waved her arm grandly over the machinery. "They're playing my soup."

"Cute, Martha."

"C'mon, Asher. Give it up. You've been working at this since you were twelve years old. You're staring fifty in the face."

"Thanks for reminding me." A flatbed truck filled with bags of chicken pieces passed underneath. "See that?" I said. "New supplier. I dealt with the last guy for eighteen years. Funny old man. Hell of a storyteller. One night a virus hit his chickens and by the end of the week he was out of business." I had to stop and swallow down the sudden lump. So goddamned sentimental lately. Cry at the flick of a chicken.

"I'm missing the point here, Asher. What do diseased chickens have to do with anything?"

"The point is, every day I'm surrounded by drama, heartbreak, success. Why should I leave this?"

"Twenty million dollars is why. Finally getting to travel is why. No more sixteen-hour days is why. More time with Sarah is why. Besides, the contract gives you five more years to hang around and put your two cents in."

"It won't be the same. I was wrong, Martha. This is too soon. Maybe next year."

"If you're holding out because you still hope Jeff will change his mind—"

"I'm not—"

"Then you might as well go ahead and sign the contracts. Your son is not coming into the business, Asher, no matter how long you wait."

"It's not about Jeff. I'm not ready."

"You'll never be ready. Until you're in your grave you won't be ready."

Across the plant, a couple of Pinstripes walked out of my office onto the catwalk and leaned on the railing, watching us. I wanted them out of my office, out of my plant, out of my life.

"I'm happy here," I said. "Why should I sell?"

"Am I saying you're not happy? But I'll tell you something, Asher, more than happy, you're afraid."

"Afraid of what? Retiring with twenty million?"

"Afraid of change. Afraid of maybe having to do some of the things you've always talked about."

"Like what?"

"Like travel. You were the only kid I knew who read the world atlas instead of comic books. Now that you have a chance to pack your bags, you're chickening out."

"So now you're a psychiatrist?"

"Might have been if you'd popped for med school."

"Everything's my fault. Want to blame your divorce on me, too?"

"Sell, Asher. It's time."

"I'm not going to let that group of mumsers run my life's work into the ground." I slapped my hand on the railing. Sticky. Needed a good washing. Funny, the things I'd been noticing lately.

"And *I'm* not going to let *you* get away with *this* again.

Superior Foods happens to be the best food company in the United States. They are, you will please remember, the one company you said you'd be proud to sell to."

"You love them so much, you go sign the contract." I didn't look at her. Didn't have to. I felt the swell of her anger push out in all directions, gathering force, the quiet before—

Her body went rigid, arms straight at her sides, hands fisted, neck muscles bulging. Voice so quiet I could hardly hear.

"You. Are. Just. Like. Mama." Martha whirled away, striding along the catwalk toward my office. Way to push those buttons, Martha.

"You're crazy," I called over the plant noise.

"Of course I'm crazy. I'm one of the Rose kids. But that doesn't make me wrong. Mama wouldn't leave the house, and you won't leave Rosie's Soup Company. The only difference is," she yelled, rounding the far end, "Mama knew she was sick."

"I'm nothing like Mama." She kept walking. "Nothing."

I leaned on the railing, looking at people I'd worked with for years, pieces of equipment I'd designed, soups cooking to my recipes. I willed myself to feel the old spark. Nothing. Nothing and nothing and nothing. My heart wasn't in this anymore. Hadn't been for nearly a year. So why was I holding on? Maybe Martha was right.

She stood in the office doorway, staring across the catwalk at me, arms folded, head tilted, right foot tapping. "All right, all right," I muttered, heading back around, "stop nagging."

The Suit recapped his Cross, flashing a glint of Rolex as he slipped the pen inside his jacket. I picked up a ballpoint with a Rosie's soup can eraser and flashed my buck-ninety-eight Bears' Super Bowl watch. Martha bent to point out the lines to be signed. Then there was only the scratch of cheap pen on paper. Plant machinery beat in time to my heart. My life flowed out of the pen onto the paper.

"Done," said Martha, tearing the contract away as I finished.

"Done," said the Suit, reaching across to shake my hand. From a great distance, I watched myself extend a hand. The man had a fish handshake, limp and cool and lacking heart. What kind of company makes a fish-hand its boss? I pushed back my chair and stopped, not quite sure what came next.

"The champagne," coaxed Martha.

"Right." I pulled Paul's gift of Dom Pérignon from the ice-filled wastebasket under my desk. Linty gum and candy wrappers stuck to the bottle. "Martha, there are some paper cups in the bathroom—"

"Asher . . ."

"You're right! I forgot. Excuse me." I smiled at the Suit. "My friend Paul bought the champagne and special cups for the occasion." I opened my bottom desk drawer and took out the package of Smurf paper cups. "Let's do this up right." The bottle held just enough for a small drink each.

The Suit raised his cup. "A toast," he said.

"A toast," said the Pinstripes.

"To the finest soup maker in the country. Your customers thank you. And we at Superior Foods thank you."

"Hear! Hear!" The group drank up.

I sat at my desk a long time after they'd gone. Martha kissed my cheek and left. She'd always known when to leave me alone. The twenty million had nothing to do with me and Rosie's. Numbers say how you're doing, not why. Rosie's wasn't about numbers. It was about the excitement of the *doing* of the thing. If I still felt that, I wouldn't have signed Rosie's away no matter how big the numbers. But Rosie's had lost something this past year, or I had. It was time to shake up my life. An hour passed, then another hour.

Finally, after twenty-nine years, the former Owner/President/ Chief Cook and Pot Scrubber of Rosie's Soup Company walked out the door, step lighter, mind easier. First I would go home and take off the damned suit. Then I would make love to Sarah.

4

Marko Fazio dismembered the portfolio I had agonized over for days. Which costumes to put in, which to leave out? His white-blond hair bobbed over the drawings and photos strewn across his butcher-block table.

"Where'd you get such a strong sense of theater?" he asked, shuffling through twenty years of costumes I'd made for school

plays, local theater groups, commercials, industrial shows, docu-
mentaries.

"My mother was an actress back in the dark ages. I grew up
watching wardrobe women fitting costumes."

"It shows." He returned to the drawings. A small fire burned
in my stomach. I stood and walked around, too tense to watch.

Marko had converted a Printer's Row loft into an acre of
varnished wood floors, jungle greenery, eclectic art. Gigantic Nav-
ajo baskets overflowed with fabulous fabrics. Sun streamed
through skylights spanning the vaulted ceiling. I coveted this
studio. Not that I wasn't happy in mine. It beat working on my
dining room table, threads and scraps littering the carpet, fallen
pins finding Asher's bare feet like heat-seeking missiles. What
crazed me most was having to clean up for company when I was
in mid-project. I loved my studio, even if it was two windowless
rooms in a damp basement. Even if Asher didn't understand why I
couldn't work at home.

Marko hummed over my sketches. I am not nervous. I will not
throw up. Beautifully framed renderings lined the walls; Marko's
costumes for the Lyric Opera, The Goodman, plays all over the
country, feature films. Last week, a collection of his original
drawings for *Henry V* sold at auction for twelve thousand. It hurt
not to be able to draw like that, to capture body movement and
fabric drape with a few bold lines. How had I let myself believe
my work looked professional? Here in Marko's studio, surrounded
by his genius, my portfolio screamed "Amateur!"

"Espresso?" he asked, stretching, yawning. Great, my work put
him to sleep.

"Yes, thanks, I'd love some."

"Be right back."

Not "I love your work, we must do a film together." The offer
of espresso sounded like "Thanks, but no thanks." Sewing machines whirred at the far end of the loft. Behind a wall of fabric
screens, Marko's workroom turned out the costumes he designed.
He specialized in difficult period costumes, his brilliant construction allowing actors full physical movement without sacrificing
authenticity.

I ached to work with Marko, to study under the master, to sink
my designing teeth into a feature film. I'd dreamed of designing
for movies from the time I made wardrobes for my Margaret
O'Brien paper dolls. But, until Marko, I didn't believe a designer

could be successful outside Hollywood. So, all right, he hated my portfolio. I wasn't good enough to work with him yet. But I was one interview closer. I'd work on technique, strengthen my portfolio. My mama didn't raise no quitters.

The front door opened and a young man walked in carrying two bags of groceries. "Ahhh"—he walked slowly and with some difficulty toward me—"you must be *the* Sarah Rose."

"Why, yes I . . ."

"Greg?" Marko called from the kitchen. "That you?"

"It's me."

"Want an espresso?"

"Absolutely." He dropped the bags on the table and sank into the chair next to me, offering a hand. I took it. "My name's Greg Waller, and Marko hasn't stopped raving about you all week." *Moi?* "What do you think about the job?"

"Job?"

"Oh-oh!" Greg winced. "Marko's going to skin me."

"What now?" Marko carried in a lacquered Chinese tray stacked with three cups of espresso and cookies. I pushed aside my drawings to make room.

"I think I upstaged you," said Greg.

"What's he been saying?" Marko asked.

"He wants to know what I think about the job."

"Thanks, Greg."

"I assumed you would have asked her by now."

"Here's the thing of it." Marko sat next to me, arms crossed on the table. My heart chugged. "You've probably heard that my design assistant has escaped to Hollywood." Hooray for Hollywood!

"Gone off to do B movies and make *important* contacts," said Greg.

"Don't be bitchy," said Marko. "I started the same way. Greg refuses to understand costuming tradition. We apprentice to a master, learn all we can, then move out on our own." I hear you loud and clear. "Of course, if I lived in California, my assistants might hang around a bit longer. But I'm committed to staying in Chicago."

"You should be committed *for* staying in Chicago." Greg dropped three sugar cubes into the tiny cup. Marko ignored the dig.

"I've signed to do a made-for-TV movie being shot in Chicago." Be still my heart. "A couple of people I've worked with before are unavailable right now." And? "I asked around, agency people, independent producers, and your name came up a few different times. You've made some fans out there. They say you're dependable, thorough, professional, and a few other things hard to come by in the arts. I'd like to hire you as my assistant for the project." Yes! Yes! Yes!

"*Whatever he offers, don't look excited.*"

"*I know, Asher.*"

"*Don't clap your hands, jump up and down—*"

"*Asher!*"

"*—kiss his ring, shine his shoes.*"

"*Asher, I can negotiate a simple business deal.*"

"*I've seen you play poker.*"

"*Oh.*"

I screwed on my blankest expression.

"What does the job of assistant involve?" Walking on rusty nails? Hanging from my thumbs? No problem. I sipped the espresso, trying to keep my hand from shaking.

"We'll go over the script. You'll help me shop the show. And then, of course, you'll be on location during the shoot."

"Ahhh." I nodded. Yesyesyesyes.

"*Remember to ask for what you want.*"

"*Right.*"

"Will it be possible for me to do any designing?" A little pushy, aren't we? Greg coughed and smiled. Marko rubbed his chin.

"There are one or two minor characters I could let you have a crack at. But I'll have to approve the designs before our presentation to the director." *Our* presentation.

"And what's the time frame?"

"The shoot begins in three months and should last five to six weeks." Three months! Aaaarrrrgh. "It's a contemporary piece with two flashback forties scenes. Shouldn't be too hard for us to put together." Us. Us. "The director's coming in a few days to scout locations and talk over ideas. What's your schedule like?"

"Me?" Who can think? "Let's see. I'm finishing a job for the phone company and one for Nabisco. I can get those out of the way by the end of this week." If I don't sleep, eat, go to the bathroom, talk to Fanny, or make love to Asher. "And my husband and I are going to California a week from Monday. We'll be gone ten days."

"Mmmmmmm." Was that a yes mmmmm or a no mmmmm? Was it unspeakably unprofessional to mention a trip with my husband? To mention my husband at all? Marko chewed his lower lip, his eyes scanning the brightly painted overhead pipes.

"You know, Sarah, filmmaking hours are horrendous. They put tremendous strains on the best of relationships."

"A-men to that," said Greg.

"Do you think your husband will have a problem with you working long hours?"

"Asher?" I laughed, as in "Surely you jest." "He's worked twenty-five-hour days since he was a kid."

"All right, then." Was this a yes? "I'll give you the script to read and you can fax me your notes and preliminary sketches from California. That sound all right?" Like a reprieve. Like heaven. Like a giant step forward in a mid-life career. Mother, may I?

"Fine," I said. "It sounds just fine."

Bloodless Cold. Even the name of the film excited me. And the characters! I started scanning the script in the elevator, reading the first page three times before I calmed down enough to make sense out of the words. I read it every chance I could all the way home. There are never enough red lights when you really and truly need them.

Asher's car in the driveway startled me. I'd been so lost in the script I'd forgotten he'd be home. Of course he would. I forced myself to leave the script in the car. If I brought it inside it would follow me around, screaming for attention. And today was Asher's day.

"Hello?" My voice drifted off through the house, unanswered. "Asher?" No sign of him. Mail still in the box. No nibblings left out in the kitchen. "Asher?" Up the stairs, no lights on.

Our bedroom door was closed. It was never closed. "Asher?" I turned the knob, pushed. Hundreds of giant balloons filled the room. A few escaped as I walked in. I waded through to the bed, punching them away, pushing them aside, until I reached Asher, naked and smiling on the bed.

"So," I said, unbuttoning my blouse, unzipping my skirt, taking off my stockings. "So," I said, climbing on top of him, bombarding him with balloons, "what's new?"

5

" 'Morning, lazybones."

"Mmmfph. Hey!"

"You have the world's saltiest earlobes."

"C'mon, Sarah. Stop. Tickles."

"Sleeping to the crack of noon."

"Time!? Six. Clock says six."

"Take that pillow off your head, Asher. You have a boss to answer to. Remember?"

"Uhhhnnnggghh. Scratch. Lower. Higher. Half inch to the right, there, there, harder. Ahhhhmmm."

"You had some wild dreams last night."

"I never dream. Ouch! Not so hard. Do the whole back. Yes. Great. What were you doing up?"

"You kidding? I kept waiting for the Fraud Squad to come crashing through the door and arrest me. How 'bout scratching me as long as you're not busy? Mmmmm. I feel like I put one over on everyone, pulled the scam of the century. Assistant to Marko Fazio? C'mon."

"Fairy tales can come true . . ."

"You have the world's worst voice. No. Don't. Just kidding. No. Asher!"

"So, you like being in the movies."

"Naw. Me? Sarah Rose? The kid who practiced ballet legs in the bathtub so I could understudy for Esther Williams?"

"That's why you were always wrinkled. Ouch! Hey! Now my head. Scratch. Harder."

"Gotta get going. You too, sailor. Up and at 'em."

"What are we going to do with all these balloons?"

"I think they kind of brighten up the carpet."

"I thought they'd stay up the whole weekend."

"Asher, love, nothing stays up a whole weekend."

"I resemble that remark."

"How about we see who can pop the most in five minutes."

"What's the prize?"

"Winner gets to choose tonight's position."

"Mark, get set, go!"

6

For the first time in my life, I was driving to work as an employee. No responsibilities until I walked into the plant. None after I walked out. Whistling, I turned off the tollway and headed west on the two-lane road.

This was exactly where it all started, halfway between Herman's Tulip Farm and Bartoli's Fruit Mart. Maybe I should erect one of those road shrines, let people know something important happened here. Used to be, climbing this small rise in the road, I'd spot the distant tips of Rosie's smokestacks and adrenaline hit my system like cold water on a hot skillet. Juices flowing, mind kicking into high gear, I'd push the gas to the floor and fly down the road to work. That rush, that high was always there, nothing I ever thought about.

Until the day it didn't come.

Until the day, catching sight of Rosie's smokestacks, nothing happened.

The void, like silence after sound, stopped me cold. I pulled over, shaking, sweating, dizzy, nauseous, pressing my forehead against the cool steering wheel. It passed in a few minutes, and I figured it was some kind of flu. A month later, it happened again. Not the flu, heart attack. I barely made it to Rosie's nurses.

"Your EKG is perfectly normal, Mr. Rose. Possibly something you ate didn't agree with you. Oh, if you have a second, I'd like to talk to you about this carpotunnel problem we're starting to see in some of the veg-prep workers."

And again. This time to my doctor.

"Can't find a thing wrong, Asher. I'm making an appointment for you at the hospital for a thorough physical, stress test, the works. You're due."

This past year the "spells" came closer and closer together.

"Well, whatever it is, it isn't physical. You check out A-OK. Something bothering you? At work, maybe? At home? Under more stress than usual? I can give you the names of a couple of good therapists."

No chance. I came from a generation of men who worked things out by themselves. How did people go around spilling their guts to strangers? Besides, I didn't have anything to open up about. I held on.

Now none of that mattered. The smokestacks up ahead were just smokestacks. Rosie's was someone else's headache. I was an employee. A hell of a well-paid employee, but an employee, nonetheless. For the next few years, give or take a healthy number of four-day weeks and three-week vacations, all I had to do was punch in and help out where I was needed. No fuss, no muss, no worry. This past weekend for the first time ever, I didn't go in to work, not to look through the mail, not to see if the cooker's repairs held. Here it was Monday and Rosie's was still standing. Amazing.

The shifts wouldn't change for another half hour. I swung into the quiet lot, pulled into my parking space and took three steps before it hit me that it wasn't my name painted on the This Space Reserved For sign. One of Kirk Kimball's first changes was to put his name on my space. Not a big deal. Especially since I didn't intend to move my car. He wanted the space? Let him get his skinny ass to work at a decent hour.

I rounded the corner of the building, working up a good anger. Ten-to-one he was out jogging. Fists clenched, teeth gritting, nostrils flaring, I stopped just outside the door, closed my eyes and took deep breaths to get my heart rate back down.

"Breathe in through the nose, out through the mouth." I could hear Sarah's voice. "Sloooow in. Sloooow out." Some sort of yoga she'd learned passing through India. "I want you to live long enough so I can see how you look with gray hair." The good news was, all the Rose men died with full heads of hair. The bad news was, only one uncle lived past fifty. Hell of a legacy for a forty-nine-year-old. The breathing calmed me.

"Bulldog" Charley nodded from the security desk, setting his magnifier down on the *Wall Street Journal*. Years back, he stood when I walked in. But the wear and tear of school football, twenty-five years as a Chicago beat cop, and fifteen years of walking Rosie's as my security chief, had taken their toll on his knees. Standing was a painful courtesy.

" 'Morning, Mr. Rose."

" 'Morning, Charley." He made a move to get up and I motioned him not to bother. You have to give a man his pride. Skinnyass Kimball better bear that in mind. "Going to make my rounds. If Mr. Kimball comes in, have him catch up with me."

The name threw a shadow across Charley's face. Looked like his take on Kimball was the same as mine. What the hell, Charley's police pension and Rosie's profit sharing would keep him in *Wall Street Journals* the rest of his life. No one was forcing him to stay at Rosie's. One of the many things I promised myself this past year was I'd stop feeling responsible for everyone. Might as well start now.

I found my assistant production manager in the minilab checking sample cans in the incubator for leakers.

" 'Morning, Cliff."

" 'Mornin', Asher."

"Ready?"

"Let's do 'er."

We put on our hair nets, holding on to them as we walked under the powerful Bug Blaster fans that kept flying critters out of the soup-making area.

"Everything okay last night?"

"Had an accident around four this morning. A hose pulled loose on a guy cleaning a cooker." He checked his sheet. "Victor Martinez. Caught the steam on his left leg and arm before the other guys could get to him." I couldn't put a face to the name.

"He new?"

"Five months."

"How bad?"

"Not too. Should be back next week."

A year ago I would have known Victor Martinez. Would have known something about his family, his problems, what mattered in his life. It took energy to care about people. Hadn't had a lot of that, lately.

"Anything else?"

"Marge and Gail over in Silicon Valley want to switch to night shift so they can take courses at Clayton College."

"Think this means they'll all want to go to school?" Cliff laughed. Marge had breast implants the year before and three women working with her thought she looked so great they all had them done.

"They want to know if the new owners will still pay part of the tuition."

"I'll check with Kimball."

We made our morning rounds, kibitzing with people as we passed, too many new faces, too many people I didn't know. I picked up a couple of steam-scrubbed carrots from the conveyor and tossed one to Cliff. We swung past the cast-iron cookers, stepping over patches of water left from the five million gallons the night crew used to clean up. Pasty globs of potato starch, chicken fat and carrot puree slopped off cans spinning along the conveyors. This slurry had to be hosed down every four hours. I'd like to see Kimball's Italian leather shoes after a few days of making these rounds.

We held our ears past the Cluster Buster as the little forklift hoisted a frozen forty-pound block of cut beef eight feet into the air, then dropped it onto a thick metal plate. We might still be hacking the beef apart with picks and hammers if I hadn't seen a bartender drop a bag of ice cubes to break up clumps. I used to get ideas for improving Rosie's everywhere I looked. That changed, too, this past year. The creative part of my mind shut down. Now that I'd sold Rosie's and didn't have to worry about day-to-day headaches, maybe the fun of the work would come back to me.

"Anything else?" I asked.

"Nothing much." Cliff looked at me over the tops of his glasses. "Except I'm supposed to pump you for information on our new owners."

"I figured. People worried?"

"Rumors blooming like mushrooms after rain."

"Like?"

"We're in for major layoffs. Or no layoffs but big salary cuts. Or they're closing the plant altogether. You name it, someone's sayin' it."

"I'll talk to Kimball. Tell him to get down here and press some flesh. Tell him to write a little hello note in the newspaper."

I left Cliff to his rounds and walked out past the casks of wine used for beef burgundy. When I found out workers were siphoning nearly a hundred gallons a month into jars and bottles to take home, I took the salt that went into the recipe and added it directly to the wine casks. End of loss. For every problem there is a solution. If you just think about it long enough.

The fifty-two steps to the catwalk never got any easier. I climbed to the top and waited for my knee joints to forgive me. Drop cloths and paint cans barricaded the door to my office. The room had been skinned and gutted. Workmen stapled acoustical ceiling tiles over holes where the fluorescent fixtures used to be. A painter coated the dingy gray walls with primer the color of baby lima beans. A third man perched on a stool in the doorway, methodically scraping off the name Sarah had painted on the door nearly twenty years ago.

I didn't know the workmen. Looked like the maintenance and engineering teams that handled Rosie's' in-house construction, electrical and decorating weren't up to Kimball's snuff.

" 'Morning," I said. "Kimball in yet?" The name-scraper-offer looked up.

"Ain't seen nobody."

"Any idea where they put the stuff from this room?" Shrugs all around. "Thanks."

Edie would know. I walked along the catwalk to her office. She whipped around the room on her caster-wheeled chair, rebounding from file cabinets to desk to phone like a pinball. Several pencils jutted from her frizz of red hair. I sat on the edge of her desk while she juggled a couple of calls, checked through files, jotted notes and memos that greased a considerable number of Rosie's' cogs.

A bout with Bell's palsy had knocked out the muscles on the right side of her face. She flashed me her cockeyed smile and tilted back in her chair.

" 'Morning, Boss Man."

"How're you doing, gorgeous?"

She nodded toward the activity in my office. "Looks like we're finally getting some class around here."

"Go ahead, cut me to the quick. Any idea where they've put me?"

"Boiler room."

I grabbed a handful of jelly beans. They were always in the jar on her desk, like the gray paint was always on my office walls. Never thought about them before. I picked out the licorice ones and tossed them back. "How many tons of this garbage have you bought the last fifteen years?"

"I keep a running tab. Figure I'll hit Rosie's with the bill when I retire."

"Thought you were going to work till you dropped."

"Thought you were, too." She stopped and looked away, pretending the philodendron needed her attention. It was plastic. I reached over, gently squeezing her shoulder. Her eyes were watery when she looked back, but her smile was in place. "I don't think it's going to be as much fun around here. Although"—her eyes followed a muscular young painter hefting a ladder onto his shoulder—"the scenery's definitely improving."

"You dirty old woman."

"Not so old. And don't whine. You had your chance."

"You're all talk."

"You'll never know."

"So, where'd they stick me?"

"Mookey's office."

"Where'd they put Mookey?"

"In Mookey's office."

Among other quirks, my brother had a prodigious output of gas. "There isn't room for two people in there."

"It's cozy."

"Thanks." I slid off her desk and grabbed a handful of beans for the road. She reached into a drawer and tossed me a book of matches.

"Here, a little room deodorizer."

I threw them back. "Think I want to blow up the place?"

Her laughter followed me down the catwalk to my new office.

For once I was happy Mookey didn't come in one minute earlier than he had to. I could set up without him getting in my way. I flicked on the light. Some decorating genius had put our desks facing each other in the center of the small room. Great. Mookey and I could spend our days staring each other down. He barely spoke to me since I "sold Rosie's out from under."

I shoveled bags of cookies, candy wrappers, old magazines and other assorted junk to his side of the office. My little brother had the personality of a halibut and the metabolism of a slug. He never volunteered to do a damned thing, and never felt other people did enough for him. Just the sort of person to run Rosie's. Right into the ground.

I should never have made him vice president. Martha the Mediator's bright idea. "It'll make a great thirty-fifth birthday present," she said. She got her friend Sarah to work on me at home. "Being vice president is bound to make Mookey more responsible. Inspire him to take charge." The trouble with both of them was they'd read too many Oz books. They thought making Mookey vice president would give him business sense, the way a diploma gave the Scarecrow brains. Mookey started strutting around, issuing orders, writing memos. He didn't do any harm, but he never did any good that I could see.

Was there no end to his junk? Mookey oozed into unoccupied space. Maybe it was the fifthborn's attempt to establish territory. Not all his fault. From the day he was born, Freyla and Pearl fussed over him, carried him, dressed him, fed him, played with him like a huge doll. Martha and I warned them they'd spoil him but did they listen? His feet didn't touch ground until Mom popped out a new baby for them to spoil. Mookey was four when Norm was born. By then the damage had been done.

Finally clearing my half of the office, I began unloading stuff the movers had shoved into the desk drawers: wedding photo, industry awards, cube photos of Maxi's family in California and Jeff's in Boulder, two chipped coffee cups, assorted well-chewed pencils and pens, an old metal Rolodex with tattered cards. Boxes in the corner held the overflow: personal stationery, business cards, train and plane schedules for Paris, London, Hong Kong, Brazil. Not much to show for a lifetime of work.

Palpitations. *Your EKG is fine, Asher.*

Rush of sweat. *Not a thing wrong with your heart.*

Blurred vision. *Are you under stress? Something at work? At home?*

Hang on. Hang on! Here it comes—

A life force hit from behind—*hang on*—ramming me into the chair—*hang on*—hurtling me full speed into a great cosmic swirl—*a mild anxiety attack*—sucking me into a bottomless black hole—*nothing life-threatening.*

I threw my head down between my knees, gasping. Ribbons of childhood dreams squiggled through my thoughts like noodle dough through an extruder. Europe, Asia, Africa. I'd promised myself. Why was I still here? Why had I agreed to stay at Rosie's during the transition? Why not make a clean break instead of torturing myself like this? Breathe deep. There was a world out there waiting for me. Breathe again. Easy.

"What did the doctor say?"

"He said, 'Tell Sarah not to worry so much.' "

"Asher."

"Really. He says I'm in top physical condition. Just working too hard."

"Surprise, surprise."

"I'm going to sell Rosie's."

"Yes, dear."

"I mean it this time."

"Yes, dear."

"Sarah, I swear."

"Yes, dear. Asher? Asher! No! Don't. Ha ha ha ha ha nofair-nofairnofair I wasn't ready. Let me up."

"Repeat after me. I."

"I."

"Asher Rose."

"Asher Rose."

"Am going to sell Rosie's."

"Am going to sell Rosie's."

"And travel around the world with my wife, Sarah."

"And travel around the world with my sexy breathtakingly beautiful wife, Sarah."

"Did I say breathtakingly beautiful?"

"And sexy."

"What a smart man I am."

The dizziness passed. Was Martha right? Could I be taking after Mama? Was I coming down with a slight case of agoraphobia? She'd been, what, thirty-seven, thirty-eight, when the grocer found her standing in front of the meat counter—blade roast in one hand, whole fryer in the other—shaking, crying, unable to move? I was in my father's shop, sewing buttons on a suit, when the call came. I knew it was serious when he took off his leather apron, put on his suit jacket and actually left work to go get her. She never went out of the house after that. Not for weddings, not for funerals, until her own.

I sat up slowly, wiping the sweat off my face and neck. I sold Rosie's to save my life. Go explain that to Mookey. Sold Rosie's to get control again before these spells sucked me down into the center of whatever the hell this was, before I disappeared forever.

I finished organizing my desk and left the office. Mookey wouldn't like our cozy new arrangement, and I wasn't in the mood to hear him complain. Not before I'd had my coffee.

"Good morning, Asher." Kimball, bright, sunny and squeaky clean, sidestepped the paint-splattered drop cloths. "Sorry about this mess. Looks like it will be a week before I get situated—files in order, room the way I want it, that sort of thing. Can't function in disorder." He dropped a hand on my shoulder, patting me like a pet Pekingese as we walked around the catwalk. "I spent the weekend reviewing company records, getting to know the operation."

"A whole weekend? You must have everything pretty well nailed down." The sarcasm skidded across his moussed hair.

"Yes. I think I have a pretty good handle on things. If you want to take off until after your California trip, that'll give me time to settle in."

"You don't have any questions?"

"About?"

"About how the company works, about employees, about procedure, about how to find the men's room?" He laughed. I didn't get the joke.

"You've done a splendid job here, Asher." Splendid? My life's work was going to be managed by a boy who said "splendid?"

"I'm sure if I have any problems or questions during the week your people here can help me."

Edie scrunched her face at me as we passed her office. I caught a glimpse of Kimball and me reflected in my old office window. Country mouse, city mouse. Did I really look that old or was it the lighting? Why would the same lights make Kimball look like high school? I sensed a direction to our walk. He was leading me to the stairs.

"Oh, Asher, about all those travel posters on your walls. I had the men roll them up and put them in a bag. Didn't know if you wanted to keep them. I'm afraid a few of them tore."

"You can toss them."

"Are those places you've traveled?"

"Places I'm going to travel. I've waited my whole life for this. Tacking up those posters made me feel like I wasn't so cooped up, like I was in the middle of the Sahara or the Alps or—"

"Um-hum," he said, stopping at the top of the stairs. His bored gaze wandered out over the plant below.

"Well, if you're sure you don't need me, I have things to take care of. You've got my home number?" He shook my hand and hurried back to my . . . his office. Wanted to oversee the painting of the molding, no doubt. A few months of this kind of attention to detail and Rosie's was going to be the prettiest plant to go belly-up.

Nine o'clock and I had the whole day ahead of me. My stomach grumbled for its chocolate donut and two coffees. Maybe I'd take Sarah to breakfast. Why the hell not?

One of the two cafeteria pay phones kept spitting back my

coins. I made a note to have Edie call the company. Sarah's studio phone rang five times before she picked it up.

"Hey, sexy," I said. "Let's play hooky."

"Asher?"

"How does scrambled lox and eggs at Belden North sound?"

"Like cholesterol city."

"All right. I'll treat you to brunch at Crickets, champagne and all."

"Aren't you supposed to be smoothing out bumps for the new owners?"

"They won't need me for a while. Thought we'd have breakfast and see what develops."

"Oh, honey, great idea, lousy timing. Wait—" She talked to someone, then someone else. I shifted from one foot to the other. My stomach grumbled again. The cafeteria smells were getting to me.

"Hello?" I whistled into the receiver.

"Sorry," she said, "it's a madhouse here. The Krispy Korn choreographer just walked in with two of the agency people and a couple of dancers. They need to see how the costumes move. Why don't I call you when I'm squared away? Around three?"

"That's too late for breakfast and a long decadent day in bed."

"What? Wait—" Someone else interrupted her.

"Never mind."

"Wait, Asher—"

"I'll talk to you later."

I grabbed a tray and joined the long food line. Pretty funny. All these years, Sarah said I wasn't spontaneous. I'd say, "It's easy to be spontaneous when you don't have a job. When you don't have responsibilities. I had five brothers and sisters to take care of and a mother who wouldn't leave the house. You think I didn't want to take off? You think I didn't want to thumb around the world like you? It's easy to do what you want when you're an only child."

"No," she'd say, "it has to do with personality. Either it's your nature to seize the moment or it isn't." Well, I'd just seized. Where was Sarah?

My world shifted, giant land plates heaved and collided, gearing up for ten-point earthquakes and massive destruction. I grabbed the tray rail until the flash of dizziness passed. Twice in one morning? A new world's record. Selling Rosie's was supposed to cure this.

Another wave of dizziness. The edges of my day crumbled. I had to get out of here, make it home, wait out the day until night, until sanity, until Sarah.

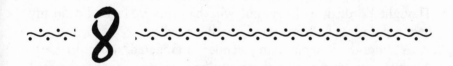

"Sarah? Sarah?"

"I'm down in the den."

"You coming up soon?"

"I can't get these corn tassels to sit right on the headpieces."

"Come to bed."

"Soon."

"It's two in the morning."

"Asher, please. I've got to finish everything before we leave for L.A."

"Work on them tomorrow."

"Tomorrow I meet with the ad people from the phone company."

"Tomorrow night, then."

"Tomorrow night I have that meeting at the Ritz with Marko.
   Asher?
   Asher?"

Fifteen minutes, sitting in the Ritz lounge waiting for Marko, and not one man showed the slightest glimmer of interest. Not a nod. Not a wink. I felt polyester double-knit in a silk-on-silk world. Frayed and nubby from nonstop days of too much work and too little sleep. I could do with a little innocent ego boost. I signaled the waiter for more coffee. The gin and tonic I really wanted would have to wait until I got home. Meeting the director was one first impression I didn't want to blow.

The Good Thing was, the last ear of Krispy Korn finally danced out of my studio at six this evening. Now all I had to do was sew sixty push buttons, and hot-glue them onto five pay telephone costumes. After that I'd be free and clear to concentrate on the movie. Sort of. Asher was so excited about our California trip, I didn't have the heart to tell him I was bringing work along. I'd work on my sketches after we made love and I tucked Asher in for the night.

I wished I didn't feel guilty leaving him tonight.

"I don't like your driving downtown alone," he'd said, sitting in bed, surrounded by boxes and bags of photos.

"I won't be late."

"Don't park in the underground garage. Give your car to the valet."

"Yes, Daddy."

"And be careful that—"

"You want to come with me?"

"Are you kidding? I still have two million photos to sort through. I've already filled two albums and I'm only up to our fifth month of marriage."

"You're so cute when you're gluing."

"Up yours."

"Mmmmm." I gave him a kiss to remember me by. "We'll have a quiet cuddle when I get back."

"It's a date."

The waiter refilled my cup and I checked my pocket mirror for the umpteenth time. My eye bags had bags. When I hit fifty, I'll hoist my saggy body skin into a topknot and cut off the excess. Thought I'd do it at forty, but who had time? Maybe I'd do my own nip and tuck. Pretty handy with a needle.

A smooth-skinned man, slender, mannered, born to wear Armani suits and Gucci shoes, walked up and sat in the small settee opposite mine. We exchanged half-smiles and nods. Not my type at all. Aquiline nose, thin lips, too ordered, too contained. No guts, no substance. French, most likely, from the cut of his jabot. Still, I wanted to feel attractive to someone who didn't already love me, and there are worse things than being noticed by a gentleman. I accepted his smile—*No, you are not invisible, Dear Lady, au contraire, you are attractive and charming and I wish to bear your children*—with grace and dignity, straightening my back, tilting my chin. The daughter of the famous Fanny Feldman knew how to do elegance.

"There you are!" Marko rushed through the posh lounge like a crazed Ichabod Crane, long limbs jutting, ankle-length coat billowing, leather shoulder bag grazing a crystal table lamp. "Sorry I'm late. Ready?" He breezed past without stopping. So much for the elegant me. I threw money on the check, grabbed my coat, and hurried after him into an elevator, using the ten-floor ride up to slash on lipstick, smooth my hair, and blend my eye shadow crease. Deodorant. Had I spritzed on deodorant? I'd find out soon enough. We all would.

"Is there anything I should know about Pace before we go in?" I asked.

"This is preliminary preliminary. Nothing at all for you to do, but I thought you'd find tonight interesting. It'll do you good to get your feet wet before the floodgates open. You might find some of the shtick confusing. Just watch me." Huh? Verbal communication was not Marko's strong suit. His brilliant clarity began and ended at the drawing board. The yin and the yang of the man. No matter, I'd sort through everything soon enough.

The door to the suite stood slightly open and we walked in on a subdued gathering. "Marko!" A shaggy man in a plaid shirt and corduroy pants came at us with open arms. People in the room turned to watch. I hadn't expected Group.

"Good to see you! Good to see you!" He hugged Marko, slapping his back, then turned his smile on me. "And you must be Sarah Rose." Everything about the man was puppy friendly. "I'm Mel Pace." Enter the director. "Glad to meet you. Come in, come in." He kept hold of my hand, leading me around the room, performing introductions.

Half the people were clothed in the most expensive and elegant garments sold up and down Michigan Avenue. The other half, many of whom Marko seemed to know, looked like flea market refugees.

"Who?" I whispered to Marko between introductions.

"Backers," he said.

The odd mix clicked. Mel Pace presents "The Money People Meet the Movie People." Tonight's party was about putting artists on display. I wanted to kick Marko for not warning me. I could have dressed more artsy for the part.

"Bernard, Janice"—Mel brought us to two of the Beautiful

People in the corner—"I'd like you to meet our costumers Marko Fazio and Sarah Rose." Mel rattled off the extensive list of Marko's credits, implying by omission that they also belonged to me. Bernard and Janice stopped looking bored.

"Yes, of course we know your work," said he.

"Loved your *Carmen,* adored your *Streetcar,*" said she.

"And your costumes for the New York production of *Nightmare at Northpark* were absolutely brilliant. Much more exciting than the ones at the London opening." Quite.

Yo, Sarah. What are you doing here, playing dress up, pretending you're a for-real costumer? Fraud. Con. They're gonna find you out, take away your Vogue Fabrics charge card, sentence you to a lifetime of summer stock.

"Circulate, circulate," said Mel, dropping us off in front of the bartender. "Enjoy. Have a drink, something to eat. Talk to you later." I lifted an eyebrow at Marko.

He handed me a glass of wine. "This is window dressing, fru-fru, has nothing to do with our work. Mel's lining up backers, wants to produce and direct his next film. Gotta romance the money men. We're part of the dog-and-pony show."

I stood quietly at Marko's side, watching, taking detailed mental notes. All the years I dreamed this scene, now here I was. Who wudda thunk it? Movie making was a who-you-know, word-of-mouth industry. People hired school friends, social friends, friends of friends. Most California directors used L.A. designers. Granted, Marko was a genius. But even a genius had to be doing other things right to be able to live in Chicago and still work in film. I intended to learn them all.

Men gathered around the special effects supervisor and stunt coordinator imported from L.A. Women gravitated toward Marko, me, and the head of makeup. Sweetie Wright, Chicago's notorious do-it-yourself socialite, pushed to the front of the group.

"Do you ever design for private clients?" she asked.

"Occasionally," said Marko. "This year I've done a few things for Oprah, Cher, and of course Ardis Krainik's dress for the Lyric's opening night." He dropped big names into the conversation like blood into water. The sharks circled.

"I need a dress, something eighteen hundreds, for the photo on my new book jacket," she said, making sure everyone heard.

"Forget it, Sweetie," said the socialite she had elbowed aside.

"His dress will cost more than your ghostwriter." Uneasy smiles all around. Not my sort of folk.

"Unfortunately," said Marko, "I've been swamped. On location in Rome for two months, then Mexico. Now I'm starting this new film."

"May I give you a call?"

"You can try," said Marko, "but I can't promise anything." His business cards materialized and several jeweled hands grabbed them up, tucking them into purse and pocket. Hey, everyone, I sew. No one asked.

I smiled, trying to look pleasant and to nod at the right times. I had friends who would kill to be in this room hobnobbing with the money men, the socialites, the movie mavens. But I'd grown up in theater, spent some of the most boring hours of my life watching Fanny coax production money out of rich "angels." This was the same play, different cast. By the end of an hour my feet throbbed, my eyelids felt like lead, and my sleep-deprived mind couldn't focus. I'd rather be cuddled in bed with Asher, sewing my phone buttons, sharing a bowl of popcorn and watching David Letterman. Nirvana is in the eye of the beholder. Another few minutes and I'd slip out. If Marko said okay. Had to remember I was an employee.

The door to the suite banged open and a group swarmed in, laughing, talking, generating their own force field. The rat pack cranked up the energy level in the room, increasing the volume of conversation, pumping up the laughter. The Gathering began to feel like a Happening. I supposed I could stay just another few minutes.

A compact hard-bodied man paused in the doorway, his dark eyes scanning the room. Dressed completely in black, he looked every inch the cat burglar, except for a large leather case strung bandolera-style across his chest. His coal-black braid reached halfway down his back. Even at rest, he was electric. His eyes swept back and caught me staring. Who was this masked man? He smiled, nodded, then moved into the room. I followed him out of the corner of my eye as he flowed from group to group, talking a few moments, then moving on. He circled closer.

I lost sight of him. Marko and I fell captive to some woman going on and on about her ever-so-amusing moment in a dressing room at Valentino's, that black taffeta gown pulled halfway down over her head when the dressing room door opened and—*I felt him move in close behind us, silent, waiting*—a man walked in on her, and she thought it was her husband, and—*The force of him, the power, little electrodes washing like waves over the nerve endings down my back.* He moved up between Marko and me, gripping our shoulders. Marko looked around.

"Zack!?"

"Excuse me"—his voice slid past me to the woman, deeper and huskier than I would have guessed—"but I need to steal these two." The heat of his touch burned through the silk as he steered Marko and me toward the bedroom.

"Oh, yes, well—" The woman sputtered, confused at having her little moment upstaged.

"Zack, Zack, Zack!" Marko grabbed the man and swung him around. "I didn't see you come in. What are you doing here? I thought you were in Bolivia or something."

"I was." His eyes moved from Marko to me. "Some guys in khaki kept shooting up our equipment. We had to pack it in. Mel had asked me to do this movie a while back, so I called and he still wanted me."

"No accounting for taste."

"Glad to see you, too."

"Sarah, this is Zack Mandan, one of the best production designers in the business. Sarah's my assistant on the project."

"I know." He knew. "Mel told me." He took me in all at once. "If you two have a minute, I want to show you . . ."

He unzipped his case, tossing batches of sketches, photos, diagrams onto the bed. I recognized the "look" of our movie immediately. Marko picked up a photo of an old building. "This for the old couple's apartment?"

"Right."

"Where'd you find it?"

"Pure accident. Took a wrong turn off Ogden Avenue and there it was."

"No such thing as accidents in this world," I said. My voice, Fanny's words.

"I agree," said Zack. A person could get lost in those eyes. "And here"—he burrowed into the photos—"here's what I was thinking of for the bridal scene. This feel, this kind of space." An elaborately tiled entrance hall rose into a wide central staircase.

"You can almost feel the bride walking down," I said. Marko nodded.

"Long satin train trailing down those stairs."

"We can backlight that stained-glass window on the landing," said Zack, "filter the light through the lace."

The three of us kicked off our shoes and curled up on the bed, going through the photos, batting around ideas. I'd barely had time to scan the script, wouldn't have time to take it apart scene by scene until the flight to California. But even with that one short reading, I'd developed an idea of how I'd like the movie to look. And I'd braced myself for the worst. Marko was head designer and he might see the characters entirely differently. The set designer might have another idea altogether. And the director, overlord of us all, might not agree with any of us.

But Zack's vision was perfect. A thousand times more exciting than my half-formed ideas. We moved out of ourselves into the world of the film, throwing ideas on top of ideas.

"What if . . ."

"Yes, and how about . . ."

"Do you think we could . . ."

Conversation darted in and out of possibilities. My mind, so fatigued ten minutes ago, raced over characters, colors, styles, locations. The person I'd been in that outer room, the polite, small talking, socially correct lady, disappeared. I was back in my element.

The makeup man drifted in, and the stunt coordinator. We scrunched together on the bed. More people wandered in and we spilled over onto the floor until the room was crowded with a core group all focused on the same project, like musicians playing different parts of the same symphony.

"Hey, Zack, remember how we lit the tavern in *Father Jim?* We might be able to . . ."

"If you're going to need snow after March you might want to contact . . ."

"The CTA's pretty good about letting us shoot from the . . ."

It wasn't until a thunderclap of snoring in a corner stopped the conversation cold that I thought to look at a clock. Three in the morning?

Asher would be frantic!

He knew where I was.

He could have called.

He would have called if he was worried.

I could have called.

I should have called.
It was too late to call.
Shit!

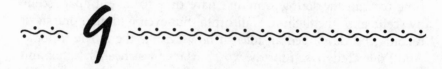

No easy way out. This was going to be rough. I lay on
my back staring at the ceiling, watching dawn push pale stripes
through the blinds. Asher's breathing shifted from deep to shallow.
He didn't move but I felt him wake. I slid a leg over to his side,
making the lightest of contact. He didn't slide back. But he didn't
pull away, either. A spark of hope.

"'Morning," I whispered. A moment of silence, Ladies and
Gentlemen.

"So you finally decided to come home." Hurt, anger, with just
a soupçon of accusation. He rolled onto his back, cradling his head
in his hands.

"I'm sorry, Asher. I lost all track of the time." Silence. Icy cold.
I risked a hand on his chest. His heart thudded.

"You didn't think I'd worry with you out there all alone,
driving around Chicago all hours of the morning?"

"I wasn't driving around. I was at a meeting."

"Until four in the morning?" So, he'd just pretended to be
asleep when I climbed into bed.

"I said I lost track." We stared at the ceiling together. C'mon,
say something. "You have every right to be angry."

"Thank you very much." He rolled off the bed and stormed
into the bathroom.

All right, I was wrong. I apologized. At least that part was over.
Now, if I was careful enough, and gentle enough, I might be able
to end this. When Asher came back to bed, if we made love . . .
The shower started. Asher never came back to bed after his shower.
He wasn't done being angry. This would go on for a while. Damn!

"It wouldn't hurt to lie once in a while, Sarahlah."

"I don't lie, Mom. Not to you. Not to the children. Not to
Asher."

"Everyone lies. It helps smooth out life's little bumps."

"I'm lousy at it."

"Try."

"I'm sorry I was late Asher but the elevator jammed and I was stuck between floors with five other people one of whom had just eaten a clove of garlic and I had to pee so bad the whole time and we sang songs to keep our spirits up."

or

"Asher, I had two little glasses of wine and the room was so hot that I felt woozy and went into the next room and sat down in a big chair and I must have passed out or something because the next thing I knew it was three in the morning."

"You're right. You're a lousy liar. But you're also not so terrific with the truth."

Is it my fault Truth's so pitifully lame? Better I should have crashed on the Outer Drive and been rushed to a hospital. At least then I'd have a worthwhile excuse. Well, if this ever happened again, I'd be sure to plow into a pole on my way home. That way, I wouldn't have to lie if I lived.

I walked through the house toward the kitchen. The den was a shambles. While I was at the Ritz, Asher had given up pasting photos in albums and dumped out all his dresser drawers on the den floor. It looked like drop-off day at the Salvation Army: jumbled mounds of T-shirts, socks, jockstraps, sweaters, bathing suits, Jockey shorts, cabana suits, long underwear, tennis shorts, pajamas. Hangered clothes draped over sofa backs. He'd even raided the attic racks and the out-of-season clothes I stored in the kids' old closets. I hoped he wasn't counting on me to help sort through everything. The phone company people were coming tomorrow to check the costumes and I still had to stitch and glue sixty push buttons.

I started the coffee, poured oat bran into Asher's bowl, sliced a banana on top, and sprinkled on a handful of raisins. Maybe I should run to Ganache for a couple of brownies. Buying him a treat might make me feel less guilty about coming home so late. Especially since I had to leave in a few minutes to go to my studio. I brought in the morning papers and poured myself a cup of coffee. The least I could do was keep Asher company while he ate breakfast.

He read the sports, stock report, comics and news. I cleared his dishes and refilled his coffee cup. He never looked up. I cut two thin banana slices and placed them over my eyelids.

"Oh, Daddy Warbucks, ain't you never going to talk to Little Orphan Sarah again?" I heard him sigh and put down his paper.

"So tell me, Sarah, what were you doing until four in the morning?"

"He speaks!" I lifted the banana slices and ate them. "I told you, we were talking about the movie." Boring, boring truth. "The director was there, and crew from lighting and special effects, and set design, and all sorts of people who will be working on the film. It was exciting, Asher. I wish you'd been there. We started throwing around ideas—"

"Marko was there?"

"Yes, of course Marko—"

"You can't do this talking during the day?"

"Asher, it happened. It just happened."

"Is this what movies are like? Are these the hours you're going to keep?"

"I have no idea what—"

"Because if they are, I don't want you doing this." Cut. Print. That's a wrap. Let it go, Sarah. Let it go.

"You don't want me doing this?"

"That's right." He slapped his hands on the table, pushed up and walked out of the room. Let it go, Sarah. I chased after him into the den. He settled into the middle of the clothes piles and started sorting.

"You can't ground me. You're not my mother." Silence. "You're my husband. I'm your wife. Doesn't that give me some equal rights around here?"

"I never stayed at Rosie's until four in the morning."

"If that's when they needed you, that's when you would have been there." He jammed his hand into sock after sock, tossing ones with holes into a large basket. "In all these years I've been designing for theaters, for ad agencies, for the kids' schools, have I ever once let my work interfere with our lives?"

"So why start now?"

"A lot of nights I'd work after you went to sleep just so I could be with you when you came home from Rosie's. But now I'm working around someone else's schedule and I don't make the hours and I don't make the rules." I sat next to him, picking up single socks, trying to find their mates. I couldn't leave like this, couldn't go through my day surrounded by anger and hurt. "Asher, I promise that if it is humanly possible, I will never again as long as I live do anything as stupid as forgetting to call."

"Good."

"But I need to do this movie. Need to get away from neurotic ad people who change their minds three times an hour and want everything done yesterday. And I am tired of trying to costume plays for theaters with no budget. And it would be nice for once to see the costumes I create live longer than a five-week run. I have no idea what working on a movie will be like. All I can promise is to be as considerate of you as I possibly can."

"Well"—he took the socks out of my hands and set them on the other side of him—"I guess that's it, then." End of discussion.

I filled a thermos with the rest of the coffee and left for my studio. A heaviness the size of a pressing ham pushed down on my heart. What was wrong lately? This guilt-laying wasn't Asher's style. The Asher Rose I knew and loved would be the first one to tell me to grab for that brass ring. Something was going on in his life that I didn't understand. Maybe it was selling Rosie's. Maybe it was facing fifty. Well, it was too late for me to back out of the movie, even if I wanted to.

"The Good Thing is," I said, sifting through the ashes for some small spark, "Asher doesn't expect me to help him sort through his clothes."

10

She held the large flower over her ear, her arm drooping with fatigue. "Almost done," I said, attacking the canvas faster, bold brush strokes painting her strong brown body against a backdrop of violent island colors. With a flick of the palette knife I slashed an appendix scar exactly like Sarah's into her firm belly. Gentle winds blew strands of ass-length hair across her nipples.

My arm muscles burned with fatigue and I switched the brush to my left hand, filling black holes that kept opening in the canvas, trying to suck me inside. A ship's bell sounded. Tips of a three-master rounded the reef and sailed into harbor. My ship. Had to finish the painting. If I didn't get it all down now, I'd lose it forever. The ship's bell sounded again. My arm exploded in pain. The third ring woke me.

I tried to reach for the phone but my arm was paralyzed. Must've slept on it. Nerve endings prickled and stung as the blood rushed back. Where was I? Beverly Hills. The Beverly Hills Hotel. Right. I grabbed with my other hand, hit the phone off the nightstand, fumbled with the receiver.

" 'Lo?"

"Oyyyyy. Oyyyyyy." The moaning dragged on, followed by silence. Gasps. Silence. "Oyyyy, oyyyy."

"Fanny?" The web of dream threads broke and floated off. Mouth dry as cotton. I shook my head, trying to clear the fog left from wine with lunch and five hours poolside in the California sun. "Fanny?"

"Let me talk to Sarah. Oy."

Sarah's lusty voice echoed in the shower: "Shave his belly with a rusty razor . . ."

"Fanny, what's wrong?"

"I'm sick. Dying, maybe. Sar-rah!" Her voice hacked like an ax—*whack!*—through my skull.

"Fanny, please, calm down." I stood, carrying the phone around the room, reaching for the dream. I had a feeling it was special and I wanted it back.

"I need Sarah!" *Whack!* I held the phone away from my ear.

"Do you want me to call an ambulance?"

"Don't talk crazy." *Whack!* "Where's my Sarah?" *Whack!* "Oy, I'm dying." Oh, the ear bone's connected to the eyeball nerves. I pressed thumb and forefinger against the lids to hold my eyeballs in.

"Sarah's busy. If you're sick, I'll send help."

"I can't breathe. Last night I didn't sleep a wink the whole time. I thought . . ." Fanny launched into her disease-of-the-week monologue. I opened the heavy drapes, squinting against the sunlight. Two women in string bikinis and see-through coverups passed our cottage on their way to the pool. I'd always had a thing for tall Eurasian women with long showgirl legs. It was God's little joke to package Sarah as a mid-size frizzy brunette. The fates were not without humor. I pulled the drapes closed.

Fanny's complaints picked up steam. "Aaah," I said sympathetically, shifting the phone to my other ear. "Uhmmmmm."

I didn't like this new hypochondria. All those years Fanny made digs about my "sick" mother. Why didn't she recognize "sickness" in herself? Where was the Fanny I knew and loved? The tough lady with the funny stories?

"— and I don't know what's the matter with me. I want to talk to Sarah."

"Fanny, what do you think she can do from here?" Silence. Labored breathing. "You want her to call your doctor? An ambulance?" She slammed down the phone. *Whack!* I put the phone on top of a pile of papers covering the desk. What was all this stuff? Sarah must have been up working last night. I thought we were supposed to be on vacation.

I peeled off my clothes. The body was still pretty good, chest, legs, tush, probably from walking all those miles around Rosie's every day. I sucked in my stomach. It had expanded the last few years like a slowly inflating tire. I'd start doing sit-ups, maybe take off a few pounds. Not much point being a multimillionaire, not much point at all, if I didn't stay fit enough to enjoy it. All the money in the world couldn't buy me health. It was time I started taking care of myself, hire a personal trainer, work out an hour a day, maybe two, get my endurance up, cholesterol down. The shower stopped and Sarah shifted into "The Twelfth of Never." I called room service.

"Send up a bottle of champagne and salt-free caviar on whole grain toast points," I said, examining my face in the dresser mirror.

"I don't think we have salt-free caviar, sir."

"Right, then, give me the fish eggs. No yolks."

What was this puffiness around my eyes? Something new? Probably from too much sun. And this soft wad of skin under my chin? Maybe I'd check out one of the L.A. plastic surgeons who kept America beautiful. Of course, if I became too gorgeous, it wouldn't be fair to all the women in the world who couldn't have me.

Sarah floated out of the bathroom wrapped in a silk kimono, smelling wet and delicious. God, I loved this woman, loved everything about her. Why was I so hard on her lately? She came toward me—oh, that sexy walk of hers. I had no right to be jealous of her new job, of the time it took away from us. Not after all the years she put up with Rosie's. Not after all the years she devoted to me and the kids. Her robe opened slightly, exposing the slightest curve of breast, the tiniest hint of inner thigh.

"I wouldn't scream," I said, falling back spread-eagle onto the bed, arms and legs lashed to imaginary bedposts, "if a beautiful, sexy woman were to attack me and ravage my body."

"Oh"—she clasped her hands together—"I do declare, you are so very very brave." She stood next to the bed, slowly untying her robe, trailing the ends of the belt over my body.

"What'cha got under the robe, lady?"

"None of your business. Turn over." I rolled onto my stomach.

She tuned the bedside radio to soft jazz. I closed my eyes. The bed shifted as she climbed on and straddled my rear. Warm oil drizzled down my spine and Sarah's strong fingers worked the oil into my body to the rhythm of the music. I drifted into the feel of her hands, her breasts brushing my back as she leaned forward to nibble my neck. Her fingers worked up my back, out my arms to my fingertips, and back again. After a long while she turned around, massaging deep into my thighs, my calves, my feet, and back up. She turned around again, laying her warm body on top of me.

"Think you're ready to have me do the other side?" she whispered, outlining my ear with her tongue, raising goose bumps. I rolled over, reaching up for her, pulling her down to me.

And oh the feel of Sarah on me under me with me her shower-warm skin sweet with soap and oil and lust and sweat her rhythms my rhythms her body familiar and surprising sweat-smacking against my body skin soft under my hands stroking probing Oh she says and Oh heating slowly and slowly warm to hot to flaming her passion stoking mine firing hers red molten at the core and Oh we say and Oh longings and wantings goddamn it bubbling and burning Oh God forcing up through fissures and Oh please urgent now and Oh God errupting and exploding and Oh God I shout and Yes she says and God I cry Oh yes she says and God I shout bursting beyond lust into loving into lust and I shudder with need and want and yes love all right love why not love until I

    until we

        until I

        until we

            until I

            EXPLODE

                and DIE

and it is all Sarah all Sarah all Sarah.

Something wet and cold brushed my mouth. I opened one eye. Sarah dangled a clump of green seedless over my lips.

"Thought you was a goner," she said.

"I was." She placed a grape in my mouth and I sucked her fingers on their way out. "Miss me?"

"Dunno. Thought I'd get to drink this whole bottle of bubbly myself." I hadn't heard room service come and go. She filled two glasses and fixed a plate of caviar. "Fanny weaned me on this stuff." Fanny.

"She called," I said.

"What?"

"You were in the shower."

"Asher!"

"What's the big deal"

"You know how nervous she was about our leaving Chicago." Sarah dialed Fanny and I swigged the first glass, wincing at the bubbles. Sex and sun work up a thirst.

"No answer." Sarah slid into bed, pressing her body against mine. I fed her caviar. "Did she say why she called?"

"Yes. She was dying."

"Ash-er." She threw a grape at me. "Really, what did she want?"

"Really, she said she was sick, dying."

"How could you forget to tell me?"

"Something else came up."

"Grrrr." Sarah dialed again. "Hello, Mr. Francosi? This is Fanny Feldman's daughter. Apartment three-oh-five?" She held the phone away from her ear. The building's super, half deaf from years of banging on boilers, tended to shout. "Yes, that's right. I'm in California and I was trying to reach my mother but there was no answer and I wondered if—"

"I just saw her," yelled Francosi.

"Oh?"

"Sitting in the lobby with the ladies."

"Ask if she looks dead," I said. Sarah hurled two grapes at me. Woman's got one hell of an arm.

"You want I get her for you?" asked Francosi.

"No," said Sarah. "Just tell her I called and I'm glad she's feeling better."

I dipped my fingers in the champagne and traced wet patterns along her body.

"Don't be nice to me while I'm mad at you," she said. She turned and spooned her naked body into mine. I cupped her breast in my hand and fell into a deep dreamless sleep.

11

"Here." I handed Jason to Asher. "Go and buy your grandpa an ice-cream cone."

"C'mon, Sport," said Asher. "I guess we know when we're not wanted."

Asher hugged our grandchild, that miracle of all miracles, and headed down the street. Maxi and I watched them. And now, Sarah, what are you going to tell your daughter? What have you learned in forty-five years that might be of any use? I took her hand in mine and we strolled up Rodeo Drive.

"Will we see Ben this trip?"

"Yes, of course. You know he loves both of you."

"It's just our daughter he's having problems with."

"Something like that." The sunlight caught red highlights in her hair. Thick strands like Asher's, curls like mine. The best of both. Fanny never warned me it could hurt so much to love a child.

"Is he beating you?"

"Ben?" She looked at me like I was crazy. "Of course not."

"Belching in public, talking in movies, moving his lips when he reads?" I saw the beginnings of a smile.

"Mom."

"So?"

We walked into a courtyard bordered by shops. "This one's fun," she said. I followed her into Wearable Art, letting her show me painted gowns and woven jackets, outrageous prices for mediocre talent, waiting until she was ready. We settled in front of a large mirror, trying on hats and head wraps. "It's not any one thing," she said. "I'm just not happy anymore. I'm restless all the time. If it weren't for Jason I think I would have left weeks ago."

"About the time you started your new job?"

"It has nothing to do with that." She set Asher's square jaw in righteous indignation. I played with a painted length of silk, wrapping it different ways around Maxi's head.

"You haven't suddenly run into more interesting people?" I asked. "Maybe someone at work you find particularly exciting?"

"That has nothing to do with Ben and me." Bingo. I put a dramatic straw hat on my head, angling its wide brim down over one eye. Maxi laughed. "It's you, Mom."

"In my next life. Elegant takes too much time." I swapped the antebellum South for a baseball cap studded with jewels, mine for just ninety dollars and a future draft choice.

"I don't expect you to understand," she said. "You and Dad never had problems."

"Oh? In twenty-five years we never had problems?" I tossed the cap back in the pile and stood up. "If you believe that, my dear, I have a bridge in Brooklyn to sell you." We walked back out into the courtyard, slowly circling the shops. How much do you tell your child? As much as she needs to hear.

"But you and Dad have always been so much in love. I used to be embarrassed when my friends talked about how awful their parents were. I wanted to make up bad stuff about you so I could fit in."

Sunlight sluiced through the open roof, pouring sharp shadows into the courtyard. We walked in and out of sunlight, hot to cold to hot again. Around and around. "I love your father, Maxi."

"I hope so."

"But before I loved him, I liked him. Liked the straight set of his back, the determination of his walk, his laugh, his eyes, his boyishness, his enthusiasm. All the time we were growing up, I could go to him with any problem and he would listen to me. He loved me for me. And let me tell you, that wasn't always easy. I love your father. But even more than that, he is my best friend in the whole world."

"I like Ben. I'm not saying I don't."

"Good. If you like each other, anything is possible. If you're friends, there's hope."

We stopped in a shaft of sun, staring into a diamond-studded window. Sixty-thousand-dollar bracelets, twenty-thousand-dollar earrings. They seemed to be doing a brisk business inside. Strange world, southern California. Maybe Maxi and Ben needed to come home, ground themselves in midwestern soil, send down roots. As if unhappiness didn't weed up into everyone's garden.

"Marriages move on waves, Maxi. All marriages. You ride the crest a while, then slide into the trough. There have been times I wasn't thrilled with your father, and times I felt him fall out of love with me." How much do you tell?

"I don't believe it. Daddy adores you."

"You aren't listening to me. Marriage cycles come and go without invitation or permission. One day you're crazy in love, can't get enough of the man, and the next you're thinking of hopping in the car and leaving. Am I right?" She looked away. I'd hit a truth.

"Maxi, you show me a woman who hasn't fantasized getting in the car and leaving home and I'll show you a woman who doesn't drive." She laughed. A good sign. "You don't think an occasional young girl at work has looked more exciting to your father than a tired wife with two children? You don't think an old boyfriend ever called to see how I was and, oh, by the way, had I heard he just divorced his wife? Of course there are temptations. Of course you wonder 'what if?' But if you love someone, you get through it. If you love someone, you grab hold of the good times and hold on for dear life through the bad. Give your marriage a chance, Maxi. Ride this out."

"Why?"

"Because each time you do, the marriage gets stronger. Because loving someone is the greatest joy and the hardest work in the world, and you are barely at the beginnings of it."

12

"Shu-shu?"

"Yes, Jason?" His small body twisted in my arms as he pointed to one of six white Rolls parked on the block.

"Caw?"

"Right. Carrrr." I hugged him, nuzzling my nose into his sweet little neck—baby powder and pink lotion and something all his own—until he pulled away giggling.

"See caw?"

"Carrrrrrrr. You got it, Sport." Black-suited chauffeurs

schmoozed in the shade of a curbside tree. I bent down, lowering Jason so he could look into the car. Maybe I'd buy Sarah one of these for her birthday. Not that I could ever pry her away from her old station wagon. That woman had some weird tastes. Jason wriggled in my arms, grabbing for the pristine paint with chocolate-covered hands. One of the chauffeurs straightened, on alert. I swung Jason away.

"Caw!" he cried. "See caw!"

"Oh, Jase! Look! Look at the doggie. See the doggie?" Please let there be a dog. I swung him around like an airplane—"Whirrrrr, whirrrrr"—hurrying up Rodeo Drive toward Sarah and Maxi.

"Seeeee caaaawwwwww!" yelled Jason. Maxi turned and laughed, throwing her arms open to us. Jason lunged for them.

"What's wrong?" asked Sarah.

"Your grandson wants a Rolls-Royce."

"A man of taste," she said, wetting a tissue with her tongue, wiping ice cream and tears from Jason's face. "Just like your grandpa." They walked ahead and I held back, loving the view. My family. Wife, daughter, grandson. Living long-distance, sometimes I forgot the pride of creating a family. Maybe Sarah and I should stop in Boulder on our way home, spend a couple of days with Jeff, get to know his wife. So he didn't want to work at Rosie's. So all right. It's over. Rosie's is gone. Maybe Jeff and I can be friends now. I dug in my pocket for a Kleenex. Getting sentimental in my old age.

Sarah waved from under a white awning, signaling that they were going inside. I waved and ambled on. An elegant couple nearly knocked me over as they ran laughing out of Armani's. She was a stunner. Short little skirt, blond hair, expensive gold and diamond jewelry. He looked late forties, but his stylish clothes and vigorous attitude made him seem years younger. Suddenly, my beige sports slacks, off-white shirt and woven belt that had looked so dapper in Marshall Field's felt downright dowdy. I stared as he helped the woman into a white limo. How did he do that, put the outside together to reflect the inside?

I could buy anything on this street I wanted. The simple idea hit me broadside. Anything! No reason I couldn't be like that man. Armani, limo. Sarah and I could move here. Good weather. Closer to Jason and Maxi. What kept us in Chicago? Rosie's? I had the feeling Kimball would be happy if I never came back to work. Fanny? We'd bring Fanny along.

The sweater in the window of Pierre LaTour had my name on it. I strode in and asked the salesgirl for a medium.

"What color would you like?" she asked. I nearly said beige.

"What do you suggest?"

The girl studied me a moment, then pulled a black sweater from the pile. "With your coloring . . ." she said, handing it to me. "This is a fabulous sweater. Four-ply cashmere."

I never wore black. Black washed my mother out and made her look sick. She raised all six of us on beiges and blues. I pulled the sweater over my head. Fabulous! It built up my shoulders and trimmed down my stomach. I looked powerful in black. Important.

"That's made for you," said the girl.

Clothes absolutely positively make the man. I'd been dressing old my whole life. Not anymore. A wardrobe of clothes like this would knock off ten years. Now that I didn't have to worry about vats bubbling gravy on my clothes or rough-edged crates snagging fabric, I could wear whatever I wanted. I took off the sweater and tossed it on the counter. I'd get a few pairs of new pants, some Italian shirts, a couple more sweaters.

"Will this be all?" The salesgirl slid behind the counter. She smelled like fresh strawberries and ocean mist. Yes, I would move to California and live happily ever.

"I'd also like—" The price tag flipped over as I pushed the sweater across the counter. $2,500! "That is, I'm looking at some pants down the block that might go with this. I'll be back."

"I'll just set this aside for you."

I escaped to the street. Looking great was one thing. Being a schmuck was another. My father stocked four-ply cashmere to make robes and scarves for a few wealthy customers. The goods cost two hundred a yard, tops. That sweater took a yard and a half. Not that it wasn't beautiful. Not that I didn't look important in it. Not that I couldn't afford it. But I couldn't buy it. Every time I put it on I'd feel like I'd been taken.

"There you are," said Sarah, coming up behind me. "Thought I'd lost you. Find something?"

"Not really." We walked arm in arm down the street. "Having a good time?"

"How did we manage to have the world's most beautiful, brightest, happiest grandson?"

"Spoken like an unbiased grandmother. Enjoy your girl talk with Maxi?"

"She's going through a little bit of a rough time. She and Ben are seeing a marriage counselor." Her words stacked like bricks on my chest.

"What's wrong?"

"Now, don't get all upset. If you remember, we had a few things to work out in the beginning, too. They'll be all right." I couldn't draw a full breath. The world started squeezing in. "Asher?" Sarah helped me over to a bench. She held me close, rocking slightly. "Come on, honey, all the kids today go to marriage counselors." A part of my life broke off and floated away.

Maxi hurried down the street toward us, Jason bouncing on her hip. "I just called home to collect phone messages," she said. "Grandma's sick."

"We know," said Sarah. "Fanny called us at the hotel. She's a little tense with us away."

"No, this is for real. Dr. Fishman called. Grandma's in the hospital. A gallbladder attack or something."

Sarah didn't touch her food on the flight home. "Seems a shame to pay for first class and not eat," I said, trying to coax a smile out of her. Later: "It's not your fault Fanny's in the hospital." Still later: "She'll be all right."

I leaned my head against the window and stared down at the clouds. Was Fanny faking? My mother was too sick to do any of the things we needed, but she was sure well enough to have friends over playing poker and mah-jongg two days a week, every week, year in and year out.

The cool window felt good against my forehead. I couldn't go through this again. One invalid mother in a lifetime was enough. Damn Fanny's broken hip. She was so healthy until then. It sure didn't take her long to enjoy the attention she got living with us while she recuperated.

I wasn't being fair. The doctor said Fanny had a gallbladder full of stones. Still, the dangers were the same. I'd let my parents walk all over me, but I'd been a kid. Well, I wasn't a kid anymore. I'd take control of this right away. We'd find Fanny a housekeeper, a nurse, whatever it took to get her well and give Sarah and me peace of mind.

13

I felt around in the dark closet, cracking my baby toe against a shoe box, tearing a thumbnail on a hanger. This was stupid. Why hadn't I laid my clothes out last night? I pulled the closet door closed and risked turning on the light.

"Sarah?" Damn! I opened the door.

"Sorry, Asher. I didn't mean to wake you."

"I don't see why you always need to be at the hospital at dawn."

"It's not dawn." Maybe dawn-and-a-half. "I like to be there when Dr. Fishman makes his rounds."

"You can't call him at his office?"

"Asher, please. This is my mother." I grabbed what had become my uniform: a black jumpsuit with something thrown over for color. A real no-brainer, like slopping different sauces on the same old chicken. I tossed the clothes on the bed and stripped off my robe. Asher patted the bed next to him.

"Oh, no," I said, dressing. "Yesterday you made me an hour late."

"What am I going to do all day?"

"You might try going to work."

"That's good for about two hours' worth of Mickey Mouse things to do."

"Call Paul. He's always up for playing hooky."

"Meet me for lunch."

"Can't. Marko and I start shopping the show today."

"You have to eat."

"I don't know where I'll be."

He sat up, smoothing the blanket across his lap. "Is there something going on between you and Marko?"

"Yes, Asher. We're costuming a movie together."

"Is he married?"

"No."

"Going with someone?"

"Long time."

"She in the movies, too?"

"*He's* an architect. Hey! No! Asher, put down that pillow!" I ducked too late. The pillow hit me head-on. I picked it up, climbed onto the bed, and hit him back. He grabbed me and pinned me down, pressing his nose to mine.

"Why didn't you say something?"

"Because you're so cute when you're jealous." He kissed my nose, my eyes, my ears. This morning he made me only half an hour late.

The hospital elevator doors slid open. I hurried past the central station, avoiding the nurse's eyes. God only knew who Fanny had offended since I left last night. This time they'd put her in a room at the end of a long corridor. Did Fishman think she'd disturb fewer people if he tucked her away? Gimme a break, Doc. Fanny threw her voice to the last row of the third balcony for more years than you've been alive. Banishing her to the boonies just gives her more emoting room.

Even at seven-fifteen in the morning, before her pipes were properly warmed, Fanny's voice echoed along the bright corridor and out to the desk. "Nurse," she called. "Oy [beat] oy [beat] NuRRRrrrssse!" I tiptoed down the hall, past room after room of perfectly behaved patients who rested, finished breakfast, read. "NurRRSSE!" My luck. Fanny was not the type to go gentle into the night or day.

"NurRRSSE!!" This last slid up one whole octave, hurtling me back to 1950. Douglas Park Theatre. Second act of *The Little Foxes*. Anyone who hadn't sat mesmerized in that dark theater night after night, anyone who hadn't watched little Fanny Feldman grow ten feet tall on stage, anyone who hadn't heard that exact brilliant vocalization note for note, pitch for pitch, might have thought this modern-day Fanny was dying instead of recovering. I knew mid-performance when I heard it, but I refused to run around trying to explain an actress's need to perform. It was not for me to apologize for my mother's behavior. Well, perhaps just a token gesture, a simple ten-pound box of Godiva chocolates to the nurses and a promise to write them all into my will.

" 'Morning, Mother." I set my gift of fresh flowers in the vase on her dresser. "Where's your roommate?"

"Out for tests." She thrust out her arms, the skin yellow and blue from IVs. "Look at this, Sarahlah. They're trying to kill me!"

"Has Dr. Fishman been here yet?"

"Mumzer. Goniff. All his fancy society patients. What does he care about an old lady?" I kissed her forehead. No fever.

"Dr. Fishman adores you."

"Bah."

"You're the only patient who outshouts him."

That coaxed a small smile. She waved her bruised hand grandly toward the closet. "Bring me the gold."

The tiny space overflowed with bed jackets left over from Fanny's last hospital role, The Grand Dame of the Broken Hip. I'd sewn jackets for several of her personalities. Delicate laces ("Oh, Doctah, Ah do believe Ah have the vapahs"), rich brocades ("The Queen will see you now"), diaphanous silks ("How frightfully terribly wonderfully sweet of all you handsome young doctors to come visit"), all trimmed with sexy boas, elegant feathers, playful buttons. The gold was the heavily studded number she favored in her more flamboyant moods. I took it as a sure sign of recovery.

"You should see how they push me around in here." Blood coursing through her veins brought a glow to her cheeks. "Two of them dragged me out of bed and made me sit in a chair!"

"Sit? In a chair? How dare they!" The heavy jacket weighed her down. She was much too frail. Like Asher's mother near the end. Stop it! This was not the end! This was gallbladder. Fanny and Mrs. Rose had absolutely nothing in common. Mrs. Rose was the type to die.

Eight-thirty. Where was Fishman? He always came by eight. Fifteen more minutes and I'd have to explain to Fanny why I had to leave, or call Marko and explain why I'd be late to work. The old rock and a hard place. The fire in my stomach heated up.

Fanny flipped up the tray mirror and popped open the jar of Ponds Cold Cream. Best smell in the world. The smell of Mother at Dressing Table, accepting flowers and praise after a performance. The smell of Mother the Princess/Witch/Orphan/Daughter/Neighbor/Lover/Wife magically transforming back into Mother the Mother. The smell of Mother at Rest listening to her daughter babble on and on about school and boys and whatever else she wanted to talk about. I drank in the smell of memory as Fanny slathered Ponds over her face.

"How could you let them stick me in this godforsaken room?" she asked. Here we go.

"You will please remember that I put you in a private room and you carried on until we moved you."

"That was not a room. That was the Black Hole of Calcutta."

"You just don't like playing to an empty house."

"This room's in Kishnev." I handed her the box of tissues and helped wipe off the cold cream. "Who can see what's going on? You couldn't find one next to the nurses' station?"

"The ward's SRO. It was this or the broom closet."

"Is it closer to the nurses' station?"

Dr. Fishman raced in, coattails flapping, residents trailing, wisps of white hair flying off in all directions.

"Gary!" Fanny eased into her brave-but-weak mode, clutching the bed jacket around her thin shoulders. Dr. Fishman bent to receive a kiss and to give one.

"Looking sexy today, Fanny," he said, feeling her pulse, checking her eyes, scanning her chart. Fishman did a minimum of three things at any one time. Fanny beamed at his attention. He examined her skin color over the tops of his glasses. "Looks like we got rid of that yellow."

"It's not my best color."

"How're you feeling?"

"Oh [beat] as well as can be expected."

"You're going to outlive us all, Fanny. Hi, Sarah." I nodded as he turned to what Fanny called his "doc-lings" and launched into a rapid-fire rundown of Fanny's condition.

My stomach pain eased and, for the first time all morning, I actually felt relaxed. Fishman, tough as a barnyard rooster, with infinitely less finesse, happened to be the best diagnostician in Chicago. He loved celebrities, skied with them in Vail, danced at their weddings, appeared regularly in society and gossip columns. Fanny latched on to him early in his career and made him the doctor of choice among her actor friends. The more he insulted her, the better she liked it.

"I want out of this place," said Fanny.

"How about tomorrow?" *Whomp!* Back came the pain. Really should mention it to the doc when I had time.

"You sure that's not too soon?" I asked.

"Don't worry, Sarah." He put a comforting arm around my shoulder and zeroed right in on my problem. "I'll give you the names of a couple of services that supply nurses. It'll be all right."

"I don't want nurses," said Fanny. Here we go again.

"You want to go home?" asked Fishman. She nodded. "Then you need nurses. You can't take care of yourself just yet."

"I have a daughter. She'll take care of me."

"I work, Mom."

A weakened Fanny turned to the doc-lings. "She works." With great effort she turned her head to me. "I'm your mother. What's more important?" Just drive those rusty nails through her frail body and into the cross, boys.

"Behave yourself, Fanny." Fishman took Fanny's hands in his. "You're going home, you're going to be nice to the nurses, you're going to let Sarah live her life, and in two months—*if* you behave yourself—I'll take you out dancing."

"Moscow at Night?"

"It's a date."

Speeding toward Marko's, I liberated a bottle of Pepto-Bismol from the glove compartment and swigged mightily. I wasn't crazy about this stomach pain. It wasn't gas and it wasn't needing to go to the bathroom. This was something other and it hurt like hell. I'd better update my will so the kids wouldn't kill each other fighting over my Betty Boop watch and collection of topless Tupperware. No way I'd leave my treasures for Asher's next wife. Slut. Bimbette. Firm-thighed treasure hunter. I prayed he'd have the strength to wait for someone who would love him for him and not his millions. It wasn't as if he'd had a whole lot of experience with women. Oh, the pain. I'd make an appointment as soon as I got to work.

Three swigs doused the raging flames to embers. A checkup would have to wait until I had time.

First I'd get Fanny squared away, line up nurses, buy groceries, drop them at her apartment.

Then I'd steel myself for at least one week of Fanny doing Death. She'd rehearsed it during the Broken Hip and had it pretty well honed by now. It was an exhausting role, physically and emotionally, especially for the audience.

Then I'd finish working on the movie. And THEN I'd help Asher pick an exotic place for our first trip. He wanted to go away for a month. Two weeks, I told him. Can't leave Fanny longer than that. Not to mention my work—which I didn't.

14

"So I say to the guy, 'You show me where it's illegal and I'll stop doing it.'" I nodded, staring out the front windshield, wishing Paul would too, since he was driving. He whipped his newest in a long line of red Porsches in and out of Loop traffic, swinging west along the river. "Awww, what the hell. I've been thinking about going into something else. Maybe now's the time." He turned into the East Bank Club lot, beating out a BMW for the last space. "Maybe I'll open a restaurant near the Merc, put fax machines on tables for orders, break each item down to its cholesterol, fat, protein. Hey, maybe some of your nutrition experts at Rosie's could help me with that. I don't know. I'll think of something."

We grabbed our gym bags and cut across the lot past rows of Mercedes, BMWs, Cadillacs, Nissans. Eleven-thirty on a Friday morning. Who were all these people who had nothing better to do than sweat in a gym?

Two uniformed women smiled from behind the marble reception counter. Paul stood in line to check us in. In the lobby, near-naked bodies draped over crushed-leather sofas and sprawled in cushy suede chairs. A parade of people, shiny from sweat or oil or both, hurried around gigantic potted plants, gripping hand weights, squash/tennis/racquetball rackets, bottles of juice, exercise mats.

So this was Paul's club. He'd flaunted it often enough, calling from the club lounge while he sipped a pre-lunch martini. I'd answer my beeper, picking up one of the plant's floor phones, barely able to hear over the roar of the overhead can conveyor or the *chuka-chuka-chuka* of the veggie slicer. But nothing Paul had told me about the club prepared me for the reality of the place. I felt an old anger rise up and dust itself off.

"Doesn't anyone around here work?" I asked.

"I've been trying to tell you," said Paul. "There's life after chicken noodle."

The line moved up and I stood aside, watching the stream of exercisers. All around the city, poor saps sweated their balls off so these people could play. Like when I was young and my brothers and sisters rode bikes, played ball, visited friends while I shopped, met with their teachers, and did whatever else parents were supposed to do. History, Asher. Ancient history. Put it to rest.

It was easy for Paul to rag on me about working too hard. He had a nose-to-the-grindstone partner who took care of business. I had had Mookey. The few times I went to New York on business or out to L.A. to see Maxi, Rosie's was a mess when I got back. How could I leave? Well, Rosie's wasn't my problem anymore. Kimball made that clear every time I showed up, humoring me with make-work jobs like I was some ancient relic.

Two women came at us, nipples jutting, behinds wiggling, perfume lingering. Their short shorts and tank tops were cut from scraps so tiny even Sarah would throw them away. Maybe this place wasn't all bad. I smiled and nodded. They didn't smile back.

"Try not to slobber on the carpet," said Paul, leading the way up plush carpeted steps to the locker room, past the sauna, steam room, and whirlpool.

"This ain't the Y," I said.

"Haven't thought about that place for years." He laughed. "Remember that dingy locker room—"

"Showers with no water pressure—"

"Handball courts with potholed walls—"

"A pool too crowded for laps."

Paul shook his head. "We thought it was a palace."

"For twenty-five bucks a year we didn't get ambience."

"For twenty-five bucks we got a sliver of soap, a towel thin enough to see through, and foot fungus."

"Yeah," I said, "those were the days."

I hung my clothes in a locker the size of Nevada. A kid Jeff's age sauntered in from the showers, rippling muscles as he toweled off and pulled on leopard-print bikini briefs. Maybe that's why the women in the lobby hadn't smiled back at me. They sensed I wasn't the leopard-brief type. That didn't mean I couldn't be. Work out every day. Build up my chest and firm this stomach. Five grand, ten grand, how much could it cost to join? What difference? Coming here wouldn't be a bad way to spend time. It beat cleaning closets and sorting through forty-nine years of photos.

I unzipped my duffel and began suiting up. The only white socks I could find, one in Maxi's old room and one in Jeff's, were different lengths and had different colored bands at the top. Why didn't Sarah keep all the sport socks in one place? She used to be efficient. Maybe, when I finished organizing my things I'd put the whole house in order.

"So this is how the other half lives," I said, pulling on my old sweats. Under the fluorescents, they looked more blotchy green than I'd remembered. The bikinied man glanced over, unsmiling. Paul groaned.

"Weren't those things condemned?"

"You picking on me?"

"Sorry, Asher, I forget. You can't afford new clothes." He shoved his Gucci bag into his locker and slammed the door.

"What's with you?" No answer. "You mad at me?"

"Mad? Me? I'm not mad. Do I look mad?"

"Sorta like your grandpa looked that day we flushed his teeth down the toilet." Paul came over, snarling.

"Unless you're sitting around counting your money all day, you probably have a few minutes to go out and buy a pair of decent sweats. And those socks. You're wearing those socks to antagonize me."

"I just love it when you're angry." I pinched Paul's cheek, ducking his swing.

"It's not like you're still working twenty-hour days, seven days a week. You're filthy rich, goddamnit, and you've got nothing but time. It should only happen to me. Damn, forgot my shoes." He attacked the combination lock.

You could never tell Paul's bank balance by looking at him. He floated in and out of serious debt, but always dressed like a millionaire. "If you look like a winner and think like a winner, you are a winner." He believed it and made it come true. At the moment, he had two kids in Swiss boarding schools, and lived in a penthouse apartment with his socialite bride. Well, you couldn't tell my bank balance by looking at me, either.

"Know what I think?" I said.

"Can't wait to hear."

"You're jealous because I have style."

"Right."

"These pants have history."

"Yeah, like Pompeii and the Roman Empire." He flicked me with a towel. "C'mon, Numbnuts," he said, taking the stairs to the gym two at a time.

It wasn't like any gym I'd ever seen. Metallic hoists, pulleys, gizmos, gadgets, a room straight out of a science fiction movie. "Just follow what I do. It's easy."

I followed him from machine to machine without reducing the weights. Four machines into our workout, facedown on a leg-weight bench, my calves cramped, pain hammer-gunned into my shoulders, and my face pressed into leather that reeked of VO5. The adult in me hurt like hell but the child wouldn't let Paul beat me. We'd competed our whole lives, running, swimming, golfing, bowling. I wasn't going to let him beat me now. A trainer came up to me.

"This your first time?" Sweating, panting, the veins of my neck ready to burst, I nodded.

"You're going to hurt yourself that way," he said. "Come on, I'll take you through step-by-step."

He saved my life. Away from Paul, I was free to reduce the weights. Working out became a possibility. Yes, I would definitely join this club, build myself up when Paul wasn't around, get my old strength back.

After the machines, we crossed the hall into a room ringed with mirrors. Sculptured bodies crowded into rows.

"Don't stand near me until you buy new sweats," said Paul. "I don't want my membership revoked."

I gave him the finger and wedged between Rambo and Jane. Rambo's satin T-shirt strained across his chest. Jane's tiger-striped leotard matched her tights and headband. My reflection taunted me from every wall of this room of mirrors. Baggy clothes, baggy face, baggy body. A sobering sight.

Paul moved to the row in front of me, striking up a conversation with the beauty on his right. How did he do that? Made it look so easy. Not that I had trouble flirting with the women at Rosie's. But these ladies were a different animal. I wouldn't know how to begin.

The instructor bounded into the room, hopped up on the stage and switched on the music. Full breasts, tiny waist, no hips. I tried to work out and stare at the same time and kept bumping into people. Five minutes into the warm-up, I noticed the mean set to her mouth. She barked like a drill instructor, "Keep going! Don't stop!" Another five minutes, I realized she wasn't at all pretty. Ten minutes into the "abs," flat on my back, straining to bring my head and knees together over my stomach for the seventh time, I wondered what I ever saw in her.

Paul sailed through the exercises, laughing with the woman next to him. This was a trick, right? I couldn't be this out of shape. No breath, muscles burning, vision blurred, I was two jumping jacks away from passing out when the instructor shouted a command and jogged the class out of the room onto the quarter-mile track. A few minutes later, Paul jogged back into the room, running in place next to my corpse.

"You all right?" he asked.

"Yes, Paul." Sweat flooded out of my pores and pooled on the floor. I concentrated on sucking air. "I am lying here . . . staring at the ceiling . . . composing a farewell letter to Sarah, because . . . I feel so damned fine."

"I can't believe you let yourself go like this."

"Some of us . . . had to work . . . every day. You know, jobs."

He stopped running and knelt next to me. His knees didn't crack. "Asher, be serious, this isn't good. Tiffany barely worked us. The hard part starts after we run ten minutes on the track."

"You're kidding." He wasn't.

"You should have a thorough checkup."

"I'm just a little out of shape."

"Right." He pulled me up. "C'mon, let's get you into a shower."

"Fresh."

Paul waited while I stripped off my soaking sweats, then started the water for me.

"After the shower, take a whirlpool, sauna, steam, the whole nine yards."

"Where you going?"

"I have half a class left. Want a massage? They got 'em here."

"I'll take a pass. How much happiness can one man stand?"

"Asher"—he shook his head and smiled—"you don't know the half of it."

15

Wood shavings and sawdust littered the back porch. But I was so happy to be coming home, so exhausted from eight hours of costume-hunting in mildewed basements and spidery attics, that I stepped over the warning signs and into the minefield.

"Asher?" No answer. I slung my purse on a kitchen chair and tossed my coat on the table. "Asher?"

No signs of anyone doing anything about dinner. The housekeeper I'd hired until Fanny approved a nurse and went back to her apartment usually had *something* cooking by the time I walked in the back door. Where was everyone? I flicked on the kitchen tap and sprinkled Ajax on my hands and arms, trying to scrub off the top ten layers of grime before I touched anything.

Oh, no, I'd forgotten to call home. How could I have gone the whole day without calling? No wonder no one answered. I was probably in deep shit with everyone. In the rush from house sale to house sale, who had time to call? Where was there a phone? Besides, when was the last time I'd had to phone home, now that Asher called me a minimum of five or six times a day? Where do you keep this? he'd want to know, or What do you plan to do with that?

I dug out a Brillo pad from under the sink, cleaning around what was left of my fingernails. All those years he worked, I tried not to bother him unless I was in hard labor. After all, I'd read the secretaries' letters to Ann Landers making fun of clinging bosses' wives. I wasn't about to pester *my* husband with the children's squabbles, repair problems, household decisions. I was an independent woman capable of running a home and raising a family without any help, thank you very much. Wish Asher read Ann Landers.

My hands were as clean as they were going to get without a serious soak in a hot tub. I walked through the house looking for signs of life.

"Asher?" The morning newspapers and afternoon mail lay unopened in a pile on the foyer table. Asher Rose *never* began a day without his newspapers and *always* opened his mail. I started up the staircase and caught the smell of fresh-cut lumber, heard a buzz saw rip through a piece of wood. A fine film of sawdust covered the banister, carpet, everything. "Asher?"

The door to Maxi's old bedroom opened and Fanny peeked out. The back of her thinning hair, mashed from lying against pillows, fanned around her head like the tail of a weary peacock. "Thank God you're home," she said.

"What's going on?"

"He's been at it all day long."

"Where's Mrs. Cunningham?"

"She couldn't stand the dust. Allergic. Said to tell you it was real nice working for you. She'll send a bill." The saw whirred alive and screeched through another length of wood. Fanny winced. "Who can rest?"

"What's he doing?"

"Do I know?"

"You didn't ask?"

"I asked. He wouldn't tell." She coughed and clutched her robe around her. "I'm not feeling so good. You talk to him. That's a good girl." She closed the door.

Lumber in assorted lengths lay in the hall outside Jeff's room. I stepped over, trying to avoid nails, screws, tools. All Jeff's furniture was gone except for his old clock radio, now aimed at the closet door, playing a staticy WXRT. I walked toward the closet that up to this morning had been filled with clothes, coin collections, comic book boxes, scuba gear, old hockey sticks, missing-pieced games, baseball/soccer/golf shoes, beer cans, *Playboys*, hats, baseball cards.

Asher, in sweaty T-shirt and old bermudas, stood on a ladder drilling holes into the closet wall. From the time I'd left home at seven this morning, Asher had ripped out Jeff's custom closet system and replaced it with floor-to-ceiling plywood shelves.

"Hi," I said.

He looked around, surprised. "Sarah. You're home?" He looked at his watch. "I can't believe it. Did this day ever go fast." He sat on the ladder, wiping the back of his arm across his forehead. "Well," he said, "what do you think?"

"What are you doing?"

"Can't you tell?" I looked at the deep closet shelves, the empty room.

"Give me a clue."

"Wait, wait." He clambered down the ladder and took me out

into the room. "Okay, picture this. An eight-foot-long, twenty-seven-inch-high table in the middle of the room, lots of compartments underneath to store things. A grid of bright lights overhead . . ." He went on and on, excited, energetic, enthusiastic. This was my Asher. The take-charge kid I fell in love with a lifetime ago. The man I couldn't wait to come home to at night. He'd been fading these last few months. I sure as hell missed him. Didn't like that humorless irritable old man trying to move into his body. ". . . window seats under the bay. The tops will lift for extra storage."

"You're making a workroom?"

"Yes! Do you like it?"

"I love it." He put an arm around me and looked out over a vision only he could see. "I was lying in bed this morning and it just came to me. How stupid we've been to waste this huge room storing stuff Jeff doesn't want."

"You didn't throw—"

"No, no. I thought about it but I knew you'd get crazy. I hired a couple of guys to cart everything to the basement."

"It's fabulous. When did you— How did you— What made you decide to finally build yourself a workroom?"

"Me?" He laughed. "No, not me. You. This is for you." And, oh, the joy on his face, the proud child gifting the parent his treasured dead frog. I heard the small ticks of my heart, like pins pulled out of live grenades. "See, here's where you'll keep your fabrics. And I'm putting up a pegboard on that wall for threads, scissors, that sort of stuff, and the sides of the table will be hinged to open out—"

"Asher—"

"—like this, see." He smoothed out a sketch done on a Rosie's cafeteria napkin. Damn that new manager for not keeping Asher busy, for not exhausting his many talents, for not keeping his worklife the hell away from mine. "You can cut a tent on a table this size if you want. And this—"

"Asher! What are you talking about? I have a studio." He looked at me as if I wasn't understanding.

"That's the *point*, Sarah. There's no need for you to go out of the house to work. We have more room here than you could ever want."

"I can't work at home."

"You *couldn't* work at home. Not in the dining room. I mean,

I understood your problem with that. Having to set up your sewing machine, cutting board, iron, all that stuff, then put it away when we needed the room."

"You hated the mess."

"Yes, yes, I know, I know. Hated coming home to a messy house, hated stepping on pins. But here you can be as messy as you want and just close the door. Oh, this is going to be so great!" He climbed back up the ladder. "Hand me that Phillips, will you?" I picked up the long screwdriver and handed it to him, watching him tighten a bracket.

Whose movie had I stepped into? Who wrote this script? Was this Woody Allen or Stephen King? Do I laugh or scream? Go easy, Sarah. This is meant as a gift of love. Careful where you tread.

"I think this would make a super workroom for you," I said as cheerfully as I could. "I'll help bring up your tools. That musty corner next to the boiler can't be a healthy place to work. Think of the things you could make and fix and tinker with in a room like this."

"Oh, no. I'm not going to take over your room."

"I don't want it." He froze in mid-screw. Careful. At least take off your cleats before you stomp all over his ego. "I appreciate this, Asher, I really do. All this work, the time and planning you put into it. But I can't work at home." He sat on the top of the ladder and clamped his hands on his knees.

"What's so special about that studio of yours? You complain that it's freezing in winter and damp in summer."

"It is. But it's mine. And a basement's all I can afford to rent just now. Don't give me that look. I've always paid my business expenses out of my profits. All your money doesn't change that."

"It's our money."

"I didn't earn it, Asher."

"You stayed home and raised our children and took care of the house so I could earn it. You're my partner."

"I understand. But it doesn't feel the same as the money I earn doing my work."

"Why can't you work at home? People do it all the time. Look at Lyn Metcalf. He's a pretty damned good architect. Runs a hell of a business out of his home."

"And Ruth Metcalf goes crazy trying to keep the children away from Daddy's office, running to answer doorbells, the house

phone, preparing lunches for his meetings with clients. You show
me a man with small children who works out of his home and I'll
show you a wife on the brink of a breakdown."

"I'll be your Ruth Metcalf. I'll tackle vacuum salesmen on the
front step, keep Girl Scouts from knocking on your door."

"Home is different for a woman, Asher. Home is not where we
come to relax after work. Home *is* our work. It's an oxymoron to
say a woman spends her day off at home. It would be like your
spending your day off at Rosie's."

"You can work anyplace you set your mind to."

"Not here. Here only part of me's at work. The other part's
thinking I should run to the grocery store, or start dinner, or take
in the dry cleaning, or pick up shoes from the shoemaker, or
answer the doorbell, or be civil to friends who drop by to chat
because, after all, I'm just working at home. When I worked at
home, I had to do important projects after midnight when there
were no interruptions."

"It doesn't have to be that way. You can make the rules."

"And then go crazy trying to enforce them? What if you knock
on the door to ask a question? Or the doorbell rings and no one
but me is home to answer? I like my cold, damp dungeon. People
take me seriously at my studio. I take myself seriously. I get
dressed in the morning and leave the house and go to work. I'm
efficient there, Sarah the Costumer. And I make Sarah the Mother/
Wife/Daughter wait outside the studio until I'm ready to go home."

Asher sighed, nodding at the shelves. "I never thought you
might not want this."

"I'm sorry, sweetheart. Honest I am."

He climbed down the ladder and folded it against the wall, then
looked around at the last eleven hours of his life. "What did I do
all this for, then?"

"You should have asked me."

"Wouldn't have been much of a surprise, then, would it?" He
walked out of the room.

"I'll start something for dinner," I said, following him out.

"I'm not hungry."

He closed our bedroom door behind him and I stood in the
hall, on top of piles of lumber and layers of sawdust I knew I'd
have to deal with. "I love to cook/paint/build, but I hate to clean
up." What egocentric idiot coined that phrase?

The house would have to wait. First I'd go down and make

Fanny dinner, and then I'd call around and find a nurse. Had to get Fanny out of our house and back into hers. Had to find something for Asher to do that would excite him as much as building me a workroom. I'd seen the old spark flare for a moment and I wanted to see more. Made me remember the real Asher Rose, realize how much I missed him. Turning, I walked a plank toward the stairs, and went down to start dinner.

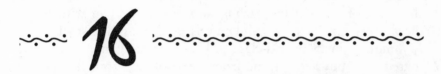

Paul was the only one of us who looked like he belonged at the best table at Ditka's. Groomed like one of the wise guy hoods we grew up with, impeccably tailored, workout trim and tanning booth brown, he led Byrd, Herb and me through the packed room to the table under the huge TV screen.

One of the perks of going places with Paul was getting the best seat in the house. I could never figure how he did it. It wasn't like I hadn't greased my share of palms over the years, but it didn't seem to seat me any faster or any better. Besides, I hated doing it, passing lines of waiting people, slipping a folded five or ten or, upon occasion, twenty into a willing hand. Self-conscious, always. I hadn't seen any money change hands tonight. At Ditka's the VIP currency was Chicago connections, and Paul's socialite bride was plugged in at the top.

The Monday night Bears' game wouldn't start for another hour. Gayle Sayers, bigger than life on the large screen, answered an interviewer's questions.

"He's in the building," said Paul. "That's a closed-circuit hookup. Think Jeff would want his autograph?"

"Naw. I just moved all that junk to the basement. Should probably toss it." Jeff was a fanatic Sayers fan, collected articles, photos, stats, anything he could find on him. I'll bet if Sayers had owned Rosie's, Jeff would have gone into the business.

Herb, his stomach draped over his waistband, slathered butter on a roll.

"Linda's got me on this killer diet. No salt, no sugar, no eggs, no meat, no ice cream."

"You got cholesterol?" asked Byrd. "Mine's one-ninety." He waited expectantly, his head bobbing toward each of us, always needing to compare everything in his life with everything in ours. Herb shrugged.

"Do I know? Cholesterol, heart, gout. Whatever cockamamie disease is in those magazines Linda reads is what I got. Remember her gribenes? Pickled herring? Chopped liver?" Herb shook his head sadly. "She used to be such a great cook."

Strong feelings stirred in the deepest part of me, a longing for the smell of chicken fat sizzling in a hot frying pan with finely diced heart, gizzards, liver and onions, cooked until crispy brown. My mother made world-class gribenes, trusting me to cut the ingredients, but keeping me from the cooking, from the hot fat that spit red burns up her arms. "Gribenes," I said. Juices flowed into my mouth. "When was the last time anyone cooked any of us gribenes?" We heaved a collective sigh.

"That stuff'll kill you," said Byrd.

"Get off it, Burdowsky," said Paul. "Your mom's the one who gave us cold schmaltz spread on matzoh." Paul kissed his fingers to the memory.

"We were kids then." Byrd snapped a breadstick and nibbled one end. "You eat like that now, it's like pouring hot grease down a cold drain. Clogs everything up. Your heart can't pump blood through that sludge, arteries start popping and *ka-blooey*, that's all she wrote."

"We'd die happy," I said.

"I keep telling Cheryl, 'Cut out the fat.' " He'd been down on Cheryl for a few months. Paul thought Byrd had a girlfriend. But then, Paul thought everyone had a girlfriend. Byrd shook his head, sneering. "Cheryl goes crazy when I try talking to her. Says her mother cooked that way and her mother's mother and she's not about to change."

"Invite me to dinner at your house," pleaded Herb.

"I tell her, 'All the young girls I work with cook healthy, why can't you?' "

"Real smart," said Paul. "Mention the young girls."

"Cheryl's stuck in the old ways. Won't try anything new."

"Count your blessings," said Herb. "Everything Linda serves tastes like cardboard."

"Lots of fiber in cardboard," said Paul, waving the waiter over.

"You guys are spoiled," I said. "I can't remember the last time Sarah cooked dinner more than two days in a row."

"Awwww."

"Think it's funny? Let your wives go to work full-time and see how you like it."

"Right," said Byrd. "The day Cheryl gets a job, I'll be named Pope."

"I thought she got a job at Sak's."

"I didn't like her clerking like some teenager. Didn't look right. What if some of my clients saw her? I told her to look for a nice office job, maybe part-time, something near the house so she could get home to do what she has to do. You know what she said? I should let her work full-time. What? I can't support my family? Part-time, all right, to break up the week a little. Where does she come up with these ideas?"

"Soaps." Herb signaled for more butter. "I watched some when I was laid up after that periodontal work. You wouldn't believe what they get away with—people jumping in and out of bed, women wearing see-through nighties, guys in bikini under-pants so tight you can tell which way their religion's hung, kids murdering parents, parents kidnapping kids. Tell me that stuff doesn't rot women's brains."

"Don't talk to me about soaps," I said. "Fanny has those damned things blaring all day. Drives me crazy, all that whining and crying. I made the mistake of suggesting to Fanny that she might need a hearing aid. She didn't talk to me for two days."

"She still living with you?"

"We're trying a new nurse now. If she works out, Fanny's on her way home. Don't get me wrong. I love the woman. But I can't live with her."

The waiter came for our orders. Gribenes and schmaltz were not on the menu. I ordered broiled chicken and waited for the others.

When we were kids, it was funny the way Byrd hated everything. But his complaining wore thin over the years. Why did I think age would change him, change any of us, into something better? If anything the years acted like magnifiers for our quirks, beliefs, hatreds, fears.

"Second wives," said Paul. "I've told you guys, but you won't listen. Second wives are like second kids. Get all your mistakes out of the way with the first."

The waiter poured the wine and Paul hoisted his glass. "To Asher," he said.

"To Asher." Herb and Byrd lifted their glasses.

"The last of us to get laid—"

"Heyyyy, watch that," I said.

"—and the first to retire."

"Hear! Hear!"

"Asher, may your days be filled with fun and your nights be filled with love."

"Just don't let Sarah find out. Ha, ha."

"And may you share your newfound wealth with your three best friends since kindergarten."

"Share?"

"With the three brave souls who let you experiment on them. Oh, the sacrifices we made, the soups we ate."

"Three best friends?" I scratched my head. "I don't remember any three best friends." Herb threw a roll at me.

"Not to worry." Byrd patted my arm. "Paul's secretary is drafting a memo. Tells you where to send our checks."

"I'll drink to that," said Paul. We all did. A cheer went up from the crowd, loud whistles, grunts. Walter Payton walked onto the screen, shook hands with Sayers, and joined the interview.

"You should come to my office," said Byrd, "set up some investments."

"Bo-ring," said Herb. "First you should spend a little."

"What do I need?"

"Clothes," said Paul.

"Now *that's* boring," Byrd said. "What about going to some of those exotic places you've always talked about?"

"Sarah can't get away right now."

The crowd cheered again as the television switched to live coverage of the Monday night game. After the opening credits, the shot cut to O. J. Simpson and Arnold Palmer standing on a cliff overlooking the ocean.

"Pebble Beach," said Paul. "Talk about a dream of a golf course."

"That's something I'd like to do," I said. "Play some of the world's famous courses." Paul slapped me on the back.

"Be a sport. Play 'em all."

"Like *The Swimmer*," said Byrd. "That movie where Burt Lancaster swims from pool to pool across Beverly Hills? You could start golfing in California and work your way across the country."

"Around the world," said Herb.

"When do we leave?" Paul looked at me dead-on, smiling.

"How did you get in on his vacation?" asked Herb.

"You think he's going to take Sarah to Pebble Beach?" Paul swigged his wine. "C'mon, Asher. You know it's gotta be the four of us." He was right. I did know. A new energy came over the table.

"When?" I asked, feeling expansive from the wine.

"Tomorrow," they said.

"You don't think I'm serious." I hoisted my glass. "I'll make the plans." Right after I break the news to Sarah.

Paul narrowed his eyes at me. "I am not going on any golf trip with you—even if you are paying, which is, of course, the only way I'll put up with your short game—unless you buy some decent clothes. I will personally pay for your shoes."

"We'll all chip in," said Herb.

The food came and we dug in, watching the game, talking, eating, laughing. I felt high beyond the wine. This was what it was all about, sitting with friends, eating good food, drinking good wine, talking about a golf trip. For four poor city kids, it was a fantasy come true.

"You think I'm kidding," I said. Paul slid his gold toothpick out of its case and worked it through his teeth.

"Face it, Asher. You're not exactly Mr. Spontaneity."

"I declare this my fiftieth birthday present to myself. For once in my life I'm going to do something completely and totally for me."

"Well, well, well," said Paul, lifting his glass, "here's to the new Asher Rose. Welcome to the world."

17

"How do machines know?" Sarah yanked a jumpsuit off its hanger. The plastic snapped in half. "Four years I've had that machine, never a problem. It was just waiting until I had two lace inserts, one smocked dress, and six shirt alterations. Bobbin keeps jamming, snapping needles in half."

I sat up in bed.

"You're not going to work?" I said.

"Have to. Maybe I can hook up my old Singer—"

"But I leave tomorrow."

"Oh, honey." She sat on the bed, kissing the tip of my nose. "I'll try to come home early. Promise. But I have to do all this stuff for the first scenes they'll be shooting."

"I'll be gone ten days."

"C'mon, Asher. I can't."

"Stay. Help me pack." I pulled her down and kissed her neck, running my hands down her body. She pulled away.

"No time to play. I laid everything out in piles on the table. I think you can manage to put them into the suitcase without me."

"I won't see you for ten whole days. How can you go to work?"

"Turn it around, Asher." She ran a finger over my lips. "Pretend—"

"I don't want to turn it around."

"Pretend *I'm* going off to play golf in California and *you're* staying home to work at Rosie's. Would you take the day off to pack my suitcase?" I blew out my cheeks like Dizzy Gillespie. She laughed. "No you would not. Would you have spent last night going through my drawers, laying out my clothes, matching socks to slacks, shirts to sweaters?" I bugged out my eyes and made fish lips. "No you would not. Would you have used your lunch hour to buy the fill-in items I needed?" I wriggled my nose. "No. Turn it around, Asher." She kissed my nose, then climbed off the bed. "I'll call later. Love you. 'Bye."

I turned it around and around and around. This was a new part of our lives, this turning around. It made issues fair and even and clear. I hated it. I'd married a woman who wanted to be a wife and mother. Where did this career of hers come from? Who said we could change rules in mid-game?

I closed the bedroom door while I packed. Fanny considered an open door an invitation to walk into a room, and I wasn't in the mood for company. I wanted her out by the time I came home. I'd tell Sarah before I left. Sure I would.

Sarah called at three, saying she'd canceled the reservations I'd made at Spiaggias for our farewell dinner.

"Prepare for a surprise," she said.

"How should I dress?"

"For a surprise."

I met her at the door wearing my father's old tux jacket, cut-off jeans, one black shoe and one gym shoe. She threw her head back and laughed, then planted a world-class kiss on my mouth.

"Perfect!" she said. She ran upstairs to say hello to Fanny, came down wearing a fake diamond tiara and sweats, then herded me into the car.

"Don't you want me to change?" I asked.

"You're dressed just right."

She drove into Wilmette, to Gilson Park. It was one of those perfect fall evenings when a warm air mass floating up from the south mixes with the wet leaves and earth. It took both of us to carry the large picnic hamper to the grassy knoll bordering Lake Michigan. Sarah spread out a huge blanket while I popped the cork on the champagne. The basket was crammed full of my favorites: duck pâté, cheeses, cold chicken, grapes, Nicole's French bread, tomatoes, caviar, and Matt's Chocolate Chip Cookies.

Sarah pushed ten candles into the sand and I lit them while she set out the food. We ate in silence, relaxing to the lapping of the waves and the smell of warm breezes. After a while we began the sharing.

"Phones going all day, Paul and Herb and Byrd. Worse than my sisters getting ready for their proms. The last one was Byrd wanting to know what I'm wearing on the plane."

"You tell him the pink lace?"

"Then Linda called to see if I could special-order vegetarian meals on the plane for Herb. Herb called warning me not to." Sarah laughed. She told me about her battle with her sewing machine, the work she was doing on her costumes. How did people live without someone to share their lives?

Candle flames bobbed and weaved in the breeze, the melting wax puddled on the sand. Full, content, I stretched out, resting my head in Sarah's lap listening to the shouts of Frisbee players, laughing children, birds calling. Sarah hummed softly, stroking my face with cool fingers. I drifted in and out.

She bent and kissed my eyelids. "I'll miss you, Asher." I reached up, weaving my fingers through her hair.

"Sarah, Sarah, Sarah, what am I going to do ten whole days without you?"

"You are going to have a wonderful time."

"Paul isn't as pretty as you."

"Yes, but he has a lower handicap."

"Good point."

She peeled an orange, dipped sections in honey, and fed them to me. "Do you realize," she said, "that this will be our longest separation?"

"What about the two years you lived in Europe?"

"I mean since we've been married."

"You'll be so busy working you won't notice I'm gone." She rumpled my hair.

"Think you can go without sex for ten days?"

"Do I have to?"

"Asher . . ."

"I'll try. But no promises."

"Then I'd better give you something to remember me by."

On the way home, she pulled into a motel and checked us in as Mr. and Mrs. John Deaux. We wanted to enjoy our last night together, to shout and yell and laugh. Something we couldn't do, hadn't been able to do, now that Fanny was in our home, like a shadow.

18

Delicious warm bed clothes, soft smelling, sweet scented. I stretched, slipping toasty toes toward Asher. Freezing sheets jolted me awake before I remembered. Pebble Beach. Asher's at Pebble Beach. I curled back into the warmth on my side.

Driving home from my studio after midnight, eyes burning from strain, back aching from hunching over the old Singer, I'd promised myself this whole Sunday off. No meetings, no shopping, no nothing. I'd follow my own rhythms, do exactly what I wanted. And, right now, I wanted to stay in bed, drifting in and out of sleep. Delicious.

Three whole days without Asher. I'd been too busy to miss him, too exhausted to feel lonely. I worked late, pouring over library books and old magazines for fashion details that would make the flashback scenes authentic to the forties, making sketches and jotting ideas to show Marko.

I tried to be home for at least one meal a day with Fanny. Not that I had the time. I tried working at home so she wouldn't feel abandoned, but she couldn't *not* interrupt. Would I like a little tea? Did I think the house was chilly? Where did I keep the Tums? This new nurse was working out. It was time for Fanny to go back to her apartment.

I squinted at the clock. Seven forty-eight. Practically midday. Sunday morning used to be our special time together. I'd put up coffee, make a bagel run to New York Bagels & Bialys, head to Kaufman's for lox, cream cheese and a *New York Times*, come home and layer thick slices of onions and tomatoes onto a platter and have everything ready before Asher came downstairs. The rest of the morning we'd cuddle on the pit, reading the papers, sharing articles, rubbing toes. But that was before I took this job. I hadn't had time for our Sunday mornings lately.

The phone rang. Let it ring, let the machine take it. But what if it woke Fanny? I grabbed the receiver before the second ring.

"Hello?"

"Sarah, Sarah, Sarah." Mookey practically screamed into the receiver. "So good to hear your voice."

"What's wrong, Mookey?"

"Wrong? Why should anything be wrong?"

"It's eight o'clock on a Sunday morning."

"You and Asher never sleep past dawn, heh, heh." And you never get up before noon.

"Asher's in California, Mookey."

"Exactly why I'm calling. We're on our way to Barnum and Bagel and want you to come with us."

"Oh, thanks, that's sweet, but—"

"No buts, Sarah. Asher's off having a good time, no reason you can't do the same. When the cat's away, heh heh. Pearl will be there, and Freyla." Yargh.

"Since when are Pearl and Freyla talking?"

"They fall out, they fall in. But when push comes to shove, they're sisters. Family. We're all family. And family is what counts, Sarah. Family is what matters." Did he want violins with this?

"I'm glad you feel that way, because you'll understand why I can't join you. You see, my mother is ill and—"

"I'm sorry to hear—"

"She's living here at the moment and I really can't leave her. Thanks so much for invit—"

"Don't say another word. It's not like I don't know from a mother who stays home, heh, heh. We'll buy brunch and bring it over to your house. No problem." Big problem. If they came to the house I couldn't get up and leave when I was bored or offended or angry, at least one of which usually happened within the first two minutes.

"I couldn't put you through all that trouble. You know, Mom's still asleep. Maybe I could sneak away long enough to meet you for a quick bite."

"Wonderful. We'll be there eight forty-five." He smashed the phone in my ear. There went my morning.

I rolled out of bed, splashed water on my face and sat at the dressing table to do battle with my face. Mookey was up to something. Asher's family never invited me anywhere without him. And how many times in the last twenty-five years had Mookey dialed our number unless he wanted to talk to Asher? Never, that's how often. If Mookey called and Asher wasn't home, he panicked. "Hold on, hold on, I'm sure Fran would love to talk to you." Then he'd throw me into Hold Hell, where I'd go into a slow boil until poor Fran—dragged from washing the dog or diapering a kid or baking bread or darning socks—picked up the phone and the two of us sustained a strained conversation until a decent enough interval passed so we could hang up. All of which meant, cynic that I was, that Mookey and his sisters wanted something from me besides the pleasure of my company.

I finished with a light dusting of rouge. About as good as my face was going to get. Passable if not spectacular. I tiptoed into the hall and listened. No sounds from Fanny's room. Since she'd been recuperating at our house, she shifted her life four hours to the right, getting up at eleven, watching old black-and-white movies into the wee hours. This newest nurse—she seemed to be working out, please God—slept when Fanny did.

Downstairs, I put on coffee and decided to pay bills before every utility was shut off. Plenty of time. If I got to the restaurant by nine-fifteen, I'd still have to wait for Mookey and the crew. It killed me not to be prompt, but Asher's siblings considered anything earlier than half an hour late compulsive behavior.

I opened the rolltop and uncrammed the bills from their cubbyholes. How long had it been? I used to pay bills every

Wednesday night after I finished the dinner dishes. When was the last time I cooked a dinner, let alone paid bills? Between my work, Asher's demands for attention, and Fanny's illness, my daily schedule lost all form. Old rhythms fell apart.

I spread out on the dining room table. Cup of coffee, adding machine, envelopes, stamps, scratch paper, stationery, checkbook. I positioned the artillery in front of the stacks of bills. Not what I'd intended for the morning. But there was no sense settling into the Sunday papers when I had to leave to meet Mookey. I liked my pleasures uninterrupted.

Maybe now that Asher was semiretired he could take over the bills. Getting through the maze of Medicare, AARP, doctor and hospital bills still coming in for Fanny's broken hip should keep him busy a few months. Lots of small jobs he could help with: calling workmen for repairs, waiting for deliveries, taking the cars in for servicing. I felt lighter just thinking about it. Instead of Asher moping around, depressed at being frozen out at Rosie's, angry that I wouldn't leave work to play with him, I could keep his life as busy as he wanted. Maybe then he'd leave mine alone.

Five minutes into the utility bills, an upstairs toilet flushed. Fanny or her nurse? I listened to the ceiling, waiting for footsteps. Please don't come down. I need time to regroup, put order back into my life. The slow steps shuffled toward my room, stopped, came down the hall to the stairs. Fanny was up and around. I waited for her to call me. Instead, I heard the creak of a tentative foot on the stair. For the first time, Fanny was coming down on her own. Now no place in the house was safe.

" 'Morning, Mom." I rose, kissed her and pulled out a chair. Fanny Feldman, quickstepping imp of the stage, shuffled over, pulled her robe tight and lowered herself into the chair.

"Ummmmmph." Bravely muffled pain accompanied by a hand, fingers splayed, pressed to her stitches.

"Sleep well?"

"Not too good. That mattress is like a rock." She scanned my makeup and clothes. Two plus two equal: "You're going out?"

"Yes, Mom. Mookey, Freyla and Pearl are taking me to Barnum and Bagel. Can I make you some tea?"

"Mumzers. What do they want?"

"They thought I'd be lonely with Asher out of town. Maybe a half grapefruit?"

"They want something." I shrugged. "I hope you told them you've got a sick mother to take care of."

"Of course I did."

"That you can't go running off like that."

"Mookey sends his love." Liar, liar, pants on fire. "When I told him how sick you are, he offered to bring bagels here—"

"We got bagels."

"—along with Freyla and Pearl."

"Oh?" Warm bodies were warm bodies. An audience of Asher's self-serving siblings was better than no audience at all. What's the point of living if nobody's watching?

"Not to worry." I patted her shoulder. Too much bone, too little meat. "I know how you feel so I arranged to meet them out." I did it for you. "Let me toast you a bagel." I escaped to the kitchen.

Slice a bagel, pop it in the toaster oven, fill a mug with water, plop in a tea bag, put it in the microwave, slice a lemon, unwrap the cream cheese. Fanny taught me efficiency in the kitchen, in life. No wasted movements. Everything in sync. Her passion for split-second timing had made her a great comedienne. It was also the reason—okay, one of many reasons—Asher's family drove her crazy. Freyla never *considered* taking butter out of the fridge until *after* the toast popped up. Pearl didn't look for her coffeepot (I'm sure I saw it around somewhere just last week) until the dinner dishes were cleared, rinsed, and in the dishwasher. Their drummers beat dirge time; Fanny's played rhumba.

"Asher and Martha are mutants," she'd said after a grueling three-hour Thanksgiving dinner at Pearl's house. "Not like the rest of them at all. You got the pick of the litter."

The toaster oven dinged. At this rate, I'd be done in another minute. I slowed down, not ready to face Fanny, to tell her it was time she went home. Today. Like a sick toddler allowed to sleep with its parents, Fanny had begun reading permanence into a temporary situation. I wanted her settled in her apartment with her nurse, give the two of them time to smooth out their daily schedule, before Asher came home.

"Want a little honey in your tea?" I called.

Her voice trickled in, weak and trembly. "I don't want to be a bother." A command if ever I heard one.

I banged the encrusted honey jar cap against the counter, ran it under hot water, gripped and turned, pried and pulled. Arthritic hands be damned, Fanny shall have her honey. The cap gave and I stuck the jar in the microwave to liquefy the crystals. If I were still a full-time housewife, if I were free to make my own schedule the way I was when she broke her hip, I might think about letting Fanny stay. But I wasn't and I couldn't. Not with a full-time job. Not with Asher home most of the day.

"I set the thermostat at sixty-eight," he'd complained the last time, "Fanny moves it to eighty. I go out, she tells me to put on a sweater. I'm eating lunch, she moves my water glass away from the edge of the table. I lived through one mother at home. I'm not up for a repeat performance." Without me around to act as a buffer, they'd kill each other within a week. And I'd have to clean up the mess.

"Here you are." I set the tray on the table next to Fanny. "Need anything else before I go?"

"Why don't you stay home, Sarahlah? You look tired."

"I'm fine, Ma." Exhausted, run-down, nervous about work, worried about you. "Really."

"You run here, you run there. Go to this one, go to that one." Did I detect a hint of jealousy? I opened the napkin and smoothed it onto her lap.

"You know I'd much rather stay home with you than have breakfast with the Odd Bunch."

"So?"

"So, they are Asher's family and I'm not going to start trouble by snubbing them."

"Family? They should grow like onions with their heads in the ground."

"I'll just go up and wake Miss Johnson."

"Leave her sleep." Fanny poured a little tea into the saucer and clamped a sugar cube in her front teeth, sucking the tea through it.

"Ma."

"Go. Go."

"Should I turn on the TV?" Silence. I went.

19

The four of us huddled near our clubs. A gust of wind hit us broadside, whipping drizzle like hailstones.

"Extra! Extra!" called Paul. "Four Chicago men found frozen to death waiting for caddies."

"Shit!" Byrd pulled his slicker closed. "This is stupid."

"No," I said, "this is Pebble Beach in October."

Once we started moving, the pain of the penetrating cold would ease a little.

"You couldn't have retired in July?" asked Herb.

"Freak weather," I said. "Who knew?"

Paul opened his wallet and took out a bill. "Cough it up," he said, wiggling his fingers at us until we each laid a one-dollar bill in his palm. He shuffled them behind his back and let us pick. I studied my serial numbers. 58525928. A couple of pairs and three of a kind. This was my day.

"Pair of twos," said Paul.

"Three threes," said Herb. Ten minutes later, I was five dollars richer. Byrd, the other winner, would be my partner for the day. Our caddies came out of the shack, two young, two old. Byrd and I picked the old men. The young ones couldn't track balls or judge distance. Their advice on how to play a shot was useless. They talked nonstop about themselves, their girls, how much they drank, and how caddying was temporary until they found the right job.

The old caddies plodded along quiet and steady as pack mules, faces craggy as shoreline rocks, their rutted skin the color of weathered clay. There wasn't a shot we hit, a joke we told, an excuse we made that they hadn't heard hundreds of times before. They were as quiet as we wanted—invisible, if we liked. But, if we let them, they played the game for us, leading us shot by shot through the knee-high sawgrass and bottomless sand traps of Spyglass, and over the blind hill shots and deep ravines of Pebble Beach. They wanted us to play the best round of our lives because the better we played, the bigger we tipped.

Byrd and I led the caddies to our bags. This was a delicate moment. Byrd's bag, a fiftieth birthday present from his wife, was hand-tooled leather, the size and weight of a small horse. A couple of caddies refused to carry it. One tried putting Byrd's clubs into a carry bag but Byrd was afraid to leave his good bag behind. I would have bought him a lightweight nylon travel bag in a second, but becoming a multimillionaire is a delicate business around old friends. Byrd, especially, watched for signs that I might start thinking I was somehow better.

The smaller of the two caddies looked at the bag, looked at Byrd, then looked back at the bag. Dragging deep on his cigarette, he gripped the handle and heaved the clubs onto his shoulder. He sank a couple of inches into the wet ground. "Ahhhhhhhhhssss," he breathed, like air escaping a tire, then led us off to the first tee.

This was our third straight day of gray gloom and penetrating drizzle. I took out a couple of clubs, swinging gently, trying to warm up. My right shoulder and hip, achy after the first day, felt like they'd been mule-kicked. The Good Thing (Sarah insisted there was always a Good Thing) was that the pain in my joints made me shorten my backswing. This straightened my cronic hook and gave me more distance and accuracy. Screw the pain. I was playing the best golf of my life.

Lines of golfers and caddies stretched out in front of us. The drizzle stayed steady and I peeled off my sopping glove to keep the club from slipping in my hand. Three holes later, I felt a few preblister burns on my fingers. My nose ran nonstop. Little Kleenex packets Sarah'd tucked into my golf bag soaked through, disintegrating in the rain.

The rain was the least of it. The wind, brutal enough the first two days, joined force with the tail of a storm coming in off the ocean. Unable to walk upright, we bent in half like Aruban divi-divi trees, lunging into sixty-five-mile-an-hour gusts. With the wind at me, I could take my clubs back, but couldn't swing forward. Balls I managed to hit took off, crashed into the wall of wind, and dropped like dead birds. When the wind blew from behind, I strained to take the clubs back, but a hit ball sailed forever. Putting was impossible. The putter waggled crazily in my hands and gusts of wind blew the ball across the green.

"Think we should play winter rules?" I shouted, my ball half buried in a fairway divot.

"Winter rules, hell," yelled Paul. "I've been teeing up every shot."

We almost made it. The light drizzle held steady to the seventeenth hole. Then a bank of clouds, black as grease fire smoke, dumped water so hard I couldn't see the ball on the ground in front of me. Byrd lunged against the wind, his lips blue, water streaming down his cap and off his glasses.

"Let's go back," he shouted. "This is crazy."

"We are going," yelled Paul. "But we might as well play in. A hundred says I win the last hole."

"You're crazy," said Herb.

"With or without handicap?" I asked.

"Your handicap's bogus," said Paul. "I'm talking scratch."

We yelled back and forth, arguing over the bet as we battled the headwinds to the eighteenth.

"A hundred's too much," I said. Byrd looked relieved.

"So name it."

"Ten?" They all nodded. Paul knew we wouldn't play for a hundred, but it got our juices going. One way or another, he could always rev us up. In seconds he'd changed us from dreading the last hole to gearing up for it.

My mind shifted away from my pain and into the problems presented by the eighteenth hole. Had to keep ego out, play the smart shot. Paul would go for the flash, power a driver off the tee instead of his more controlled three wood. He'd try to cut across the dogleg that bent around a treacherous bit of rocky shore, hit the ball too far out over the ocean because he figured the wind would carry it back to the fairway. A good idea, if it was possible to depend on the wind. I was betting the erratic gusts would grab hold of his ball and hurl it into the ocean.

My game was as conservative as his was wild. Herb and Byrd fell somewhere in between. Golf exposed who we were in a way no other sport could begin to. A golfer is totally alone in picking shots, weapons, strategies. Even the ball is completely stationary. The blame and the glory of a shot sit square on a player's shoulders. The one great variable in golf is personality. Even, steady, safe, I won the hole. As usual, Paul had the most fun.

"You need a good stiff scotch," said Paul, trying to lead us into the Lodge bar.

"Send mine to the room." I sloshed through the lobby. "I'm going to soak in a scalding tub until my skin falls off." Herb and Byrd slogged along with me.

"Don't worry about a thing." Paul slipped his arm around a passing waitress. "Me and Peggy here will take care of everything." Peggy, a moonfaced girl with an astonishing overbite, giggled and blushed furiously. "We will bring food and drink to the room, tuck you in for a good nap, and have you ready to do some serious partying tonight."

The pain in my neck fused my head to my spinal column. I had to turn my whole body to look at Paul.

"Don't even joke. I'm not leaving the room until we tee off tomorrow morning."

"A-men to that," said Herb.

"Ditto," said Byrd.

"Sure, guys, anything you say." Paul led Peggy off to the kitchen.

"I don't like the way he said that," said Byrd.

"He gave in too easy," said Herb.

"Well"—I opened the door to our suite, the sharp-edged key popping a thumb blister—"you guys go boozing if you want, but this body is resting up for tomorrow."

"Right," said Byrd.

"Right," said Herb.

20

Red flag, red flag! Dive. Dive. Mookey's navy blue Lincoln with the gold trim, Continental tire, and wire wheels occupied the Handicapped space nearest the deli's door. He'd arrived ahead of me. Why now, after a lifetime of keeping people waiting, did he decide to come on time—nay, early? Danger. Detour!

Cars waiting for spaces blocked people trying to pull out. Horns honked, people yelled, nothing moved. A car pulled in behind me, cutting off my escape route. Minor stomach pain. Purely normal. Certainly nothing to worry about. I waited for something to happen. A young man chauffeuring two cigar smokers in the Buick ahead of me jumped out of his car and began directing traffic, hitting car hoods, waving his arms, whistling, calling. Little by little, cars began moving.

I swallowed against the sudden lump in my throat. That was just the take-charge sort of thing Jeff would do. Sometimes the pain of being a long-distance mother got to me. Sure I raised Maxi and Jeff to be independent, but why did they have to listen to me? Maybe I'd buy a dozen bagels and ship them out in the morning. Jeff wouldn't take money from us, but could he refuse a bagel? Could he even buy one in Boulder? I pulled up, in line for the next spot.

A little black Corvette whipped around the lot the wrong way, trying to take what was about to become my space. I hit the gas, lurched forward, and blocked him, covering the space protectively until the car pulled out and rolled away. Because of my awkward angle, it took a while to maneuver into the space. The Vette's driver wouldn't back up to give me room. More stomach pain. I needed this?

"That was my space," he snarled as I walked past. "Bitch." He gunned his engine, intending to speed off. The old macho hit-and-run insult. A car pulled around, blocking him. I walked over to his window and leaned down. He hid his eyes behind dark sunglasses, but I saw him swallow and tighten his mouth.

"I'm sorry," I said sweetly, "I didn't quite get what you said."

"I said, that was my space."

"Didn't your mama ever teach you to wait your turn?"

"Screw you." He dragged on a cigarette and exhaled in my face.

"I'll be sure to mention to my daughter that you and I ran into each other. She's told me so much about you." Little dots of perspiration exploded on his forehead. Whose mother had he insulted? What girl? I smiled and walked into the restaurant. The mob-in-waiting jammed the entrance.

"There you are!" Mookey waved his cane, nearly decapitating a passing waitress. I pushed through to where the name-taker, clipboard in hand, dispensed booths and tables. "We're all here," Mookey told her. "Rose party. Four people."

"Be just a few minutes," she said, ticking off names.

"We've been waiting," said Mookey.

"Sir, I have a few parties ahead of you. It won't be long. Goldstein, party of four? Goldstein." She led the Goldsteins off.

"So, Mookey," I said, "how've you been?"

"Can you believe her? Wouldn't seat us until you came. I thought you and Asher were always on time. Me and the girls were on time." And you had to wait, poor baby.

"Rose. Party of four."

"Here!" Mookey took a few steps before remembering to limp. His cane was as bogus as the orange Handicapped card on his windshield.

"Your party all here, sir?"

"Yes, yes. The girls are in the ladies' room. In fact, I think I'll visit the men's. Sarah, you go ahead, get the table. We'll catch up."

I trailed behind the hostess into the large dining area, following her to the table. A couple of women wore appliquéd sweat suits I'd made years back when Maxi started high school and I had entire days to myself. I'd sold the suits in North Shore beauty shops, synagogue boutiques and church bazaars.

"Here you go," said the hostess.

"Thanks." I settled in to wait for the others.

Funny how seeing those early sweat suits gave me a rush of warm fuzzies. They were old friends from the days when I'd worked at home, curling up next to Asher, sketching designs while he watched TV. Night was our time to be together, reading or watching television, stretching out next to each other, our feet or hands or *something* touching. I did all my sewing during the day. How simple it had been back then.

But business picked up. A couple of community theaters asked me to costume shows. Designing plays felt like coming home. I began sewing a couple of hours before Asher woke up in the morning, adding more hours at night after he went to sleep. More theaters called, a couple of ad agencies.

By the end of the year, working full-out, I moved into my own studio, hiring sewers or using contractors when the work load got too big. Now I was working on a feature film. And it all started with a few appliqués.

"Not here!" Mookey limped up to the table. He waved the hostess over.

"Yes, sir?" she said.

"I told you we wanted a booth." The woman gripped her clipboard.

"You said you wanted to be seated right away."

"In a booth."

"I don't have a booth. I have this table. If you want a booth, you'll have to go back out and wait."

"What about that booth?" Mookey swung his cane toward the windows.

"That's for six or more."

"It's empty."

"I'm bringing my party now."

"This table's fine, Mookey," I said.

"It's not fine."

My stomach twisted. I should never have come.

"Mookey, Fanny is too ill for me to leave for very long. Either we take this table or I'll have to go."

"No! Don't go." He yanked out a chair. "All right," he said to the hostess, "bring us some coffee."

"I'll send your waitress, sir." Mookey lowered his mass into a chair. Sometimes I think he believed he was disabled.

"So, Mookey." Why am I here? What do you want? What are you trying to pull off behind Asher's back? The idea of woman-as-intelligent-life-form was foreign to Mookey. "How's Fran?"

"Fine, fine." He scanned the room, tracking a busboy. A Mookey without food was a Mookey in panic. He wouldn't hear a thing until he had possession of a piece of bread and butter. Might as well save my breath. I cringed as he snapped his fingers at a busboy. "We need some coffee over here, some bread on the table."

"Saaaa-rah!" Enter Freyla.

"Saaaa-rah!" Enter Pearl. The dynamic duo. So good to see you both, kiss kiss.

"So, Sarah," said Freyla, hands on vacuumed hips, lifted eyes scanning the room, "what do you hear from Asher?"

"He called last night."

"Coffee here?" The busboy materialized gripping a coffeepot in each hand.

"Decaf all around," said Mookey.

"Regular for me," I said.

"Me too," said Freyla, still standing, posing. "And a little pitcher of skim milk."

"I think I'd like tea." Pearl wiped the chair seat with her napkin before perching. Preheadache pressure pushed in my temples. Hang on, Sarah, this is only for an hour. Breathe in through the nose, exhale through the mouth. It could be worse. They could have brought brother Norm the Depressed.

"Anyhow," I continued, "Asher said Carmel is cold and rainy and—"

"Oh, you don't have to tell me how cold northern California can be." Freyla shivered, shimmying her shoulders prettily. "John and I went there for our honeymoon. The fog never lifted before noon. That cold gets right down into your bones."

"For chrissakes, Freyla." Mookey buttered his second roll. "That was twenty years and three husbands ago."

"So? It was still cold."

"What does that have to do with anything?"

"I was just saying."

"You mean," said Pearl, tiptoeing around the conflict, "Asher went all the way to California, spent all that money, and now he can't play golf?" At forty-one, Pearl still played the wide-eyed ingenue. Once cast, a Rose had the role for life. Asher the Protector. Martha the Levelheaded. Freyla the Flirtatious. Pearl the Timid. Mookey the martyr.

"A little monsoon isn't about to stop Asher from golfing," I said. "In fact—"

"Oh!" Freyla waved to someone across the room. "There's Suzanne and Sharon. Would you excuse me just a minute."

"Not *now*," Mookey said. "Stay and *talk*. Sarah's got to *go* soon."

"I won't be a minute. Besides, you're the one who's going to tell her. Order me eggs hard scrambled with nova; be sure they make the onions well cooked." Freyla threw her henna-rinsed head back, implanted bust out, and walked toward her friends as if forty cameras were filming her. Whether married or between husbands, Freyla was perpetually predatory.

"She'll be right back," said Pearl.

"Thinks she's a goddamned Perle Mesta." Mookey snapped his fingers toward the waitress, who came immediately. His kind of woman.

"What can I get for you folks?"

"I'll have a half grapefruit and dry wheat toast," I said.

"C'mon, c'mon. Eat something."

"No thanks, I'm fine." I wasn't about to squander calories or raise my cholesterol to please Mookey.

"I'll have the bagel and lox sandwich," began Pearl. "I'd like the bagel cut twice crosswise so I get three slices, and I want it lightly toasted. Instead of the onions, I'll have . . ."

Directions, instructions, substitutions. The Rose family took forever to order. Even water was "without ice" or, if "with ice," was with a specified number of cubes. Why did I do this to myself? When Mookey called, I should have told him I was going to a funeral, recovering from heart surgery, being held captive by Martians. Why didn't I?

Because these were Asher's siblings.

Because I was an only child and took my cues from Asher on how brothers and sisters were supposed to treat each other.

Because I loved Asher Rose and he had spent the last forty years taking care of these people.

Because one breakfast out of my life wasn't such a big deal.

"I'll have the lox platter," said Mookey.

"That serves two," said the waitress. Two ravenous normal people.

"And let me have a couple of onion bialys, pick me ones with lots of onions, toasted dark and . . ."

Give me strength! This was Asher's fault. He'd spoiled his brothers and sisters so they wouldn't notice that Father worked sunup to sundown seven days a week and Mom never walked out of the house.

The waitress raced off, leaving an awkward lull in her wake. Mookey sipped his coffee. "Boy that's good." He gazed out into the packed room. "They sure do some kind of business here. Wouldn't mind a piece of this action." Mookey often let his conversation meander to camouflage the direction it was going. I'd come from a family of straight lines.

"So, Mookey, what's on your mind?" He looked at me quizzically. "Freyla said you were going to tell me something."

"Well, I wouldn't want to ruin a nice breakfast by talking business, heh, heh, but since you ask, we're real worried about a few things going on at Rosie's."

"Rosie's? What do I know about Rosie's? You should talk to Asher."

"You think I haven't tried? Asher's been strange lately, not real easy to talk to." So I wasn't the only person who noticed. It wasn't my imagination. Whatever Asher was going through was affecting other people in his life, too. "Besides, I'm just his younger brother. How much can I know?" Time to change that old record, Mookey. "These new guys at Rosie's don't know how to run the business. I know Asher sold out for a lot of money, but he didn't plan things out right."

"Mookey, Asher spent months agonizing over every last detail of the sale. Believe me, nothing was done lightly."

"Yeah? Well, he sure didn't protect us from these guys."

"What happened?"

"They're not family. They don't understand." Ring around the issue, all fall down. Get to the everlovin' point.

"They put Norm on probation," Pearl said quietly. "As soon as Asher stopped coming in every day to work—"

"That's not his choice," I said. "Asher's been given the clear impression they don't want him around. What happened with Norm?"

"He wasn't feeling well," said Mookey. "Took a little time off."

"How much time?"

"A month," said Pearl. "So far." Wonder why Asher never said anything to me.

"Time's not the issue here!" Mookey's face turned red. The waitress brought our food and Pearl left to retrieve Freyla. Mookey hacked off a chunk of cream cheese and frosted a bialy. "The point is, you don't fire family. You make adjustments. You make allowances. Family is family. We all feel Asher let us down."

I sucked in a deep breath and counted a slow ten. Mookey owed his fancy car, home, and life-style to Asher. All of them owed Asher. They'd been riding his back their whole lives. Even the cousins still in the family's tailoring business came for loans off and on over the years. Asher let you down? You lazy, useless, overstuffed leech. How dare you!

"Tell me, Mookey"—easy, Sarah, this is for Asher to handle—"how is what happened to Norm Asher's fault?"

"If Asher sold the company to family, there'd be no problem."

"You have twenty million lying around?"

"Sarah, this is business. You wouldn't understand."

"You know, Mookey"—easy, Sarah—"I read an article once about a woman—I think she was from Parkersburg, West Virginia—who actually understood a business concept. Why don't you try me?" He waved a cream-cheesed knife.

"You don't charge family like that. You let them pay back little by little. Out of profits."

"Profits only happen if the family doesn't run the business straight into the ground."

"Right," he said, missing the point. "And the family understands Norm. We know that sometimes, every now and then, it's hard for him to go places." Like mother, like son.

Pearl returned and began arranging her food into three equal sections on the plate. Freyla, bracelets jangling, spotlight following, took a quick last look around the room in case there was someone she might have met at some point in her life and had neglected to say hello to, then sat down to breakfast.

I toyed with my grapefruit, playing the knife along the rim and section edges. So now I knew why they invited me. If Rosie's new owners could suspend Norman, youngest of the Rose clan, none of the many relatives working at Rosie's was safe. Add in spouses and children, and you had a lot of lives up for grabs. But it didn't make sense. Asher had been so careful to protect them all. I thought Martha drew up iron-clad employment contracts between Asher and his siblings, contracts binding to the new owners.

"How much have you told Sarah?" asked Freyla.

"You want a recap? Next time, don't go visit every damned table in the place."

"Did you tell her about me?"

"Not yet. I told her about Norm."

"You know my condition," said Freyla. "I can't take Chicago winters."

"She's got a delicate system," explained Pearl. "She gets colds and flu real easy."

"Yes, I know," I said. Especially on Passover, Chanukkah, Rosh Hashanah, Yom Kippur, and any other time she might be asked to pitch in and help in the kitchen.

"So I go talk to them. I tell them every winter I go to Florida January fifteenth to March fifteenth. Ten years I've been doing that. And they tell me if I go I don't get paid. And I'll have to come back to part-time." She leaned toward me, jabbing an egg-filled fork in my direction. "I've given good years to the company. I've got pension money built up. I get insurance. I don't want to be part-time."

I busied myself with the grapefruit, cutting, scooping, eating. Whatever they wanted from me was not mine to give. Mookey said he'd tried talking to Asher, but Asher never mentioned any of this. Maybe he didn't want to worry me. Maybe I'd been so busy with my own problems I didn't leave time for him to tell me his.

"They're bringing computers into my department," Pearl said softly.

"Yeah." Mookey snorted. "Can you picture Pearl on a computer?"

"Yes," I said to Pearl, "I can. Will they teach you how to work it?"

"What difference?" Mookey dug food out of his back teeth with a toothpick. "They're just trying to scare her out. Bring in some snot-nosed kid to run her section. You ask me, they're figuring ways to get us all out of there. Ways that aren't covered by those contracts Martha and Asher cooked up."

Pearl buried her hands in her lap, nervously rubbing the chaffed skin. "I have the files exactly the way I want them," she said. "I developed the system. Everything has a certain place, a particular order. I don't think I could work there if they changed all that."

"Pearl," I said, "you have a genius for order. Computers were made for minds like yours. I'll bet, if you learn computer, you could make the changes the way you want them."

"I'm not good with machines." Case closed. Poor Pearl. Still living in her childhood home, same room, same furnishings. Change terrified her. The family built a bubble around her. Looked like it was about to burst. Fatigue set in, pressing down on my shoulders, trying to fold me in half. I needed Asher with me when I faced his family.

"What is it you want from me?" I asked.

"Talk to Asher," said Freyla.

"This is none of my business."

"Of course it is. You're Asher's wife."

"And you're his brothers and sisters."

"He doesn't listen to us. He listens to you." I didn't have the strength to face all three at once.

"Rosie's isn't Asher's anymore," I said. "He has no more clout than you. There's nothing he can do for you that you can't do for yourselves." They looked at me blankly, like I was speaking Swahili. Asher *always* took care of them. Asher *always* made things right. Always.

"Just talk to him," said Mookey.

"I'll try," I said. "When he comes home. But don't get your hopes up." I felt a sudden need for air. "I have to go. I've been away from Fanny too long. Thanks for breakfast."

I stopped the waitress on my way out, gave her a healthy tip and paid the check. Mookey, Freyla, and Pearl would act surprised when she told them the bill was taken care of. The truth was they expected Asher's wife to take care of it. Now all I had to do was go home and kick my sick mother out of my house. All in all, one hell of a morning.

21

The four of us held up a wall inside The O.K. Corral. A constant line of people squeezed past, like cans on a conveyor, toward the bar and dance floor. Music blared beyond sound, vibrating off the graffitied walls and into me.

"My caddy said this is where the action is," shouted Paul.

"Your caddy was fifteen years old."

"Nineteen."

"Whatever." Two Twiggys giggled as they squeezed past Byrd. He ran a nervous hand over his new hairpiece. "I feel like someone's grandfather."

"You are."

"Might as well have a drink as long as we're here." Paul moved into line behind a pointy-breasted girl. The hem of her tight leather skirt ended at her crotch. "I'm in love," he shouted.

"What took you so long?" I slapped him on the back. "Come on, I'll buy the first round."

The schoolroom-size nightclub was dark except for dim spots over the dance floor and bar. I kept bumping into people, apologizing, trying to avoid body contact. No way. Too many people in too little space. In the moist darkness, the blend of perfumes and hair oils, colognes, and deodorants smelled exotic and sensual. A few girls breast-pressed as they passed. Probably some native custom, give the old boys a thrill. After a few days without Sarah, it didn't take much.

I hoisted myself up on a bar stool, gripping the edge of the bar against the pain in my hip. Bone spur. Maybe arthritis. I still couldn't turn my head without pain shooting down my shoulder. Having fun was crippling me.

I shelled out for the first round and pressed my blistered hand against the frosty glass. Stung like hell. No way I could hold a golf club tomorrow. Maybe ever. A slower song started, quiet enough for us to hear each other talk.

"I could have humbled that course," said Herb.

"Please," I said. "Anything but golf."

"On a decent day, my drive on three would have put me right on the green."

"Three's the par five," said Byrd.

"No it's not." Byrd reached into his jacket pocket and pulled out a scorecard.

"I can't believe you carry that around with you," I said. He tilted it, trying to capture some bar light.

"You apes gonna rehash the entire eighteen?" Paul downed his drink and motioned the bartender for another round. He said something to two young girls next to him then turned to me. "C'mon, let's dance."

"Why, Paul, this is so sudden."

Seconds later I was on the dance floor, my arm around a bit of pink angora fluff named Kimberly, trying to keep my eyes from falling down her canyon of cleavage.

Years of guiding Sarah around dance floors had spoiled me. I liked to dance with the person I was dancing with. Kimberly jerked like a decapitated chicken, all fits and starts, twists and turns, looking for people, waving, calling, laughing. The Eau de Cheap she'd bathed in burned my nostrils and brought tears to my eyes.

"So," I tried, "you from Monterey?"

"Nobody from California's *from* California. Munster, Indiana."

"Yeah? I'm from Chicago."

"Chicago!" She squealed. "We're like neighbors, y'know? Wow. I have an uncle in Chicago. Lives north. I think. Y'know?" She cracked gum that smelled like watermelon. It occurred to me I was dancing to the longest song ever recorded. "Ginny!" Her scream pierced my eardrum. "Here, over here! It's me. Kimberly!"

The beat changed to hard-driving music.

"Thanks for the dance," I said.

"You done?"

"Hip's a little sore from golf." I limped her back to the bar. "Now, here's one of the best dancers in Chicago." Herb wiggled his eyebrows approvingly. "Herb, this is Kimberly. Says she'd love to dance with you."

"My pleasure." He led her off, winking at me over her head.

I settled into the safety of the bar stool and started working on my second drink. Byrd swiveled my way.

"How'd you like my chip shot to the green on sixteen?" he asked.

"Give it a rest, Byrd. I'm drinking to forget."

"I put that baby two inches from the cup." He rambled on and I shut him out. When we were kids, caddying weekends for rich south siders, an old caddy taught us to play bridge. It saved our sanity on rainy days. From the beginning, Byrd remembered who played what card when. I hated being his partner. Days later he'd still be at me for a dumb bid or failure to finesse. The game never ended. He beat the same dead horse with golf. How did Cheryl stand it?

"Hey," said a man next to Byrd, "can I take a look at that scorecard? I play Pebble Beach tomorrow." Byrd turned his back on me, glomming onto this soulmate who would let him rehash the course hole by hole ad nauseum.

The scotch softened the noise of the music. I leaned back, relaxing into the drink, watching Herb glide Kimberly through the mob on the floor. Paul danced full-out, his shirt sweat-stained, his face going through its range of seductive looks. If they slowed down the beat, I'd get up and dance again. The women sure seemed willing. I'd have been a lot more social when I was young if I'd grown up with girls like these. Nothing like rejection, or the fear of it, to put you off your dancing shoes.

The drinks worked their magic. Started me thinkin'. How comes it that everyone got a chance to do this but me? Paul, Byrd, Herb. Sarah, even, travelin' around Europe, writing me about this boyfriend and that boyfriend. I was the only one pressing the old nose to the old grindstone while they were out having a good old time. When was I gonna get a chance to kick up my heels? My old fun-o-logical clock was runnin' out.

The music shifted into something familiar. Visions of John Wayne and Hopalong Cassidy. Yeeee-haaaa! Git along little dogie.

"Excuse me." Pretty young girl. Where'd she come from?

"Yes?" says I.

"Do you do the Texas two-step?"

"Me? Little Lady, I came two-steppin' out of my mama's womb." I hopped down from the stool—screw the hip pain—and led my darlin' out to the floor, where everyone danced in a circle. I copied the way the men held the women, and plunged in. Three steps later she stopped.

"Are you trying to humiliate me?" Penciled eyebrows frowning, pink lips definitely not smiling. Oops.

"What's wrong?"

"You don't know how to Texas two-step."

"Well, maybe not exactly. Might be more like the Chicago cha-cha."

She stormed off the floor. Goin' to wrangle up another two-stepper, I reckoned. I slunk back to my seat. Didn't see what her problem was. I was kinda enjoying myself. Yeeee-haaaa!

A woman inhabited Paul's chair. She leaned one elbow on the bar and stirred an olive around a martini glass. No wildly costumed, she. Nah-ha. She wore something soft and drapey that flowed over the curves of her body. Her light brown hair fell shoulder length. What was a classy mid-thirties lady doing in this kiddie club?

"That was fast," she said, husky voice, friendly smile. Eyes smiled, too.

"My pardner didn't have much sense of humor."

"A lot of that going around." We watched the dancers circle. I tried to figure out the two-step but my mind wouldn't focus. "Want to dance?" she asked.

"Do you do the Texas two-step?"

"Naw, can't say as I do."

"Great."

We slipped onto the dance floor and she folded into my arms, following me effortlessly. Not that I was all that great a dancer, not like Paul, who'd mastered every dance since we'd been forced to learn the box step in Mrs. Quaid's fourth grade gym class. But I liked to dance, liked holding women in my arms. For a shy kid, it was the only chance I got to put my arms around girls.

"I'm Asher Rose," I said.

"Jane Gregory. Pleased to meet you."

"Likewise." The two-step ended and a slow song came on. "Want to keep going?"

"Love to." I closed my eyes and settled into the dance. Her body nestled against mine, friendly without being obvious.

I pressed my cheek against her soft hair. "You smell gingery."

She laughed. "Is that good?"

"Uh-hum."

We danced quietly for a while. Why would a woman come alone to a night spot? To meet men? Most of these "men" were boys Jeff's age. Maybe she liked them young. Then why ask me to dance? Maybe she was a hooker.

"You here long?" she asked.

"We came a couple of days ago."

"Golfers?"

"You wouldn't know it to see us play."

She laughed. "I've heard *that* once or twice before."

I hugged her closer and spun her around. Nice. She unbuttoned my jacket and slipped her hands inside around my waist, pressing soft breasts and round hips. *I could have her if I wanted.* The thought flashed in neon. Excited or nervous? A little of both. A *lot* of both.

"My, you have strong muscles," she said, sliding her fingers up and down my back.

"Comes from a lifetime of lifting crates, moving boxes. You don't need Nautilus machines when you work in a warehouse."

"I'll bet people don't mess with you."

"You mean fight?" I laughed. "I haven't been in a fight in years."

"Yeah? This place has nearly one a night." I spun her around, looking at all the strong young men trying to catch the eyes of all the sexy young women. Why didn't I ever get a chance to do this?

"Those kinds of fights are just young turks showing off, I said. "When I was growing up, me and my friends would get into it with kids from other neighborhoods. Those days no one carried knives and guns. It was all fists and speed. I never had a problem holding my own."

"Well, whatever you're doing, don't stop. A woman likes to feel a man could protect her if she needed him to."

"You come here often?" My voice squeaked. Dumb question. Try to get my body parts to behave.

"Every night like clockwork."

"You must love to dance."

"Not especially. Besides, I'm usually too busy. It's just that you had a nice look about you and I'm feeling a little sorry for myself tonight. It would have been my twelfth wedding anniversary."

"I'm sorry."

"Happens."

"Must be hard losing a husband so young."

She narrowed her eyes. "You putting me on?"

"Wouldn't joke about a thing like that." I guess she saw how deeply sorry I felt for her. She smiled.

"Well, he didn't die, exactly."

"Didn't die?"

"No." She laughed. "I mean, as far as I'm concerned he's dead. But . . . but." She laughed again. "Well, actually"—and again—"aw hell, he took off . . . took off . . . with the . . . night manager." She let out one of those gutsy laughs that made me laugh. Especially after two scotch rocks and some interesting dance moves.

"T-t-took off?" I asked.

"Y-y-yes."

"N-n-not dead?"

"N-n-no." We laughed, we howled, we held each other up, laughing at ourselves laughing, holding our jaws because they ached from laughing. We moved off the dance floor, finding a friendly piece of wall to lean against while we gasped for air. It took a while to come down.

"Whew." She let out a long breath. "That felt absolutely terrific!"

"Been a while since I laughed like that." I wiped the tears off my cheeks. "Sort of cleans you out." Against the dark wall, her eyes looked mysterious and exotic. I reached up and wiped the tears off one cheek, then the other. Soft skin, warm.

"You're too pretty to be sitting in a bar every night," I said.

"Got no choice."

"Of course you have a choice. We all have a choice."

"Naw, not really." A wonderful smile aimed directly at me. "I own the place."

"You—"

Shrieking electric guitars cut off any chance of talking. She reached a hand around my head and gently pulled my face toward her. Soft lips, full and warm. The short kiss left me thinking about more. She moved her lips to my ear.

"I have a room upstairs. It's quieter. We could have a brandy. Get to know each other better."

Time froze. That's all there was to it? A quick dance, then "I have a room upstairs." Just like that. Do you or don't you want to? Oh, Jane, where were you all those years when I was single and horny?

"Can't," I said. Let her down easy, Asher. "I'm here with friends. You understand." Whatever that meant.

"A shame," she said. "Could have been nice."

"I know."

She reached up and tugged my ear. "Good luck with your golf. And thanks for the pick-me-up." A quick kiss and she moved off into the crowd. I always thought a proposition would have more drama. Still, it's a kick to be asked to the prom.

22

The blinding Carmel sun picked the next morning to finally come out. The four of us squinted from behind polarized sunglasses, which didn't begin to protect our bloodshot eyeballs.

"Whose idea was it to go out last night?" groaned Paul.

"Somebody throw something at him," I said.

As rough as the stormy weather had been, the heat was worse. By the fifth hole my mouth was parched and my lungs wouldn't fill. In my youth I caddied two full bags for eighteen holes to pick up double tips. Life had lousy ways of reminding me I wasn't eighteen years old anymore. When I'd left the bar last night, I felt virile, hyped and sexy. Now, grunting as I chugged up and down hills, hip and neck pain dogging every step, I wondered if I'd make it.

Paul didn't even break a sweat. That did it! When I got home I was going straight to the health club, lift weights, jog. Maybe I should drag Herb with me. His face glowed red on the uphill climbs and he had to stop every few yards to catch his breath. I was so worried about Herb that it wasn't until Byrd said "What's Paul doing now?" that I turned.

Paul stood on the edge of a deep sand trap, both hands pressed against his heart, like a silent movie actor pledging his love. He looked puzzled.

"Paul?" He didn't move. "Paul? You all right?" His head turned slowly toward me, eyebrows drawing together.

"Oh," he said. Such a small sound. Then he pitched headfirst into the trap.

"He's never going to grow up," said Byrd.

"Paul?" I ran over. He lay facedown in the sand. "Paul!" I

jumped down next to him, heaving against the weight of his body, turning him over. Coarse grains of sand stuck to his skin. His eyes stared at me. "Paul?" I brushed the sand off. A few grains flew into his open eyes. He didn't blink. "Oh, Jesus! Paul!" I shoved my fingers into his mouth, pulling his tongue, clearing the air passage. "Someone, go get help." No one moved. "Dammit, go get somebody!" One of the caddies took off, sprinting toward a home bordering the golf course.

Breathe. In. Breathe. Out. I don't know how long I worked on him. Sometimes the wind blew his hair and I mistook it for life. Breathe. In. Breathe. Out. I willed my breath to be his breath. Breathe. In. Breathe. Out.

Herb gripped me from behind and tried to pull me away. I shook him off until help came, men who didn't know Paul, who had nothing to do with him or me or our lives, men who couldn't begin to understand what Paul meant to me for as far back as I could remember. These strangers moved into my place, trying to perform the miracle I couldn't.

There was room for only one of us in the ambulance. The strangers said there was no point in any of us going. That their insurance wouldn't let me sit in back. But how could I let Paul ride through this strange place alone? I threw the car keys at Byrd and climbed in with Paul.

"Where should we meet you?" asked Herb.

"Should we call his wife?" asked Byrd. I sat comatose as the driver shut the door.

My world telescoped inside this one small van sitting on this one small seat. I had no interest in what Byrd or Herb did. No interest at all. Let them take care of themselves. I couldn't be responsible for the entire world. Not now. Not just now.

23

I couldn't straighten up to answer the phone. Nauseous from caffeine, woozy from lack of sleep, I shuffled L-shaped across my studio. How many hours had I been bent over the sewing machine? Two A.M.? Lost all track of time.

"Hello?" I said. A voice floated in, muted, strained, distant.
"S-Sarah—"

"Asher? Asher, is that you?"

"Sarah? Oh, God, Sarah."

"Asher, what is it? I can barely hear you."

"Paul."

"What about Paul? Asher? Are you all right?"

"One second he was joking around, the next . . . the next . . ."

"Paul?"

"He's d-d-dead."

"Oh, Asher, no."

"W-we're b-bringing him home. And I . . . and I . . ."

"Oh, baby. Hushhhhhh."

"It hurts so much, Sarah. It hurts so much."

"I'm sorry. So sorry. Sssshhhhh. I wish I could hold you." I strained to pick out the few coherent words. It was so horribly difficult for him to speak. Some arrangements needed doing at my end. I jotted them down. "I love you," I said. "Hurry home." I kissed him good-night but couldn't tell if he heard.

How could Paul die? He's Asher's age. I closed the studio and drove home, hoping to grab a few hours' sleep. I couldn't do anything about anything until morning. No, not morning. Had our first production meeting at Marko's studio at nine. The stuff for Paul would have to wait until afternoon.

Four hours later I woke up bloated, my ring finger throbbing where the flesh swelled around my wedding band. I'd have to soap off the band before gangrene set in. The carpet felt like nails under my feet. My ankles had disappeared completely. Where were my water pills? Why wouldn't my gynecologist just slice me open and yank out the plumbing? "Who," I asked her, "needs this anymore? It's not like Asher and I are going to have more babies." My luck, hysterectomies were out of fashion.

The face in the medicine cabinet mirror was not one I'd care to meet in a dark alley. Puffy eyelids, double bags, pale green complexion. Could use a few days' R&R. A few hours, even. Five minutes would be heaven. I soaped my finger, tugging at the wedding band.

Asher said he'd call Bambi in the morning, but asked if I would double-check and make sure she was all right, comfort her. Sure, Asher. Nothing to it. I've got nothing better to do right now than baby-sit Paul's child bride. What about Byrd's wife? Or Herb's? They didn't work. Why was I expected to do everything?

The ring wouldn't budge. I plunged my finger into a tub of Vaseline. Good thinking. Now the ring was so slippery I couldn't get a grip on it. Marko had told me to be at his studio by eight. He wanted to talk over something before the meeting. I gritted my teeth, shut my eyes, and worked the ring—ouch!—worked the ring—damn!—worked the ring . . . off! Barely seven o'clock. I'd leave by seven-fifteen. Even with rush hour, I'd have plenty of time.

The phone!

Don't answer it.

I have to answer it.

Monitor the answering machine.

Why? Am I going to *not* talk to Fanny?

What makes you think it's Fanny?

Get real.

"Hello?"

"She [i.e., the nurse, also known as "her"] left the bathroom cabinet open. She can't close up after herself?"

"Hi, Mom. How're you feeling today?"

"As a matter of fact, not so bad." Don't touch that line. It's booby-trapped.

"That's great."

"I been thinking, maybe after my dentist appointment Thursday [dentist appointment?] you'll take me to lunch." No way I could take her. Have to deal with that later. Marko and I were in overdrive getting ready for the film. And now with Paul's funeral, and Asher . . . Taking Fanny to her appointments was one of the jobs I hired the nurse to do.

"You know, Sarahlah, I been thinking. Why don't I come stay with you while Asher's away?" Because I'm working thirty-two-hour days. Because I like not being responsible for another human being's eating, sleeping, clothing, mental health, physical well-being, psyche, appointments.

"Asher's on his way home, Ma."

"I thought he was going ten days." Do I tell her about Paul? Why depress her so early in the morning? Then again, she'll find out in a little while, anyway. The obits preceded Ann Landers in Fanny's morning stroll through the paper. If I don't tell her now, she'll wonder what other earthshaking information I'm keeping from her.

"One of the men on the trip died. You remember Paul?"

"The wild one?"

"He had a heart attack."

"Oh [pause] tsk, tsk, tsk. Such a young man. [Deep sigh.] Well, at least *he* wasn't sick."

"Gotta run. I have a meeting at Marko's."

"Which reminds me, Sarah."

"Yes, Ma?"

"You should remember you have a mother who knows from acting. If a small part for a mature woman should come up at your meeting. Now that I'm feeling stronger."

"I'll keep it in mind. Talk to you later."

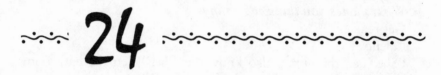

My lane hadn't moved in three minutes. Nothin' like morning rush hour to macramé every internal organ into double half hitches.

"Nice going, Paul." I rammed my palm—*Whomp!*—against the steering wheel. "Just up and die whenever it suits you. Do whatever *you* want to do. Why not? Why shouldn't you go out the way you lived?" *Whomp!* "Let everyone else clean up after you. Ex-wives, employees, attorneys, Asher. Always someone in line ready to help. Why should a little thing like death change your style?" *Whomp, whomp!*

I fanned my fingernails out from the steering wheel, a grotesque variety of lengths, cracks, chips, like a poor man's Freddy from Elm Street. I'd forgotten to nibble them even and slap on polish. You're not working alone in your little studio anymore, Sarah. You're out in the real world, part of a team. Shape up!

"Move it!" I shouted, hitting my horn a split second before the light turned green.

Actually, the jagged nails put the perfect finishing touch on this Week from Hell. Paul's death piled one more heaping helping on my plate. On top of everything else, I had to call Bambi, the funeral home, contact the rabbi, arrange for chair and coat rack rental, food trays, coffee urns, booze. And now, please direct your attention to our center ring as the Great Sarah Rose juggles flaming torches, buzzing chain saws, husband, mother, children, job.

Sarah Rose, Paul is dead.

Yes, I know.

You might be a bit more . . . more . . .

More what?

Compassionate, sensitive, feeling. You're sounding just the least little bit selfish, here. After all, he is dead.

Dead, my Sweet Sarah, is never having to worry ever again. Dead is out of the game, off the field, and into that great locker room in the sky. You want me to cry, to beat my breast, to stop my life to mourn his? Paul's the one who's selfish, arrogant, and self-centered.

But, he's dead.

Exactly! Just look where he decided to die. Did he keel over at his health club where nubile young maidens with freshly toned glutes and tight little triceps could carry him off into the sunset? Not Paul. That would have been too easy. I am not going to put my life on hold waiting for his body to come back to Chicago. And I am not going to take off work, work that I dreamed of doing and struggled to get, to help his bride pick out a casket. The same bride who attends every Chicago social gala but has not had time to pen a little thank-you note for the wedding gift we sent. You will please excuse me if that seems a little unfeeling.

Paul was Asher's best friend.

Asher likes everyone. Asher is the original Mr. Nice Guy. Stop trying to make me feel guilty. Look, turn it around. Pretend I'm the one who died in California.

And?

Asher calls from California with the sorrowful news of my untimely death, and gives Paul a list of things to do.

But?

Paul's got two tickets for the last playoff game before the Super Bowl.

Good seats?

Fifty-yard line, two rows up from the Bears' wives.

So?

Do you for one second suppose Paul would miss that game to help pick out my casket?

I see your point.

Thank you.

The man in the car ahead stared at me through his rearview. There was a time I might have pretended to be singing along with the radio instead of ranting to myself. Not now. Not anymore.

"That's right, mister. Got yourself one hell of a crazy tailgating lady."

I swung out onto the outer drive and clicked on my fuzz-buster. If I traveled just under the speed of light, I might make Marko's by eight.

25

He sat at the long table under the skylights. The harsh sun outlined his sunken eyes, gaunt cheeks. His beautiful Mediterranean olive skin had gone waxy white.

"Marko, what's wrong?" He didn't look at me. "Marko?"

I waited while he opened a new pack of cigarettes, tapped one out and tried to light it. The gold Dunhill shook so violently he had to hold the lighter with two hands. He wasn't looking me in the eye because he couldn't. He was ashamed of what he was about to tell me. He'd hired another assistant, someone with movie experience, someone unencumbered by the day-to-day demands of an aging mother and retired husband. He knew what a louse he was about to be for firing me after all the hours I'd put in on the project, after all the resale shops and flea markets we'd been through together. Hang on, Sarah, brace yourself.

"I haven't smoked for two years," he said, frowning at the cigarette as if trying to think how it got into his hand. I picked up the pack and smelled it.

"Gaulois," I said, trying to keep the hatchet from falling for another few minutes. "I smoked these when I lived in Paris. Only thing I could afford. Can't forget that smell. Like ripe manure." Marko dragged long and hard, releasing the smoke slowly through his nose and mouth.

"Greg is dying." His words drifted out with the smoke. I was so ready to be fired that it took a moment to understand what he was talking about. I was *not* being fired, *not* losing this movie. This was not about me at all.

"What do you mean, he's dying?" Marko walked over to the windows, looking out at a day of sunshine and blue skies.

"He's been HIV positive for a few years. Last week he developed a blood clot on his brain. They biopsied and he had a bleed at the site." He wet a finger and drew abstract designs on the windowpane. "He's not able to talk very well. I'm bringing him home from the hospital tomorrow." He came back and sank into a chair, bracing his elbows on his thighs, studying his shoes. Scuff marks ran along the toes and sides. The heels sloped inward. "Greg didn't want me to say anything to anyone. But I told him I owed it to you."

"Is there anything I can do?" Like what, Sarah? Chicken soup does not cure AIDS.

"I have nurses 'round the clock but I don't like being away too much." The long ash on his cigarette drooped. He tapped it into his palm. Red embers glowed on his skin and died. He didn't seem to notice. "Working straight through the shoot is impossible. I can come for parts of each day, but I'll need to lean on you pretty heavily." I couldn't imagine going on without Marko. I didn't know the steps to this particular dance.

"What if I louse up? This isn't like costuming a burger commercial."

"I wouldn't ask if I didn't think you could do it," he said. "My reputation's on the line here, too. Once we start shooting I'll be on set every morning to start you off and you can reach me by phone any time night or day. Two of the gals in my workroom have run wardrobe with me before and they'll do most of the grunt work. I already talked to Mel, explained the situation, and he's okay with it. I promise I'll walk you through this, but if you honestly think it's too much, tell me, and I'll try and figure some other way."

"Like giving the job to someone else?"

"Might be someone available."

"Over my old pressing ham, you will. This is our show. I've spent some of the dirtiest hours of my life preparing for it." He patted my hand.

"You're not bad for an old lady."

"Careful," I said, covering his hand with mine, "you'll catch my liver spots."

"I'll put up coffee." He headed for the kitchen. "They should be here soon."

"Okay if I make a couple of calls?"

"Be my guest."

I took out the list and started at the top. A woman who identified herself as Bambi's sister answered Paul's home phone, her voice seven degrees to the cool side of friendly. "Asher should have called me before he called Bambi," she said. "I could have come over here and broken the news."

"You're absolutely right." No point mentioning we never knew Bambi had a sister. "But please try to understand, Asher is terribly upset. He's not thinking clearly. How is Bambi?"

"The doctor's given her something to help her rest. We've contacted Paul's rabbi"—I checked "rabbi" off my list—"and he's taking care of the funeral arrangements." Check off "Weinstein's." "Bambi's not up to entertaining"—I'd never heard sitting shivah called "entertaining"—"so Paul's sister volunteered to receive mourners."

I'd done charity work with Paul's sister. Carol was a crack organizer. She'd order chairs and coat racks, food, the whole bit. I checked them off. I crossed my fingers. "Anything I can do to help?" I asked.

"Nothing really," she said, warming sightly. "I'll be sure to tell Bambi you offered."

A tremendous weight lifted. Sorry, Paul. I take it all back. You didn't die in California just to make my life miserable. Don't know what on earth possessed me. One part stress, one part PMS, one part lack of sleep, one part guilt. Dangerous mix. Gonna spontaneously combust if I don't calm down.

Magazines and week-old newspapers cluttered the table tops, sofas, floor. I stacked some in piles, and tossed the rest. Why hadn't I noticed how lousy Marko looked lately? Really noticed. I used to be sensitive to other people. When did I start casting myself as the center of everyone's universe? The phone rang.

"Can you get that?" called Marko.

"Got it. Hello?"

"Sarah?"

"Mom? What's wrong?"

"I have a nosebleed."

The studio doorbell rang. Footsteps echoed up the stairwell walls. This was what it was all about. All I needed was a couple of hours.

"It's probably just the dry air," I said. Zack walked in. He'd changed his braid into a ponytail. Eerie how he filled up space.

"I'll bet that's all it is. Every winter you get nosebleeds from the radiator heat. Tell Johnson to fill the humidifier."

"I want you to call the doctor." Mel came over and kissed my cheek. What if I was on a world cruise in the middle of the Indian Ocean and Fanny's nose started bleeding?

"Mom, I honestly can't leave right now. Fill the humidifier." She hung up.

I sat across the table from Mel and Zack, clasping my hands together, biting my tongue to keep from trying to explain my designs and ideas. "Mel's bright," Marko had told me. "Some directors want you to talk up your designs. Mel likes to look through, concentrate on what you've done, understand your concept, then discuss it."

They went through the designs again, then again. Mel slipped off his leather jacket, rolled up his sleeves, and sorted our work into piles. Zack changed a few drawings around.

"Yes," said Mel. "Yes. Good. I think we agree on the look of the film?"

"It's what I had in mind," said Zack. "Nice work." Aw, pshaw.

"Fine, fine. We're in agreement, then. Now, let's start with Jac's character." Mel pulled out Marko's sketches of the lead's costumes. "What I'd like to see here is . . ."

The four of us huddled as, sketch by sketch, he told us his ideas, changes he'd like to see, facets of characters we'd introduced that he liked and wanted to keep. My creative juices started flowing, washing away concerns for Fanny and Asher, carrying me willingly, happily, eagerly out of this world and into the world of the movie.

26

The pain.

"And what can we say about the fra-JILLL-ity of life? That GOSSSSS-amer thread that can SNAP . . . at any second?" Paul's rabbi paused, his neon blue eyes speed-scanning the crowd at Weinstein's Funeral Home, challenging each of us for an answer. Come on, come on, get it over with.

Oh, God, the pain.

Female sobbing leaked through the silence. Male throat-clearing. The crackling of hard-candy wrappers. Paul, in a plain pine box on the fifty-yard line, played to a sold-out crowd. His rabbi paced up and back across the front, cordless mike in one manicured hand, other hand waving wildly, talking to us, talking to Paul, talking up through the acoustical tiled ceiling di-RECT-ly to God.

He milked the crowd like a revivalist preacher. Mar-Joe does Yahweh. I searched his clichés and platitudes for something that had anything to do with Paul. Nothing. I stared at the casket, willing the top to open. C'mon, Paul. This whole death thing's a hoax. Just push that lid up a quarter inch. I won't tell anyone. Cross my heart and hope to die.

"What does it tell us when a man in PER-fect health, a man of vi-TAL-ity and EN-ergy, a man who had just be-GUN to hit his

    Mid.

      Life.

        Stride.

is strickendown and takenfromus? In the BLINK of an eye?" He blinked. That did it!

"If he doesn't shut up—"

"This is for Paul," whispered Sarah, locking her arm in mine, stroking my shoulder. "Just hang on a little longer."

Rabbi Gold dipped and swayed, shouted and whispered. A wail rose and fell somewhere in back. Paul oh Paul oh Paul, why'd you pick a holy man who wears a pinky ring and dyes his hair and works the crowd like a carney barker? What was wrong with Rabbi Friedman? Remember? Remember how he stood and swayed, davening with his eyes closed? Remember how he wrapped himself in his great white tallis, shutting out the world while he talked one-on-one with God? Remember the day at Hebrew School you said he was really wacking off under there and all four of us cracked up and got sent home with notes and our fathers had to come to synagogue—our *fathers*, Paul—to meet with the rabbi and our bottoms were so sore we really couldn't sit down the rest of the week? Remember Rabbi Friedman? Gimme that old-time religion. It's good enough for me. Why'd you always need different? Please, Paul. Open the damned lid.

"He left behind four children, four fine young adults just be-GINN-ing to make their WAY in the world." The rabbi sighed toward Paul's children in the front row. They'd formed a protective barrier between Roberta and Bambi. "Four young lives torn apart, never again to know the guidance of a loving and wise father. Four young . . ."

Who's this mythical Jewish man he's talking about? Come on, Paul. You gonna hold still for this? Climb on out and tell him. You hate kids. Never go near a little person unless you're on the make for its mother. What the hell. I'm not criticizing. We're from a generation that left for work before the kids woke up and came home after they were in bed. It was good enough for our fathers. Right, Paul? You just going to lie there?

Oh, the pain.

Roberta sat in front of me, rigid and regal, not an out-of-place hair on her newly blond head. Her beautifully tailored black suit was set off by a black hat with a black veil tilted slightly to the right of center. I. Magnin does Death. "A woman is a reflection of her husband's success," Paul said, occasionally becoming crazed if Roberta was less than impeccably dressed. "But does she need silk underwear? Who's going to see that shit besides me?" Paul paid for facade. Give him the best Italian marble out front. Let the lead pipes rust, the tube-and-nob electric fray. Good thing he couldn't see the plain brown wrapper Bambi picked to mail him to his final address.

"His beautiful bride"—the rabbi's voice fell to a hush, forcing the audience to lean forward—"so young. Just starting out. How well I came to know Bambi as she took the classes that would make Paul's religion her own. A greater LOVE hath NO woman."

"I can't take this," I said. Sarah tightened her grip.

"Just a little longer. For Paul."

I focused my eyes on the back of Roberta's head. She held her chin high. You gotta give it to her, Paul. The lady has spunk, coming here because your kids begged her to come. No way Sarah would come to my funeral if I'd done what you did. Tossing Roberta aside after the years of scraping and making do, living in seedy walk-ups, trying to stretch tuna and hamburger, while you went to work in silk suits. Facade. Roberta stayed through the hard times, then you turned around and handed her future to the fancy ditz with the pouty mouth. Don't mean to sound disloyal, but I figure, if Roberta wants it, she's earned the right to the best seat in this particular house.

"When a young man like Paul goes—so SUDD-enly, so unex-

PEC-tedly—it forces us to look into our own lives. How did each of us live today? Did we spend our precious minutes well? Is there some good deed we might have, should have, COULD have done but didn't? Is there some PLEAS-ure we de-LAYED taking because we thought we had . . . tomorrow?"

C'mon, Paul. Did this joker ever meet you? When did you deny yourself any pleasure, any experience, any adventure? You lived every day like it was your last. Sarah stroked my hand and I lifted hers, pressing it hard against my cheek. Let's go home, Sarah, let's go home and climb into bed and hold on to each other until this pain goes away.

After the service, I walked to the front with Herb, Byrd, and the other pallbearers. I'd carried my father in this sort of casket, hand-sanded lengths of pine. Interesting that Bambi was so suddenly smitten by the elegant simplicity of orthodox Jewish burial rites. The plain wood casket was so much more authentically Jewish than the top-of-the-line models. And perhaps just a tad less expensive.

I wanted to carry the casket to the hearse, to bear Paul's weight. He's not heavy, he's my goldbricking friend and he's going to jump up and yell "Gotcha" any minute. But Weinstein's put their caskets on a cart that we wheeled to the hearse. Attendants slid it inside. I couldn't look at Byrd's puffy-eyed wreck of a face. Herb wasn't much better. Paul's death twisted in my heart. I hurt too much to cry.

"How d'ya like this casket?" Byrd whispered as the attendant shut the hearse doors. Herb snorted.

"Think Bambi got it on special at K mart?"

"If you ask me," I said, "Paul wouldn't be caught dead in something like that." They groaned. I listened for Paul's laugh. Still not talking. Looked like this time he was going to play the joke to the end.

27

You're green.

What do you mean I'm green?

I mean I'm looking at your ugly face, Paul, and it's the color of split-pea soup.

You should be so ugly, Asher. Paul floated over me, a Chagall refugee.

This isn't funny anymore, Paul. Stop messing around and get down here.

Not ready. Got people to go, places to see. Paul started to fade.

Wait! Take me with you.

You never went anywhere in your life, Asher. You'll just hold me back.

I grabbed for him. My arms passed through his body. He grew transparent.

This time I'll go. I went golfing in California, didn't I?

Oh, yeah, right. Fat lot of good that did me. See ya, Asher. Keep the faith.

I lunged for him again but Fanny came up behind me and pinned my arms to my sides. "Let go! Let go!"

"Asher?" Fanny shook me. "Asher?" Out of breath. "Asher?" Pillow soaked with my sweat. "Wake up." Not Fanny. Sarah. Sitting on the bed, rubbing my back. "Shhhhhhh. Shhhhhh. It's all right. It's all right." Dry mouth. Heart breaking through my chest wall. "Would you like some water?" I nodded, felt her leave. She came back with a glass of ice water and a wet washcloth. "It's five-thirty," she said. "We should get ready to go."

The room swam. Hard to breathe. I forced myself to sit up and dangle my legs over the edge of the bed. Sarah knelt behind me, pulling off my shirt, wiping my neck and back with the cool cloth. "We don't have to stay late." Her lips pressed against my left shoulder. "You need sleep." She kissed my right shoulder. The room spun in slow circles. I'd had two hours' sleep in four days. "Asher?" Whatever I'd dreamt left a two-ton weight on my chest. "Are you sure you're up to going tonight? Carol would understand if you—"

"Gotta go." If I could just get the room to stop spinning. "Would you run me a shower?"

"You got it." She draped the cloth on my neck, kissing my forehead lightly on her way.

Later, showered, dressed, a cup of strong black coffee shoring me up, I felt almost human. It wasn't until I climbed into the car that I remembered.

"I need my tallis," I said, stumbling out of the car and back into the house. Where was it? Not in its place on top of the prayer books on the shelf. I tore through my dresser. Not there. The drawers in the den were filled with old Word Finds, crayons, yarn, fabric scraps. Where *was* it!

"Asher. They'll have everything at Carol's." It was the soft level voice she used to calm hysterical children. I pushed past her to the hall closet, pulling out boots from the floor, scarves and gloves from the top shelves. Not there. The guest bedroom, closet and drawers still full of Jeff's baseball trophies, uniforms, school awards. "Why is this still here?" Throw it out on the floor.

"Asher . . ."

"You don't want to deal with it? Ship it to him. And send him all that stuff I took out of his bedroom. Let him toss it. We don't need it here."

Not in the library. Maxi's old room. Not in the closet, not in the drawers. More fabric scraps, buttons, threads. "How much space are you going to take up with this? I thought that's why you needed a studio outside the house." Sarah silent, sad-eyed. I gripped her arms. "Paul's grandmother made that tallis for my bar mitzvah. I'm not going to pray for him in some rent-a-shawl!"

Sarah found the shawl where it had fallen behind the prayer books on the library shelf. We didn't talk all the way to Carol's house. That suited me just fine.

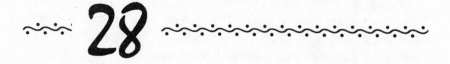

"Saaaa-rah." A shorter, blonder, heavier Paul rushed out of the crowded kitchen to greet us. "Aaaa-sher." Carol threw her arms around us. "Oh," she whimpered. "Ohhhhh." What was my pain compared to hers? I lost a friend. She buried a twin.

"It's all right," I said into the curly hair that smelled of perfumed spray and fresh-brewed coffee and just-baked coffee cake. "It's all right." I hugged the trembling body split from Paul's egg, flesh of his flesh. The anguish idling inside me took off at full speed. I held on for dear life. Sarah did the same. Our hands met behind Carol and locked. I squeezed Sarah's hand. I had no right taking my anger at Paul's death out on her. Sarah squeezed back, understanding.

"I can't believe it." Carol dug a handkerchief from her apron. "I can't believe he's gone. Tell me, Asher," her voice a whisper, "tell me what happened." He birdied the hole, couldn't take the excitement. "I need to know." He did a dead man's dive headfirst into a five-foot-deep bunker, and I had to dig his face out of the sand. Don't make me do this, Carol. I can't. Sarah squeezed my hand. I think I can.

"He was just joking around," I said, "walking up to hit a golf ball. He fell down. That was it. No warning, no pain."

"Just like Papa." She wiped tears off Paul's eyes. They'd had their lids and brows lifted on their forty-fifth birthdays and were planning a twofer face-lift for their fifty-fifth. "Papa died at fifty-one. Sometimes I think that's why Paul lived so crazy. Afraid he'd die young, too." If fifty-one scared Paul, I should be terrified. My father died at forty-eight. Why wasn't I afraid? No time. I'd been too busy working. Not anymore. Now I'm retired. Got all the time in the world for fear. "I'm glad you were with him when he died," said Carol. "At least he wasn't alone." She hugged me again and left for the kitchen.

"I'll go help," said Sarah. "You okay?"

"Fine. Go ahead."

The house smelled like Lysol and fresh baking, furniture polish and mothballs. A real old-fashioned house. Our house had no smells anymore. People came up to me. "Sorry, Asher. I know how close you and Paul . . ." "Can't tell you how sorry we are that . . ." "At least he lived a full life." "Left a beautiful family to . . ."

Who were all these people? The friends I knew. But who were the others? People from work, the country club, East Bank? I found a space on the sofa and settled in.

"You're Asher Rose?" I nodded at two enormous eyes the milky caramel of taffy apples. "Marguerite Maxwell." She perched on the end of the sofa, one cheek off, one cheek on, diddle diddle dumpling, and held out a delicate white hand lined with the palest of blue veins. Chipless manicure, ringless fingers. She withdrew the hand. Had I forgotten to shake it? "Paul told me so much about you." I couldn't place her. "We met on convention last year? In Anaheim?" Was she asking or telling? "It was my first time out in the field and Paul absolutely saved my life."

A little mouth-to-mouth? An emergency chest massage? The name clicked. Those long fingernails dug tracks up and down Paul's back. He couldn't wait to show us. On our couple's theater night, he dragged us into the men's room during intermission and pulled up his shirt. Red lines crisscrossed his back. Paul faked a cold for two weeks, sleeping in pajamas instead of the nude until the evidence healed. He thought Bambi might not understand.

"You simply wouldn't believe the way some men lech on convention." The delicate detail of Marguerite's lace bra showed through her thin white sweater. I studied the outlines of the perfect circles around her dark nipples. "I mean, would they behave that way at home?"

"I wouldn't know," I said. "Soup people aren't big on conventions."

"But you must travel on business?" Want dates? Times? Flight information?

"The few times I traveled I took early flights out and came home the same day." Because I had Sarah to come home to. Because if I wasn't at Rosie's the place would fall apart. Still, it's hard to meet taffy-eyed ladies that way. Hard to have time to unbutton little white sweaters and unhook delicate lace bras.

Marguerite raised her left eyebrow prettily and rested her hand on my arm.

"Trust me," she said. I trusted her. "Most men away from home are all hands." Look who's talking. She glanced around secretively, then leaned in close to me, her breast pressing my shoulder. She smelled dusky pink and powdery. I could almost taste her. "Paul was different." The world tilted and I felt myself falling into her eyes. "He was a real gentleman." Did he say please and thank you? "He opened a car door for a lady, held out a chair." Was that all it took? Here, let me open the door, your place or mine?

"Asher?" Sarah stood over us, energetically wiping her hands on a towel. Marguerite eased back.

"Sarah, this is Marguerite Maxwell, a . . . uh . . . business associate of Paul's." No way hawk-eyed Sarah missed Marguerite's white-sweatered body against mine, but she chose to ignore it. And Marguerite.

"Carol would like the chairs set up in the living room for the service. They're in the den." She spun on her heels and returned to the kitchen. Marguerite, put off by the smell of wife or work or both, levitated from the sofa and drifted toward a group of men I didn't recognize. They straightened, sucking in stomachs, checking hair with nervous hands. Who *were* all these people?

Byrd and Herb guarded the den, Byrd stretched out on the plaid sofa bed, Herb tilted back in the tweed La-Z-Boy. No Louis XIV chaises on this shag carpet, no etched glass tables or Chippendale chairs. Not like the eclectic mix of expensive furniture at Paul and Bambi's that dared you to put your feet up and your drink down. It was only right this was the shivah house. Only right.

"Wondered where you guys were," I said. Byrd, balancing a glass of schnapps on his stomach, rolled his head in my direction.

"It's time?"

"Carol wants these set up." I walked to the piles of gold plastic chairs stacked behind the rented coat racks and lifted six chairs at once. A muscle snapped on my left side. Getting old, Asher. I pretended to be adjusting the chairs until the pain eased. Herb released the footrest and rocked forward out of the recliner.

"Rabbi here?" he asked.

"Not yet."

"Think we'll need all these chairs?"

"A lot of people walking in."

"You happen to run into a Marguerite Maxwell out there?" Byrd winked at Herb.

"She made a point of saying hello," I said.

"Oh, Asher." Byrd put his hand on my arm. "Paul told me so much about you." His falsetto was perfect.

"When you think about the way Paul lived," said Herb, "it's amazing he didn't die a lot sooner."

We grabbed a couple of chairs in each hand and threaded through the living room crowd. People spilled over into the dining room and hallway. So many strangers. Paul didn't mix his drinks or his groups. Took life full-strength.

Up and back, setting up one row after another, excuse me, coming through. So many chairs. How many would Sarah have to rent for me? There'd be Sarah, Maxi and Jeff. Well, Sarah, anyway. Martha, probably. The rest of my brothers and sisters, if there wasn't anything good on TV. What about the crew at Rosie's? Edie, Cliff, and Bulldog for sure. None of the new people would know who I was. Byrd. Herb. Acquaintances from the synagogue. Where did Paul meet all these people? Even four chairs were too heavy, now. Down to three at a time. Have to work faster. Too many people. Maybe Bambi called Rent a Mourner.

"Asher?" No time for chitchat. Work to do. "Asher, it's enough." Sarah took the chairs out of my hands and handed them to a young man.

"What's wrong?"

"It's enough with the chairs."

"But—"

"It's enough." She sat me down. "I'll bring some water." No air in the room. Hot. Dizzy.

"Oh, Uncle Asher." Patti came at me. Little Patti, crying into my shoulder. I swung a leaden arm up around her.

"There, there, baby. It's all right." Patti, Patti, finnan haddie, will you come cry at my funeral? "It's all right." My own family might be too busy. "Your dad was so proud of you, honey." I stroked her hair. "So proud of everything you did. He talked about you all the time."

"Really?" Paul's eyes, Roberta's mouth.

"Yep. Bored us silly." She smiled and I saw the baby she'd been just yesterday. No harm in a small lie. Paul probably was proud of Patti, might have talked about her if he'd thought about it. I just passed on what he would/could/should have said. "That's my girl. Your dad wouldn't want you to cry."

The rabbi had traded his blue daytime contact lenses for emerald green. Sarah sat beside me, rubbing my back, keeping me calm while Rabbi Gold swung into his evening show. No room to move. People overflowed the living room, crowding into doorways and halls. They pushed the air out of the room. Walls buckled. Sarah's strong fingers soothed my neck and shoulders.

Paul's children sat up front with their Aunt Carol. Their mother had not come. Roberta went to the funeral for her children's sakes. No need to suffer the intimacy of a home gathering. She'd called me the day Paul married Bambi.

"Why'd he marry this one, Asher?" Drunk, crying. I'd never seen Roberta touch liquor. "Why couldn't he just screw her like all the rest of 'em, then come back home?" She knew about Paul! All those years he thought he was getting away with something, Roberta knew. I never told anyone.

The crazy thing was, their marriage lasted as long as he fooled around. But the times caught up with him. "Between herpes, AIDS, and being caught," Paul said, "there's no way I'm going to fool around anymore. Hell, I'm even afraid to play with *myself*." Without his affairs, he couldn't live with Roberta. He craved passion and excitement. "I need someone younger, less used up." So what if he was the one who did the using.

Each of his children gave a tribute: loving poems, funny anecdotes, warm memories. In the end, a lousy father was still a father. Even in this throwaway world, there were some things we couldn't replace. I felt a small glimmer of hope. Maybe Jeff and Maxi would find a few kind words in their hearts for me.

Our father sent us to Disney World once. He couldn't go himself, of course. Too much work to do. But he paid for us, made all the arrangements and even called the cab to take us to the airport. Wotta guy.

And what about my work? Rosie's Soups made millions of people happy, healthy, soothed, loved. There had to be something somebody could say about that.

Asher Rose made one hell of a beef barley. Never scrimped on ingredients. Wotta guy.

Soft sobbing in the room. Who were these women daubing their eyes, risking runny mascara in front of their husbands? I recognized a few from the neighborhood. How many had slept with Paul? He was always at it.

Asher Rose was a faithful, loving, dedicated husband. He had sex with two women before he married Sarah and, in twenty-five years of wedded bliss, never strayed once. Not that he didn't enjoy looking. He wasn't dead. Like Paul. Wotta guy.

His children sounded as if they loved Paul. Maybe death burns warts off memories. Long live the altered state.

". . . and I am proud to carry on my father's work. Being

together with him every day at the office this past year gave me a new appreciation for all he accomplished." Tall, good-looking boy. Twenty-four? Likable. Nice enough. Not sharp like Paul, not hungry and hustling. Why couldn't my children have loved Rosie's like I did? What would have been so terrible? What's the use of twenty million dollars if it's blood money for selling your baby?

A room full of crying now. Noses blowing all over the place. Sarah's fingers kneaded, massaged, trying to soften the steel in my shoulders. So I'm rich. So I finally showed my father. Asher the Dreamer, he called me. Asher, the one the family would have to take care of. What kind of man spends time cooking soups when he could be sewing suits? Well, who wound up taking care of who, Papa? And why did you have to die before you saw any of it? I'd spent my life proving something to a dead man.

I couldn't hold back anymore. "Excuse me," I said, stumbling down the row, stepping on feet, crushing purses, "sorry, excuse me," making a break for the door. Outside, I held my face up to the cold air. "Oh, God." Billions of stars in the moonless sky, a great wide universe there before we came, there after we'll go. Crying full-out now.

"Asher." Sarah's arms around me. I grabbed her and held on. "I know you miss him."

"It's not about Paul. Not only about Paul."

"What, then?"

"Me, Sarah. It's about me."

"What's about you?"

I held her, trying to keep my world from spinning off center. "I'm nearly fifty, Sarah. My business is gone. My best friend is dead. I've alienated my son."

"Jeff's just going through—"

"If I die tomorrow, Sarah, if I drop dead like Paul, what did all of this mean? What did any of it mean? 'Asher Rose died with a large bank account, personal papers in order, and clean drawers.' That's one hell of an epitaph. Don't look at me like that. I'm telling you, there's got to be more to life than this."

"Of course there's—"

"Come away with me, Sarah. Please. Now."

"Asher, you know I can't—"

"Tibet. Tahiti."

"You're upset. Let's go home." Oh, the softness of her face, the long black lashes, the pale gray eyes.

"I'll be all right. Just need to get away. With you. We can do the world alphabetically. Start with the A's. Africa. Amazon. Arkansas. Don't look so sad. I'm serious. Any letter. Pick a letter. Come on, Sarah."

"Asher"—tears in those beautiful eyes—"I will go with you. I will. But I can't right now. We've been through this. Please don't do this to yourself. To me. To us."

Her lips kept moving but a black wave pushed up from somewhere deep inside of me and I lost what she said in the horrible, terrible, deafening roar.

29

I wheeled my basket from line to line. Chains closed off six of the ten checkout lanes, causing long lines at the other four. I studied the overflowing baskets, envelopes crammed with coupons, trying to guess which line would move fastest. What are all you people doing here at eleven in the morning? Why aren't you home eating bonbons and watching Geraldo?

Eleven-o-one.

C'mon, we're going to start fitting the Stars today. Hey, World, listen up, I'm talking big-time stuff, here. Little Sarah Feldman Rose is finally getting a peek behind a very closed door. I do not have time for grocery-line waiting. Except Fanny is not eating. Except I am watching her wither away in front of me and don't know how to stop it. So, when she casually mentioned having a taste for cottage cheese and bananas . . .

Only seven people in the ten-item-or-less line. Eleven items in my basket. Close enough. I'd perform a little unloading sleight of hand, set the sixty-tablet box of Efferdent on top of the Tums three-pack.

Eleven-o-two.

Nothing moving. Two checkers crammed into the small space behind the register. The woman in front of me finished leafing through the *Star* and exchanged it for a *National Enquirer*. Thirteen items in her basket. That was pushing it.

"What's going on?" I asked.

"Dunno, it's been slow." I took out my checkbook and started filling in the information. There were a million little ways to save time if one only thought ahead. I felt the woman's eyes on me and looked up. "This line's cash only," she said, nodding at the three-foot-tall flashing neon CASH ONLY sign.

The five and two singles in my wallet wouldn't cover every appetite-tempting thing in my basket but I wasn't about to give up my place in line to cash a check up front. I jiggled my purse. Two dollars and seven cents in coins fell to the bottom. Found a crumpled single in my lipstick case. Damned bar code, how was I supposed to add unpriced items? I'd have to guesstimate.

Once upon a time, I knew prices to the penny. Long, long ago, in a faraway land, the minutes of the hours of the days of my life were strung together with trips to the grocery store, meat store, bakery, fish store. I loved it, thrived on it, couldn't get enough of price comparing, coupon clipping, living a real honest-to-goodness normal life. Me. Fanny Feldman's daughter who grew up thinking postperformance forays through all-night markets was how *every-one* shopped. And I lived happily ever after. Until Jeff and Maxi grew up and moved away. There's no adventure in shopping for two. Getting five cents off on one bar of soap lacks impact. Now I shopped for speed. Nine dollars and seven cents. This was going to be close. I might have to leave an item or two behind.

Eleven-o-five.

The first person in line finally passed through. And then there were six. Had to stop at my studio, get my notes and supplies together. Please hurry.

"Excuse me"—a man's voice behind me—"but all I have is this pack of cigarettes." Ignore him, Sarah. Just keep digging for dollars. Another three cents inside my bank statement envelope, a quarter in my little tissue pack.

"Excuse me," he said again, pushing into my space, "I just have this one item."

"And a lovely item it is, too."

"Would you mind—"

"And I just have these eleven items, and the woman in front of me, who has been waiting since Booth shot Lincoln, just has those thirteen items"—easy, Sarah—"and what the *hell* makes you think your time is so much more valuable than mine or hers or the four people in front of her that you can just push your way in because you just have that one item which by the way can be bought at any grocery store drugstore gas station newspaper stand I'm talking serious options here but I have this cottage cheese which can *only* be bought at a grocery store which is why I'm stuck here waiting in the world's slowest line and you can jolly well wait your turn."

Eleven-o-seven.

"Bitch," he muttered. Yes, well maybe sometimes I have the right. He strode out of our line and tried his "I only have one pack" on two other lines before an elderly lady let him in front of her. Someone behind her said something which he ignored. It's amazing more people aren't murdered in grocery stores. Good thing they don't sell guns on the checkout candy racks.

In my Original Plan, Fanny's nurse did all the shopping. A fine plan, a lovely plan, a plan designed when Asher was newly retired and Marko was in absolute charge of this movie and Fanny was safely recuperating in the hospital. In those halcyon days of clear thought and connective logic, I'd lie in bed in the wee small hours, cataloging, ordering, prioritizing my responsibilities, blithely shaping the world to suit my needs. I conjured Mary Poppins for Fanny's nurse. The pert and perfect Poppins kept an impeccable house, cooked nutritious and enticing meals, and loved going grocery shopping. Best of all, Fanny adored her.

Then came the dawn. "Green bananas she brings me," said Fanny. "At my age, you buy ripe. Three pounds of coffee? Who am I, Rockefeller? Oranges she gets the size of grapefruits." None of which had anything to do with food, and everything to do with fear, fear that if she said she liked Mary Poppins, I would not come to visit anymore.

Eleven-o-ten.

The tampon holder! I liberated it from the purse bottom, extracting a tightly folded emergency twenty-dollar bill. Home free. I could buy it all. The line next to mine moved up. A lady with two full shopping carts began unloading. A man rushed up to her waving a jar of pickles. The checker took him first.

Eleven-o-twelve.

"What's the problem?" I called. The checkers didn't look up. "I SAID," I shouted—easy now, Sarah—"WHAT SEEMS TO BE THE PROBLEM."

"We're training a new girl, here, ma'am," said the nontrainee. "Please try to be patient."

"It's rush hour! Mothers shopping before the kids come home from school, workers on lunch hour buying food to cook for

dinner, people with sick mothers who need to get to their houses.
How can you train someone at rush hour?"

"You'll just have to be patient." A mother hen protecting her
new chick. "She's doing the best she can." The trainee looked
ready to cry. Great, Sarah. Strike terror into the hearts of checkout
clerks who lay their lives on the line for a few bucks an hour and
all the stale bagels they can eat. What's happening to me? I used
to be a nice person.

30

I abandoned the basket, fled the store, drove forty miles
an hour over the speed limit to the little corner grocery near Fanny,
bought the same items I'd left behind for four times the amount,
and whipped my car into the bus stop in front of her building.

An elderly man, gripping the bus stop signpost for support,
waved his cane at me. "You can't park here," he said.

"Emergency medical delivery," I said, grabbing the bag out of
the car and racing into Fanny's apartment building. I rang her bell.
No answer. Waitwaitwaitwait. Rang again. No answer. Her keys
lived in the junk jungle at the bottom of my purse. I'd have to start
digging. One more try. The intercom clicked.

"Whoooooo [cough cough] izzzzzzz it?"

"Mom," I shouted, "it's Sarah." Not this again, Fanny. Not
now. I'm in no mood.

"Whoooo?" [Cough.]

"Sarah."

"Whoo [cough] ooo?"

"Mom, it's me, Sarah." Where's the nurse? "Buzz me in or I'll
post your real age on the mailboxes." She buzzed.

Waitwaitwaitwait. No elevator. I jammed my finger into the
button again. One elevator started its crawl down from the twenty-
fourth floor. Someone had the other one locked on eighteen. Acid
poured into my system, burning through arteries, eating away
stomach walls, roiling up my throat until the elevator came to my
rescue.

Silly me. Why did I think Fanny's door would be open? I

knocked and waited. I knocked again, longer and louder. No answer. Waitwaitwaitwait.

"Mom? Mom, I know you're in there! I just talked to you on the intercom!" A couple of doors opened along the long hallway. Smells of frying and baking wafted into the hall. People peeked out. In an apartment building of retirees, a crazed woman shouting and beating on a door rated as the day's main entertainment.

A small man wrapped in a large bath towel padded down the hall toward me trailing water. His head of thick white hair came up to my eyebrows. He wore the towel with the unselfconscious ease of a man who had done hard time in the Luxor steam baths. His teeth clamped on an unlit cigar the size of a broom handle.

"A problem?" he asked.

"Not really. Mom's just a little hard of hearing." A sudden violent rattle of chains, bolts, locks. Fanny, who must have had her ear pressed against the door, flung it open.

"I am *not* hard of hearing," she said, burning me with a look that could render chicken fat. For Mr. Towel-Around-the-Waist she had another look altogether.

"Hello, Leon." She extended a hand.

"Fanny." He took it, kissed it, patted it. "You had me worried there a second."

"Not to worry, Leon. I was [demure flutter of eyes] indisposed. [Stage whisper.] My daughter is the hysterical type. If I don't answer the instant she knocks, she thinks a mass murderer has come and hacked me into a thousand pieces." She stood aside so I could enter her apartment. I smiled at Leon.

"I'm Fanny's daughter, Sarah," I said.

"Charmed." He might have released Fanny's hand long enough to shake mine if she had let him.

"You can put those groceries away, dear," she said to me. "I'll be right in." Class dismissed. Fanny, I noticed, hadn't coughed once.

The apartment sparkled. I brought the groceries to the kitchen and began unloading. A box of spaghetti stood on the counter next to a pot of steaming water.

I thought Fanny wanted cottage cheese for lunch. Where was Nurse Johnson? I yanked open the refrigerator door. No need for me to shop after all. Fanny never wanted the cottage cheese, she wanted me. Somewhere in the back of my heart I knew that. A few interesting items lined the shelves of the mold-free, clean-smelling refrigerator. Fanny came into the kitchen.

"Caviar?" I held up the open jar. "I don't remember buying caviar."

"A gift from Leon," she said, taking it out of my hand, putting it back in the fridge. Beluga caviar. The last time I priced it, a two-ounce jar went for half the national debt.

"Did he also bring this pickled herring, wine, and—" Fanny walked out of the kitchen. Conversation over. "And where," I asked, following her, "is Nurse Johnson?"

"She no longer works for me."

"You fired her?"

"I should pay someone to sit all day?"

"I pay. And she didn't sit all day. Someone cleaned your refrigerator, your apartment. You're not strong enough yet to—"

"I don't need anyone here. I can take care of myself."

I collapsed onto the sofa. Johnson was a prize, one of those fabulous caretakers passed from household to household along the north shore. Before she came to work for us, we had an unsmiling Swede who couldn't cook and a talkative Hungarian no one could understand. If Fanny wouldn't keep a gem like Johnson, she wouldn't keep anyone. Now what would I do?

She began coughing, one hand pressing a tissue to her mouth, the other clutching her chest. This whole cottage cheese caper was about letting me know she fired Johnson. Fanny wanted to be alone, but not so alone I wouldn't come around.

"You don't sound all that healthy to me, Mom. Let her come back for another week or two."

She coughed again, tossing her tissues into the garbage bag under the sink. The bag overflowed with tissues. Maybe I should mention this to Dr. Fishman. Eleven fifty-seven. I had to get out of here.

"What's this?" She inspected the items on the table.

"The groceries you wanted."

"Who needs such a big jar of applesauce?"

"It was the only size they had."

"It's not from the Jewel."

"No. The Jewel was too crowded. I went down the block to Marty's Groceries."

"You're so rich you can throw money away? I can't eat all that."

"Mom, it'll keep. In a week, two weeks, you'll eat it."

"Mold I'll have."

"So you'll toss it."

"Take it back." She shoved the jar at me. With the nurse gone, I moved back into the primary caretaker space. Not now. Not now. Too much to do. Fanny had to know that. I picked up my car keys and put the applesauce in my purse.

"Where you going?"

"I have to get to work. I won't be here tomorrow. Probably not until next week."

"What are you talking?"

"If you're so healthy you don't need help, I have other matters to attend to." She began coughing so hard she had to sit down. I forced myself to turn away and walk to the front door.

On my way out of the building, a panhandler hit me for a handout. I reached into my purse and gave him Fanny's jar of applesauce. He didn't look thrilled with it either.

I approached the juncture on my way to the studio where I could veer off to the right and take the expressway home. Fifteen minutes to get home, a quick half hour lunch with Asher, then back to the shop. He'd been so depressed since Paul's death that I felt guilty being gone all day.

You don't have time, Sarah.

But he's so unhappy. If only he'd get out and do something. So what if they're freezing him out at Rosie's? It's not like there's nothing to do in this city. Lately he stayed in his pajamas all day. When was the last time he left the house? I shuddered at sudden childhood memories of his mother peeking out through her curtains at the world. What if agoraphobia was hereditary? A little gene that didn't like to go out? I'd ask Dr. Fishman when I called him about Fanny's coughing.

31

The front doorbell rang for the third time. Where, I'd tried to explain to Sarah, where is it written that I had to answer a ringing telephone or doorbell? Someone coming unannounced took his chances. Salesmen, mostly, pushing magazine subscriptions, Watchtowers, Environmental This, Save the That. People with no concern for the homeowner teetering on top of a ladder (or the edge of the Earth), or sitting down to a meal, or making love to his wife. Not that there was a whole lot of that going on around here lately. But still. But *still*. What gave these uninvited bell ringers the right to demand we drop everything? Sarah said she couldn't ignore a ringing bell. I told her she could do anything she set her mind to.

Another ring. This was a persistent one. And there's Marisha again, banging around the hall with her brooms and buckets, making noise to wake me in case I'm sleeping, not understanding why I don't come out of the bedroom and answer the doorbell. Why I don't want her answering it. None of her business.

It occurred to me a few days ago that I really didn't need the entire house. Why mess the sofa? Television shows, for what they were worth, were as crummy upstairs as down. I did make it a point to take my meals in the kitchen when Sarah was home. No need for her to know where I spent my days. She'd be upset if she knew.

Have to get this TV tuned up. Color's off. All these food commercials. Haven't seen one for Rosie's since I've been home. We used to run a few a day. There, that's better, not so much green in the picture. Soap stars were looking like Martians. I'd kidded my employees who talked about these TV characters as if they were real people facing real crises. Sometimes, at lunch, they'd have me read "What Happened on the Soaps" from the newspaper. I'd ham it up. They'd laugh. I was a funny man. Very funny. Stop crying, Asher. You can be funny again. Someday. Just not right now.

A knock on my door. Well, I don't have to answer that, either. Another knock.

"Asher?" Man's voice. I knew that voice. "Asher? You awake?" I hit the TV's mute button.

"I'm busy, Michael." Michael might not consider my watching "The Young and the Restless" as being exactly busy.

I could picture him outside the door, hands clasped behind his rumpled overcoat, rocking back on his worn heels to peer up at the ceiling. "Too busy for an old friend?" Rocking forward to examine the carpet. "What's so important"—smudged eyeglasses slipping down his nose as he pursed his lips—"that you don't have a minute?"

Ghosts of childhood Yiddish wrapped softly around his words. No way out of this. Michael the Patient would stand a year in my hall if he needed to. An effort to get up from the bed. Body achy, head throbbing. I unlocked the door and swung it open.

Michael's eyes spoke first, large tears pooling over deep sadness. A rabbi should learn to hide his emotions better. I bet Paul's rabbi-of-the-fur-coat didn't get all bleary-eyed. Couldn't risk crying on his silk suits. All Michael's suits were tear-stained.

He nodded silently, slipped an arm through mine, and led me down the stairs. Lines of small talk . . .

So, how's the family?

You know who I ran into last week?

Why don't you and Sarah come over for . . .

. . . lines once soft and flowing as spider's silk, broke into brittle pieces. Somehow, as we passed through the front hall, he wrapped my coat around me and slid my feet into my shoes. I was still grasping for something to say when he walked me out the front door. The latch clicked like a gunshot behind me.

"I can't," I said.

"You already have." His arm through mine again, we strolled down to the sidewalk and turned left. I'd forgotten the feel of fresh air on my skin. The day was surprisingly warm. A last hurrah before winter. The air carried smells of dead leaves, lake fish, things cooking. Sounds trailed out in great distances, moving without end around the world. Too much to think about. Too much to deal with.

"I have to go back," I said.

"In time." It was all right as long as he held on. If he let go, I'd float off. We turned the corner, starting a new side of the block.

"I've never done this before," I said.

"Done what?"

"Walked around this block. Eighteen years we've lived here."

"You were a busy man, Asher. A very busy man. But now you have time to take a walk around the block. Two blocks, even."

"Let's not get crazy."

"Do you know how lucky you are? You have good health. A happy home. You're young enough to enjoy the pleasures this world has to offer. To hide all day in a dark room—"

"I'm not hiding, Michael."

"—watching make-believe people on a tiny screen jump in and out of bed in fifteen-minute segments—"

"Twelve, tops."

"—is, perhaps, not the best use of your considerable talents and blessings."

"This is better? Block walking? Tell me, Michael, what makes this use of my time so much better?"

We came to another corner but continued straight, crossing one street, then another, until we reached Lake Michigan. A concrete gray sky pressed down into the still gray water and disappeared.

"No horizon," I said.

"There's always horizon, Asher. Only, sometimes, we can't see it."

"You're wrong, Michael. There's nothing out there. Maybe there used to be. But it's gone now, and it ain't a gonna come back. No time. No way. No how."

We sat on the crumbling brick ledge bordering the sand, took off our shoes and socks, and rolled up our pant legs. I dug my toes into the cold sand *Paul died in sand like this* and followed Michael to the shoreline. I could keep walking straight out into the water and disappear.

"We've missed you at services, Asher." Michael picked up a black stone, rubbed off the sand, then tossed it back. "You have the only voice strong enough to stand up against Leonard's monotone." I found two flat stones side by side. Keepers. "Sarah tells me you have not been well."

"Is that what she said?" She'd been going behind my back? Something ugly stirred inside. "That I've been sick?"

"Not sick, exactly." He squatted at a pile of stones, sorting through. "Troubled. Not yourself."

"I'm exactly myself. Just a part of myself I haven't used very often." I lifted a flat stone, worn smooth from the sand, and hefted it in my hand. Hunching down, I curved my forefinger around its outer rim and whipped the stone sidearm along the surface of the water. It skipped once, twice, three times before sinking. "Not bad, for an old man."

"Watch this and weep," said Michael, setting his overcoat and suit jacket on the sand. He unbuttoned his shirt cuff and rolled the sleeve up to his elbow. Picking up a stone, he wiggled his wrist to loosen up, shifted his weight, hauled back his arm, and whipped the stone into the lake. The shiny black disk skipped in long arcs across the surface of the water. "One! Two! Three! Four!"

"Two out of three." I ripped off my overcoat, swinging my arms, loosening the muscles.

"You're on."

The stones I'd gathered—fine for a casual lob, an idle toss, a friendly skip—no longer satisfied. I dug through the tidal offering of sticks, dead fish, weeds. No way Michael could beat me. I'd worked with my arms my whole life, lifting, stirring, moving. I raced from stone to stone, looking for the right shape, size, weight. My arsenal.

"You first," I said. Michael selected his stone, tossing it up and down a few times to get the feel of it.

"I could use a man with time on his hands, Asher," he said, bringing his arm back. "We've grown so much this last year we need to restructure our organization." He whipped his arm around. The stone shot out, hit the water, and sank. His surprised laugh startled a group of gulls into flight.

"I'm not your man, Michael." Coiling my body, I brought my arm back and sprang around, hurling the stone low and hard. "One, two three, four five six! One all." Michael selected another stone.

"With your organizational know-how, you could really make a contribution, maybe come in an hour each day—"

"No."

"All right, a couple hours a week."

"Michael. I'm cleaning house. Divesting. Skimming the fat off the top of my life. No more responsibilities. No new ties."

"Stand back," he warned, miming a comical pitcher's warm-up on the mound. The stone skipped the still water in four long arcs before sinking. "We should get points for distance."

"Can't change rules in mid-game," I said. "I tried to tell Sarah that."

"If you make the rules, you can change the rules."

"Look out. This is for all the marbles." The stone, hurled nearly horizontal, skimmed the top of the water, skipping seven times. "Yes!" I yelled, throwing up my arms, running around in a victory circle. Michael laughed, clapping his hand on my shoulder as we gathered our coats and headed back to our shoes.

"Asher, sitting around the house all day is no good for a man like you."

"Sarah shouldn't have called you."

"I'm honored she did."

"This is no one's business."

"She loves you. She's worried about you."

"She's wrong to worry. I am not without my projects."

"Like?"

"I happen to be gathering and organizing travel information. We'll go away as soon as Sarah can leave."

"What if that's another month, or half year, or year?" A stone dropped in my heart. "You going to spend another year sitting in your bedroom?"

"Michael, go play rabbi somewhere else. We've been friends too many years for you to start butting into my life." I broke into long strides, reaching the wall ahead of him. He struggled through the last bit of sand and settled next to me.

"Remember Donald Kaminsky?" he asked.

"Scrap metal?"

"Right. When he retired, he was like you."

"Have him call. We'll compare soap operas."

"No hobbies. Not even golf."

"That should make the *Guinness Book of Records*."

"Somehow he found out his old grammar school auditorium— you remember Clinton School near Devon and California?—well, the roof leaked and plaster was falling. Kids hadn't used the room in years. He paid for all the repairs."

"The man's a saint."

"When the arts funding was cut, he financed a music program."

"You're boring me, Michael."

"He promised each Clinton kid who finished high school he'd pick up their college tuition." I pulled my socks on over the sand and jammed my feet into my shoes. Never should have come out. "And he's made good on that. Kids who never would have—"

"I get the picture. Since when do you have to hit me over the head with an idea?"

"Since you stopped living in this world." I got up and headed home. He ran after me, shoelaces clicking against the sidewalk. "Think of the good you could do, the lives you could touch. You need to get involved with something meaningful, Asher." I wheeled around.

"Involved! That's the last thing I need! I've been involved my whole life!" The sand on my feet ground into my skin.

"There's no need to yell—"

"I'm tired of taking care of the world, Michael. Tired of being responsible for everyone and everything. Since I was nine years old, I've done for others, my mother, my father, my sisters, my brothers, my family, my employees. I'm sick to death of it. You want to do good deeds with my money? I'll give it to you. Take it with my blessing. I'll have Martha draw up the papers. You feed the hungry, clothe the naked, house the homeless, do whatever you want. But leave me out of it."

"This isn't for me, Asher. It's for you."

"For me? For my own good? This is for my own good? This hurts you more than it hurts me? The check is in the mail? Go away, Michael. Go home. There's no work for you here."

~~~ **32** ~~~~~~~~~~

I flicked on the studio light and walked toward my desk. The monstrous pile of **THINGS YOU MUST DO THIS VERY INSTANT OR YOU WILL DIE A CERTAIN AND TERRIBLE DEATH** growled and shifted on its haunches, drooling fabric scraps and invoices. Had it doubled in bulk since yesterday? Must be feeding on something when I went out. I sat, careful not to get too close.

Deep breath in. I mustn't let Fanny get to me. Deep breath out. Can't let her manipulate me. Breathe in. It was her choice to let Nurse Johnson go. Breathe out. I have my first feature film fitting in half an hour. Breathe in. Have to get jars of applesauce out of my mind. Breathe out. Good. Think. Focus.

I closed my eyes, visualizing entering the suite at the Drake
Hotel. I am charming, witty, bright, helpful. Enthusiastic. Don't
forget enthusiastic. Or, it might be better to work quietly; Marko's
efficient, indispensable right-hand gal.

My studio door opened and Asher walked in. He hadn't left the
house in days! How did he pick this exact moment to break out?
The day took on the feel of a sitcom. In today's episode, a harried
Sarah picks the wrong grocery checkout lane, learns her mother
has fired the nurse, suspects something evil lurks under her office
clutter, and finds her housebound husband at her office door the
exact moment she needs to leave for a meeting. Punch up the laugh
track.

Asher planted a huge kiss on my forehead.

"What a surprise!" I said. He'd showered, shaved, put on a
clean shirt and pressed pants. "You look devastatingly handsome."
Asher beamed. So what if his fly was open a few teeth and he'd
popped the third button on his shirt. He was up and out.

"I'm tired of feeling tired. I thought, maybe, if I forced myself
out I'd feel better. I took a walk to the lake. Skipped stones."

"Really?"

"Yep. And I said to myself, 'Self,' I said, 'who in this world do
I want to spend such a beautiful day with?' So, here I am."

I stood and gave Asher a massive hug. "I've been worried about
you," I said. His arms slid around me, pulling my hips to his. He
kissed me. Made me remember how little he'd done that, lately. I
hugged and kissed back.

"Spend the day with me, Sarah."

"You know I can't."

"You're always begging me to go to the art galleries with you.
Let's do that today. Really, I'd like to."

"Asher, you're breaking my heart." I eased my body away from
his and started cramming supplies into my large work bag. "Remember? I told you. We're working with the film's stars today." I
unearthed my production notes from the desk. Had I forgotten to
pack anything I might need?

"You can spare an hour for lunch. Gotta eat."

"Honest, I can't." He curled out his lower lip. "Not the lip!" I
pressed the back of my hand dramatically to my forehead. "Please,
please, not the lip." He curled it out farther, his eyebrows drawn
mournfully together. "Ooooooooooohhhhhh, you're making me
feel guilty."

"Good."

"I'd love to have lunch with you. But—"

"I'll drive you to the fitting. . . ."

"Yellow-handled scissors. Where'd I put the— There they are."

". . . wait for you in the car."

"It could take hours. I'd worry about you sitting out there. Blue tape measure. Do you see a— There."

"I'll come in and wait." I looked up, about to laugh. He wasn't kidding.

"Asher, be serious. Can you imagine me sitting in on your meetings at Rosie's?"

"I would have loved it."

"Sure, easy to say now." Asher deflated. "Let's make it dinner. We'll have a special romantic dinner."

Too late. Whatever energy he'd mustered to get out of the house drained onto the fabric-strewn floor. I found the pack of tailor's chalk and scrounged around for a plastic bag to toss it in.

"What am I supposed to do all day?" he asked. Hell, Asher, I don't know. I hoisted my bag on my shoulder, trying to move him toward the door.

"Why don't you go to Rosie's?" Why don't you go out and play with the other kids? "Dust off your desk. See your old friends. You haven't been to the plant for a while." He shook his head slowly.

"Noooo," he said. "I don't think so."

"How about a movie?"

"You know I don't like doing things alone."

"Who does?" Stop it, Sarah! "Honey, you're going to have to find things to amuse yourself."

"What about us? What about our plans, all the things we were going to do when we retired?" I set the bag down and folded my arms tight across my ribs.

"Five years, Asher. Remember?"

"I don't—"

"You sat me down in the kitchen and told me you were going to sell Rosie's and work there for five more years."

"That was—"

"And *I* said, 'Can't you retire now?' "

"Who knew—"

"And *you* said, 'No, five more years.' That's what you wanted, that's what you did."

"So? Things changed."

"So, I made plans to keep busy while you worked. You told me five years. I've made commitments, assumed responsibilities."

"What am I supposed to do?"

Don't say it, Sarah. "All those years I waited for you to come home from work"—don't do this, Sarah—"I found things to do to keep me from going crazy. All those nights you were in mid-crisis with a cracked cooker or broken freezer or I don't know what the hell else, I put the kids to bed and watched 'Bewitched' reruns and sewed costumes for school plays. Did I once come to Rosie's making demands on you? Did I once tell you to come home and be with me?" Great going, Sarah. Kick a man when he's down. And the truth shall set you on a collision course.

"I had no idea being home was such a hardship."

"It wasn't." I put my hand on his sleeve. He pulled away. "It was my choice to stay home and raise our children. I loved those years."

"Sure doesn't sound like it."

"All I'm saying is you worked long hours and sometimes it got lonely. So I found ways to fill that time. Now it's your turn to find ways to keep busy. You said five years, Asher. I want them."

He looked at me without speaking, then turned and walked out. Something about the droop of his shoulder, the slouch of his back, the shuffle of his feet, reminded me of every zombie movie I'd ever seen, horrific tales of the living dead.

33

Heads turned as Marko walked down Michigan Avenue, his white-blond hair flowing over the vintage khaki greatcoat he'd unearthed during one of our resale shop digs. Fragile Ego Rule #1: Never go anywhere with a man more attractive than you, especially when you have designer bags under your eyes.

Not that Marko looked his best. Greg's illness had beaten him down, worn him out, stolen his smile. Still, his less-than-best was sensational, especially against the backdrop of the Magnificent Mile's somber business suits and predictable ties.

I struggled behind him, pulling the box-filled luggage cart with one hand, lugging a canvas bag the size of Rhode Island with the other.

"It's not fair," I said, hoping to slow him down.

"What's not?"

"It's so easy for men. Put on a suit, shirt, tie, and walk out the door. We women need a uniform, too."

"I can't picture you wearing anything anyone else would wear."

"Don't be logical while I'm being pissed." That got a smile out of him. Or maybe it was a trick of light. We turned into the Drake Hotel.

Jac Green opened his own door. No publicist, no secretary, no entourage to guard him from the Attack of the Wild Costumers. Just Jac Green, star of every other action flick made in the last ten years, alive and up close in skintight T-shirt and jeans. And short. Very, very short, like a Shrinky-Dink Schwarzenegger.

"Comeincomeincomein," he said, smiling. "You can set up in there." He waved a bulging bicep toward the dining room. "I'm just finishing up an interview. Be with you in two seconds. Coffee's in the kitchen. Might be a stale donut or two. Help yourselves." He walked back to the living room, where a woman waited, steno pad and pencil in hand.

"Love these measurement sheets," said Marko, tossing the specs onto the dining room table. "Check the height on that." Green's studio listed him as a smidge under six feet. "Even Stallone's taller than this guy." I started taking cords off boxes.

"Where do you want this?"

"Unload everything on the table." We unpacked a movie's worth of garments, two or three possibles for most of the scenes. Marko set his huge work bag on the floor, pulling out tape measure, pins, chalk, one thing after another. He started humming, laying out outfits in different combinations, checking his notes, hooking up the steamer. For a little while, anyway, work would take his mind off Greg. Marko was back, Jack, and all was right with the world.

A small clock on the mantel chimed the quarter hour. The fitting could go all afternoon.

"I'd better call Fanny while I have time," I said, heading back to the foyer phone. "She gets nervous if I call too late." She picked up on the first ring.

"I just called Dr. Fishman," she said. "Told him I've been

coughing up a little blood. He wants me to come to his office right now."

"Mom, I can't leave. If you wait—"

"He's leaving in an hour. I've got to go now." She stopped to cough. I remembered all those tissues in her garbage can.

"Maybe Asher can drive—"

"I already called and asked. He says he's not feeling so good himself." Which meant Asher went straight home after he left my studio. I hoped he'd find something to do besides go back to bed.

"You'll have to call a taxi."

"I don't want no taxi." In the living room, Jac Green and the woman stood, talking as she gathered her things. End of interview.

"Mom, we're just getting started here. I'll catch up with you as soon as I can. Call me from the doctor's office."

"If I make it there." She hung up. I dialed Asher, keeping my voice low so Marko wouldn't hear. He had enough to worry about without my problems.

"I talked to Mom," I said. "Please, can't you take her to the doctor?"

"I just got out of my clothes."

"So put them back on."

"I don't feel well, Sarah."

"Please, Asher."

"What if I wasn't home? What would you do?"

"But you are home. And I'm asking you please please help me out."

"Is this what's going to happen? You're going to work, and I'm going to take care of your mother? Because if that's what you—"

"Asher, for God's sake. I'm asking this one time." His answer was a long time coming.

"All right. Call Fanny. Tell her to be downstairs in fifteen minutes." He hung up. I dialed Fanny, grateful Asher would take her, furious he couldn't make the call himself.

Jac Green let the journalist out and came into the dining room. "I'm all yours," he said. "Just tell me where you want me."

I tensed as he unbuckled his belt. One of the actors in the first community theater I costumed came for a fitting with no underwear on. I refused to measure him. Not because I hadn't seen naked men, more than my share when I lived in Europe, but because it wasn't professional. He was the only one in all these years, but I never got over that nervous moment when an actor first let down his pants.

Jac Green, macho martial arts movie star, the man who single-handedly defeated every black-hearted karate-kicking villain in every one-hundred-twenty-minute film, wore underwear, God love him. Boxer shorts. With little red hearts all over. A tiny ray of sunshine in a gloomy gloomy day.

34

Three-thirty. Why isn't it three-thirty? Clock must be broken. Hands stuck on three twenty-two. Flick on the TV. Still "Win Lose or Draw." All that jumping, screaming, yelling. Chaos. Mayhem. Who needs it? Shut off the noise. Another eight minutes to "Jeopardy." Probably should get up off this sofa and do something. What's the point?

Marisha's running the vacuum again. I told her DON'T VAC-UUM. Can't believe she's doing it. Thinks I don't hear her all the way down here. Thinks closing the door stops the sound.

Seven more minutes to "Jeopardy." Now there's a real show. Neat. Tidy. Categories listed in one horizontal row across the top. Dollar amounts, listed small to big, running in vertical columns down the board. Organized. Exact. A person can depend on a show like that. Sure, every now and then a contestant goes out of order, maybe picking the $400 question before the $200. Disturbing, yes. Well, sure. Of course, disturbing. Things not exactly in the order they should be. But, in the middle of so much order, a little jumping around is manageable.

Damned vacuum. How much dirt can there be? Sarah's away all day and I hardly move. Make-work. That's all this is. Why did I think it would be quiet at home? This house is a damned resonator, like living in the middle of a motorized orchestra. Buzz/hum/whir, refrigerator solo, freezer counterpoint, bring up the water conditioner, heating unit, washing machine, dryer.

Six more minutes. When did time start crawling? All those days at work, all those years of days at Rosie's, never enough time. Run like a son of a bitch from early to late and hate to leave at night because there was still so much to do. This is why I never had enough time. All those minutes I needed were hiding here in the house, building up, growing into this mountain. I used up all the fast minutes at Rosie's. Now I'm stuck with these crawlers, these inchers, these barely-movers. A second at work is an hour at home. How did Sarah stand this all those years?

Today's obituaries were the worst yet. Three men under fifty. I cut them out, added them to my file. Gotta keep track, try and spot the trends. I talked to Michael about how I wanted my funeral services. No reason to take a chance. He says I have too much time on my hands. Why did I sell Rosie's? Stop crying. What's the matter with me? Like a broken faucet lately. Tears pouring down with no warning. How can I go out if I never know when this is going to happen? Incontinence of the tear ducts. Go diaper that, my man.

Got to take my mind off. Into the kitchen, adjust the flavorings in the cauldron bubbling since early morning. Who knows how to make just a little soup? Who would trust a person who could/ would make soup for one from scratch? Sarah brings batches to the seamstresses in Marko's workroom. They sent a little fabric flower by way of thanks. Like when I was twelve years old and people paid for my soups with bubble gum, pencils, baseball cards. Now they send fabric flowers. And in between I built an empire. And in between . . . bubble bubble. . . . She's vacuuming over the kitchen. Following me around. Tormenting me. Put the lid back so softly she can't hear. Tiptoe to the dining room. Let her think I'm in the kitchen. Let her torment the soup.

Now, now, now. Let's see, let's see, let's see. Might need to extend the dining room table. Even with all the leaves in, I'm cramped for space. Have to remember to ask Sarah where she keeps the aluminum folding table. All the years we've lived here and I don't know where the most mundane everyday things are. Took me a week to reorganize the kitchen. Sarah wasn't thrilled but, like I told her, how often does she cook anymore?

The border's filling up nicely. Stroke of genius. Photocopying the geographic entries in the back of the dictionary, checking off all the places in the world I want information on, sending the list to my travel agent. Amazing the amount of information available for the asking. Finally have brochures coming in at a steady clip.

Something satisfying about the alphabetically organized stacks of brochures running clockwise around the edge of the table.

Aachen, Aalborg, Aaist. Baroda, Barotseland, Barquisimeto. Maybe I could go to the library, look through *National Geographics*, photocopy places of interest. No, I can't go out. I'd cry over the copier, drown Dubrovnik, sink Soweto. Buy a copier. Where would I put it? Damned things always need repair. I'd have a service man coming in here every day. Don't need some stranger watching me cry. Sarah can make copies for me. She'll have to.

The map's looking good. Biggest world map I could find. Lots of colored pins stuck in, each one corresponding to a brochure, each pin a promise to go to that place. Yesterday's batch of brochures was troublesome. A few hot spots. Beirut. Tehran. Belfast. Lima. Put red pins into those. Yellow pins for warm climates. Blue for water. Green for jungles. White for civilized places.

Why didn't I travel when I was young? A person could go anywhere in the world back then. What was so important that I never made time? Mama hiding in bed because the world was too much for her, and me cooking and cleaning and raising her kids. And then there was Rosie's. I should have traveled thirty years ago when I was young and the world was safe. Now everyone was at war. Look at all the red pins. And a lot of places not at war are too hard on the body. I'm too old. Last year, when Sarah dragged me to visit Jeff, I had trouble breathing, vomited in the Denver airport, sweated and cramped in Boulder. Jeff took it personally. Like I meant to ruin his plans to hike in his hills, picnic on his mountain. Like I was still angry he turned his back on Rosie's to open a coffeehouse. He's so sensitive. Can't talk to him. Colorado was altitude sickness, pure and simple, no matter what Jeff thinks.

Which leaves out the heights of Machu Picchu. Nepal. Maybe I'll do jungles. I always liked those Mutual of Omaha shows. What was the host's name? Comeoncomeoncomeon. Milton? Marvin? M something. Wrestling pythons in the Amazon. Morton? No. Losing names lately. I'd work on it. Had to remember before Sarah came home. Make it the "time's up" on my personal Final Jeopardy. Who is —? Alex. No. It will come. Trying to remember would give direction to my afternoon. Keep me horizontal and vertical, neatly lined up. Damned tears. Getting the brochures all wet. Why'd you die, Paul? Can you please just tell me why?

Three-thirty! Hurry. A cold beer would taste good. No. Have to wait for intermission. Don't want to miss a single question. Flick on the TV. Commercial. Could make it to the kitchen for a beer. No. I can wait. Commercial. Commercial. Afterschool Special?

Wha—? Check the channel. Right channel. "WHAT ARE YOU DOING? WHAT KIND OF AFTERSCHOOL SPECIAL!?" The vacuum shut off upstairs. "WHERE'S 'JEOPARDY,' YOU IDIOTS! WHAT'S THIS GARBAGE?" Adrenaline pumping, heart racing, bile rising. Where's the phone? Dining room, on top of Afghanistan. Punch 411, demand ABC's number, punch some more.

"American Broadcast—"

"What are you? Crazy? You think kids run home from school to watch this?"

"Excuse me, may I direct—"

"It's three-thirty! Kids aren't even home from school!" Tentative footsteps creaking down the front stairs.

"Sir, if you will let me direct your call, I'd be happy to—"

"You think kids can't wait to watch other kids being abused, drinking, doing drugs? Kids don't get enough preaching in school? What lunatic's in charge of your programming? Put this show on when kids are home to see it. Midnight maybe. But leave 'Jeopardy' alone."

Now what? Now what? Half an hour to the first news. Could do with a nap. But she's upstairs. No. There she is, tiptoeing down the stairs. Good. I'll recapture the battlement.

One sure way to ease into a nap. Paul always said if God didn't intend for man to whack off he wouldn't have invented *Penthouse Forum*. Lock the doors. Don't need the Polish Patrol walking in on me. Now. Let's see. Try and get into it. Scan the old standbys. Watching Arlene Smith through my bedroom window, her in her training bra and panties, me in my tented pajamas, terrified someone would see me seeing her. "Hey, Asher, how come you always get the bed by the window?" "Because I'm the oldest." The window shade up just enough for me to glimpse the promised land. Both of us knowing I was watching. And, oh—comeon— she'd turn her back and unhook—comeon—the bra and ease the straps one by one off her shoulders and—comeoncomeoncomeon. OhpleaseOhplease. Nothing. Stop crying. It's all right. More where that came from. All right, now. New start. Scanning. Scanning.

Years and years back. Sarah pregnant, too big to make love the last two weeks. A new girl started in veg-prep and I naturally made it a point to have lunch at her table, the way I did all new employees, though perhaps not so often or for so long when they were older or uglier or less needy of someone as intelligent and helpful and understanding as me—comeoncomeoncomeon. She leaned forward when she talked, her breasts resting on the cafeteria table, pushing up, mounding, comeoncomeoncomeon. And oh that call her voice hysterical "Please Mr. Rose" and "Could you meet me early for breakfast in a little out-of-the-way restaurant before my shift comeoncomeoncomeon because I am so terribly unhappy I had no one else to turn to my husband is not a man like you who listens and understands and communicates" comeon-comeoncomeon inhaling her lily of the valley smell and in the dark privacy of the booth "let me show you the bruise where he pushed me up against the dresser and hit me because he thought I was flirting at the party when I was just being friendly and he says I drink too much but I'd rather drink my calories than eat them and I know lots of others drink plenty more and you can't imagine how tender this is. Feel? Here. Slip your hand under the sweater, yes, feel this lump just under the rib maybe just a bit higher Yes, oh yes, there." Her skin like velvet and oh so warm—comeon-comeoncomeon. Please, please. Not a twinge. Stop crying. Not the end of the world. It's okay. It's okay. Got to stop this, Asher Rose.

That crack in the ceiling is growing. Never had time to watch it before. Used to get in bed at night and fall asleep in two seconds. Sarah took care of the house. Not now. If the ceiling is splitting, what's happening at the foundation? I'm not going to lie here watching the house come down around me. Maybe Paul was right. I need to work out. Get in shape. But how can I work out the way I am? I'll look like a shlub standing next to bodybuilders like the ones at Paul's club. I could build a gym in the house, add a workout wing, hire a personal trainer. Yes. Perfect. Where's the phone book? Not up here. Downstairs. Up and at 'em, I'm a man with a mission. She hears me coming, creeps up the back stairs. Better and better.

Let's see. Equipment. Sporting goods. Dozens of listings. Which place to call? What would I say? Too many listings. Paul would know what to do. For God's sake, stop crying. Dial a number. Any number. So many. Too many. Maybe I need to eat something. Soup's not ready yet. What's in the fridge? Moldy cream cheese, leftover spaghetti, peanut butter, an old leg from one of those damned rotisserie chickens. No appetite lately.

Clothes are beginning to hang on me. Drawstring pajamas make the most sense just now. Too hard dressing in the morning. Besides, I just have to undress again at night.

The map. The key is in the map. My future neatly laid out on the dining room table. Beautiful colorful pins. When all this craziness passes, when Fanny is well and Sarah can travel and I don't cry every two minutes . . . Something's wrong. Something's changed. All those pins, all those colors. Not promises anymore. Not promises at all. Accusations. Why haven't you come here, Asher? Why haven't you visited?

Have to take this one out. Who wants to go to Beirut? And Colombia? And Syria? Take all the red pins out. No need to go to war. Got my own Apocalypse right here. And what about these mountains? Altitude's too hard on me. That leaves out Tibet and the French Alps and the Andes. Better this way. Fewer places to choose from. Now, the jungles. Not really crazy about humidity. Besides, Amazonian Indians are killing the lumber people who are killing the environmentalists. And the Congo. Poachers killing animal rights activists. And New Guinea, remember what happened to the Rockefeller kid. Screw the jungles. Out with the green pins. And the water. I get seasick in the bathtub. What am I going to do on an ocean? Out with the blue. Out with the white. Out. Out. Out.

One pin left. One place in the world for me to go. X marks the spot and I'm standing on it. Not a very big pin. How many angels dancing? Any of them doing the Texas two-step? Sharp pain flipping in my chest like a trapped bird, pecking the base of my throat, pushing into my tear ducts, setting me off again.

Oh, Lord, this time it's for real and I can't stop crying and I can't move and there's nowhere for me to go in this world and no one who loves me and wants to make it all better and there's no point in moving because that only makes it worse and how long can I cry before I'm squeezed dry and shrivel up and blow away?

A lifetime later, a gentle Sarah-breeze blows in against the blackness, wraps me in its arms, guides me away from the table, up the stairs and into bed. It crawls in beside me, holding me tight. So tight. I rest my head on its soft breast, breathe in its perfume.

"There, there," it whispers, stroking my head with a cool hand. "Hush, it's all right. It's all right."

Let me end this way. Let me go out like this. "I can't, anymore. I can't."

"Hushhhhh," she whispers. "It's all right. It's all right." Her arms tighten around me and keep me from falling off the Earth.

35

AsherFannyWorkAsherFannyWorkAsherFannyWork.
My thoughts wound tight as buttonhole twist. Visit Fanny, go to work, home to Asher. No beginning, no middle, no end. No exit. Occasional bubbles of memory, of times when I controlled my life, pushed up from the murk and burst.

I'd visit Fanny at the hospital, put on the mask and gown, sit and hold her cold hands. All that coughing—coughing to catch my very busy attention—reactivated ancient TB.

"Picture a little hard-shelled nut," said Dr. Fishman, rubbing Fanny's shoulders, talking to me over her bedbound body. "That nut was dormant inside Fanny for years. Probably from childhood. The coughing cracked it open, releasing the TB."

Fanny sat quiet, too scared to act. Oh, for an occasional "Oyyyyy," a theatrical groan, moan, curse.

"TB's not serious anymore," said Fishman.

"By you, being in the hospital isn't serious?" said Fanny. "So why does everyone come in masked like the Long Ranger?"

"I didn't say you weren't contagious," said Fishman. "You need to be isolated—"

"Oy."

"—and medicated—"

"God should only take me."

"—a little while. Once the TB's under control, you'll be good as new." I couldn't read his face behind his mask. Truth or fiction, Doc? Fanny, too, studied his eyes.

"So, Dr. Genius, when will I be able to play the violin?"

"Could you play it before?"

"You stepped on my line."

"Get new material. Now behave. I'll stop in to see you later."

We watched him go, staring at the closing door, waiting for the next act. "He's lying," she said. "I'm dying and he doesn't care.

Oh, God. Ohhhhhh." Here we go, ladies and gents. "Take me out of here, Sarah."

"I'll take you home as soon as the doctor—"

"Please, now!" Her face and body rigid with fear.

"Mom, be reasonable."

"You take me home now." I sat on the bed and hugged her until her trembling became part of me. Fanny's body, that fine-tuned instrument that played comedy and tragedy, that tiny power pack that lit up a stage and ignited an audience, had turned on her, coughing up bloody globs from mysterious depths. The masks and gowns we wore into her room terrified her. Not being allowed out of the room terrified her. Confined to solitary with no audience terrified her. Her body shook against mine and she cried into my shoulder, triggering a coughing jag. She filled tissue after tissue, lining them along her bedside tray like bloodstained soldiers.

We sat in the room, Fanny coughing, me waiting. Mother and daughter in still life. I checked my watch. Had to get to Marko's. So much to do before we started shooting.

How could I walk out?

How could I not?

Fanny is my mother and she's afraid.

I am in emotional quicksand and I am being sucked under.

If she'd only let me distract her. "Mom, let me turn on the TV."

"No. I don't want it."

"You can't just sit here coughing. You've got to get your mind off—"

"Please." Angry now. "Don't tell me what I should do."

"I have to go."

"Go."

"I'm going," I said, blowing her a kiss. She coughed as I pulled open the door and shut it behind me, stripping off the mask and gown and stuffing them into the special "contaminated" container. I couldn't shake the sound of her coughing. It followed me down the corridor, into the elevator, and out the door of the hospital.

36

I called Martha during my lunch break and asked her to meet me after work. I needed to talk to someone before I started bouncing off walls. The fact that my best friend was also Asher's sister/attorney had kept me from crying on her shoulder until now. But I couldn't carry this alone anymore.

I'd intended an intimate heart-to-heart in one of the Pump Room's comfy booths. But by the time I got to the Ambassador East, Martha had established squatter's rights on two prime bar stools near the entrance. She'd been a long time between men. We settled in and played catch-up. The bartender set a fresh gin and tonic in front of Martha. I ordered a scotch. Neat.

"So what are you going to do when Fanny gets out of the hospital?" she asked.

"She wants to go back to her apartment. How can I let her? She can't take care of herself anymore."

"Same thing happened with our father, started disintegrating after Mom died." She propped her elbow on the bar, resting her cheek on her hand. It lifted the skin of her face ever so slightly, nipping off a few years.

"I don't remember that."

"This was before you and Asher were married, when you were gallivanting around Europe."

"Studying art."

"Whatever. All of a sudden I'm getting calls from Dad's bank. He's overdrawn and his checks are bouncing left and right. Mortgage payment's two months late. So, I go over, right? 'Dad,' I say, 'what's going on?' And he starts cursing and yelling. 'These young kids at the bank are useless.' " She banged her fist, startling the stag line around the bar from us. To the untrained eye, Martha didn't look like she was looking, but she was looking. "He's yelling, 'You can't get good help anymore.' "

"He had *that* right," I said.

"And I'm thinking, Hey, here's a man who ran the best damned tailor shop in Chicago for forty-three years. He knows bookkeeping, right? Banks make mistakes, right? And now I'm getting angry at the gonzo from the bank for giving my dad a hard time. But, so long as I'm already at Dad's house I figure it can't hurt to go over his checkbook. 'Dad,' I say, 'why don't you let me take a little look?' "

"Old Milton punch you out?" I asked. Martha laughed, launching one of her Miss Piggy head tosses, swishing her long hair from side to side. It's a killer movement. Crotches across the bar snapped to attention. She pretended not to notice.

"Just about. He's yelling, 'You believe that bank? You think I made the mistakes? You think I can't take care of my own business? You think blah de blah de blah.' " She squeezed the wedge of lime into her drink, stirred, and swigged. "So I make us coffee and sure enough, two cups later he's off to the bathroom. I quick open his desk drawer." She ran her tongue over the lime, snagging the attention of the third man on the left. "You wouldn't believe the mess. Bills wadded up and crammed into the drawer, checks gone from the checkbook but not recorded, bank statements stacked in a pile, unopened." Martha rolled her large brown eyes. The man raised an interested eyebrow. I clucked sympathetically.

"Did you say something to him?" I asked.

"Think I've got a death wish? I dumped the whole mess into a shopping bag and took it home. Spent the next two days straightening everything out, then snuck it all back. He never missed it."

I thought of the dust balls in Fanny's apartment, the unflushed toilet, moldy food. "That's no solution," I said. "It's a bandage, not a cure."

Martha shrugged. "Look. I'm just telling you what worked for me. I was at law school and didn't have time to hold Dad's hand."

"What about Asher?"

"He'd just bought his first small plant and was killing himself trying to get Rosie's off the ground. And you can forget Freyla, Pearly and the boys. They would have made a whole big deal out of it. It was easier for me to just steal Dad's bills and pay them. What's so terrible?"

We played with our drinks. Our friendship spanned conversations of dolls, boyfriends, husbands, children, careers, Martha's divorce, long-distance mothering. Now we talked parents. Maybe I shouldn't bring up Asher. If I had a sister, would I want Asher talking to her about me?

Martha pulled the lime wedge open and licked it with the tip of her tongue, then slid it into her mouth and out again, verrrrrry slooooooowly. Tonight was no sight-seeing safari. The lady was out to bag game.

"How's my bro?" she asked. "Giving you trouble?"

"Asher? Always."

She smiled as if I'd said something remarkably clever, letting out line across the bar. Hooking was the easy part, the art lay in the reeling. The man turned his body toward us. Bar language for "I'm interested. Your move."

"I've tried reaching Asher a couple of times," she said, "a few details to clear up on Rosie's. He's never at Rosie's and he's never home." She brought it up, I didn't.

"Martha, Asher's always home." Her smile froze.

"What are you talking about?"

"Asher stopped going out. Stopped getting dressed." I pressed my lips together, pressing a fist against them. I didn't mean to cry. Martha gripped my arm.

"Why didn't you call me?"

"I thought he was depressed about Paul's death"—stop, swallow, get on top of the tears—"that he'd get over it." Stop. Emotions floating so close to the surface, lately, they kept bobbing through.

"You should have called."

"I thought I could handle it. I thought it would pass. And then this TB thing came up with Fanny and she's so scared. And working on this movie is taking more and more time. I sort of lost track of Asher. Now I'm trying to take care of both of them and do my work, and I'm not sleeping and I just can't think straight anymore."

"Sarah, listen to me." Her voice low and urgent. "You've got to get Asher up and out of that house. If you don't, he'll never leave."

"I've tried."

"Try harder."

"I can't."

"You listen to me, Sarah Feldman Rose. I'm the brains of this friendship, remember?" She wet the corner of a napkin and wiped away whatever damage my tears had done to my face. "Asher of all people should know better than to do this to you."

"Do you think he's becoming like your mom?"

"No I don't. When I was a kid, I read up on agoraphobia for my own peace of mind. It's not passed on genetically. Asher's no more agoraphobic than you are. Which is not to say he's not majorly depressed or male menopausal, or whatever the hell sometimes happens to men his age. The rotten thing is we learn behavior patterns from our parents, and one thing Mother really knew how to do was hide out at home."

"So what am I supposed to do? Pick him up and throw him out?"

"If that's what it takes."

"I can't think anymore, Martha. It's like everyone's pulling pieces off of me. Pretty soon there won't be anything left." I put my elbows on the bar, pressing my fingertips against my forehead. She massaged my neck and shoulders. How long had it been since I'd felt the comfort of a caring hand? Asher, who once couldn't pass by without touching me, now didn't even seem to notice when I was in the room.

"You have to prioritize," she said. "First you arrange for Fanny. Hire a nurse, put her in a home, something."

"I can't."

"You can."

"She won't—"

"She will. And if she doesn't, it's her decision. At some point, Sarah, you have to let people take responsibility for their own lives."

"Like you did with your father's bills?"

"Don't get smart. I wasn't balancing on the brink of a breakdown. Once you get Fanny squared away, you get Asher up and out of the house. Hire a goon squad to carry him out if you have to. I'm serious. Don't let this get a foothold. It's not a fun way to live."

She opened her purse and took out her lipstick and mirror, methodically applying new color. The man watched and she smiled at him, light glinting off her incisors. He smiled back. She'd played out enough line, it was time to hook that sucker. She lifted her left eyebrow his way. He picked up his drink and wound his way through the crowd toward us. I stood, tossing money down for my untouched scotch. A fortyish blonde in a twentyish miniskirt made a move for my chair. Martha slammed her purse on it, smiling apologetically. "Sorry," she said, "this seat's taken."

"Call you tomorrow," I said, sliding my drink over to her. Nothing is wasted among old friends. She waved vaguely, her back already to me.

37

Water steamed into the claw-foot tub. A few added drops of sandalwood and musk oils mellowed the air. I opened the bottle of Benedictine Asher bought on our twenty-fifth anniversary and poured the sweet liquid into tiny Turkish brass cups he'd given me as my engagement present. "These are just a deposit," he'd whispered. "Someday, I'll take you to Turkey. And Paris. And Greece. And . . ."

I set fifteen assorted-size candles on the low shelf bordering the tub and began lighting them. It had taken me a few days to accept Martha's advice, days of looking for change, hoping Asher would miraculously wake up one morning eager to start the day. But, if anything, he became worse, asleep when I left, asleep when I came home. I wanted my Asher back, his easy laugh, his constant love.

Last night, digging through dusty piles of boxes in the basement for some of Fanny's old hats to use for the film, I came across an old box of Asher's things. Flyers he'd hand-printed in grade school and put under car wipers to sell his matzoh ball soup. Soup recipes dating back to the fifties, cut from travel magazines and kept in folders according to countries. PR flyers, printed in the high school print shop, listing seven different soups, available fresh or frozen. Some of my postcards to him littered the bottom of the box. Aix-en-Provence, Como, Helsinki. I never stopped to think how painful it must have been for him, housebound in Chicago, to get those cards. I'd write about this boyfriend and that boyfriend, hoping to make Asher think of me as a woman, and not just Martha's friend. What a cruel insensitive thing to do. He was dying to go to Europe, and all I cared about was making him jealous.

When I finally came up from the basement, I understood what I had to do as clearly as if it were carved on tablets from the Mount. I made all the arrangements. Now, everything was ready. I lit the last candle and turned off the overhead lights. All that was left was to tell Asher.

He sat in bed clutching the television control, flipping from channel to channel. Nothing held his attention for more than a few minutes, not even the nonstop sports programs that once absorbed him for hours. The last color had drained from his face.

His thick hair sprang unkempt in all directions, the gray coming in thick this past month. Who was this old man in my bed? Asher was dying in front of me. I had to do something to save him from committing psychological suicide. The plan I came up with terrified me. But it was all I had.

"Come on," I said, folding back the covers, holding out my arms to him. "I've run us a bath." He shook his head, not turning from the screen. I looked. He was watching a dog food commercial. "Come on," I said, reaching down, taking the control from his hand, helping him up.

I undressed first, dropping my clothes to the floor. At least Asher watched. At least he did that. I untied his robe, unbuttoned his pajamas. By now the old Asher would be rock hard and we wouldn't make it into the tub for a good long while. Not now. Not a hint of an erection for over a month. For Asher that was a lifetime. I led him to the candlelit bathroom and climbed in the tub, easing into the hot water. Asher hadn't moved. I held out my hand to him and he climbed in, his back to me, lowering his body between my legs, leaning back against me. I kissed his neck, dipping the soap into the water, reaching past his arms to rub slow circles around his chest.

"I love you, Asher Rose," I said. I kissed his ear. He tilted his head back, resting it against me. I cupped hot water in my hand, spooning it over his chest. "But you're making yourself sick, and I don't know how to help you."

"I'm fine," he said.

"You're not fine. You sit closed up in the house. You're shutting yourself down. A little more each day."

"I'll be all right."

I took almond oil from the ledge, spread it over his shoulders, and moved my fingers strong and hard along his muscles. Thick knots tied the muscles down his back. Water splashed a couple of the candles. Flames sputtered and died. I had to be careful, watch what I did, or there would be no light left for us. No light at all.

"I'll be all right," he said again, his voice catching.

"Not unless you get away for a while." There. I'd said it. No response. "You've got to. Don't you see?"

"I thought you couldn't leave. I thought—"

"Not us, Asher. You."

The Earth stopped.

Not us. You. Not us.

My words hung in the air, strange fruit in our home.

Not us. You. I gripped him tight to me.

"Remember when Lenny committed suicide, you were so angry with him. You said, 'If life got to be too much for him, why didn't he just go off and sit on a mountain until things got better?' Remember, Asher?" Please remember. "You said, 'Because things always do get better. Always.' "

Silence. His heart pulsed under my hands, strong quick beats. It was risky mentioning Lenny but I was desperate to get through to Asher. He'd loved his funny, irreverent cousin. They'd been inseparable until Lenny swallowed his mother's pill collection. The wound of his suicide never quite healed. Maybe I'd pushed too far.

For a long time Asher didn't move. Then he shuddered and lifted his hands from the warm water, placing them over mine. His thumbs stroked my skin and my heart caught. A sign of affection. Our lives used to overflow with little touches, small kisses, warm caresses. How had I ever taken something so precious for granted?

"I was a kid then," he said. "It's easy to be smart about what you don't know."

"But you did know. And you were right. Lenny would be alive today if he'd just given himself some time. Oh, Asher, you need to go off and sit on a mountain." Nothing. "I want you to go. Travel. Anything but sit in the bedroom and die a little more each day."

"Go without you?" he asked quietly. He brought one of my hands to his mouth and kissed the fingertips one by one.

"I'll catch up with you as soon as . . . as soon as . . ."—Fanny is well and the movie is over—"I can."

"That could be months."

"It won't be."

"It could be."

"Yes," I said softly, "it could be. But you can always stop in to say hi on your way from Zagreb to Tanzania."

"Hang a left at Nepal?"

Humor? Was that humor I heard? More. More.

"Something like that," I said.

"How can I? I'll wait for you."

"If you wait, if you stay here, you'll resent me and Fanny and my work even more than you already do." He moved my hands down his body, pressing them between his legs, guiding them up and down against him. Yes. Please, God, please. Give me back my Asher.

"Come with me, Sarah." A little firmer now.

"Don't, Asher. I'd feel guilty leaving right now. I'd ruin your time and mine."

"I'll take my chances."

"If something happened to Fanny while I was gone, I'd never forgive myself, or you. And I'm too far into the movie to leave. Asher, I've thought this thing through." He filled out under my hands.

"I'm not going anywhere without you."

"Listen to me, Asher Rose. You've worked your whole life." *You could drop dead tomorrow just like Paul,* I thought, but didn't say. There are things a smart woman doesn't mention on the cusp of an erection. "You have a right to live a little."

"How little?" He arched his back against me, definitely firming up now.

"Asher, I'm afraid, terrified, that if you stay here much longer, I'll lose you." I nuzzled his hair, loving the smell of him. "I couldn't bear that."

A pinhole of light penetrated the blackness. Leave. Go. Now. Of all the possibilities I'd agonized over these past months, traveling without Sarah had never occurred to me. The light grew brighter. Not so much a pinhole as a door opening into my darkness, showing me a new way out.

I climbed out of the tub and looked down at Sarah, loving the flicker of candlelight on her face, the caress of bubbles riding the full curves of her breasts. "I am—I was a sexual animal," I said, feeling distant tremors. "When I'm . . . myself . . . I can barely go a couple of days without making love. What makes you think I can go a couple of weeks? Or months?"

"Asher"—her voice so low I could barely hear—"I'm not asking you to." Asking you to. Not asking you to. "After so many years of good behavior . . ." Behavior. Behavior. ". . . a little time off . . ." Time off. Time off. ". . . isn't going to kill our marriage." Kill our marriage. "But staying together might."

She stood and I helped her from the tub, wrapping her in a towel, gently patting the water from her skin. I bent and licked the drops off her nipples, knelt and sucked the moisture from between her legs.

We had made better love in our lives—more exciting and passionate love—but never had our lovemaking been more important. The erection did not hold. "That's all right," Sarah said, comforting, reassuring, "that's all right."

It would have to be. Not what I'd hoped for, but a faint promise, a possible beginning. And, at the moment, it was everything.

The hotel room reeked of stale cigarettes and spilled booze, and the heater had a terminal rattle. The king-size bed, desolate without Sarah, creaked and sagged and bunched up the sheets. She could have come to New York with me for the night, stayed until my morning flight to London. Would it have been so terrible to miss one day's work?

I had to get fresh air. Prying and pushing, I worked open the only unsealed section of window, a narrow strip over the heater/air conditioner. The blare of car horns and street noises drowned out the heater's rattle. I rammed the window shut.

In twenty-five years of marriage, how often had we slept apart? Sarah stayed a few days in the hospital when Maxi and Jeff were born. I'd traveled half a dozen times on business. Even on those rare nights Sarah and I weren't exactly on speaking terms at bedtime, I still felt her closeness.

One-fifteen. Enough! No use fighting it. I turned on the light. Taking out my Swiss Army knife, I unscrewed the heater's front panel. The fan's holding screw was loose, and I tightened the blades down. End of rattle. Maybe I'd go downstairs. There was some kind of bar off the main lobby. Might pass some time. But that meant dressing again. Who had the energy?

I plumped the pillows and flicked on the TV, clicking channel after channel, stopping at a rerun of the old Dick Van Dyke show. I remembered that one! He was pretending to be a car, screwing up his face and shutting his eyes, popping them open as he turned on headlights. The sound of my own laughter startled me, like the sound of a forgotten language. Van Dyke started to idle and I laughed again. Pretty dumb. Pretty damned dumb. Pretty dam dum diddy dum dum. I laughed at myself laughing, surprised how good it felt.

At the commercial I opened the small room refrigerater for a Coke. A frosty bottle of Beck's beckoned. One swig triggered a craving for pizza—green peppers, onions, anchovies, olives. When was the last time I'd eaten pizza? A cheesy, fatty, greasy, cholesterol-producing pizza pie? I called down to the bell captain.

"Sorry, sir," he said, "we have no pizza here and—"

"Ten bucks on top of the tab if you bring me a pizza within the hour. And add a couple of beers to the order."

I settled back for the second half of the show. I'd have gone fifteen bucks. Maybe twenty. Being rich had its advantages.

Mary Tyler Moore walked through her living room, long legs, fabulous smile. She used to turn me on. What was the show she did before Dick Van Dyke? Peter Gunn. She was the receptionist's voice. The camera did a slow pan up her legs and you'd see the switchboard and hear Moore's voice answering the phone. But they never showed her face. Pretty sexy for TV in those years. I remembered a few times, making love to Sarah, I thought about those legs. Well, well, well, looked like all my appetites were perking right up. Maybe Sarah was right. Maybe I did need to get away.

Marlin Perkins. "Wild Kingdom." Mutual of Omaha. It was all coming back. All of it. The pizza arrived halfway through "I Love Lucy." I greeted the bellman like a long-lost buddy, gave him the ten, let him keep the change from the pizza, and danced the warm box back to bed. Not exactly as cuddly as Sarah, but at the moment, more suited to my appetite.

The pizza—soggy thin crust, lifeless sauce, indifferent cheese, tired vegetables, delicious beyond my wildest hopes—lasted through two more hours of some of the best comedy shows ever made. During a clip from "Your Show of Shows" I laughed so hard I choked on a chunk of green pepper. Hopping around the room coughing, I tried to self-inflict the Heimlich maneuver. CHICAGO MAN LAUGHS SELF TO DEATH. DIES HAPPY. Panicked, I yanked the desk chair around and threw myself over its back. The pepper popped out. I dropped to the floor, gulping air. Had to be careful, chew more thoroughly. Living alone was not without danger.

At three o'clock, Jerry Lewis clopped across the TV screen, running white-socked and knock-kneed after the ever-cool Dean Martin. Maybe it was the beers. Maybe it was remembering the

Century Theater on a Saturday afternoon, watching this movie with Paul and the guys, our feet up on the seats in front of us, chewing the sugar coatings off Good & Plenty candy and spitting the licorice centers on the floor. Maybe it was all of us trying to imitate Jerry Lewis's walk on our way home. Whatever it was, I broke down. Propped against the pillows, Jerry screaming "Dean, OH, Dean," I laughed and cried and grabbed hold of Paul's memory.

This felt different than the other crying I'd been doing. Not self-pity. Not anger at Sarah. Not bottomless depression. This was cleansing. Like hosing out the crud. For the first time, I let myself mourn Paul's death. After a while, drained, soaked with tears and sweat, I rolled over and closed my eyes. Lights on, TV on, sleep steamrolled over me.

"Schmuck!" The wavy transparent figure solidified in front of me. He wore white socks, black shoes and ankle-high pant cuffs.

"Paul?"

"You have another friend who can walk like this?" He did a Jerry Lewis around the room. His thinning hair grew thick again, shiny, slicked back, reeking of VO5. An eerie glow pulsed from his side part, a white line chiseled through black marble.

"So, how is it?" I asked, blowing my stuffed nose into a pizza-stained napkin.

"How's what?"

"Dead, schmuck. How's dead?"

He reached for a slice of pizza and his hand passed through the box. "No pizza. No beer." He sighed. "Y'know, Asher, death's not all it's cracked up to be. Sure you got good hours, pleasant surroundings, paid medical. But, to tell the truth, it's boring sometimes. Most times."

"That settles it," I said. "I'm not going."

He sat on the edge of the bed and stared into my face. "You been crying?" I shrugged. "Gotta stop this, Asher. Enough with the moping around."

"You been spying on me?"

"Helps pass the time. Besides, I'm here to tell you don't blow it."

"Don't blow what?"

"Your wife sending you off, telling you to have a good time. This is a once-in-a-lifetime offer. No more of this sitting-in-your-room-alone shit. No more solo pizzas and beer. You think my wives ever made me such an offer?"

"They didn't have to. You did it anyway."

"I need insults?" He stood.

"Wait! We never had a chance to say good-bye."

"You're right. Let's do it. Never can tell what tomorrow will bring. I should know. Although, there are worse ways of signing off than doing a swan dive into a bunker. At least I didn't have to hit out of the damned thing." He threw his head back and laughed.

"I miss you," I said.

"Take care of yourself. I'll be in touch." He turned away from me. "Want to see a neat trick? Watch this." He waved and walked through the wall.

"Wait," I yelled, reaching out for him.

"Watch, Dean," yelled Jerry Lewis. "Watch this!" My eyes opened to the TV. I swigged warm beer through the desert in my throat. For the first time in months, I felt at peace.

The phone woke me at five A.M.

"This is your morning wake-up call," said the sleepy female voice.

" 'Morning, Sarah."

"You sleep all right?" Sure, if you don't count the cold pizza, warm beer, and occasional ghost.

"Missed you," I said. "Had to hire a warm body to fill this big bed."

"Hope he didn't snore too loud." We laughed. I pressed her voice tight against my ear.

"Tell me again why you are there and I am here, Sarah. Tell me again why we are not together."

"We will be."

"When?"

"Soon."

"I love you, Sarah Rose." How long had it been since I'd said that?

"I love you, Asher Rose."

"I know."

39

ARE YOU SURE NO ONE HAS HAD OPPORTUNITY TO PUT ANYTHING IN YOUR LUGGAGE? The sign over the Concorde luggage banding machine was not reassuring. A plane filled with rich people might make a tempting terrorist target. Maybe I should row to England. An attendant set my bag on the machine and a mechanical arm wrapped a tamperproof band around it. The stunning brunette behind the counter checked me in. I was her only customer. Afraid of being late, I'd arrived two hours early.

My stomach rumbled. She pretended not to notice. Class.

"Is there someplace I can get breakfast?"

"Well, sir," she said, a warm smile softening her clipped British accent, "you might want to have a look at our lounge buffet before you go elsewhere."

My stomach rumbled all the way to the lounge. Last night's pizza and beer had ended a long fast. I was a month behind on meals and ready to do battle with breakfast. I'd skipped the hotel lobby juice stand, offended by the three-fifty tag for a thimble-size serving of orange juice. Rosie's cafeteria sold a glass of juice four times that size for sixty cents.

A double-decker buffet table took up the center of the Concorde lounge. Bottles of liquor covered one side, every major brand plus a variety of champagnes, wines, and beers. The plates on the food side were small, but so was the food; shotglass-size muffins, tiny juice glasses, demi coffee cups, bagels the diameter of Oreo cookies. The huge fruit basket overflowed with giant strawberries, chunks of perfectly ripe melons, iridescent green kiwi, and flawless bananas. I began loading up, using a second plate for the fruit.

I spent the next hour eating, drinking coffee, and reading the lounge's seven English language papers. Oh, if only the breakfast crew at Rosie's could see me now! Other passengers entered the lounge so quietly that I didn't know I wasn't alone until I looked up. Smooth and expressionless as automatons, the few who ate anything picked a single muffin, a piece of fruit, cereal with skim milk. What kind of people didn't dive headfirst into a free buffet?

Maybe it took a food man like me to appreciate such superior quality.

The men, all wearing dark suits and spit-polished shoes, smelled like old money. I slid my scuffed crepe-soles back out of sight. On my feet all day at Rosie's, walking hard concrete, jumping puddles of water and spilled food, I never invested in expensive shoes. Well, just once, years back. Sarah, eight months pregnant, hysterical over the tiniest thing, forced me to buy one "good" pair of shoes for Freyla's wedding. Damned things nearly crippled me. Determined to get my money's worth, I wore the shoes to work. By the end of the week, the topstitching broke and the soles cracked in half.

The women in the Concorde lounge, tailored and monotone in beige suits and low heels, looked stiffer and more polished than Sarah. There were servants and chauffeurs in these women's lives. They did not sweat over sewing machines until two in the morning while their husbands waited at home. Sarah could have all this. She could have anything she wanted. Why didn't she want what my money could buy? Why wasn't that enough to make her happy?

It wasn't until later, walking back to my seat with my fourth cup of coffee, that I saw her. Photos didn't begin to capture her excitement. Sleek, white, tiny as a toy, she sat poised and waiting on the black tarmac, dwarfed by the other jets. Stone still, wings thrust back, long nose pointing into the wind, she looked like she was in motion. I shuddered. Until this moment, the trip had not seemed real.

None of the other passengers glanced at her. They sat quietly sipping tea or coffee, preoccupied with the stack of international newspapers. Even people who had walked in together didn't talk. The only sound was the wobbling wheel on a cleaning woman's cart.

What made rich people so quiet? I could just picture Edie and Cliff and some of the others from Rosie's pressing their noses against the glass window, gawking at the plane, juggling food-filled plates and beers, joking, laughing. Is that what a six-thousand-dollar plane ticket bought? The right to remain silent? Why had Sarah booked me on the Concorde? I didn't belong here.

A few minutes before boarding, three young men in torn blue jeans came into the lounge and started eating their way through the buffet. Rock stars? Actors? How else could ragged young men afford these fares?

"Couriers." The elderly Brit next to me sniffed. "You would think the companies that hire them would make them adhere to a dress code." What kind of company paid six thou to hand-deliver messages to Europe? What was so important that it couldn't fly a few extra hours on a regular jet?

On board, I settled back with a glass of wine, watching the digital display panel flash altitude and speed. Starting slowly to keep the noise level low, we picked up speed over the Atlantic. I braced as we approached Mach One, gripping the armrests, waiting for the skin of my face to pull back with the force of the thrust. The plane broke the sound barrier without so much as rippling my wine. Not a lot of bang for the buck.

When the crew began food service, I understood why the other passengers waited to eat. The menu, a three-section foldout printed on heavy paper and illustrated with line drawings, began with canapé selections which included lobster, galantine of smoked goose, and fresh asparagus.

The presentation on the plate was magnificent. I wished the food artist who designed Rosie's print ads could see what they'd done. If Sarah were here, she could sketch it. If Sarah were here I could hold her hand and whisper "Look at this!" The man next to me worked through a stack of papers, popping canapés into his mouth without looking. Might as well be peanut butter and jelly for all he noticed. What a waste. Sarah would love this. Sarah would— Stop it!

I washed the appetizers down with the Mumm's Champagne Cuvee Rene Lalou 1982, one of three wines an attendant poured nonstop. I would build a wine cellar. Why should the cases of wines I'd collected over the years sit on the damp basement floor? They deserved a climate-controlled room. I'd put in a full range. Stock the best of the best. Go to auctions, bid on rare bottles.

I opened the packet of Concorde stationery and began designing the cellar, the layout. Why had I wasted all those days sitting around watching TV? I should have been downstairs taking measurements, meeting with air-control experts. I'd probably need half the basement. Who used it anyway? We stored stuff for people wanting temporary storage space. Maxi and Jeff, my sisters and brothers, their kids, friends who'd moved and had been out of touch for years, Sarah's dad's things, my parents'. Some boxes were over ten years old, pushed against damp walls, the cardboard bursting with moisture and fuzzy with mildew. Seams tore, insides

spilled out. I'd mail out postcards, set a deadline. Anything not
removed would be tossed. I felt lighter thinking about it.

The stewardess served my main course of grilled fillets of lamb,
baby turnips, zucchini, broiled tomato, and almond potatoes. I
switched to a glass of Les Forts de Latour. The man next to me
shifted his papers to make room for his meal, a cold seafood plate
with smoked salmon, trout and caviar. Sarah's kind of food. He
asked for a diet Coke instead of the Puligny-Montrachet premier
cru I would have ordered for Sarah.

Oh, Sarah, where are you? "I'll come next time," she'd said.
But next time won't be *my* first time. Nothing's ever as fresh or
important or frightening or exciting as the first time. Maybe next
time I'll be like the other passengers: jaded, disinterested, bored.
Jesus, Sarah.

Iwon'tcryIwon'tcryIwon'tcry. I ate slowly, trying to enjoy the
meal, trying to keep the blackness from moving in. I could barely
eat half, and sat pushing bread crumbs around with my knife.
Why am I here alone? What's the point, alone?

Most of the passengers left the plane without bothering to take
the leather-encased notepad offered as a gift in the seat pocket.
There were also packets of Concorde stationery and pens. I gathered extras as I walked down the aisle, slipping notepads and
stationery into my bag next to the menu I'd taken. A Care package
for Sarah.

"Mr. Rose?" The uniformed Savoy chauffeur approached, and
the customs agent waved me through. Sarah really knew how to
treat a guy. "Have a nice flight, sir?" he asked, carrying my bags
to the waiting Jaguar sedan.

"Perfect."

He held the door while I climbed in. Part of me wanted to sit
up front. The other part wanted, just once, to see what it felt like
to be chauffeured when there wasn't a funeral at the other end.
"You settle in, sir. We have a bit of traffic ahead."

It might have been the wine, or the lack of sleep the night
before, but I didn't remember the ride into London. The next
thing I knew, the driver was shaking me awake, helping me out of
the car and into the lobby of the Savoy Hotel.

40

It was a good thing Asher wasn't in Chicago. He'd kill me if he knew I was walking down this particular stretch of Halsted Street at nine o'clock on a pitch-black night. Not that I was so crazy about it myself. A wicked wind whipped from all directions. I flipped up my parka hood, pulling it tight around my face.

A rat you could saddle galloped across my path as I turned onto Maxwell Street. I slowed until its tail disappeared down a dark gangway. My Moon Boots thudded echoes up the canyon of crumbling brick walls. The clunky boots were the footwear of choice among veteran crew members who had worked winter shoots before. The thick foam boots might keep my feet warm, but if I had to outrun an attacker, I was dead meat.

Huge trailers lined the street ahead, their shiny metal and clean lines surrealistic against the decaying buildings and dirty streets. A sea of workmen unloaded sound and lighting equipment. Assorted people hurried from place to place clutching clipboards. Extras huddled near the catering truck, hands pressed over steaming cups of coffee. The usual gathering of street people, passersby, friends of cast and crew hovered on the fringe.

The wardrobe trailer that had become my home away from home was pitch-black. There would be no lights unless I turned them on, no costumes until I got them ready. Until tonight Marko had been true to his word, coming to work every morning to get me started. But because of some mix-up with Greg's nurse, Marko couldn't get away for this night shoot.

My stomach twisted with the fear of my first solo. How was I going to do this without Marko? I wasn't ready. I'd be found out for the fraud I was. I slid my key into the trailer door. Take a deep breath, Sarah, and jump in with both feet. If you can't swim, maybe you'll at least float. A wino shuffled up and, looking right at me, unzipped and relieved himself against the trailer. I opened the door and locked it behind me.

The lights blinked on. Clothes hung menacingly from long racks, dangling pant legs, empty sleeves, drooping collars, rumpled shirts. I started pulling costumes for the first scene. The dusty

musty mothballed trailer smelled like every costume room Fanny
ever dragged me to. Deep in theater basements, waiting for Fanny
to be fitted, I'd burrow into racks of silky gowns and scratchy
burlap capes, dig into shoe bins for silver heels and pirate boots.
Fanny, endlessly patient, stood mannequin-still on a platform in
front of a mirror, kibitzing with the designers, gossiping about
members of the cast, people in the theater. Fitters, their mouths
full of straight pins, spoke rapid-fire Yiddish. I'd stare, terrified
they would swallow the pins and die agonizing deaths before my
eyes.

"You want Wardrobe and Makeup to be your friend," said
Fanny, who always brought a gift of homemade mandle brot. "If
they like you, they make you beautiful. And if they don't, you wind
up looking like death warmed over."

I checked the racks of costumes, running my hand down the
dress hanging in front.

"Hello, Heather," I said. Poor Heather would be killed during
Friday's shoot. Had I made her look vulnerable enough? Washed-
out beige, limp linen, small shoulders, little buttons down the front
of the pleated bodice. The whole outfit screamed "Victim!" Perfect. I might get through this yet.

The first hour raced by. I grouped each character's clothes with
belts, beads, shoes, hats and other accessories, then rechecked
garments for any rips, stains, loose threads and other mending I
might have missed after yesterday's shoot. I'd spent all day going
over the script, double-checking my list, panicked that I'd forget
some important garment, some necessary accessory. I'd stop at
odd moments, thinking it was time to go visit Fanny at the
hospital, or call Asher at home. But Fanny was back in her
apartment being cared for by a nurse. And Asher was safe in
London. I felt strangely free. Like the first day Maxi and Jeff both
went off to school. It was weeks before I didn't suddenly look
around for them, forgetting they weren't home.

Sandra, Mel's assistant director, stuck her head into the trailer.
"Ready to check the extras?"

"Be right there."

"And Shirley wants to see you in her trailer. She's finished in
Makeup."

"Right."

The wind nearly ripped the trailer door out of my hand. T'ain't a fit night out . . . Fifteen extras shivered in a passageway between two buildings.

"All right," I said to the assembled mass, "if you'll line up along that wall—"

"It's warmer over here," said a man, dragging on a cigarette.

"I need you under that light, to see how you look as a group. The faster you line up for me, the faster you can get back to your warm spot." Please don't let him see me shaking. I held my breath until he moved into line. Wonder if first-time drill instructors get the jitters, too. I prowled the line, tucking, turning, flipping, wrapping, looking for too-bright colors or bold prints that would "pop" on camera. "That sweater's too light."

"It's warm."

"Let me have a look." I folded back the sleeve. "The back is darker. Take it off and turn it inside out." To the next. "Those pants are too well creased. I need you to take them off, roll them into a ball and jump on them a few times."

"I just got them back from the cleaner's."

"Homeless men don't spend on dry cleaners. Go to the wardrobe truck and wrinkle the pants. I'll steam out the crease."

Mel looked into the passageway, his back to the light. Wished I could see his face, know if he liked what I was doing. "How's it going?" he asked.

"A couple of odds and ends. Ten more minutes?"

"Fine. How are you on your principals?"

"I'll get Jac and Shirley set as soon as I finish here."

"Fine."

I ran to the trailer, steamed out the extra's pant creases, grabbed flea market hats, rumpled shopping bags, a cane, and other props to complete their costumes, then turned them over to Mel, crossing my fingers while he checked them out.

"These are fine," he said. Hallelulah! "Sandra, get them placed, will you?"

"Right," said Sandra, motioning the extras to follow her. "Hey, Sarah, Shirley's still looking for you. You don't want to keep her waiting. She's the excitable kind."

Head down, I forced my way through the wind to Shirley's trailer, pounding on the door. I didn't like Shirley. Marko, who knew her much better, hated her guts.

"It's about time," she said. Steady, Sarah. She's just taking her nervousness out on the hired help.

"I'll bring your things." I forced myself not to slam her door. Spoiled little Shirley had got it into her swollen head that her credits as a teen soap star made her Grand Pooh-Bah on set. The mother in me wanted to ground her. But my Aspiring Movie Designer self knew that, without stars, there was no work.

I laid out her outfit on the long table, double-checking my list of accessories before carrying everything to her trailer.

"I have some long underwear if you want it," I said.

She slipped into the jeans, wiggling them up side to side, working them over her liposucked body. "Can hardly get these on as it is."

I'd had bigger hips and thighs the day I was born. One of the advantages of designing and sewing was I could artfully hide my bad parts. Over the years I'd spread and sagged like anyone else. It never bothered me too much. Sure I'd like a great bod, take off ten pounds, work out at a gym, swim, walk. So far, I hadn't had time. Maybe after Fanny was well and Asher was well and this job was over. Shirley stretched out on the floor to zip up the fly.

"You're going to freeze your bippy out there," I said, brushing lint off her jacket.

"I already photograph ten pounds heavier. The last thing I want is more layers." Tummy tucks loomed on her horizon. Could calf-shaping and cheek implants be far behind? It had to be hell living in terror of turning twenty.

The door flew open and Jac came in, shivering from his short run from the makeup trailer. The producers were banking that the chemistry between the two of them would be magic on screen. Marko called it "The Rich Bitch versus Jovial Jock." I couldn't see it, but I hoped the experts were right. I'd love to add a hit movie to my résumé. Jac stepped over Shirley, collapsing into one of the two chairs, smiling as she struggled to work the jeans' zipper up.

"Kinda like stuffing sausage," he said.

"Up yours."

A button hung loose on Jac's vest. I pulled a threaded needle from the collection in my collar and stitched it down. Should have fixed it after last night's shoot but I'd wanted to visit Fanny, then go home to cook her favorite foods, make packets to freeze, foods that might put some of the weight back on her disappearing body. I knotted off Jac's button and bit the thread near the knot.

Shirley finished dressing. I checked her outfit against my notes. "That should do," I said. Jac took her place in front of the mirror.

His lean muscular body had the musty smell of recent sex. Sudden crotch twinge. I pushed away unsummoned thoughts.

Sandra walked in. "Sarah, I hate to bother you, but the production office got a call. It's about your mother." Sudden cold chill. "Says she doesn't feel well."

"Who called?"

"I think they said your mother."

"Good. Thanks." A quick check of Jac's pants turned up a ripped inseam. I made him take them off and I closed the gap with quick small stitches. "What have you been *doing* in this costume?"

Sandra waited, bewildered. "Aren't you going to call her?"

"Sandra, my mother's just out of the hospital. She won't feel well for a while. She has a full-time nurse living with her. What the call is really about is that she's worried because I'm out so late. Here"—I handed the pants to Jac—"try these on."

"Want me to call her back?" asked Sandra. With a million details on her mind, she didn't need this.

"I'd appreciate it."

"What should I tell her?"

"The truth. That I'm busy. That thousands of dollars in production time are riding on how soon I can get these clothes on Clark Gable here. That I'll stop by her place when I get off work in the morning."

"How can you be so coldhearted to your own mother?" said Shirley the Shrew doing Mother Teresa. "You're lucky to have a mother who is alive."

"Thanks so much for your input." Don't call us.

An hour into the shoot, the cameraman told Mel you could tell, even in the dark street shadows, that Shirley was a woman. Mel called me in. "We've got to make the audience think Shirley's a man sneaking into this building," he said. "You've got to pad her out."

For the next half hour I fattened Shirley's body with socks and fabric remnants, binding everything in place with gaffer's tape, pulling a baggy pair of pants over it all. She sulked, whined, and complained. My job was not without perks.

41

Armed with a Michelin guide and a London street map, I pulled the door to my room closed behind me and walked down the long hall to the elevator. There'd be no breakfast in my room today. No lounging around in pajamas, watching TV, reading the paper, working the crossword. After a lifetime of dreaming and planning, it was time to go out and explore the streets of London. I'd spent the night carving the city into sections, mapping out important sights. I patted my pocket. List in place. Time to go.

The elevator doors opened onto the lobby. My legs wouldn't move. A bell clerk held the door open.

"Lobby, sir."

"Thank you." I forced myself out, step-by-step, toward the front door. A great antimagnetic field pushed me back, back, back, deep into the safety of the hotel. My heart rammed against my chest. A flash of sweat soaked through layers of warm clothing. I should go up and rest for a while. No. I'd come too far to sit in a room and hide.

I focused on the squares of floor tiles. Left foot in one square, right foot in the next square, left foot, right foot, stiff and jagged like a goddamned robot, left foot, toward the revolving door, right foot, aim straight for that diabolical rotating trap, left foot, won't you come into my parlor, right foot. Beyond the glass door, the doorman helped an elderly couple into a taxi. When he finished, he would come and spin the door for me. If he did, I wouldn't be able to enter. Had to do this on my own, at my own speed. Right foot. Into the door, sweaty hands on the railing, push against the force, left foot, turning and turning, right foot.

Tires on wet pavement, car horns, bus engines, people talking, laughter, cats fighting. Wet air, bus fumes, coffee, bakery, sewer. When I arrived yesterday, I'd crossed the six-foot strip of sidewalk from limo to hotel like a child playing musical chairs, not letting go of one before lunging for the safety of the other. I'd been so focused on making it into the hotel that I'd missed the city.

Left foot. The Savoy threaded the eye of a needle-thin cul-de-sac. I squeezed past the morning lineup of taxis making the tight turnaround to pick up and drop off passengers. It was the only strip in London where cars traveled American style, on the right instead of the left. If I was going to get hit by a car, odds were it wouldn't be on this particular patch of road.

It took a century for me to walk down the wet pavement to the main street, and another century to decide which way to turn. The only direction I couldn't go, the only direction I was terrified *not* to go, was back. It had taken every ounce of courage to get this far. If I turned back, I wouldn't have the guts to go this far again. Right foot.

I'd begin with one small area of the city. Walk directly from point A to point B. Do not pass Go. Stick to a preplanned route. Keep on line like some human connect-the-dot—eyes fixed straight ahead, body hugging the safety of building walls—and pray the sky would not fall on me. It didn't. I survived Day One.

Sarah called. "Hi, handsome. How's the Queen?"

"This is some kind of city."

"Told you."

"Where'd you get so smart?"

"Soup is brain food. What're you up to?"

"I'm in the world's most luxurious suite, spread out on a king-size bed, watching the streetlights dance on the Thames."

"Sounds beautiful."

"Be a lot more beautiful if you were here."

"Tell me everything."

I took Sarah through my day, trying to share my London with her the way she'd once shared hers with me.

"Doesn't sound like it's changed much in twenty-five years," she said. "Be sure to look to your right before you step off a curb. I seem to remember a couple of times I nearly bought the farm."

"You'd have made one beautiful hood ornament."

"You sound better already, Asher."

"You sound far away. I miss you, Sarah."

"Me too, you."

"Wish you could be here with me."

"I know. I know. Sleep well. I'll talk to you tomorrow?"

"If I'm not out partying."

42

Fanny lay back on her pillows and scrutinized my face. "What's with your eyes?"

"The caterer on the set made Chinese."

She touched her fingers to the swollen lids. Her icy hands soothed the pain. "You couldn't tell them no MSG?"

"It's not individual, Mom. Only the stars are served food you can identify. The rest of us feed at a trough of casserole catering. I planned to have a salad, but by the time we broke for dinner, I was too hungry." While I shoveled in chow mein, Shirley ate two lettuce leaves and a cherry tomato. Rumor on set was she took the edge off hunger with three lines of coke. She also disappeared into the bathroom after she ate. Hell of a life for a kid. I took Fanny's hands in mine and tried to rub heat back into them.

"Go put ice on your eyes," she said.

"Later. When I get home."

"You haven't been home? It's nine in the morning."

"And you thought theater hours were rough." She wouldn't be humored.

"You're not taking care of yourself, Sarahlah."

"I like who's talking." Her morning tray sat untouched on her nightstand next to a box of tissues. It didn't look like she was coughing up blood. But she also wasn't eating. "How about I scramble us some eggs and toast up a couple of bagels?"

"I'm not hungry. You go ahead."

"You know what they say about people who eat alone."

"Yeah"—she smiled—"they say they're hungry."

The nurse, a sturdy woman with an annoying sunshiney manner, stepped into the bedroom doorway.

"How's your patient?" I asked.

"Oh, we're doing just fine." She beamed at Fanny. Fanny did not beam back. "Our vital signs are improving but we need to take a bit more nourishment. Maybe with you here she'll eat a little something."

"What am I?" said Fanny. "Invisible?"

"Mrs. Rose, if you're going to be here, I'd like to run to the grocery for some more Ensure Plus and a few other items."

"I'll be here." I followed her into the living room. "Any problems?"

"Your mother's blood pressure drops suddenly when she stands up," she whispered, climbing into a huge down coat. "I'll mention this to Dr. Fishman when I call in my report."

"Is it anything I should worry about?"

"I don't think so." She pulled an angora stocking hat down over her ears and wrapped a matching twenty-foot-long knit scarf around her neck. "Although she does seem dizzy when she stands."

"Seems?"

"It might be normal weakness from her stay in the hospital. When she doesn't think I'm watching she holds on to the wall on her way to the bathroom. She won't say she's dizzy, of course. You know how she is." She pulled on the mittens that completed the set. Somewhere a large herd of shocking-pink goats was running around naked.

I gave her shopping money, which she pushed down into her mitten along with the apartment key, tissues, and shopping list. I closed the door after her. The MSG hung like weights on my eyelids. I had to lay down. Fanny sat, her hands folded tightly in her lap. She'd combed her hair while I was out of the room. A good sign.

"Want me to turn on Oprah?" I asked.

"Whatever."

I flicked on the set, crawled onto the bed, and curled up, resting my head on Fanny's legs. She stroked her fingers along my hair.

"Mmmmmmm," I said.

"I don't need a nurse."

"Ma, not now. I'm exhausted."

"I'm not sick."

"Having a nurse doesn't mean you're sick. It means you were sick and now you're getting better."

"If I was better, I wouldn't need a nurse."

"It's just for a little while." Silence. She massaged my temple. "Do you think Dr. Fishman and I are keeping secrets from you?" Silence. She stroked my eyelids. "You think TB is ravaging your body and Dr. Fishman has sent you home to die?" Silence. She massaged my scalp in strong slow circles. "Oh, jeez Mom, that's exactly what you're thinking. How can I convince you?"

"Give her money and send her home. If you don't, I will."

"You can't fire her, Mom, you didn't hire her."

"Then you take her." She stopped stroking my head and lifted her hands away. Abandoned! I rolled up to a sort of sitting position, my joints stiff from a long night in a cold trailer. If I didn't get some sleep soon, I was going to pass out.

"Mom, what am I supposed to do?" No answer. "You want to move into my house? Is that it?" No you don't no you don't no you don't. "It won't be like last time when I was home to take care of you. I'm working full-time. You'll still need a nurse."

"You got too many stairs."

"You want me to put in one of those chairs that takes you up and down?" Careful, Sarah. If she moves in, how're you going to break the news to Asher?

"Don't talk foolish."

"Now what's the problem?"

"Who told you to live so far away?"

"From what?"

"Everything. The stores, me, everything." There was no end to this.

"Mom, what do you want me to do?"

She turned away from me. "Nothing. I don't want you to do nothing."

She threw off the sheets, hesitated a moment on the side of the bed, then pushed herself up. The nurse was right, she did seem unsteady on her feet. I followed her into the kitchen. Fanny filled the kettle with water and shuffled toward the stove. She never made it. I caught her as she fell, her head flopping back, her eyes rolling up into her head until all I could see were the whites.

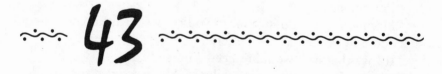

43

The pain started on my fourth day. Standing outside Buckingham Palace, waiting with the crowd for the changing of the guard, I tried to adjust the ASA on my Nikon. Damp cold seeped inside my fingers and froze solid. No gentle aching joints here. No dim discomfort. No subtle stiffness. The arthritis I'd felt in Chicago winters wasn't even an appetizer on the London pain menu. A power hammer drove eightpenny nails through my knuckles. A vise crunched bones in my wrists. Movement of thumbs shot pain up my arms, down my spine and out my legs.

The strange thing was, I found the pain comforting, like a knife cutting away layers of solid gray fog. Asher Rose had been away, but he was coming back. And part of coming back meant starting to feel again. I found myself prodding the pain, wiggling thumbs, wrists, fingers.

I walked for hours along routes I mapped out at night over dinners in my room. One by one, I visited the places on my London "must see" file: the changing of the guard, Tate Gallery, Madame Tussaud's, Tower of London, Ceremony of the Keys, pubs, Old Bailey, Hyde Park's Speaker's Corner. It would have been easier to get around in a limo or taxis, but they would isolate me. My days were lonely enough without Sarah. I needed to be around people.

I forced myself to eat breakfast and lunch out. Dinners would take a little longer. I'd tried eating in the hotel dining room my first night in London, stumbling out after the salad, barely making it to my room before I broke down, crying for no reason, no reason at all. I thought I was done with all that. Much safer to order dinner in, using nights as planning times, reading, relaxing, hot tub times.

And so I walked or, when I had miles to go, rode double-decker buses. Once, I toyed with the idea of riding the Tube. Standing at the top of the stairs, trying to force myself to enter the stream of people rushing to catch the underground trains, my head started swimming and I had to grip the iron handrail to keep from pitching headfirst down the stairs. Double-deckers were slower but safe. The worst they could do was tip over.

By the end of the week, I began to have the uneasy feeling something was missing. Maybe if the penetrating cold had lifted just one time, if my body hadn't turned on me, joints rusting in their sockets, muscles knotting from neck to toes—maybe it might have been different. Whatever the reason, I didn't enjoy going out to see something just to go and see something. And that scared me because my whole life I'd dreamed of visiting every important site in every place in the world. Now, it wasn't enough.

"Give it time," Sarah said when I told her. "You're still healing."

There was no question I was better. The stark terror of walking out of the hotel in the morning had faded to a slight palpitation.

And only once, caught in the crush of a sale crowd at Harrod's, had I broken out in a sweat and felt dizzy enough to need to sit down. Still, limping back into the Savoy one early evening, a new arthritic pain playing a rusty-knifed game of mumbly-peg deep in my right hip, I felt a great unrest.

" 'Evening, Mr. Rose."

" 'Evening, Izzy." I hobbled to the front desk. "Any mail?"

"No, sir." He looked concerned. "Have an accident, did you?"

"I think your weather's getting to me."

"If I might suggest, sir, a massage would do wonders. Would you like me to make an appointment with our—"

"No, no thanks, Izzy. All I need is a hot tub and a good night's sleep."

Fifteen minutes later, sitting in a chair in my room, trying to unbend after unlacing my shoes, I reconsidered. I'd never had a massage but I'd known a lot of guys over the years who swore by them. There used to be a bruiser at the old sweat bath. I'd watch him twist and pull the limbs of my father and uncles, who spent their days sitting crosslegged on hard floors, bent over their sewing. He'd pound their overworked bodies, dig his meaty thumbs deep into their backs and shoulders and legs. The more brutal he was, the better they liked it. Maybe a little of that would do me good. I called down.

"Izzy? Is it possible to get a massage this late?"

"I took the liberty of making a seven-thirty appointment for you," he said. "I wanted to be sure they could take you if you changed your mind." Like Mama always said, you get what you pay for in this world.

Fifteen minutes until the massage. I stripped off my clothes and climbed into the shower. No matter what kind of mindless brute the guy was, there was no need to subject him to my unwashed body. Hours of walking in layers of wool clothing made me a pungent blend of gamey balls and musty underarms. As for my feet, I wished I didn't have to be in the same room with them when I took off my shoes.

Izzy's directions led me to a small door that said simply "Spa." A young woman at the desk checked me in. "Leda will be with you in a moment, Mr. Rose. Please, have a seat. There's tea if you like."

I think I smiled. I know I sat. A woman. I was going to be massaged by a woman. Why hadn't Izzy warned me? I couldn't do this. I picked up a magazine and thumbed through, hands tingling, lips fuzzy, heart thudding, trying to look nonchalant. Had to be some way out of this. Maybe I could plead a forgotten appointment. Sweat washed away my shower. I'd stand up, say I had to go make a call, and leave. On the count of three. One. Two.

"Mr. Rose?" A magnificent Eurasian woman, her white wrap dress glowing against her dark skin, floated toward me. "I'm Leda. I'll be your masseuse. Please"—she gestured gracefully toward a long hall—"this way."

I followed. Her hair, shiny as wet black beans, coiled into an elegant bun. She was small-boned and shorter than Sarah, too birdlike to do me any good. Oh, she was probably all right for the average Savoy guest, the CEO desk-sitter, the landed gentry, the royal wot-not. But someone like me, a man who spent his life working with his hands and body, a man on intimate terms with lifting and lugging, a man like me needed a Goliath with arms like pile drivers and fingers like pickaxes. It wasn't Leda's fault. No way she could have known. I'd pay her for her time, then leave.

She reached into a closet, her delicate hands handing me two thick towels, a white terry robe, and rubber thongs. Now, Asher. Say it now. "You can dress here," she said, pulling aside the curtain to a tiny cubicle. "I'll set the timer on the sauna. How many minutes would you like?"

I started taking off my jacket, stalling. How should I know how many minutes? I'd never stepped into a sauna. Dry heat was for tall Nordic types with long legs and uncircumcised shlongs who beat each other with birch branches and rolled naked in the snow. Short Jewish men went straight for the steam, where they could talk and sweat and suck cigars, then head fully clothed to Manny's Deli to revive themselves with lean pastramis on rye, kosher dills, and chocolate phosphates. Now was the time to back out if I was going to do it. "Time?" I said. "Oh, I guess the usual."

"Five minutes? Ten?"

"Ten." No namby-pamby here. You're dealing with a Real Man.

"Ten minutes it is. The shower's just there." She pointed to a door next to the sauna. "I'll be in the massage room when you're ready. It's down that hall, first left, then first right, then two lefts." She spun around, set the sauna timer, and walked away. I waited for the rustle of her crisp uniform to disappear before I started to undress.

I could still leave.
Why should you?
Go away, Paul.
You're a grown adult male nearly half a century old. Why shouldn't you have a woman massage your body? It's not like this is some sleazoid joint on South State Street where the masseuse wears less than you do.
What if I get a hard-on?
Wear it proudly, son.
Good-bye, Paul.
I'm outta here.

A minute into the sauna I knew I was going to die. Leda had turned the heat high enough to roast a turkey. Which was, I figured, exactly what was happening. Every breath seared my throat and lungs. I stared at my watch. A minute thirty-five. A minute forty. At two minutes, I cracked open the door, checked to be sure the hall was clear, then darted into the shower. The freezing water sizzled on my skin. I opened my mouth and took in a steady stream, swishing the water around, spitting it out. When I'd gone from burning to freezing, I checked the hall again and raced back to the sauna. Never, in the annals of time, had ten minutes passed so slowly. When the timer finally clicked off I'd dripped a small river between the sauna and shower.

Showering for real, this time, I scrubbed my parts, wondering seriously what I would do if I got hard while Leda massaged me. Granted, I hadn't had that particular worry for a while. Still, who knew what would happen when a beautiful woman began stroking me. Would she cover me? Would I be laid out on the table, naked as a carp?

I toweled off in front of the dressing room mirror and put on the robe, belting it tightly. I looked ridiculous. How could I walk down the hall tied up like some scared kid? I took the robe off and thumb-hooked it casually over my naked shoulder. Too arrogant. Maybe just drape it over my shoulders. Too country club tennis player. I compromised, putting my hands into the sleeves, loosely tying the belt ends, letting the robe part slightly in front.

Sauntering down the hall, I followed Leda's directions, turning left then right, then—what was it?—right once again. A large curtain at the end of the hall covered the door to the massage room. *You're a big boy now, Asher. This experience will be good for you.* Calling up all my courage, I grabbed one corner of the curtain and yanked it open. Pigeons flew up and two startled women, barely an arm's length away, stared at me from the sidewalk. Behind them, a Thames barge hooted long and loud. I stared out the huge picture window, feeling my belt ends come undone and the robe spread open. The women, giggling, turned away.

Leda later said, her fingers like iron rods digging the knots out of my muscles, that she had rarely worked on anyone quite so tense. The Good Thing, as Sarah would say, was that, during the entire massage, I never once worried about an erection.

"Are we having fun yet?"

"Shhh." I patted Fanny's free hand. "Try and sleep."

"You try and sleep with this cockamamie contraption in your arm." Ten o'clock at night and we were three hours into Fanny's blood transfusion. Sitting in the dark room, watching red drops drip drip drip down the IV into her arm, there was nothing to do but wait for the transfusion to be over. Four hours, the nurse said, more or less.

"I used to give blood during the war," said Fanny. "Sometimes, between shows the Red Cross came. Rows of actors, we'd have, lying on stage giving blood. The men gave once a week during the war."

"Actors always overdid."

"Made for a lot of fainting. The great Jacob Ben-Ami himself fell on me during a performance of *Samson and Delilah*. The audience loved it. Best review he ever got." She stared at the bag of plasma. "They take blood out in a few minutes. Why so long to put it back?"

"Mom, you don't have to stay awake for this. It's not all that interesting."

"I don't like sleeping pills. I can wait another hour." She looked at the plasma sadly. "Told you I was sick."

"So you're a little anemic."

"This by you is a little anemic? A little anemic is you eat some chopped liver and a good steak and your blood count goes up. That's a little anemic."

"Well, anyway, anemia is not TB."

"It is also not a walk in the park." She was quiet for a while and my eyes started to close.

"You make arrangements with the Wedgewood?"

"Yes, Ma. As soon as you're released from here, I'll take you there."

"Myrtle Bloom says it's from the best. You know what a critic she is. You're sure it's not too much money?"

"It's not too much money." Asher's retirement still made her nervous. No new cash flow, no weekly paycheck. The numbers were so big she couldn't grasp them. "The important thing is you're sure it's what you want."

"Tell me again how it looks?" It looks like a nursing home. Like a hospital. Like an institution with plants and paintings. Like the heartbreaking all-American final solution. It also looks like a life raft on my particular sinking boat.

"Fine, Mom. The Wedgewood Home looks fine. Try and rest."

Bloodless Cold had switched from a night shoot to a day shoot and I'd been running back and forth from set to hospital, praying there wouldn't be an emergency on either end. Sleep got lost somewhere in between. I dozed in the chair, waking when the nurse came in. Fanny's plasma bag was empty.

"I did it!" Fanny smiled, jubilant. "Can't keep a good woman down."

I laughed, rubbing her shoulders, relieved she could at last get some sleep. Could use a day or three of sleep myself. "You sure did do it," I said. Another nurse came in carrying a fresh bag.

"What's that?" asked Fanny.

"The next one," said the nurse. Fanny sat up, yanking the covers up to her chin.

"No! Nobody said nothing!"

"Mrs. Feldman, please, there's no need to—"

"No more."

"Dr. Fishman ordered—"

"No more. I won't!"

I sat on the bed and took Fanny's rigid body in my arms. "Give us a little time," I said, waving the nurse away.

Fanny collapsed, folding into my arms like a broken bird. So little left to hold on to. I rocked her in that dark room, that foreign land decorated in early impersonal, and dove deep into my life for one thing, anything, that might bring her some small comfort.

"*Rozhinkes mit mandlen* . . ." I sang, stroking her hair in time to the old Yiddish lullaby. She cried. Not the strong wail of the aggrieved actress but the small wimpering of a frightened woman who'd had enough. More than enough. That will be all for now, thank you. I forgot what came after "Raisins with almonds," so I hummed the lullaby, over and over, not knowing what else to do. A very long while later, she sniffed loudly into my shoulder.

"You have that . . . all wrong," she said. "Just . . . like your father." She sat up and cleared her throat. Faint, pale, barely audible, the first words whispered past me. "*Unter Yideles vigele, shteyt a klor vays tsigele.*" Slowly, her years of training breathed life and heart into the words, carrying the notes like ringing bells. "*Shlof zhe, Yedele, shlof.*"

The sweetness of her voice squeezed my heart to breaking. Nurses gathered at the door. The lullaby traveled the late-night hall, quieting, soothing. Fanny sang through twice, holding the last sweet note, fainter and fainter, until it disappeared. And, oh, that special silence, that electric stillness after a great performance when the audience stays wrapped inside the magic. Then the nurses tiptoed in, patting her, praising her, ohhing and ahhing in hushed voices. Fanny smiled, nodded, graced them with a backhanded royal wave. She had converted the white-uniformed enemy into admiring fans. It was a change she could live with.

"All right," she said, hoisting the empty plasma bag, "I'm ready for a refill."

The nurse-cum-ally convinced Fanny to take a sleeping pill, then waited until she drowsed before hooking her up again. Careful not to touch the painful place on the back of her hand where the needle entered the vein, and a burning swollen spot just above her wrist, I cradled Fanny's hand until the new blood flowed into her.

"I'm like your father's old Buick," she said, eyes closing as she slipped under. "Soon as he'd fix up one thing, something else broke down. Remember?" I nodded. "Just like that old Buick."

"Sort of look like it, too." I kissed her forehead. "Except it was a prettier shade of green."

She winked conspiratorially at the nurse. "Very funny, my Sarahlah." As soon as she fell asleep I left for home. Five hours, a fraction of what I needed, would be better than no sleep at all.

45

I dragged through the quiet house up to my bedroom, punched the answering machine button and flopped nosedown into the quilt. Mistake. Should have undressed first. Didn't think I could move.

"This is Benjamin Berlin from the Wedgewood Home. I'm just calling to see how your mother is doing and to reassure you her bed will be waiting as soon as she's released from the hospital." I bet it will, Benji baby. Nothing like a hefty contribution to move Fanny's name to the top of your thirty-foot waiting list. The wait could have been a year or more and I didn't think Fanny was strong enough to take one more disappointment. What was our new money for if it couldn't buy peace of mind? He left his office number "should you have any questions."

"Three guesses." Asher. My heart flip-flopped. He made kissing sounds into the phone. I wouldn't have thought anything could make me smile just now. "I loooove you." He sounded tipsy. Or maybe he was happy. So long since I'd heard either. Asher, Asher, Asher, I want your snuggly body right here this very second. Although, as tired as I was, I wouldn't be much company. I'd try reaching him in the morning before I went to work. The next message clicked on.

"Well, I hope you're happy." Freyla? "They've fired Norman. Fired him!" Who they? Rosie's? Impossible. Asher's baby brother was protected the same as Freyla and Mookey and Pearl. "They say their medical plan doesn't cover agoraphobia. And they're definitely making me part-time if I take my usual three months in Florida. Me! After all the years I've given Rosie's." If I could lift my arm I'd fast-forward Freyla, but thirty-thousand tons of air pressed down on me. "I've called Martha to see if they can legally do that. I need my time in Florida for health reasons. You know that. Asher knows that. I told them I could get my doctor to write a note. I don't think this is right. I want you to tell Asher." Pause. Her frustration raged through the silence. Why isn't her big brother on call when she needs him? Why aren't I at home In Person to yell at? "Where are you at eleven o'clock at night?" Wadda you, my mother? Old Freyla roundheels yelling at moi? Sure, Freyla, I'll tell Asher. Hold on, I'll call him in London, wake him out of a sound sleep to lay your problems on him. Just what he needs. Right, Freyla, in my next life. She slammed down the phone.

"Hi, Sarah. It's Martha. Just calling to see how Fanny's doing. Have your machine call my machine."

"Where aaaaarrrreee you?" Asher again? "I'm lonely. Do you think of me ever? At all? Do you remember me? Y'know, lot of the women I have up to my suite remind me of you." Ho-ho. The man was feeling no pain. For a guy who hated the phone and never ever went over three minutes on a long-distance call, calling transatlantic twice in one night was a real breakthrough. Wish I'd been home to talk to him. Maybe I would call and wake him up. Naw, my mind wasn't working right. Better to wait.

"Sarah. Call me when you get in. It's important." No way, Marko. I'm in serious paralysis here. I'll see you at work in the morning.

Marko's voice was the last thing I remembered until hard rock in the key of discord blasted me up at five in the morning. With a massive act of will, I dragged myself to the bathroom and plunged my face into a bowl of cold water. I'd sleep as soon as Fanny was out of the hospital and into the Wedgewood. Just have to hang on a little while longer.

I clutched the morning *Times,* using it as ballast on my walk from the Savoy to a tiny neighborhood bakery. Shoulder pain, knee pain, joints in revolt, but I was moving forward, up and out.

"Scones and coffee, please," I said, sounding, I thought, nearly normal. No flashes of sweat this morning, no panic at the front door. Every day a little easier. Every day in every way.

Two pages of unvisited London Places to See padded my jacket pocket. Why was it that the exciting streets and sites I read about at night—settled in my suite, warmed by a brandy, gas fire burning—did not look nearly as interesting by gloom of day?

When Sarah talked about the two years she traveled I could almost taste fresh octopus in Mykanos, hear gondoliers singing in

Venice, smell spring flowers perfuming the Tuileries. She'd never
talked about her lovers. I'd never asked. Of course there were
lovers. She never pretended to be a virgin. Not that I didn't wonder.
Not that I didn't think she sometimes compared me to them. So
what? If I'd traveled instead of worked, I'd have had lovers too.
    Sure you would.
    You still here?
    Where else would I be?
    So where are my adventures, Paul? Or maybe the magic's not
in the traveling, but in the telling?
    London isn't the only place in the world.
    You're right. Paris is a short hop, Rome. Just because Sarah
made plans for me to come to London doesn't mean I'm welded
to the spot. I'll make a few calls tonight. Paris. Wonderful. Always
dreamed of going there. Why the hell not?
    I caught myself whistling as I stirred sugar into my tea and
scanned the local section of the *Times*. On page 20, the words
Savile Row jumped out from the text.

> The one-hundred-twenty-year-old firm of Hedly & Brumley an-
> nounced its plans to close its doors later this month. "Bespoke
> suits are fast becoming a thing of the past," says proprietor
> Martin Thompson, who purchased the firm fifty-four years ago
> from the founder. "Gentlemen who can afford hand-tailored suits
> seem unwilling to invest the time necessary for proper fittings.
> Other shops may not mind selling off-the-peg suits on their
> premises, but I assure you that is hardly the case here."
>   This is the third Savile Row shop to close its doors this year.
> Other owners sympathize with Thompson, citing problems which
> include a dwindling client list, increased foreign competition, and
> a critical lack of qualified workers. "Just you try to find a
> buttonhole lady today," says Thompson. "Hand-sewn button-
> holes are going the way of the dinosaur. I don't intend to remain
> to watch it happen." Thompson plans to retire to his country
> estate and devote himself to his garden.

    Savile Row. I was weaned on stories about Savile Row. Every
day after school, sweeping the floors, cutting fabric buttons, stitching covered belts, I'd listen to my father and uncles talk about that
legendary street of tailors. They'd spent two impoverished years
there, en route from Russia to America. Years later, working in

their dingy Chicago tailor shop, hand-sewing the thousands of stitches that went into the construction of a man's suit, they talked about Savile Row like it was Camelot. Savile Row. A magic name in the old days when I expected to grow up and become a tailor, before I was sent home to become nursemaid to my mother.

I swallowed back the old bitterness. The article shook me, made me realize I'd been avoiding Savile Row. Not consciously. At least, I didn't think so. Still, I'd flipped past it in the guidebooks and hadn't put it on my itinerary. I studied the grainy photo under the Savile Row article. An elegant old man posed in front of a wall of fabric bolts. I recognized his sadness. I knew how it felt to lose a business that had been a life. A world.

My father and uncles were long dead. Only two of my cousins stayed in the shop, stitching away their eyesight and lives with black thread on black wool. Most of the others had, one time or another, come to work for me at Rosie's. Not bad for Asher the Dreamer, huh Pop? What did I have to be bitter about anymore? I tore the article out of the paper and folded it into my pocket. That's what I'd do today. Go see what Camelot looked like.

The bus dropped me off at the Burlington Arcade and I walked through the exclusive area to Savile Row. Starting at Gieves & Hawkes at Number 1, I walked along, looking in the windows of Kilgour, Helman, Huntsman, Poole, turning around at Tommy Nutter's and walking back. I turned into a shop at random.

"And how may we help you, sir?" The willowy man floated toward me, his pale hands and chalk-white face jutting out of the dark three-piece suit like ghostly add-ons. Just like my dream of Paul. Just like. Just exactly like.

"Sorry," I said, backing out. "My mistake." Had to escape to the street, take long strides away from there until I could breathe. A group of laughing tourists walked toward me and I turned to a shop window, sponging sweat with a handkerchief, studying the display until they passed.

The salesman must have spooked me, sizing me up that way— my suit, my shoes, my haircut—tucking me away in some neat mental file. I knew that look, had seen it on my father and uncles often enough. So what? So *what?* Since when was I a candidate for the cover of *GQ*? Find another shop and walk in. You can do it.

"Good morning, sir." There it was, that judgmental sweep of

the eye. An older eye, less threatening somehow. "And how may we be of help?"

"Just looking," I said.

"Do let us know if we may be of service."

So far, so good. I'd start at the ancient oak tables layered with neat bolts of fabrics, walk slowly down the narrow aisles. Blacks, navys, grays, herringbones, pinstripes, row after row of muted colors in classic weaves. I tried to pass without touching but how could I not, at the very least, run a hand over the cloths? My father could afford four, maybe five bolts of this quality. Who could imagine an entire roomful?

A few times a fabric was so magnificent I had to fold back the selvage and rub the cloth between thumb and forefinger. A bolt of navy merino wool stopped me cold and, as if forty years hadn't passed since I straightened goods in my father's shop, I hefted the bolt, spun out a length in midair, then set it down. I grasped the cloth, gently crushing it, needing to feel its *hand*.

"Allow me, sir." A striking young woman in a man-tailored suit took the bolt from me and set it down. She began to reroll the fabric.

"Don't," I said.

"Sir?"

"I'm not done with that."

"I will be happy to show you what you like, sir," she said, still rolling. I put my hand on the bolt, stopping her.

"I need to feel the fabric," I said. "Is that a problem?"

"No sir, of course." She stepped back and waited, her hands folded neatly in front of her, her straight blond hair pulled back into a twist at her nape.

"Why don't I call you when I'm ready?" I said. "I like to take my time with fabrics."

"You know cloth, then, do you, sir?"

"Yes. I know cloth." She hesitated a moment, as if deciding, then left me alone.

I started up the next row, pulling out an occasional bolt, building a small pile. The vicuña had the softness of Jeff's baby blanket after four years of being dragged and carried and washed and loved. Why had I taken it away from him? "I weaned my brothers and sisters from their blankets," I'd told Sarah. "It's time Jeff gave up that ratty scrap." But Jeff wasn't my brothers and sisters. And I was too young to see the difference. Until later. Until he quietly turned his back on Rosie's and went to make a life for himself in Boulder. For the first time I understood that his gentleness was not weakness. As fragile as he seemed, he was stronger than all my brothers and sisters put together. By then, it was too late to fix the damage between us. I rubbed the soft cloth between my fingers. Maybe I'd send him a small piece. Tell him he could have a whole suit out of it if he wanted, if he'd forgive me, if he'd let me be his father. I had time now to be his father.

An elegant man and woman walked in, one of those picture-perfect couples you couldn't help looking at. In a thousand years Sarah and I could never look like them. Oh, maybe for five minutes, if our lives depended on it, we could dress up and walk with straight backs and smile with just our mouths. But who could live a regular life like that? Who would want to?

The trouble was, they looked so damned good. I pretended to study a Harris tweed while comparing myself to the man. He was American, about fifty. Taller than me, which I couldn't help. A little firmer around the middle, which I could. His hair, thinner than mine on top, was perfectly cut and combed, his clothes impeccable. The tailor greeted them by name and the three of them huddled.

I'd watched my father build a person like that, start with a body in boxer shorts, and stitch-by-stitch construct a man who could pass for nobility—*if* the man never opened his mouth. Not a whole lot of Lords walked into our Taylor Street shop. Merchants, yes, gangsters, certainly, all sorts of men from the old country who knew the worth of a good tailor. Their sons, with no sense of history and no eye for quality, bought off the rack. Tailoring was a dying art, its secrets buried with men like my father whose sons opened soup factories and wore wash pants to work.

I sorted through the pile of fabrics I'd created, pulling out three of the most beautiful.

The girl came back. "Have you done with the others, sir?"

"Yes, thank you." Just obeying orders, I reckoned. I signaled the man who'd greeted me at the door.

"Yes, sir?"

"I'm interested in a suit." Surprise, surprise.

Way to go, Asher!

"Very good, sir. Allow me." He held out his hands for my overcoat, my father's overcoat, all I ever needed for the occasional bar mitzvah, funeral and wedding. He hefted it and knew the quality. Another man materialized, took the coat, and disappeared. "Now, just what sort of suit did we have in mind?"

He was, whether he knew it or not, tilting toward the rack of ready-to-wear along the back wall. Certainly not a thing he'd do to the American across the room.

"I've always wanted a Savile Row suit," I said, "built for me from the ground up."

His eyebrows lifted ever so slightly. "You would like a bespoke suit, sir?"

"Yes, that's exactly what I'd like."

"Very good, sir. If you would be so kind." He led the way into a small office and motioned me to a chair. "We always find a little information about a client's life-style is most helpful." He opened a large book and uncapped a fountain pen. "There, now, just a little history of your habits and activities. To give us an idea of the most suitable style and fabrics." Fifteen minutes later he turned me over to three tailors who put me in a large dressing room and watched me strip to my shorts. I said a silent thanks to Sarah for packing new underwear, no holes, no stretched-out waistbands, no spots worn so thin you could see flesh through fabric.

The ghosts of my father and uncles hovered over the tailors, whispering, nodding, oohing and aahhing at the thoroughness of the fitting. Thinking of them kept my mind off the flying fingers probing, pressing, pulling, pushing, up-down-around-through.

"Sir dresses to the left, I see," said the trousermaker, kneeling in front of me, wielding his tape measure with speed and grace. A note-taker in the corner wrote the exact measurements that would create the anatomically correct fullness to the left of my pant zipper.

The jacketmaker took over, calling out measurements, endless combinations of numbers needed to construct a paper pattern. My family stored their patterns in the old coal bin behind the workroom. Hundreds of brown butcher paper chests, backs, arms, and legs hung clipped to clotheslines, crammed together like tobacco leaves in a smokehouse. Scribblings on the patterns noted the customer's hobbies, children's names, sports interests, little details that let the tailors welcome the client like an old friend, no matter how much time had passed since the last visit.

The jacketmaker finished and called in the cloth man, who

looked at the fabrics I'd selected. "Either the pinstripe or the navy will be acceptable for the style you've selected."

"I like them both," I said. "Make up two suits."

He didn't flinch. When someone said to my father "Make two suits," out came the bottle of schnapps.

"Will you be wanting fittings here, sir, or in the States?"

"The States?"

"Our fitters call every four months. New York, Beverly Hills, and Dallas."

"Here, I think. I'll be in town awhile."

They left me alone to dress. When I pulled back the dressing room curtain, the girl was waiting. I thought she looked a little friendlier. Maybe now that I was a real customer . . . "If you will follow me, sir." From the back, she had a surprisingly feminine walk. For my benefit, perhaps? I could make out a nice figure under the suit, good legs, graceful back. She led me back through the changing areas to a small ledger-filled room. "Just here, if you would, sir." A friendly smile. No mistaking it.

The small man, dwarfed by the large desk, spread out sheets of figures my fitters had given him. "Please," he said, motioning me to a chair. He opened a massive ledger with cracked leather covers, flipping through pages of numbers, comparing them with the ones he'd just figured. Running a finger down the rows, he stopped at a number, then turned and gazed through the room's small window as he asked, "Will that be satisfactory, sir?"

I took out my glasses. The total came to just under six thousand dollars. My father and uncles fainted.

"Is that for each one?"

"Oh, no sir, that will do both."

For six thousand dollars I could have had two and a half black cashmere sweaters on Rodeo Drive.

"Yes," I said. "That will be satisfactory."

He closed the book and opened a much newer one. "If I may, sir, an unfortunate necessity I'm afraid, the times being what they are, you understand, but if you could manage, say, a third."

"Of course." There was no credit card machine on his desk. I pulled out a pack of traveler's checks. "This may take a while."

"If Sir prefers"—he opened his desk drawer and with two fingers lifted the familiar machine as if it were a dead mouse—"we do accept credit cards."

Done. How many children of immigrant tailors could come

back to Savile Row and buy two bespoke suits? Why couldn't my father have lived to see this? Pulling the Taggart & Rowe door closed behind me, I stared up at the sky. A brilliant sun chiseled cracks through the clouds. I held my face to the shafts of light. Sarah wouldn't believe it. She'd been after me to get a new suit for so long.

"One suit in three years is not a lot, Asher."

"It's all I need."

"Looking a little frayed around the edges."

"Me or the suit?"

"Your choice."

"Weddings are so crowded no one notices—and funerals, who cares?"

"What if it's my funeral?"

"For you, Sarah, I'll buy a new suit."

"Then do me a favor, get it now, let me enjoy it a little."

I wouldn't tell her about these suits. Just sort of saunter into the house wearing the pinstripe and watch her pass out. I couldn't wait to see the look on her face. Made me laugh to think about it.

What now? I pulled out my London list. As long as the weather was good, I could take that boat tour down the Thames. I unfolded my map, figuring out the bus routes to the boats. The door opened behind me.

"Excuse me, Mr. Rose."

"Sorry." I moved out of the doorway. The girl passed me, juggling a package while she pulled on her coat. "Wait," I said, walking after her, "could you tell, Miss—Miss—"

"Parker. Vanessa Parker." She offered a delicate hand with a surprisingly firm handshake.

"Miss Parker, yes." I held out the map. "Can you tell me the best way to get from here to there."

"I'll try." She bent over the map and I inhaled the clean scent of her. A light fragrance, playful.

"It's not too bad a ride, actually. You'll have to change trains once, just there." Trains? Change trains? Mild panic. C'mon, Asher, macho men aren't afraid of riding the Tube.

"I'll take a bus," I said. "Lets me see the scenery."

"You don't want to do that." Yes I do. "Take you forever with traffic this time of day. Tell you what." She smiled, lovely even white teeth. "I have to drop this package off at the stop past yours. I'll be happy to show you the way."

"That's very kind." Trapped! No graceful way out. Toughen up, Asher, it's no big thing. Just a journey down to the center of the Earth.

It wasn't until I was on location, chewing the dregs from my second cup of coffee, that I remembered I'd forgotten to return Asher's call. He would think I was ignoring him, or that I didn't care, or that I was too busy for him. I hadn't told him Fanny was back in the hospital, didn't want to worry him. Maybe during lunch I could try to figure out how to make an overseas call from a pay phone. I had to.

They'd wedged Wardrobe into one small corner of the Evanston police station. Thirty extras milled around trying to amuse themselves. I knelt on the hard floor, making an emergency repair on a torn hem. The actress wearing the costume admired herself non-stop in the makeshift dressing room's mirror. Two young stud cops hovering around didn't make my job any easier. "Stand straight," I told the actress for the third time. "You're dipping."

"I wanna see."

"I'll do the seeing. You do the standing still." Marko rushed in, juggling boxes and bags of garments and costume props. He had a hard time finding space to put them down.

"You didn't call back last night," he said, dumping everything on the floor next to me, unpacking bags of new shirts, plugging in the steamer, taking the pins and cardboards out of the shirts and hanging them on the metal rack.

"Sorry. Came in late last night. What's up?"

"Greg and I are going away."

"When?"

"Saturday."

"For how long?" He didn't answer. "How long, Marko?" He shrugged.

"Not sure."

"You can't do this to me." It was tricky yelling with a mouth full of pins. Marko wouldn't look at me. He talked into his shirts.

"Calm down, Sarah. I promise it will be all right. Greg wants to see his family in California. They have a beautiful place overlooking the ocean." He tried to make it sound upbeat and happy but he was a lousy actor. Greg was going to California to die and Marko wanted to be with him.

"Stand still." I gripped the actress roughly. "Still!" She straightened, hiking the hem a full inch. A few extras walked over to watch.

I yanked a needle threaded with beige thread from my collar and started a row of tiny stitches around the hem. If I had more time, I'd set up the sewing machine, but they were waiting for her on set.

"You'll have Rita and Sonia full-time," said Marko.

"Marko, I don't want a staff. I want to *be* staff. It's hard enough doing this job without having to stop and tell someone else what to do."

"You'll be fine."

"You promised. You said you'd hold my hand through this. That you'd be here for me. I can't do this alone."

"You already have been. The two or three hours I'm here in the mornings don't count for much. And I haven't made any of the night shoots. You're doing a fabulous job, Sarah."

"Because you've been a phone call away."

"I still will be."

The actress twisted suddenly, yanking the hem in my hand, driving a pin deep into the flesh of my thumb.

"That does it!" I pulled out the pin, sucking the blood, trying to keep it from staining her costume. "You two, go arrest someone!" The young cops smiled sheepishly and backed out of the area. "All of you"—I waved back the extras—"find something else to watch. I swear," I said to the actress, "I'm going to staple you still." Marko laughed.

"Ain't show biz grand?"

"Why did I ever leave theater? It was so much more civilized, more time to do everything. And the work didn't have to be so exact."

Marko set down the steamer and knelt next to me. He set his huge hands on my shoulders. Sarah, Sarah, what a piece of work you are, carping to a man whose world is falling apart.

"Hang in, you're doing great."

"I'm scared to be in charge. There's so much to remember."

"Trust your production notes. Do one scene at a time. We've finished the designing, have all the major pieces. The work gets easier from here. I promise. Okay?"

"I have a choice?"

I spent the first half of my lunch break scrounging enough change to call Asher. Zack walked by while I was tracking down the international codes and London information I'd left at home. He leaned against the phone, looking at the piles of coins.

"Break into your piggy bank?"

"Trying to call London." He reached into his wallet and handed me his phone card.

"Use this."

"No, I—" He folded my hand around the card with strong fingers flecked with paint.

"Give it back when you're done. Lot easier than carrying around thirty pounds of coins. Surprised you don't have one."

"I think we do but I've never used it."

"Welcome to the wonderful world of technology."

I managed to reach the Savoy, but Asher was out. Where was he? What was he doing? I felt cheated that he wasn't there to talk to. Was he alone, wandering aimlessly, or had he found people to be with? I left a message that I called.

Vanessa talked nonstop on our walk to the Tube, tossing out two-hundred-year-old bits of Savile Row gossip. ". . . and in that shop a positively mad multimillionaire Hungarian came in with a heavily painted lady, if you catch my meaning, and headed back toward the dressing room and the proprietor *threw* his body across the entrance, refusing to let them use it. Now, over here . . ."

"Let me carry that," I said, reaching for her package. She hesitated, then handed it to me.

"Please, be careful."

"The crown jewels?"

"Well, I'm certain he thinks so." Those beautiful teeth again.

"Lord Morgan's new shirts." She slipped her arm through mine to steady herself across a puddle. I felt an unexpected rush. A long time since I'd had a woman on my arm. I was sorry when she let go.

"Do you give all your clients personal delivery?"

"Hardly. Depends. We turn here." She led me down the Tube stairs. Nothing to be afraid of. It'll be all right. Plenty of air. Breathe easy. Keep talking, keep talking, keep talking.

She paid for us both before I could dig out my wallet. A high-pitched ringing filled my head. Calm down. I am not under the Earth about to be crushed to death. I am not. Hope my sweaty hands don't stain the Lord's shirts.

"This way," she said, taking my arm again. Safe. Just in the nick. If I'd fainted and crushed Lord Morgan's shirts, they'd fire Vanessa and send her sick mum to the poorhouse. She moved us onto the crowded platform, too near the edge. One bump from behind and we'd fly onto the tracks. I was so focused on not falling that I didn't hear the train until it pulled in front of us. Vanessa led me on, politely but firmly rearranging two singly seated women so we could sit together.

I gripped the package on my lap. Had to concentrate on something besides riding through a tunnel hacked through millions of tons of rock. Concentrate on the warmth of Vanessa's body against mine in the narrow seats. Concentrate on the reassuring press of a woman's thigh.

"You surprised me, you know," she said, looking into my eyes. "I must say, when you first walked in I misread you altogether."

"Your eyes are orange."

"Hazel. Turn green when it's going to rain."

"Ah. And how did you misread me?"

"People almost always back off when I come 'round straightening after them. I don't much like people mucking about with my cloths."

"I wasn't 'mucking about' with your cloths. I was looking at them."

"Yes, well, there's looking and there's looking." She lowered her voice, leaning toward me. "You have a feel for fabric. I saw that." She patted my arm, singeing my sleeve. To what did I owe this pleasure? "I sometimes think I spend half my time rerolling bolts people tear apart. People I know jolly well are going to buy their suits off the peg. Not like you. You're a man who appreciates quality. You'd be surprised. . . ."

Her mouth, full-lipped and pouty, formed soft circles when she talked. How would it feel to have those lips around me? That small darting tongue? Warm. Wet. My gut tightened. Sexual stirrings. Been too long. Maybe the terror of hurtling through the belly of the Earth heightened all my senses. Then again, maybe it was her burning hand or those perfect teeth.

A few stops later we got off, hurrying through a maze of interconnected tunnels, settling on a bench next to a bald teen and her longhaired boyfriend. We had a longer wait for the second train.

"Have you had many adventures in London?" she asked. I scanned the question for clues. Adventures in fine dining? Sexual adventures? "I know I always have at least one mishap when I travel. Not that I've gone so very many places. Still, stepping foot in a new culture can make for those little unexpected moments."

I decided to take a chance and tell her the story of my massage. I wished I'd had a chance to tell it a few times to other people, smooth out the rough spots, sharpen the edges, tighten the timing. But I plunged in. Couldn't let her think I was a man without adventure. Besides, talking kept me from thinking about where I was, helped calm the panic.

". . . so there I was—peeking out the sauna and running to the shower, peeking out the shower and running back to the sauna . . ." She laughed. ". . . walking along, sort of keeping my robe slightly open, not too modest, not too"—I was about to say "cocky," but edited myself in time—"too bold." She blushed. "And when I yanked open the curtains . . ."

She laughed so hard she started coughing. The bald girl watched with interest. A success. My first new story in months. Sarah used to laugh at my stories like that. Not lately. But then, I hadn't been particularly funny lately. Good to know I still had the knack.

"Haven't had a laugh like that in a while," she said, taking a tissue from her purse, wiping her eyes. "Seems all I do lately is work and watch the telly."

"Makes for a dull life."

Look who's talking, Mr. All-work-no-play Soup King.

"Don't I know." She plucked an invisible piece of something off my lapel.

"Hard to imagine a pretty girl like you sitting home alone." Her cheeks flushed red again. I didn't think girls blushed anymore.

"Thanks, but it's true. My sister and I just moved into our own flat." Oh? "So I don't have a lot of money for doing things." Awww. "And I broke up with my boyfriend last week." Ah-ha! "Don't much feel like going out. Here's our train." We pushed onto the crowded car and stood next to each other, our hands touching on the pole. "Done much sight-seeing?" she asked, her body swaying against me. I ran down my list. Telling it sounded nearly as boring as doing it.

"Ah, yes." She smiled. "All the London highlights."

"I'm open to suggestions. Is there something special I should see while I'm here?"

"You must see *Ishmael*. It's just opened and I hear it's better than *Phantom, Les Miz,* and *Miss Saigon* all put together. 'Course, tickets are impossible."

"I'll try to remember." The train pulled into a station. She pressed against me as we braked to a stop.

"Wait." She pulled a Taggart & Rowe business card out of her wallet and wrote "Ishmael" on the back. "There, now you can't forget." The train started up again and she added her name and phone number before tucking the card into my pocket. "Your stop is next," she said.

I handed her Lord Morgan's shirts. Her hands slid along mine as she took the package from me. Hope the heat didn't take all the starch out of the collars. Her train pulled away and I stood watching it go. What was that all about?

It's called flirting. Something men and women like to do. You should try it sometime.

I did my share at Rosie's.

In the safety of the cafeteria, where you could run back to work if a woman called your bluff.

Come on, Paul, Savile Row's not Rush Street. Taggart & Rowe doesn't hire women to entertain their clients.

Men is men, and women is women.

You're reading too much into this.

Right, she wrote down her name and number because she never wanted to hear from you again.

I jogged up the station stairs. Four impeccably groomed men walked past me. Not a crepe-soled shoe or soft-creased pant in the bunch. Made me feel rumpled. Enough! I wasn't a shlepper anymore. No reason I had to look like one.

Way to go!

My suits wouldn't be ready for a while but there were other things to work on. A professional haircut, for starters. Not that Sarah hadn't done a good job all these years, cutting my hair at night while I watched TV.

"Asher, why don't you go to a stylist?"

"No time."

"Everyone else finds time."

"Can't do *this* to a stylist while she trims my bangs."

"Fresh! Stop that right now or I'll cut your sideburns on the bias."

I had time, now. And money. And I had my health. Some, anyway. More and more. Feeling pretty damned good as a matter of fact. I hailed a taxi. The tour down the Thames would have to wait. For some reason, the idea of sitting on a cold rocking boat for two hours had lost all interest.

49

What to pack? What to leave? Every inch of Fanny's closet was crammed with clothes, shoes, purses. Scarves, jewelry, and belts hung from hundreds of nails hammered into the door and walls. Just pick something, Sarah, a few basics to get her started at the Wedgewood. When Fanny felt stronger, when I had more time than a lunch break, I'd bring her to the apartment, let her decide what to keep and what to toss.

How do you sort through a lifetime? Makeup's a good place to start. Not too many decisions. I took a small box and sat down at the skirted dressing table. Sweep the whole cluttered mess into the box, Sarah.

Don't stop to play.

Lotions, powders, brushes, oils, cold creams, cotton balls, tissues, cotton swabs, pencils. I picked up a coal-black eyeliner and started drawing crow's-feet along my crow's-feet.

Don't stop to play, I said.

When I was a child Fanny taught me how to make my face old. Could she teach me to make it young?

After the crow's-feet I penciled a few faint frown lines across my forehead, then packed the pencil. With a white oil stick, I drew a thin line from the bridge of my nose to the tip.

You're playing. I can tell. Don't you have things to do?

I smoothed the line with my baby finger. Made my nose look wonderfully flat. Hundreds, maybe thousands of variations-on-a-theme-of-Fanny had been created at this table. Virgin to vamp, timid to tough, never the same two days running.

"Other men play around," my father used to say, "because they get bored. Not me. I'm married to a different woman every day." Was Asher bored? Is that why I felt him slipping away this past year? I used to wish he'd had hundreds of girlfriends before me, so he'd appreciate what a great catch I was. Maybe, if he'd done a little more premarital experimenting, he wouldn't be so restless now. Damn Paul for making affairs sound so glamorous. Asher might be sexually shy, but that didn't mean he never wondered what he'd missed. Every time he flirted with another woman I wondered if he was sorry he'd married me before he'd had more experience.

I picked up the old pipe Fanny kept on the dressing table. Sometimes my father was crystal clear in my mind, sitting in his nubby chair, slippered feet propped up on the cracked leather hassock, dipping his pipe in a round humidor, drawing the match flame down into the tobacco, filling the room with smoke that smelled like fermenting cherries. Other times I couldn't remember what he looked like. I was eleven when he died. Should at least be able to remember his face when I wanted to.

"Helloooo?"

"Jeez!"

"Sorry, sorry, sorry." A little woman with kind eyes moved her walker toward me. "Didn't mean to startle. The door was open and I thought maybe Fanny was back from the hospital. I'm Sophie Solomon from across the hall."

"Sophie," a man's voice called from the hall, "what now? Let's go, already."

"In a minute, Morrie. You're Fanny's daughter?"

"Yes."

"I could tell in the eyes. Just like your mother." Complete with crow's-feet and worry lines? Good thing Fanny wasn't here.

"Sophie," said the man, "I'm going."

"So go. I'll catch up."

"Fanny's still in the hospital, Mrs. Solomon. She'll be out in the next day or so."

"Sophie!"

"Always running, always running. Like he's got someplace to go." Sophie turned her walker toward the door. "Tell Fanny I send my best, yeah? Tell her Sophie Solomon from three-o-four sends regards." She waved over her head, hurrying after Morrie.

I stared at the door, clenching my fists so I didn't hurl something at it. It wasn't fair. What made Sophie Solomon from three-o-four so special? Who was she that God let her grow old with her Morrie?

I gripped the edges of the dressing table, staring down at the sea of goodies. All those tubes and bottles and jars. How was I supposed to predict who Fanny would want to be? Better take it all. I pushed everything into the box and taped it shut. The toolbox filled with greasepaint, fake scars, beauty dots and other theatrical goodies could wait a while until Fanny was up to performing. First we needed to put weight on her, find out why she was so weak.

Three large boxes of clothing should be enough to get her started. I packed a variety and, as an afterthought, topped off each box with a supply of thick padded hangers. Fanny took care of her clothes, kept them so long they came back into fashion, give or take an alteration. Couldn't do that with wire hangers.

I'd loaded two boxes into the car and was struggling down the hall with the third when Leon, Fanny's champagne-and-caviar neighbor, came out of his apartment. A sweat suit and gym shoes replaced the towel he'd worn the first time we met. He shifted his unlit cigar to one side of his mouth.

"How's your mother?" he asked.

"Better, thanks. We're hoping she'll get out of the hospital tomorrow."

"Good. I'll be glad to see her."

"Oh. Well, I guess you don't know. No, of course, how could you? Fanny won't be coming back here." His face crumpled, as if he'd taken a hard blow to the gut.

"Where's she going?"

"The Wedgewood Home."

"What are you talking?" He ripped the cigar out of his mouth, jabbing it violently in my direction. "That's not a place for Fanny. It's full of old people."

"She's—" I stopped myself from saying "seventy-eight." She'd kill me if I told. Besides, he looked at least that. When, then, did old age begin? Ten years past whatever we were?

"How can you do that to your own mother? A woman like that. Shame on you!"

"Me? It's not me. This isn't my idea."

"Bah!" he said, walking back toward his apartment.

"No, really. She's the one who wants to go." He wouldn't turn. "Some friends of hers told her about it and she—" He slammed his door.

Fanny, Fanny, Fanny. Still leaving a trail of broken hearts.

~~~ 50 ~~~~~~~~~~~~

The Eclectic Salon was worth the twenty-minute crawl through London traffic. I nearly fell asleep stretched out in a great leather chaise, my head tilted back into a sink while the shampoo girl massaged, cleaned, conditioned, rinsed. Shave? Why not. Manicure? Sure. Pedicure? The works.

An hour and forty minutes later, I stared at the distinguished man in the mirror. Hello. Where did you come from? So this is what I'd been missing all these years. Sarah had been right. A professional cut made a big difference. I'd find someone in Chicago. Wonder if Sarah's feelings would be hurt? The stylist whisked the finishing brush over my neck and shoulders and presented the bill on a silver dish. The Works came to a hundred twenty-five, before tips.

I walked out into an icy drizzle and ducked into a nearby store for an umbrella. For a hundred and a quarter, I wanted to look good as long as possible. Wish Sarah could see me. Wish Vanessa could see me. Wish I'd looked like this before I'd gone into her shop. Three o'clock. I'd missed lunch. Why eat if I wasn't hungry? Now that I wasn't burning up calories at work I had to get out of the three-meal-a-day habit. Wouldn't take much to lose some weight. Not much at all.

I made the rounds of the shops near the salon to keep busy, get my mind off food. Amazing how fast I could spend money, considering I'd never practiced. Four belts, all reversible. Six long-sleeved shirts. Five silk ties. Eight pairs of long socks, the ones I hated, the ones Sarah begged me to wear so my pale calves wouldn't show when I crossed my legs. I once bought a pair for a buck eighty at an outlet store near Rosie's. They kept falling down around my ankles. At twenty-eight bucks a pop, I expected the new pairs to have more staying power. If not, I could always nail them to my knees.

Damned shame to waste looking this good. I felt like talking to people. I stopped at a local pub and ordered a pint of bitters. The place, all wood and stained glass, was packed. I scanned the crowd. Everyone was attached to someone.

I sipped the bitters, wondering where all the single women were. When I was with Sarah, the world around me was crammed with sexy young girls. Sexy and willing. A friendly touch here, an innocent kiss there, just enough to let me know how interested they were. Sometimes, walking through the hordes of young women at Rosie's, I'd felt like a sperm swimming upstream. Now that I was alone, every unattached woman on the face of the Earth had suddenly grown an escort.

Loosen up, Asher.

How did you do this, Paul?

You get used to it.

Sitting alone in a bar?

You're too tight.

You always made it sound like fun.

Watch the action. The one on the bar stool over there? You don't see a pair of legs like that every day of the week.

Looks like our second grade teacher. And he wasn't all that cute.

The world is wasted on you, Asher.

And the drinks taste like turpentine.

Wasted.

All right, all right, I'll watch the action.

A little brunette wearing a pillbox hat and matador's cape climbed laughing onto the stool next to me. Sarah would wear that outfit.

This is not about Sarah.

I can't help it if this girl reminds me of her.

Everything reminds you of her.

Yes.

Sarah-of-the-second-grade would come over to play with Martha, clutching a grocery bag full of old dolls in her scrawny arms. She dressed like a refugee from a flea market: plumed hats, jeweled pins, long skirts dragging on the ground. "That girl dresses in Early Housesale," whispered Mother, rigid, disapproving. "Who knows what fleas, lice, or diseases. Shame on Fanny Feldman. Letting her little girl go out like that." As if Fanny could control Sarah, even if she wanted to.

The brunette ordered a drink. I straightened my tie, hiding the gap where the top button wouldn't close anymore. No Salvation Army clothes for the Rose children. God forbid. Every August, Mother made out a clothing list and stuffed it into an envelope along with a fortune in tightly folded bills. She watched hawkeyed as I safety-pinned the envelope to the inside of my underpants and left with my brothers and sisters for a one-hour bus-and-streetcar ride to Sears. Shlepping the five of them from department to department, I filled the holes in their hand-me-down wardrobes with new school clothes of solid construction and durable cloth. The clothes, boring as hell, lasted forever.

The brunette placed an unlit cigarette in her V for Victory fingers and propped her elbow on the bar, slowly waving her cigarette back and forth. Match. Match. I scanned the bar for matches, trying and rejecting a dozen opening lines.

Here, allow me.

Light your fire?

Come here often?

Love your cape.

A blond Adonis materialized with a flaming gold lighter. The brunette wrapped her hand around his, pulling the flame to the cigarette. Her eyes peered meaningfully into his as he swept her off to his table. If I had a million years to work on it, I couldn't look like him. All the tailors on Savile Row working their callused fingers to the bone couldn't change that.

What was the point of being alone? That's what was wrong with this picture. Sarah brought home great stories about her life in Europe because she'd had experiences with people, all kinds, all the time. That one Tube ride with Vanessa had been more fun than all the other days put together. I took out her business card.

Do it, Asher.

What if she laughs at me? What if I misread the hand on my arm, the slight body touches?

You want an engraved invitation?

All the women at Rosie's flirt, blow kisses to the guys. It doesn't mean anything. Young girls today are a different breed from the ones we grew up with. Vanessa probably never gave all that touchy-feely a second thought.

Then why give you her home phone? Why mention her ex-boyfriend and how available and bored she is?

But why me? Rich men come into her shop all the time. Handsome men.

Obviously, she's desperate.

I'll bet it's because I made her laugh.

Do it, Ash. What's the worst that can happen?

Humiliation. She'll wonder what I'm talking about. She'll have a good laugh about me, tell her sister "This old fart calls me up and—"

Cut it out, Asher.

Easy for you, Paul. You're dead.

Yeah? Well, pardner, you ain't lookin' too lively yerself.

I waited in the pub doorway. No taxis. The bitter wind tore into my joints. Maybe I'd find a better spot on a busier street. A gust ripped my umbrella inside out, yanking my arm, starting a new spot of pain. Damn this cold. No major streets nearby. Had to get out of this wind. I rode the Tube once today and didn't die. I could do it again. I hurried down the steps before I could change my mind.

The colored lines and strange names zigzagging across the Tube map were confusing without Vanessa. No direct line from here to the Savoy. I'd have to change trains. Might find a cab at the midway point. Sharp edges of my packages kept jabbing people, and in the crush of boarding a train, one of the bags broke, scattering socks on the wet floor.

"Excuse me." I tried to pick them up. "Sorry." Keep them from being dragged and trampled under wet boots. Crowds closed me in, cut off my air, pushed me up and back, forcing me farther into the car where I couldn't reach the door, too far in.

Why didn't I eat something before downing the pint of bitters? Strong stuff on an empty stomach. One stop. Two stops. Had to get out. Three stops. Had to get out. Push elbows, arms, making people give way. Lunge out the doors onto the platform, through the bodies coming at me and at me and at me, up the stairs, so many stairs, up toward the cool air of the street.

Three black-leathered punks smoking, spitting, lean against the wall, smirking.

"You awright, guv?"

I nod, sweat dripping down my face, vision blurred. Don't like the way they're moving in. The little one walks up.

"Been shopping then, have you?" Blocking my path, sticking his face into mine, eyes unfocused, breath reeking of booze and smoke.

Nod and swallow, no breath for words. Force myself past him up the last stairs, out onto the street. Desolate area. Dark apartments, boarded storefronts. No hotels, no big streets. Has to be a cab. Maybe around the block, or next block. All dark, darker. The fresh air sets me straight. No reason I can't make it all the way home on the Tube. I head back, glad for the lights of the Tube entrance.

Smell them before I see them, feel them moving around me. I know in my gut what's coming, remember this brand of fear. Growing up Chicago poor is growing up Chicago tough. These punks think they've cornered a sick old man. Good, that'll buy me time. Old street moves come back to me. I straighten up, get a good grip on the umbrella, stride toward the Tube entrance. Last thing I want to look like is Victim.

"Help you out, guv?" The little one jumps in front of me and grabs the box of shirts.

"Give me the box," I say nice and calm and this makes the little one laugh and the middle-sized one angry and that leaves the big one dancing around me like a punch-drunk prizefighter, faking sloppy jabs with fingerless gloves, each jab coming closer to my face so I turn my back and start to walk away because the best thing is to leave if they'll let me which I know they won't and the large one grabs me from behind—and Oh the smell of him onions and garlic and sweat and booze and things rotten and fetid— wrapping his arms around my chest, the heat of his breath on my neck a strange comfort against the cold squeezing, squeezing, tighter and tighter, taking my air, someone's hands ripping through my pockets and

Let's get 'em, Ash!

I raise my leg and jam it down with all my might, my heel crushing the top of his foot, smashing bone. He screams, lets me go, grabbing his foot, and I ax my arm down on his neck with the whole weight of my body sending him sprawling, and the middle-sized punk moves faster than I expected smashing my eye with his fist, knocking me down through puddles and I see stars shoot against black. He lunges at me and I kick out, catching his kneecap full-force, sending him down. I am stumbling up when the little one comes at me something glinting in his hand and I grab up the umbrella slashing at him and he laughs, threatening with yes a knife, grabbing the end of the umbrella, yanking it hard to pull me over only I let go and he tumbles back. Three down, enough time for me to escape to the Tube, back down to safety.

51

The Good Thing about Marko's desertion was it made it easier for me to leave the set. Heading up Wardrobe meant more responsibility, but it also meant I could delegate the grunt work. After I set up in the morning, I could leave Rita and Sonia long enough to sneak off to do little personal things, like pick Fanny up from the hospital and check her in at the Wedgewood.

Once I stopped feeling so antagonistic/guilty/sad, I had to admit the Wedgewood Home was beautiful. Really nothing institutional about it at all. Much more like one of those charming hotels just off Michigan Avenue with their tasteful little lobbies and subdued lighting. And the welcoming staff couldn't have been nicer. Fanny, playing the Grand Dowager, let them fuss over her and take her on tour.

Later, as the elevator doors opened on the floor where she would be living, she recast herself as the 'Umble Star. There was a flurry of activity and excitement as residents came to greet her.

"Fanny Feldman. I can't hardly believe."

"My father was a cutter, AF of L-CIO. The union gave us tickets to see you at the old Roosevelt Playhouse."

"I used to die from your singing."

"Kept your picture and Dina Halpern's taped up on my mirror. To think I'm meeting you in the flesh." These were her people. They'd seen her perform. They remembered who she was.

When they took Fanny down to lunch, I unpacked her belongings. Her side of the closet was barely two feet across. So much for
the space-hogging padded hangers. Nurses dug up a few wire
hangers—"Like gold around here." Even with those, I'd be lucky
to cram in a fourth of the clothes I'd brought. I picked out what I
hoped were Fanny's favorites and put the rest in boxes under her
bed. She'd have to go through the stuff later and decide what to
keep and what to have me take home. I unpacked her underwear,
jewelry, and toiletries into the four drawers on her side of the
narrow eight-drawer dresser. Thank goodness I'd thought to bring
some photos, books, and a few other items to warm up the space.
No reason this couldn't look as cozy as her apartment. Sure,
Sarah.

The dining room was an elegant affair with crystal chandeliers
and formal chairs set around tables of four. I searched the fluffy
clouds of white hair until I found Fanny, golden threads among
the silver, holding court at table five.

"Good-bye, Sarahlah," she said, kissing me lightly on the
cheek. I hesitated a moment, unsure. She turned back to the
companions she'd left dangling mid-story. You mean that's all
there was to it?

I practically danced out of the Wedgewood, leaving Fanny to
handsome doctors, caring nurses, gourmet meals and exciting
activities two times a day. Fanny was safe, cared for, and happy.
What more could a child wish for a parent?

I smiled all the way back to work, energized, excited, ready to
take on the world. Hot damn! There was nothing I couldn't do!
The great weight holding me down these past months since her
gallbladder and her TB and her anemia, the great boulder I strained
to push back up the hill for so long I'd forgotten what life was like
without it, disappeared. Poof!

"I know it's not possible," said Zack, as I danced back onto
the set, "but you look like you had your face lifted since I saw you
this morning."

"Had my whole self lifted," I said, dipping a rag in linseed oil,
wiping a smear of fuchsia paint off his cheek. "Does it show?"

"Nearly didn't recognize you."

Everything was possible all day at work. I had the energy of ten
people. The waitresses Mel originally wanted dressed for a nightclub had to be recostumed for a hamburger joint. No problem. I
drove to Marko's studio and dug through his stash of waitress

costumes. The outdoor scene we were supposed to shoot that afternoon was rescheduled because of snow and I had to have the airport scene ready to go by two. Could have done it standing on my head. Give me something really hard, *War and Peace* on a fifty-buck budget.

That night, turning the key to open my front door, I was overwhelmed by loneliness for Asher. Walking into the dark house, into the quiet I had craved—*Careful what you wish for, Sarahlah*—making my new limited rounds from mail slot to bedroom, I wanted Asher home with me. Now that all was well I could tell him Fanny had been in the hospital. Now that I knew I could handle the job, I could tell him Marko was gone. This was what mattered, what I missed most, this sharing of our lives, the parts of our days.

There were no messages on the answering machine. Asher was probably angry that I hadn't returned his call this morning. He had every right to be. How would I feel if Asher sent me halfway around the world, then didn't bother returning my calls? I had a lot to make up for. It was four in the morning London time. Too late to call. I put on my nightgown and slid into the cool sheets.

Tomorrow I'd call the travel agent. As soon as we finished filming I'd meet Asher in London and we'd go on from there. I'd make our time together so special he'd forget all about this time apart. Not that I was unhappy I'd sent him away. As difficult as that was, I would have been a wreck with him home, Fanny in the hospital, and Marko jumping ship to California. Piece by piece, my life was falling back into place. The worst was over.

The night call jolted me awake. Asher! Something's happened to Asher. That's why I haven't been able to reach him. Something terrible. Oh, God. I fumbled in the dark for the phone. "Hello? Hello?"

"You come get me out of this place!"

"Mom?"

"You come get me right now."

"Mom? Wh-what's wrong?"

"She snores. Who can sleep with that racket?"

"Mom"—I switched on the table lamp, squinting into the light—"it's one o'clock."

"Come pick me up."

"I am not coming at one in the morning." Oh, yeah, then why

are you climbing out of bed? A woman's voice on the other end gentled Fanny away from the phone, complimenting her on her beautiful nightgown and robe.

"Hello?" said the voice.

"Yes," I said, "this is Fanny Feldman's daughter. She seems . . . upset."

"Don't you worry, miss. All my new ladies take a while to settle in." I listened but couldn't hear Fanny yelling or screaming. Either she'd settled down or the nurse had bound and gagged her.

"I'll call in the morning, see how she is," I said.

"She'll be jest fine. I'll fix her a nice cup of cocoa, set and talk a bit till she's feeling sleepy. She'll do all right. 'Night, miss."

Damn it, Fanny. Damn damn double damn. What the hell was I crying about? Just because the weight of the world suddenly redropped on my head? Is that any reason? Just because, for a brief instant, I had remembered what it felt like not to worry? Is that some kind of reason?

I went downstairs, poured myself a stiff scotch, and brought it back to bed. A drink was a lousy substitute for what I wanted. I sat in the dark room, holding the tumbler in both hands.

"Oh, Asher, I need you." If Asher were here, he'd take me in his arms. He'd hold me close and we'd be quiet together, or he'd say something wacky to make me laugh. Then he'd make love to me. I wanted the silky feel of his skin under my fingertips, the sexy salt taste of him on my tongue. I slid the cool glass down my nightgown between my legs and pressed it against me. Been too long, my girl.

I picked up the phone and called the Savoy. Hang the time. No answer in his room. ASH-er, where ARE you? Had he gone out early in the morning, or was he perchance still out from the night before? A sudden violent twinge. It took a while to recognize the old feeling. Jealousy. The same gut-wrenching jealousy I'd felt watching Asher walk a girl home from school. The torment when Asher flirted on the phone while I was over playing with Martha. Now Asher was out in the London streets, somewhere other than moping around his room. Wasn't that why I sent him off? So he'd heal? Then stop complaining, and stop being jealous. I left a message that I'd called.

I waited out the night sipping scotch, staring into the dark, the phone resting on my lap. In case Asher called. In case Fanny called. What had happened to my world, so full of hope a few hours before? The alarm went off at five and I tried Asher one more time before dragging myself out of bed.

52

The shoot should have ended by eight. We were still at it at eleven at night. Stupid reasons, stupid mistakes. After the mid-morning break, we lost the extra in the blue sweater.

"So use someone else," Fanny said when I called. "It's not like you misplaced the star."

"Mom, all morning he sat right behind Jac Green in the master shot. We need him back for the close-ups. Otherwise, when they splice different camera angles together, it'll look like the man is appearing and disappearing."

"This means you're not coming to see me?"

"I can't leave now."

"What about later?"

"This afternoon we've got a loft shoot over on Clark Street." She sighed into Wedgewood's hall phone. The dayroom TV blared in the background. "Mom, I'm sorry."

"I understand from work, Sarahlah. When you come, bring two bananas, on the green side, yeah?" She'd developed selective hearing. Neither of us mentioned last night's phone call and she didn't ask me to come take her home. Maybe nights were rough on her, too. "I need a touch-up. Make an appointment at Bliss for next week. Whenever you can take me."

"How about trying the Wedgewood beauty shop?"

"You think I want blue hair? Get me color with Linda, cut with Bob. That's a good girl."

Ninety-six cast and crew sat around Lake View High School's auditorium playing cards, reading, knitting, kibitzing, pacing, cursing. Thousands of dollars ticked away for want of a fifty-dollar-a-day extra. When the casting director finally climbed up on stage and started going down her list of extras name by name, an elderly lady came forward.

"My Joseph didn't want to do this," she said, gripping her pocketbook like a shield.

"Where is he?"

"It was all my idea. To get him out of the house, around people, away from that damned television set." Oh, lady, I hear you loud and clear. "All day he watches." I had one of those at home. "It's not healthy." A-men. "He didn't mean anything by it. He couldn't take all this waiting around. He said he'd come back after the four o'clock news." In plenty of time to pick up his check.

They sent a car for her Joseph, finished the close-ups, then let him go back to his TV. He'd put us three hours behind schedule. I'd give Mel one of my Pepto-Bismol bottles wrapped in a red ribbon.

Afternoon at the old loft building didn't go any better. The ancient boiler wouldn't throw up heat. I sent Sonia and Rita home. No point in the entire wardrobe department dying of pneumonia. Then two pieces of lighting equipment broke down. More hurry-up-and-wait while they found replacements. The hair stylist read our palms. Someone ran over to Reza's and brought back dolmas.

Had I ever been this bored in theater? Once I finished costuming a play, I was pretty much done. There was none of this sitting around sets for hours. How many more years of grunt work lay ahead before I started landing my own movies? I was too old to play apprentice for long, too old to freeze my bippy in a con-demned building when I could be in London with Asher.

Sandra handed out pieces of her homemade fudge. The key grip put out a tray of tostados and his special salsa. Catering passed around bags of carrot and celery sticks, bowls of miniature Milky Ways, crates of soft drinks. Our stone-faced cameraman did biting imitations of the actors, director, crew.

The Good Thing about being stranded with artists was they could create a center ring where there was no circus. And if we were circus, Zack was ringmaster, captivating us with stories about dodging bandits in Borneo, eating hundred-year-old eggs in Guam. Even seated, he gave the illusion of movement, current running out in all directions.

Asher had been like that, cooking soups on all four burners, hammering out publicity on an old Royal, organizing all of us to put Rosie's order forms under windshield wipers, in mailboxes, on grocery store bulletin boards. Bright, aggressive, great sense of humor, steady income. What more could a girl want?

"Marry me, Asher."

"You're too old."

"I'm only ten."

"How can I marry a woman with a milk mustache?" He reached over and wiped the milk away. Asher Rose touched me! I didn't wash my mouth for a week. Amazing, really, how much Zack reminded me of how Asher used to be. Made me want to cry.

I curled up in a corner, shivering, watching. I loved this group, so alive. I'd bonded with them that first night at the Ritz when we'd stayed up to three in the morning going over the movie's plans. What was it about the arts that transformed strangers into family? Long hours of working together? The sheer joy, the euphoria of the doing of our art? Whatever it was, I felt closer to my true self with these people than with all the acquaintances on PTA boards, Little League parent groups, and synagogue sisterhoods put together.

What would Asher think of this group? Fanny's theater friends made him uneasy. I understood that. They tended to be overly emotional, bigger than life, on and off the stage. But movie people, especially this crew, seemed more down-to-earth. I bet he'd like them, if he'd give them half a chance.

Near the end, a small group of us sat in a corner, huddled together for warmth. I snuggled between the makeup assistant and the stunt coordinator. Zack sprawled across our legs, wrapped like a pupa in his long black coat, his head on my lap. I automatically reached out and stroked his head, the way I stroked Asher's. It took a few seconds before I realized what I was doing. Zack didn't seem to mind.

"Quiet, please," called Mel. "Background settle. Thank you."

"Here goes," I said.

"Let us pray," said Zack, reaching up to take my hand.

"We're rolling," said Takeuchi.

"Speed," said the sound man.

"Background," said Mel, starting the extras in motion. "And action."

Two actors ran at each other. One picked up a chair and hurled it through a window. This time the prop chair didn't break apart in his hands. This time he didn't flub his lines. This time an extra didn't stand staring right into the camera. This time the chair flew through the fake window. This time the window frame did not fall over.

"Cut. That's a wrap."

"Sweetest words in the world," said Zack.

"You got that right." I tugged his braid, shooing him off my lap. "Up, up, up. I've got some serious shlepping to do."

"I'll give you a hand."

"You kids go ahead. I'm fine."

"Kids?" He raised an eyebrow at me. "What are you? Grandma Moses?"

The crew started packing up and I called for wardrobe. I couldn't leave until I'd checked every item back in, exchanging the actors' clothing for their time sheets so they could get paid. Someone put on the tape from *The Big Chill* and people danced the kitchen scene, miming the cleanup, dropping dishes, throwing glasses over their shoulders. Half of me thought they were hysterically funny, but the exhausted half wanted to pack up and go home. Come on, Sarah. They're just kids having a good time. Don't be a grinch. I slumped into a chair to wait them out. Zack winked at me, moved into the group, and danced actors over one by one, helping them strip off the garments I needed. Half an hour later I was finished.

Sandra danced over with the rest of the rat pack. How could they look so fresh after the day we'd put in?

"We're going to Pearl's Pub," she said. "Wanna come?"

"You kidding?" I stacked my boxes on the dolly and headed for the door. "I have a thirty-minute ride home. See you in the morning."

Zack caught up to me as I unlocked the back of my wagon.

"Give me a lift?" he asked, helping me load.

"Where to?"

"I'm staying at the New Heatherton."

"Zachary, that's all the way back toward downtown."

"Just five minutes from here."

"Everything by you is just five minutes from here."

"California time."

Oh, what the hell. If he hadn't helped me, I'd still be upstairs packing. I could drop Zack off, then whip out onto the expressway at Ohio. Probably get home just as fast.

"Come on, Romeo," I said, "get in."

I turned west off Rush Street the exact instant an afternoon of diet Cokes hit my bladder.

"Need to use the ladies'," I said, pulling into the No Parking zone in front of Zack's hotel.

"This is Lincoln Towing's favorite spot," he said. "You should pull around into the lot."

"I'll be back before they hook up the chain."

The vintage hotel was in mid-face-lift. Her lobby smelled of old mildew, new paint, and a daub of pine-scented Lysol. A Closed for Repair sign blocked the lobby rest rooms. Figured. While Zack checked for messages and mail, I rang for the elevator, trying not to think about how much I had to go. All in the mind. Sometimes I lasted nearly all day without a bathroom break. But the second I walked from my car to my house, I'd feel my bladder bursting. Zack shuffled his messages like playing cards. As the elevator rattled up, I distracted myself by reading over his arm. Several of the pink pieces of paper said "Lisa called" and gave the time. He caught me looking.

"Someone back home?" I asked.

"She thinks so." He stuffed the messages deep into his pocket.

Zack's room was at the end of a three-mile-long hall. He unlocked his door and I burst past him. "First door on the right," he said, flicking on the light.

And to think I'd nearly worn a jumpsuit. Never would have made it. Sitting on the wicker-encased throne, feeling the bladder pain ebb, it occurred to me that few things in life were as satisfying as being able to go to the bathroom when you really needed to go to the bathroom. It also occurred to me, as I washed up, that I could use lipstick, a comb, and a good night's sleep. After looking at all those fresh young faces at work, my own came as something of a shock. It wasn't fair to store a vital mind in a haggard package. I ran a comb through my hair and put on lipstick. If I'm going home, why do I need lipstick? Good question.

"Better?" He'd put Vivaldi on a portable disc player and set two glasses of wine on the coffee table. Zack moved through the room, turning on low-light table lamps, opening a bag of pistachio nuts and pouring them into a bowl. "I have some brie if you want."

"Can't stay, Zack. Thanks anyway." Faint warning drums.

"Wine's poured. Just one glass."

"I don't want to drink and drive. Not as tired as I am." I started buttoning my coat.

"Wait. I just want to show you this one thing." He pulled a large portfolio from behind the sofa and opened it onto the coffee table. "Here." He patted the sofa next to him.

"Just for one minute," I said, sitting. He flipped open the portfolio and pulled out several Polaroids and a few renderings.

"This is the set we'll be working on next week. I told Mel we have to tear up this wood floor. It's too fifties." I bent forward to look, my arm brushing against his. An arc of energy leapt across. "I pried up a corner and found the original white tiles underneath. They make the place look like an authentic Italian restaurant. Will a stark white tile floor affect your costumes for the scene?" My, Zachary Mandan, what big eyes you have. They make it powerful hard for me to remember what characters are in the restaurant scene.

"Let me think. No. The men wear dark suits. I might have to mute the waiters' aprons, but I'll see when I get there." His eyes wandered over my face a moment. My skin caught fire. I looked back down at the drawings so he couldn't see.

His renderings were beautiful. I'd thought so the first time I saw them—last week, when he brought them to the set. Maybe Zack didn't remember showing them to me. Maybe he did remember, but it was all he could think of to keep me from walking out the door. The drums beat louder.

Zack shrugged off his coat and bent over the portfolio, lifting one drawing off the other. His energy moved into my space. A little hard to breathe, difficult to swallow. I stared at the back of his head, the thick black braid wanting to be untied, the head asking to be stroked. I clenched my fists and folded my arms. I would *not* place my hands on his broad shoulders. I would *not* massage my thumbs up his neck, down his spine to the dimple at the base. I'd had a lover in Spain built like Zack. A lousy lover as it turned out, full of sound and fury. But that was Before Asher, when I was young, and experimenting. It was enough in those years for a lover to be gorgeous, attentive and frequent. It would not be enough anymore. Not after Asher. Not after love.

I studied Zack's profile, the sharp-lined features of a Mayan god. It wasn't as if I didn't look. I might be faithful, but I wasn't dead. How could I not notice the catlike way he moved, the natural way he took over, the effortless way he attracted both women and men? The drums beat relentlessly now. No way to ignore the pressure building between my legs. I grabbed my wineglass and took a swig. It had been a long time between times. Too long. Had to get out of here.

Zack looked up from a drawing, his face inches from mine, too close to focus. I stared into a blurred image of black eyebrow, thick eyelash, black pupil, sharp-edged nostril, parted lips. He smelled faintly of soap and shampoo. Clean and male. I didn't move. He took my wineglass and put it down on the table. This was not going to happen. This was a figment of my oversexed imagination. Oh, Asher, why are you in London? A shark is circling and it's all your fault. The drums, the deafening drums inside my head. I pressed my thighs together to stop the aching.

I'm going now. And oh the sweet softness of his lips pressing against my left eyelid. Gently now. Right eyelid. Oh, yes. Much better with my eyes closed. Losing myself to the dark. *Thank you so very much for the use of your bathroom.* Warm lips kissing the tip of my nose. Left cheek. Slowly. Right cheek. *And for the wine. Lovely wine. A chardonnay, you say?* Lifting my chin with his finger, bringing my mouth to his mouth, his sweet sweet mouth and oh Lord the cruel pain of wanting. *I don't suppose a little kiss can hurt.* The tickle of his tongue tip along my lips. His arms around me now, pulling me closer to him *just a friendly kiss after all* somehow laying me down *a special shared moment between two close friends* the great length of his body moving over mine *a way of acknowledging just how swell we think each other are* his kisses shifting from probe to passion.

Just for a second. Just let me know this for a second. Let me kiss him and hold him and remember how it is to feel the white-hot spark of passion between two people. It's been so long. So long. So long. A sound forced its way through the drumming, my sound, my sobbing.

His knee wedged between my legs, his hard-muscled thigh pressing slowly up into me, against me, while his mouth held me steady, steady. And I rode him, damn him, and rode him, damn him, and felt him harden against me, damn him, and in the seconds it took him to back away and loosen his belt—*now, Sarah, get up now!*—and unbutton his button—*the longer you wait the harder the break will be*—and work down his zipper—*think of the emptiness after all those fine young men. Remember the emptiness*—and move my hand around to touch him—*the emptiness and the sadness and the knowing there was something better.* And oh the steely hardness of him. I'd forgotten, I'd forgotten. The pulsing heat. I opened my hand. He closed it around him again, along silky taut skin mapped with ridges and veins. A world waiting to be explored. I let go.

"What's wrong?" His voice urgent with the wanting of me. "What is it?"

I didn't answer. Not with my breath jagged from desire. Not so I'd have to lie. I pushed away, panting, forcing myself down from the high. Nothing I could say would be right. Nothing I could say would be truth. Truth was I wanted him. Truth was Asher had been depressed and distant for so long I'd forgotten how it felt to be wanted like this. I ran my tongue over my dry lips. Zack reached up, trailing a finger along my mouth. I took his hand and pressed it to my cheek.

"I didn't mean this to happen," I said.

"I know."

"Do you?"

"I didn't think we'd make love, but I was seriously hoping." He smiled, his black lashes dewy with moisture, sweat glistening on his forehead. "You're a helluva good kisser, Sarah Rose." He didn't know the half of it.

"You're not bad yourself." Smiles. Friends. "Thanks for understanding."

"If you ever change your mind . . ."

"You're first on my list."

My car was still in front of the hotel, untowed, unticketed, hubcaps intact. The gods must be pleased. At least I'd made someone happy.

The digital panel on my answering machine logged in one call at seven-o-four P.M. I was tempted not to take it. Didn't feel like talking to Asher just now. I was angry with him for being so far away when I wanted him here. Why was he out having a good time without me? It was his fault I'd gone to Zack's instead of home to an empty house. His fault I'd even *thought* about what I'd thought about doing. I pushed the message button.

"Mrs. Rose, this is Mrs. Fisher from the Wedgewood Home. Sorry to trouble you, dear. But . . . is your mother with you?"

The trick was to walk without my eyeball falling out. I could tell by the throbbing that the little punk's right hook had rearranged my face. My clothes hung on me, wet and filthy from mopping up the streets. The Good Thing was I didn't have to fight crowds on the Tube back to the Savoy. People took one look at me and backed away.

The floor valet brought an ice pack and double scotch and took my clothes to be cleaned. Or burned. I sat staring into the bathroom mirror while the tub filled. The red skin around my eye was already puffing up. The lid would be welded shut in the morning.

"You're one ugly mug," I said, toasting myself in the mirror. "Not that you were all that great to begin with." I took a swig of scotch and pressed the icy glass against the bruise. "What are you smiling about? Pretty damned proud of yourself, aren't you? Punching out a bunch of street thugs." I touched the puffy skin with my fingertips. "Ouch!"

Thirty years since I'd had an eye like that. I'd just invested in an industrial scale and found out a spice supplier I thought was my friend was shorting my order. Went to his place steamed as hell and we got into it. I left with an eye every bit as red as this one. Three days later he walked into Rosie's, his eye turning as black, blue, and yellow as mine. Said he checked around and found one of his drivers skimming goods off his trucks. He apologized, I apologized, and we went to the Black Angus for steaks. "Bring four," he told the waitress. "Need a couple of raw ones for our eyes." Ah, the good old days. Used to have fun.

It wasn't until I'd soaked in the tub a while, head back, scotch working, ice pack hurting like hell, that the terror of what happened out on that dark street hit me. I could have been killed. Just like that. Done. Finished. That's all she wrote. What if those punks hadn't been slowed down by booze? What if I hadn't bought that umbrella? What if they'd attacked me when I was three or four blocks away from the Tube instead of a few steps from the entrance? I could have been killed.

As much as Paul's death had ripped me open, torn me apart,

left me raw, it was still death one step removed. This time the old grim reaper came stomping across my field. I could have been fucking killed.

Sarah. I had to talk to Sarah. Needed to hear her voice. I had to tell her I loved her. What if I'd died without doing that? I called our house. No answer. The production office number. Where the hell'd I put it? I shuffled through the pile of papers the valet had removed from my suit jacket—Thames tour information, maps, sales receipts from my shopping spree, the Taggart & Rowe card with Vanessa's number—and found the pocket phone book Sarah had made for me. An answering machine clicked on at the film's production office.

"Doesn't anyone answer phones anymore?" I slammed down the receiver and thumbed through the phone book. Sarah had written down addresses and phone numbers for Byrd, Herb, my brothers and sisters. Martha, I'd call Martha.

"Kanter, Roberts, Wein and Rose," said the receptionist.

"Martha Rose, please. This is her brother calling."

"I believe she's in conference, Mr. Rose. Could she call you back?"

"I'm calling from London."

"Oh, one moment please."

"Asher? That you?"

"In the flesh. Sorry to get you out of your conference."

"What conference? I'm hiding from our family."

"What's the matter?"

"Ah, that's right, Sarah was trying to spare you this. Our little brother was fired."

"What are you talking about? You and I drafted a contract."

"Only applies if Norman shows up for work."

"Where is he?"

"Holing up at home."

"Have you talked to him?"

"He won't take my calls. Tina's running interference for him, says he's too sick to come to the phone."

"Has he seen a doctor?"

"That would be too logical."

"You've got to do something."

"Norman is a big boy, Asher."

"Come on, Martha. I can't do anything from here. Just help out until I get home."

"Me and my big mouth. I should never have told you. How's by you?"

"You're changing the subject."

"You always were sharp. All right, I'll see what I can do, try to buy Norm a grace period at Rosie's until he shapes up. Ooops, gotta go. Client just walked in. Everything all right with you?"

"Terrific." I pressed the ice pack to my eye.

"Great. Talk to you soon."

Why did I call? What made me think I'd feel better if I talked to someone back home? Couldn't they take care of themselves? Did I always have to come to their rescue? Would it have been too much for Martha to fix things up for Norman? All the aggravation I'd been trying to get rid of moved back on me.

Nothing on the room service menu appealed to me. Better eat something. Hadn't eaten since those scones in the morning. Was that only this morning? This felt like one of the longest days of my life. I ordered up dinner. Another meal in my room.

You don't have to eat alone.

It would be nice having someone to talk to. I picked up the Taggart & Rowe card. It didn't have to mean anything besides dinner.

And what if it did?

I turned the card over and over in my hand. *Ishmael.* Sarah probably knew the play.

What's this got to do with Sarah?

She saw every piece of theater that came to Chicago. A hot ticket item like *Ishmael* probably cost someone like Vanessa a week's wages.

You'd be doing a good deed.

The money was nothing to me and it would be a treat for her.

Call her.

I put on my clothes—my eye throbbing with every move—and went down to the lobby.

"I need two tickets to *Ishmael*, Saturday night's performance." The concierge looked up at me like I'd dropped in from outer space. My mangled eye might have had something to do with it.

"I'm sorry, sir. That's impossible."

Nothing's impossible.

Go away, Paul. I can handle this. I peeled off twenty pounds and set it on the counter. The man didn't move.

Yo, Asher. The last of the big spenders.

Yeah, well my business didn't go under fifty different times.
You want tickets to this play, or what?

"There's another twenty on top of that if you get me the tickets." The bills disappeared off his counter.

"Very good, sir, I'll see what I can do."

I walked slowly back to my room, concentrating on keeping my head as still as possible. The phone was ringing as I walked in the door.

"Asher, I can't believe I've finally reached you."

"Hi, Sarah. I know. I've been trying to reach you, too."

"We've been working long hours."

I stretched out on the bed, pressing the ice pack on my face. "I called home, the production office—"

"I didn't get any messages."

"Didn't leave any. Got pissed at all those damned machines. Why don't you check into one of those answering services? At least I'd hear a human voice."

"When I have time. How're you doing?"

"Well, right now I've got an ice pack on my eye."

"What happened?"

"Got mugged coming out of the Tube."

"Mugged? Are you all right?"

"I look worse than I feel."

"Did you see a doctor?"

"I'm all right."

"Do me a favor, take taxis from now on."

"Yes, Mommy. How's the movie going?"

"Pretty good."

"You sound down."

"Just a lot of things on my mind."

"Like?"

"Maxi's called a few times. The counseling's not going well. I asked her to try another counselor before she gives up. Maybe, when you're out, you can look for a little something to cheer her up. A bracelet or something."

"You know I'm lousy at gifts. Why don't you get something?"

Sarah laughed. "When? I barely have time to go to the bathroom. It doesn't have to be anything special. Just to let her know you're thinking about her."

Feeling a little sick to my stomach. Too sick to go shopping.

The way I looked, I wouldn't go out for a few days. Stay in my room and read some of the books I'd brought.

"I talked to Martha a little while ago. She told me about Norm being fired."

"Damn."

"He's my brother, Sarah. I should know what's going on."

"Sorry. I didn't want to worry you."

"Anything else I should know about?"

"How depressed do you want to get?"

"That bad?"

"Fanny's been going AWOL from the Wedgewood. She won't tell me where she goes and I don't know what to do about it."

"Poor baby. You'll work it out. Talk to me. Tell me what's going on in your life."

"I'm putting in sixteen-hour days, fourteen of them spent waiting on set. This isn't the glamour industry everyone thinks it is."

"Then quit and come join me."

"Don't tempt me. Actually, it's a good thing you're in London. I'm never home. At least you're having fun while I'm working."

Didn't feel like fun to me. We talked for a while but I felt her mind was somewhere else. It was almost a relief when we finally hung up.

The phone rang immediately.

"Mr. Rose? This is the concierge. I was able to arrange for two tickets to *Ishmael,* quite good seats, for Saturday night's performance."

"I knew you could do it."

"Not without great difficulty, I assure you. But it was my pleasure. I'll hold them at the desk for you." What the hell, I'd tip him fifty.

I stared at Vanessa's card a long time before dialing. What's the worst that can happen? She answered on the second ring.

"Yes?"

"Vanessa?"

"No. Hold on." The phone banged down. Hang up, Asher. Hang up now while you still can.

Don't you dare.

Put the phone down. Now.

Don't be a wuss.

"Hello?" she said.

Now! "Vanessa?"

"Yes?"

"This is Asher Rose calling." Too late. Now I've done it.

"Why, hello, Mr. Rose." She sounded happy to hear from me. *Told you.*

"Wait, let me turn off the telly. There, now. How was your boat ride?"

She did most of the talking. A lot more fun than my conversation with Sarah. She laughed, told stories. Later I couldn't remember all the things we talked about. Except, when I invited her, she said, "Oh! I can hardly— How did you— Tickets are impossible for— Oh. *Ishmael.* I can't *believe* it. That would be lovely. Absolutely lovely."

Absolutely.

~·~ 54 ~·~·~·~·~·~·~·~·~·~

Fanny parked us in two wingback chairs facing the lobby aquarium so we could stare at something besides each other. She glued her eyes to a darting fish with a neon blue racing stripe down its side.

"Mom, you can't just walk out of here without telling anyone."

"What am I, a prisoner?"

Bubbles drifted up from a thin air hose, making small blip-blipping sounds as they broke the surface. Two angelfish swam back and forth with a hypnotic fanning of fins.

"There are rules here."

"They are not my rules."

A deep-sea diver bobbed along the aquarium floor, the victim of invisible currents that swept him past pearl-filled oysters and chests overflowing with treasure. Most visitors to the Wedgewood came during the day or on weekends. Only families of the seriously ill or terminally naughty visited seven-thirty mid-week.

"Would it kill you to sign out?"

"Yes."

I ran a thumb around my fingernails, rolling pieces of dead skin into tight coils, tearing them away until I bled. Ah the glamour of nonstop sewing, pinning, mending, washing, bleaching, dying, ironing, steaming. This wasn't fair. There were six Rose children who didn't have a parent to care for, and only one of me to take care of Fanny. Maybe I could adopt a couple of Roses to help me out. Forget Mookey, Norm, Freyla, and Pearl. Fanny hated them. Only two good Roses in the bunch. Martha was too busy playing Perry Mason, and I'd sent Asher away.

"Where do you go, Mom?"

"Out." What do you do? Nothing.

"Will you stop?"

"I'll stop when I leave this place."

Two nurses padded through the lobby on crepe-soled feet, their cheery voices coming and going, dropping us into a deeper silence. Fanny and I studied the fish, hoping for solutions. Upstairs, other residents prepared for bed. Seven-thirty at night. This alien world wound down about the time Fanny geared up. Another nurse came through and flicked off the overheads, casting us in the soft glow of three table lamps. If I closed my eyes and concentrated real hard I could pretend I was in someone's living room. Unfortunately, it was no one I liked. The furniture was too formal, the smells too sterile. This was not my mother's home. How could I ask her to stay? What other option did I have?

"My roommate snores. And when she's not snoring, she's clopping back and forth to the bathroom. That woman has enough gas to heat Cincinnati."

"I have your name on a waiting list for a private room." Next-in-line cost me another couple of thousand. There was no other way to rush the process unless I bumped off a private-room resident. The thought had occurred. I reached over and took her hand.

"Your skin's dry. I'll bring lotion next time."

"Lotion won't help anything. The water from my shower is acid rain."

"Acid rain?"

"On Tuesday," she sniffed, shrugging her shoulders up straighter, "we get current events. I know from acid rain. I also know they're chopping the rain forests into toothpicks, and that we're all going to cook to death from the greenroom effect."

"Greenhouse."

"Whatever." The fish slowed with the dimming of the lights. Fanny flicked a finger against the glass to stir things up a bit. "And the food here," she said to the darting blue neon, "the food tastes like Aunt Leah's old stockings. Creamed this, mashed that. If you can't gum it, they don't serve it."

"My first break, I promise I'll come and take you to Fluky's for a hot dog with the works and fries. Meanwhile, would you like me to see about getting you a new roommate?"

"Forget the roommate. I'm well enough to go to my own apartment and lead my own life."

"You're well enough because the Wedgewood feeds you three squares a day, and gives you your medicine on time, and keeps tabs on your health. That's why you're well."

"I can be well at home."

"Not unless you let me find a companion to live with you."

"No."

"Mom, even if you came to live with me, you'd need someone. I can't stay home and take care of you."

"Am I asking?"

She didn't have to. I accepted guilt, needed guilt, welcomed guilt. What kind of daughter lived her own life at the expense of her mother's happiness? After my father died, Fanny raised me, sacrificing who knows what? She dragged me everywhere, included me in her world as much as possible. How could I not stop my life for her? Sure I slowed it down here and there, shuffled up a few things. Like work, like my marriage. But it wasn't nearly as much as I might have done. The very least I could do was feel guilty.

It didn't look like the fish planned to do anything amazing. A few circles, a few dives, a few quick passes to knock over the deep-sea diver. He always lands on his feet, Ladies and Gentlemen. How about a big hand? Fanny stood. My audience was over. I walked her to the elevators.

"How is Asher?" she asked. The old twist-of-the-knife encore.

"Fine. Asher's fine. He sends his love."

"You sure there's nothing wrong between you two?"

"No, Ma. He just needed to get away for a while."

"I still don't understand why he went away without you."

Because he was too sick to stay and you were too sick for me to leave. And now I'm involved in other things.

"As soon as this movie's over, I'll meet him in Europe."

"You don't leave a man like Asher alone."

"You left Daddy when you went on the road."

"Those were different times. Besides, your father was not Asher and you are not me."

"What does that mean?"

"It means what it means." The elevator came and Fanny went.

Seven-forty and not a creature was stirring in the Wedgewood lobby. I signed out on the visitor ledger wondering if Fanny was upstairs preparing for bed or plotting another Great Escape. Couldn't help smiling. When in her life had Fanny Feldman done anything anyone expected? Why should she change with age?

"Mrs. Rose?" Uh-oh. The chief honcho, eyeglasses dangling from a chain around her neck, every dyed black hair lacquered solidly in place, stood in the office doorway.

"Yes, Mrs. Lipshultz. How nice to see you."

"You have not returned my calls."

"I'm so sorry. My work schedule is hectic right now. What can I do for you?" As if I didn't know.

"We called you three different times, trying to locate your mother. We can't possibly assume responsibility for this type of behavior."

"I've just had a long talk with—"

"Can you imagine what would happen if all our residents walked out without telling anyone? There are reasons for rules. . . ."

Her Clara-Bowed mouth opened and closed and I was suddenly seven years old standing in front of the school principal whose mouth yacked at me that same way because I'd fallen asleep in class. Again. I never squealed on Fanny, never told the principal my mother kept me out until two in the morning drinking Russian coffee at the Royal Cafe, or that I sat in the lap of *the* Dina Halpern while the cast of *The Little Foxes* celebrated a fabulous opening night. How could a woman with chalk dust for blood understand a mother like Fanny? Even at that tender age, I understood my future would be a variation on the theme of US against THEM, my lifeline strung with sour-faced administrators complaining to me about my mother. I chose sides early, never giving it a second thought. I stared into Lipshultz's mouth. Had I now abandoned Fanny to the enemy?

". . . and it could be dangerous for some of our people with Alzheimer's, or short-term memory loss, or serious medical needs, to go gallivanting off. Your mother is setting a bad example."

"Don't you pay the nurses on the floor to watch who comes and goes?"

"Your mother is an extremely inventive woman." Tell me about it. "She doesn't pass the nurses' station, nor does she go through the reception area in the lobby. We haven't quite figured out how she does it."

"Maybe she knots sheets together and lowers herself from the fourth-floor window."

Mrs. Lipshultz failed to see the humor. "If this continues, you may need to arrange a private nurse for her."

"What a wonderful idea," I said. "I bet she'd just love that. Why don't you suggest it to her?" Then duck real fast.

I pulled my coat around me, bracing for the biting winter wind. It didn't surprise me that Fanny walked out of the Wedgewood from time to time. Worried me, yes, but didn't surprise me. What did surprise me was that she walked back in. I didn't know if I would.

~·~· **55** ·~·~·~·~·~·~·~·~·~·~·~·~

By Saturday my eye looked like someone had melted purple and yellow crayons around it. The pain wasn't bad as long as I didn't make any sudden moves. Public transportation would have to get along without me. I had the concierge, my new best buddy, arrange for a limousine. That morning I went shopping for a gift for Maxi.

"This makes quite a special gift, sir," said the jeweler, laying a thin strand of diamonds on a strip of black velvet.

"Do young women wear these?"

"Oh, indeed. A number of gentlemen buy these as tokens of friendship. Tennis bracelets, I believe the Americans call them. Quite popular."

While he wrote up the sale, I made out a card telling Maxi I loved her and thought about her and hoped she liked the bracelet. Sarah was the gift buyer in our home. I felt awkward trying to figure out what people would like. It was easier for me to send the kids checks for special occasions. Jeff always mailed his back, as if taking a few dollars from me meant he couldn't make it on his own. Why did he deny me the pleasure of helping him out a little? I would have been thrilled if my father had given me anything. Jeff kept the funny little things Sarah sent: toy cars, joke books, wild ties. I'd given up trying.

I looked through the cases for something to buy Sarah. It would be so easy to shop for her if she wore diamonds. "Serious jewelry bores me," she said. "Give me pieces that light up or move or make sounds." A dazzling opal necklace on black velvet seemed to drink in the room's light and hold it inside. Thirty-five thousand. Another fifteen for the earrings. Magnificent. I turned my back on it. All my millions weren't going to transform my ragtag flea market maven into Zelda Got Rocks. Vanessa was the type to wear serious jewelry. I bet she would appreciate a little gift.

On impulse, I had the jeweler wrap a second bracelet.

"I'll take this with me," I said, slipping it into my pocket. The bracelet made me edgy the rest of the day.

Because buying it was spontaneous.

There's no way I'm giving it to Vanessa. I hardly know her. I should have thought this through.

Takes away all the fun.

When would I give her a thing like that?

How about when the Cubs win the World Series? Or maybe the next solar eclipse?

I'll bring it home to Sarah.

Diamonds?

I know. I know.

I kept the bracelet in my pocket that night as we drove through a steady rain to Vanessa's apartment building. Not that I intended to give it to her. How could I? But it excited me to carry it, like putting a condom in my wallet in junior high. I never took that out, either.

She waved from an upstairs window as we pulled up, motioning that she'd come down. I waited, watching as she stepped out onto the stoop, stopping briefly at the top of the stairs, closing her coat against the cold. The driver ran up with an umbrella, and as they walked down, I pretended they were a couple I didn't know. No doubt about it, I envied him his good luck.

Vanessa climbed into the back seat, pouring life into the car.

"Oh, look, champagne."

"I thought getting tickets for *Ishmael* called for a celebration."

"Your poor eye," she said, delicately touching the multicolored bruise.

"I should have worn an eye patch, to spare you having to look at this."

"I think it's quite dashing, actually. Gives you a certain air of danger." She pulled the bottle out of the cooler and I reached to help.

"No, treat's on me," she said, tearing off the foil. "You should have seen my sister when you pulled up. Thought she'd have an absolute cow. I said to her . . ." I sat back, listening, watching her slender fingers untwist the wires around the cork.

A classic beauty, this one, elegant, exciting, the kind that scared me silly my whole life. I'd stayed with the safe ones, warm friendly girls with spunk and personality who seemed to notice I was alive, and to care. I never went near the knockouts who'd walk stiletto-heeled over guys like me to get to the captain of the football/basketball/swim team. In high school I fantasized finding an ice princess who would see through my ordinary exterior into the terrific person inside. It never happened.

The champagne cork exploded against the ceiling and Vanessa caught the bubbling foam in a glass.

"You look beautiful," I said.

"Thanks." She poured our drinks, then settled back onto the seat, resting her hand on mine like it was the most natural thing in the world. "Do you like my coat?" She smoothed the dated fur. On her, a potato sack would look good.

"It's very nice."

"Borrowed it from my sister. Had to promise to guard it with my life." I forgot Vanessa was connected to other people. That she didn't begin to exist the day I walked into Taggart & Rowe. "Elva's the pretty one. A raving beauty, actually, *and* the brains in the family. Got more than her share if you ask me. Now, my brother . . ."

She launched into her family history, stories about this one, secrets about that one. So maybe I wasn't the only person with weird brothers and sisters. Tart as young wine, Vanessa spoke with the absolute authority of youth. I remembered how it was to have all the answers, to be so sure of myself. Where did that go? When did the sharp blacks and whites muddy into gray?

Moriarty's coat-check girl helped me off with my overcoat while I unwrapped Vanessa. The red miniskirted knit dress under her fur coat was so tight—how tight was it?—I could count nipple hairs. The girl took Vanessa's fur from my hands, which was just as well since I seemed to have gone into shock. Vanessa slipped her arm through mine and we followed the maître d' through the restaurant to the intimate back booths. Heads turned as we passed and I recognized the look in the men's eyes. Lust for her, envy for me. What, they wondered, did I have that they didn't? How did someone like me land someone like her? It was a kick to be on the receiving end of that look for a change.

Vanessa was one sexy lady. Not that Sarah wasn't beautiful, not that at all.

Why are you thinking about Sarah?

But Sarah's beauty was quiet. More gentle. Subtle.

Get back on track, here, Asher.

I began to get the idea that the only subtle thing about Vanessa was her Taggart & Rowe clerk's suit, and she'd left that at home. The maître d' pulled out our table and we slid into the tufted curved booth, settling in knee to knee.

Every detail delighted her: the floral china, the tiny orchid in a miniature cut glass vase, the artistic way the chef curled the butter, the wine steward hovering. She was like a little wind-up doll talking nonstop, gushing over the restaurant, gossiping about friends, family, work.

"Not that I didn't like working at the boutique—oh, yes, just a drop more, thanks—but the male clientele were a bit free with their hands, if you know what I mean. So when my uncle, he's a cutter, said there was an opening at Taggart & Rowe I thought why not give it a try? I knotted up my hair, bought a positively boring suit and blouse, and went for an interview. Just been there two months, now. A bit staid for my taste, but the pay's good and—oh, whatever are these little things? Mmm, delicious—I'm working 'round a much better class of customer. That's what bent my boyfriend's nose right out of joint. He said I was getting fancy, putting on airs. I say there's no harm in a person bettering herself and that maybe he should try. . . ."

The waiter brought menus and Vanessa asked me endless questions. Why had I been so worried about what we would talk about? She was a nonstop talker and, the one time she asked my input about what to order, I knew all the answers. Food was my arena. I helped her make a selection.

"I can't believe how I've been going on about myself," she said as the waiter brought our appetizers. "I hardly know a thing about you."

"Like what?"

"Everything."

In the intimacy of the booth, in the safety of her approval, I dusted off stories I hadn't told in years, funny stories about experimental ingredients in my early soups—"*The* Rosie's Soups? But of course I've heard of them"—poignant stories about leading my mother through panic attacks, stories that snaked through the entrée, salad, desert, coffee and after-dinner drinks, stories that made her laugh and cry and, most important of all, made her see me as more than just another of the wealthy middle-aged men she dealt with at work every day.

Vanessa laughed at all the right places, made all the right sounds. She reminded me of the fresh young girls at Rosie's, that endless crop of new employees who tiptoed around me because I was the boss. It never took long to win them over. I'd sit with them at lunch, telling stories, polishing anecdotes, honing my timing. Until last year. Until the tiredness and palpitations and sudden sweats came to call. It took energy to make people laugh. You had to care enough to want people to like you. I folded up my act and stored it away. Vanessa made me remember a little of how it used to be, how I used to be. Pretty funny guy, when I wanted to be. It felt good to haul a few old pieces out of mothballs, play to a new audience.

"We'd better go soon," she said. "Don't want to miss the overture."

"Let's not. Let's stay and talk."

She laughed and gathered her things. Sarah would have known I wasn't kidding. I'd slept through every musical she dragged me to. The more expensive the production, the deeper I went under. On the old Boredom Chart of Life, I'd take a cricket match or international chess tournament over a musical any day of the week.

The heat in the crowded theater mixed with the darkness and the bottle of wine we'd finished over dinner. Couldn't keep my eyes open. Lord, keep me from snoring. Every time I jerked awake, I forced my eyes wide, trying to keep from going under again. No use. Even the gut-tightening excitement of Vanessa's shoulder resting against mine couldn't keep me awake. Vanessa must have noticed. She'd have to be dead not to. In the second act, I woke up with my head on her shoulder. She never said a word. A lady.

After the play, long lines crammed the popular post-theater spots, occasionally trailing outside and down the block. How could I have forgotten to make an after-theater reservation? That was the sort of arrangement Sarah always took care of.

"I'd invite you up to my flat," said Vanessa, "but Elva's having friends over."

"Then we'll go to my place."

I had meant the Savoy. I had meant the lounge area, where we could sit with coffee and desert and talk about the play and life and the idea I'd been toying with of going over to France for a week while I waited for my first fitting. I had meant a friendly end to a friendly evening. Hadn't I?

Why, then, when Vanessa walked straight to the elevators didn't I steer her to the lounge. And why, then, did I follow her into the elevator, up to my floor, into my suite? And why, then, did I let her call room service and order an assortment of food that could feed a medium-size army? And why, then, when the tray came and the valet went and Vanessa said "My, you look a bit weary, why don't you put on that handsome Savoy robe while I fix you a plate?" didn't I say "Oh, no, really, I'm comfortable."

By the time I went to the bathroom and changed, she'd created an intimate setting around the fireplace. Vanessa sat, shoes kicked off, long legs curled up under, the hem of her miniskirt hovering around the promised land. I settled onto the sofa next to her. Could she hear my heart pounding? She lifted the plate she'd prepared, picking up a thin apple slice, laying on a piece of cheese, feeding it to me, taking one for herself.

The jewelry box, which had burned a hole in my coat pocket all evening, the one with the bracelet I was not going to give to Vanessa, now burned a hole in my robe pocket. When do I do it? If I give the bracelet to her now, will it look like I'm trying to buy her? But I bought the bracelet this morning, before I knew she'd be here in my room feeding me apples.

Give it to her, Asher.

When I leave London. As a good-bye present.

Now, Asher. Be a romantic once in your life.

But then, if we, if we—

Share a meaningful moment? Make love? Do the F word?

How will I know it was because of me and not the bracelet?

What difference?

All the difference. I want her to want me.

Why? So you can believe you're attractive to her, that your stories delight her, that she's never met anyone like you before?

I wouldn't mind.

C'mon, Asher. Everyone wants to be loved. It's overrated.

Not by me.

You think if you were some poor schmuck in a cold-water flat this chippy would be feeding you apple slices on a Saturday night?

Go away, Paul.

Give her the damned bracelet.

"And I adored the part where Ishmael swung from the mast ropes." She hummed a tune I'd never heard, sung during a scene I never saw. "Makes me cry every time. I've just about worn through the song on my tape." Note: buy Vanessa a new *Ishmael* tape. Maybe an entire series of musicals.

Now, Asher, give it to her now.

I slid my hand into my robe pocket.

"You know what I'm going to do?" she asked, setting her wineglass on the table, taking my plate from me.

"Wh-at are you going to do?" She unfolded from the sofa and held out her hands. I left the box in my pocket, took her hands, and stood up. She led me to the bed.

This is the big one, Ash, baby. Go for it.

I couldn't. Had to stop this. Sarah's fault this was happening. "Just a little time off," she'd said. "After all these years, it's not going to hurt."

Sarah sowed her oats when she was eighteen. When you gonna sow yours, Ash? Time's running out.

Vanessa's hand was small and warm. I'd never held a hand so fragile.

"As a reward for taking me to the best restaurant and the best play of my entire life, I am going to give you the best foot rub you've ever had." Thank God. Just a foot rub. See, Paul, not what you thought at all. "You lie facedown on the bed and I'll get the lotion."

Do I lie down on top of the spread or pull it back? And what if I get a hard-on? And what if I don't? I'd worked at it off and on since I arrived in London, halfheartedly at first, then a little more, finally reaching orgasm the night I met Vanessa, and nearly every night since. Rehearsals were going great. But was I up for a performance? And was this opening night? I pulled back the bedspread and slid facedown onto the sheets.

"Ah!" The sudden touch of her hands on my feet startled me. She laughed.

"Sorry. Wanted to relax you, not send you through the roof. Now I want you to close your eyes and enjoy."

Her hands cool on my feet, her thumbs pressing hard against the insteps, her fingers rubbing circles along each toe, tugging them gently. No need to be tense. Nothing wrong with my feet. High arch, good toes. Damned sexy feet. I was, in fact, terrific from the back. Walking miles every day at Rosie's firmed my ass and steeled my leg muscles. Wish it helped my stomach. I wasn't fat, not yet, not sloppy fat like Mookey, not as soft as Norm. But if I didn't do something soon, I'd wind up like the old men in the steam baths, their great guts hanging over stick-thin legs, little mushroom tops resting on sagging balls. Why hadn't I started shaping up before? Why didn't I work out, do sit-ups, keep firm and fit just in case of an emergency like this?

"Feel good?"

"Mmmmmmm. Where'd you learn this?"

"My boyfriend, *ex*-boyfriend, is a physical therapist in hospital. He says we have dozens of nerve ends in the feet. Relaxing them soothes the entire body."

So this was just a foot rub, after all. A thank-you for a lovely evening. I relaxed. Nothing sexual going on here. All in my mind. I'd listened to too many of Paul's stories. She added lotion to her hands, rubbing it into my heels, up into the ankle. And the ankle bone's connected to the leg bone, and the leg bone's connected to the calf bone, and the . . . phone. Vanessa lifted the receiver and handed it to me.

"I was hoping you'd be out on a Saturday night," said Sarah, her voice warm and sexy. "You still recovering from your mugging?" Vanessa went to the bathroom and came back, rolling me onto my back, laying a cool compress over my eyes.

"Better every minute."

"What are you up to?"

"Well, I went to dinner, then I saw *Ishmael*."

"Did you give him my regards?"

"He sends his love."

"I can't wait to see it. I've already memorized the score. Was it fabulous?"

"A whale of a show."

"Groan."

"The parts I didn't sleep through seemed all right."

She laughed. "And what are you doing now?"

"Right now?" I cleared my throat. She'd know a lie. "I am being massaged by a beautiful, young woman." The old frontal defense. I tried to decipher the transatlantic pause. Vanessa walked to the bathroom and closed the door. Probably wanted to give me privacy. Had she been with husbands before?

"Cute, Asher. Be sure to practice safe sex." I couldn't tell if Sarah believed me or not. No point pressing the issue. And where did I put Sarah's gag gift of Trojans? And was it a gag gift?

"How's by you?" I asked.

"I'm worried about Fanny." This was not a moment I wanted to think about my mother-in-law.

"What now?"

"She doesn't want to stay at the Wedgewood."

Jolt of head pain. "You have to leave Fanny there, at least for a while. She's got to get her strength back."

"You sound angry."

"I don't understand you. After all you went through with Fanny in her apartment, trying to find help, running her errands, cooking her meals, how can you even think about taking her out of the home?" I pressed the compress against my eyes. The bathroom door clicked open. Vanessa padded across the floor, slid her hands under my feet and moved my legs apart. More lotion, more rubbing.

"I know, Asher, I know. But you should see how much she hates it there. Maybe I could find another place." Up the foot to the ankle, up the ankle to the calf.

"Sarah, it's going to be the same thing no matter where you put her."

"Maybe if I find the right nurse. Or a companion."

"I can't believe I'm hearing this." The bed shifted and squeaked as Vanessa climbed up between my legs. The better to reach your thighs, my dear. She brushed against my legs. No clothes. The woman had no clothes on. Sweet Jesus. Half of me wanted to take the compress off my eyes and half of me didn't dare.

"You should hear her, Asher. She calls me on the phone, crying."

"Then don't"—my voice cracked—"don't answer the phone."

"Easy for you to say."

"Why are you even *thinking* about taking Fanny out?" Stockings. I felt the silky rub of stockings. Not totally naked.

"The way she—"

"Sarah, do what you want. You're going to anyway."

"You don't have to yell at me." Oh, yes I do. I need to be very, very angry at you right now. "Try to understand—"

"I'll call you tomorrow. I'm busy now."

Vanessa took the phone and dropped it in the cradle. She found a soft music station on the bedside radio, then undid the sash to my robe and unwrapped me. When I reached for her, she took my hands and put them back at my sides.

"You relax," she said. "This is my treat."

Lordy, lordy, all those years I'd fantasized this seduction scene. But I was always the seducer, arranging the right moment, music, lighting. I'd remove the woman's clothes slowly, bit by bit. Sometimes. Sometimes we flew at each other, wild and violent, like fighting cocks clashing in midair, ripping-tearing-yelling-screaming until we fell to the ground exhausted and mortally wounded. It never occurred to me I would be the seducee. And the times they are a changin'.

She started at my feet again, this time teasing the tip of her tongue up my body. Would I be able? The thought paralyzed me. All those married years when I flirted, playing footsies under dinner tables, pressing myself into all manner of willing women at parties, playing dueling tongues with hostesses during the thanks-for-inviting-us-we-had-a-great-evening kiss—all those years of feeling slightly naughty, like a kid playing with matches. Now, when I'm handed the goddamn torch to ignite the infidelity Olympics, have wifely dispensation so to speak, now when I'm ready and willing, I am terrified I won't be able.

Every time Vanessa did something wonderful, like every five seconds, I'd feel the fire of excitement, immediately dowsed by fear. After spending most of my sex life playing mind games to delay climax, it felt strange to have to try to arouse myself. I was so tense, even my old standby fantasies weren't working.

Then Vanessa lifted the compress off my eyes. "Now, you can play too if you like," she said, placing my hands on her breasts. I liked. And there it was. No need for fantasy, no need to worry. My body remembered what my mind forgot, and for the first time in months, I came violently, explosively, joyously.

Lying in bed later, Vanessa's head resting on my chest, I stared

at the ceiling. I'd done it. I'd joined the millions of men around the
world who wouldn't think twice about doing what I just did. And
I'd loved it. Of course I'd loved it. Why wouldn't I love it?

So why did I feel sick to my stomach? Why did my bowels
churn into painful cramps? Maybe I was brain damaged. Maybe
this strange behavior was a result of the attack, a remnant of the
beating. I drifted off, dreaming of buildings crumbling. Vanessa
woke me, ready to play. Sarah would have let me sleep.

The one disappointment, and it was at the same time small and
big, was that the Seduction of Asher—taking my marital virginity,
as it were—did not seem to be a major moment in Vanessa's life.
Somehow, I'd always thought an affair would be more.

In the morning, Vanessa ordered a huge English breakfast, not
bothering to dress before the tray arrived. I sat at the desk in my
warm-up suit, directing the waiter as if a naked young woman
weren't across the room in my bed, the sheet barely covering her
breasts. I was the only one who seemed uncomfortable.

Vanessa talked through breakfast. I hadn't noticed the high
pitch of her voice, almost annoying. She talked on and on about
people I didn't know, places I'd never heard of. I tried to feel
connected to her. Nothing. I felt nothing. No lust, no nervousness,
no intrigue. Vanessa was simply a pretty young woman who had,
for whatever reasons, decided to pass time with me in London.
Nothing wrong with that. Nothing wrong at all. Then why did my
gut feel empty?

The first palpitations began after breakfast. Vanessa came over
to sit on my lap. I wanted her to go. Now. Wanted her off my lap,
out of the room, out of my life.

"I have an appointment," I said, moving her away, standing.
She pouted. Her mouth was built to pout the way Sarah's was to
laugh. "I'll have my driver take you home."

Luckily she didn't press me for information. I don't know what
I could make up that might sound convincing. At the door, I
handed her the damned bracelet.

"Oh, Asher, this is lovely." No polite attempt to decline the
gift. "Help me put it on?" She lay the bracelet over her wrist, thin
blue veins pulsing under pale white skin. Next to her, my strong
workman's hands with their stubby fingers and coarse nails looked
as clumsy as baseball mitts. I fumbled with the clasp. Sarah had
never once asked me to help her put on anything. Helpless Female
was not one of her favorite roles. That suited me just fine. I'd had

enough of dependent women with Mom, Pearl and Freyla. For some reason, Paul loved women who didn't know a screwdriver from a wrench. When I married Sarah, her dowry included a three-tiered fully stocked toolbox.

I finally closed the clasp and Vanessa held out her arm, admiring the sparkle of diamonds. Please go. "Will I see you later?" she asked.

"I . . . I'm going away for a few days." I am? "I'll see you when I come back to Taggart & Rowe for the fitting."

"I look forward to it." Leave. Now. That's a girl.

The instant the door closed, I started shaking so violently I had to brace myself against the wall to keep from falling. It all came back. All of it. The shakes, sweats, dizziness, crying.

How did I expect to travel anywhere? Maybe I could hide out in my room and pretend to be gone. No. I was done hiding in rooms. Had to go out. It had taken too much out of me to get this far. One step forward, two steps back. I couldn't stop now or I'd slide all the way down to where I'd started, bedbound days of waiting for "Jeopardy," watching the clock until Sarah came home. Only, next time I wouldn't have the strength to claw my way back up.

I called the ticket agent before I changed my mind. When everything was in place, I called Sarah. I had no idea how she would react, except she wouldn't be happy.

". . . apologize. Didn't mean to blow up on you like that. Fanny's your mother. You have to decide what's best."

"And I didn't mean to upset you, Asher. There's just so much going on, with work, with Fanny. I don't want to think about it right now. Talk to me. Tell me what you're up to."

"I think I've had enough of London for a while. I've seen everything I wanted to. Besides, this cold is killing me."

"How about coming home?"

"What will I do at home?"

"I'll be here."

"Sarah, you leave at dawn and come back at midnight. What are you asking me to come home to?"

"Are you picking a fight again?"

"I'm going to Paris."

"Paris?"

"Yes. Tomorrow. I thought—"

"You can't. I want to show you Paris. I've always wanted to

show you Paris. That's my city. How can you think of going without me?"

"I'll get a room with a king-size bed."

"Asher, I'm serious."

"So am I. I'd much rather see Paris with you than by myself."

"Then wait for me."

"I should sit around London and let my joints rust because you can't get away just now?"

"I've waited years for you. Can't you give me a few weeks?"

"A few weeks? Is that a guarantee, Sarah? You'll meet me here in a few weeks? Your movie isn't going into extra innings? Fanny isn't going to get sick again? You aren't going to take on another job?"

"You want guarantees? Never mind. Go to Paris. If that's what you want. Go. Have a great time."

Mel paced in front of us, threading through the Styrofoam coffee cups, donut boxes and bodies littering the production office floor. Our eyes hung at half-mast. Five A.M. was not our best time. I was so furious with Asher for going to Paris without me that I hadn't fallen asleep until after three.

"Last night's fire burned the hockey rink's seating area, half the railing, and damaged the cooling system. There's no way to shoot around the burnt area and they're not even sure they can make ice anymore. I've located another rink in Napoleon, Ohio—" The chorus groaned.

"Where the hell's that?"

"We fly into Toledo. The rink's a few miles out."

"Why so far?"

"Every rink around here's being used, hockey season, skating classes. Napoleon's just built a new rink, which means this old one's available. It was the closest one we could find. Believe me, I don't like it any more than you."

"When do we leave?"

"I'll post travel plans as soon as they're finalized. I'm hoping to leave this Sunday night, start shooting Monday morning, and wrap up by Wednesday, Friday the absolute latest."

I took a swig of coffee. Thank God I hadn't talked Asher into coming home instead of going to Paris. If he flew all the way back to be with me and I went off to Ohio . . . Don't even think about it. But what would I do about Fanny? There'd be no one around in case she needed someone. No me. No Asher. She'd be safe in the Wedgewood, if she'd stay there. Maybe Martha would let me leave her name and number with the home in case of emergency.

Mel flipped the papers on his clipboard. "Zack, I need you to go there, slap some paint on the rink, get it in shape." Zack grunted. He sat across the room, straddling a chair backward, propping his head on his crossed arms. Zachary Mandan was not a morning person.

A lighting assistant sat on the floor at his feet, leaning against his leg. Cute young things attached themselves to Zack like leeches. With all this young meat, why had he come on to me? Not that I was complaining. Our little wrestling match in his apartment had jump-started my ego. It wasn't dead, exactly, just in need of a charge.

"Sarah"—Mel handed me a slip of paper—"here's a list of the scenes we'll be shooting and the name of the Detroit casting company. Give them a call, let them know how you want the extras dressed. They'll meet with you in Toledo Saturday. Check with Sandra for flight information. You know the scenes we're shooting here while you'll be gone. Any problems?"

"No, nothing my assistants can't handle."

"Good. Now, Mavis . . ." Mel and his clipboard moved down the line.

Zack smiled at me from across the room and I smiled back. He'd never know the good he'd done, making a pass at me when he did. Asher's decline this past year had been gradual. I felt him become increasingly distant, emotionally absent, sexually indifferent. Why couldn't he have broken a leg or had a heart attack—something I could see, something we could treat, instead of this insipid depression that had eaten deeply into our lives before I even knew it was there? Work helped fill some of the hurt, some of the loneliness. But work is no substitute for love.

Zack reminded me how Asher used to be. Could be again. Please, God. I wasn't sure how much longer I could shut down my emotions, put my passion and need for love into hibernation, awaiting the passing of Asher's winter. If I was honest with myself, Asher's plan to go to France was a good sign, the sign of a healthy person. Just because I picked London didn't mean he had to stay there. No one ever told the old Asher what to do.

Mel finished his briefing and we roused ourselves to start the day's shoot.

" 'Morning, Sarah." Zack, smiling and leechless, blew me a kiss on his way out of the room.

" 'Morning, Zack." Slight tummy flip. Probably the coffee.

I caught myself whistling several times during the morning, once while the cameras were rolling. Embarrassed at stopping the shoot, I pretended not to notice Zack hoist an eyebrow, smiling as if he thought my whistling might have something to do with him.

He took the chair across from mine at lunch, our feet accidentally bumping a couple or few times under the long table. Nice that he wasn't angry with me, that if we couldn't be lovers we could still be friends. Nice that I'd started using full makeup again instead of the careless slash of lipstick and flick of mascara that were all I could manage during the rough times with Fanny and Asher.

At the afternoon break I called home for messages. I thought Asher might try to call back, apologize for being so rough on me. I'd tell him I'd thought it over and France was a fine idea. We had to stop this long-distance bickering. These small cracks in our relationship, stress fractures in what was once solid steel, felt wider than the ocean between us.

The bad news was, no call from Asher. The good news was, no call from the Wedgewood, either. Evidently, Fanny-of-the-itchy-foot stayed put last night. Another message on the machine took a while to decipher. Norm's wife, Tina. That much I made out. She was crying so hysterically I couldn't understand the rest of it. I dialed, trembling, certain Asher's little brother must have died. All the Rose men died young. Why else would Tina call?

No, she said, she hadn't called about Norm. She'd called about her. *They* were coming over *again* tonight. Mookey, Pearl, Freyla. Every night, lately. Like a shivah house. She couldn't face *them* alone. *They* were beating her down. She needed an ally, someone else who had married into the Rose clan, someone in her corner to give her strength.

"I'll be there," I promised. No one should have to face Asher's brothers and sisters alone.

Zack stood over me as I finished packing up for the night. "Come to dinner with us."

"Can't." I pulled on my coat. "Family business to take care of."

"You're cockeyed," he said, sliding his hands under my collar, tugging me closer to him, undoing the top button, which I'd put into the second buttonhole. I shivered as he readjusted and rebuttoned me. Staring into my eyes, he buttoned the next button, and the next, working each one through the holes ever so slowly. Not so long ago I would have laughed at his youthful obviousness and persistence. Not now. Now I felt grateful as hell.

"See you tomorrow, Zack." His eyes held mine.

"Sure you won't come to dinner?" I nodded and sent him off with his fan club.

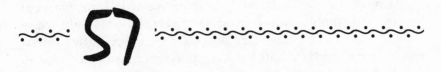

I emptied the drawers into my suitcase. Paris! A lifetime of reading about it, dreaming about it. Paris, France. Nights I couldn't sleep, I'd say it over and over—ParisFranceParisFrance-ParisFrance—an incantation against the prison of my life. Paris-FranceParisFranceParis. Shut up said Mookey, and Shut up whined Norm and ParisFranceParisFrance until I fell asleep.

I pulled open the heavy drapes. Lines of barges slogged through the rain, their mournful signals floating up and down the Thames, gray barges, gray water, gray people rushing down streets, across the bridge. I was grateful for the time I'd spent, but I couldn't take this climate, couldn't live in this perpetually gray world. I rang for the floor valet.

"Please send someone for my bags," I said, "and have my car brought around." I opened all the drawers again, checked under the bed, in the closet. This had been a great room, all in all. I felt like I'd spent a lifetime in it. In a way, I had. I'd put a few old ghosts to rest in this room. I wondered if anyone on staff would notice that a different man was leaving than the one who'd checked in.

Traffic to and from the airport crawled bumper to bumper. I

should have called Heathrow before I left, checked on my flight.
That was one of those things Sarah, with all her travel experience,
always remembered to do. Weather delays had stopped incoming
and outgoing flights. A logjam of travelers sprawled out on the
floors and aisles. It might be hours before I took off. No point
trying to buck that traffic back to the city. Might as well settle in.

I walked through the airport, looking for gifts I could buy and
send home. Nothing appealed to me. I stared into a rack of maps.
A woman passed by, her perfume sparking thoughts of Vanessa,
reminding me what I'd done. How could I be walking along like a
regular person, like I was the same man I was two days ago, like I
hadn't tossed my whole life up for grabs?

"I am a sexual animal, Sarah."

"I know."

She knew. Then why the guilt? Why the empty feeling? She
knew.

"Streets of Paris." I pulled the map off the rack. I could start at
the Arc de Triomphe, follow the streets that radiated out like wheel
spokes, a different street every day, see the Louvre, Eiffel Tower,
Montmartre, walk the Left Bank, stop in small bistros for café au
lait or vin ordinaire, rent a car, drive south to Provence.

The print blurred. Damned tears. I'd been so jealous of Sarah
living there, flying off at eighteen—"If you won't marry me, Asher
Rose, I have to find something to do with my life"—while I had to
stay and work and take care of my family. She wrote twice a week,
never caring that I rarely wrote back. She began proposing at least
once a month. I once laughed about it to Martha. She punched
me. "You are the only living creature on this planet who doesn't
know how much Sarah loves you. Although I have no idea what
she sees in you."

I refolded the map and put it back on the rack. Sarah might
still live in Paris if she hadn't come home to be Martha's maid of
honor.

"You're staring again, Asher."

"Shut up, Martha."

"Had your eyes glued to Sarah all week."

"Don't you have to go be fitted for a diaphragm or something?"

"Wish I had a cattle prod to get you going."

No need. I'd been hit by a thunderbolt. Martha was right, I
couldn't stop watching Sarah, kooky and colorful in a monotone
world. I understood as clearly as I'd understood anything before

or since that the few women in my life until then were tin, and that Sarah was solid gold. I proposed, terrified she'd turn me down. "It's about time, Asher Rose," she said. "I'd about given up on you."

I started walking around and around the airport. It was my fault Sarah hadn't been back to Paris since we married.

"Let's go in spring," she'd said. "Paris is magic in spring."

"I can't get away. We'll be hiring farm labor. Much too busy. You go."

"I'll wait." Two years later: "Fall in Paris is even better than spring."

"I can't get away then. Tomato season's our busiest. You go."

"Winter?"

"Too cold to travel and besides machinery breaks down in winter."

"Summer?"

"Too hot and besides tourists cram the cities, you can't get in anywhere."

And the times between were filled with our two children and sick parents and family crises and work problems and as many excuses as I needed to stay right where I was. Martha was right. I said I wanted to escape Rosie's but I never did. And I found a world of things beside my own fear to blame it on.

And now I was going to Paris without Sarah. First chance I got, I'd robbed her of the joy of showing me the city she loved.

It's not your fault. You offered her Paris and she turned you down. Go. Have a good time.

I checked on my flight. Paris was still fogged in. No telling when we'd take off. I walked around the airport again. The Concorde lounge was filling up. Must have a flight leaving soon. Didn't Sarah tell me, "You can always stop in to say hi on your way from Zagreb to Tanzania?" Stopping didn't have to mean staying. Paris would still be there tomorrow. And who the hell said I wasn't spontaneous?

I asked at the desk. A Concorde to New York was waiting to leave. And, yes, they had a seat available.

58

Tina yanked the door open before I got to it. She looked positively postmortem.

"They're upstairs," she whispered, her bloodshot eyes wild. She clutched at my coat and pulled me inside, quietly easing the door closed. "Mookey, Freyla, Pearl. They come every night and sit with Norm."

"Why?"

"Why?"

"Yes, Tina, why do they come every night and sit with Norm?"

"Shhhh, they'll hear you. Come into the kitchen." She clamped my arm in a death grip, cutting off circulation by the time we reached the kitchen. "I'll make us tea."

"Nothing for me, thanks."

Tina didn't hear. She had company, she'd make tea.

I sat on one of the high-backed leather stools that stood like sentries around the center island. This was not a kibitzing kitchen, no smells of cooking and baking, fresh brewed coffee or last night's dinner. This was a designer kitchen: chrome, glass, and black metal, all style and no heart.

"What's going on?" I asked.

She opened the naked refrigerator door—no Oreo magnets, family photos, shopping notes, wedding invitations—and took out cheesecloth-wrapped lemon slices and a small pitcher of milk. After all these years, she knew I took my tea straight. But she was ready in case I changed my mind.

"Tina, stop. Come sit. Talk to me."

"In a minute. Nearly done."

Her endless fussing wore me down, much as my free-fall life-style made her nervous. We tolerated each other in small doses, for the sakes of our respective husbands, who had this thing about family togetherness. Over the years Tina and I grew neither close nor far, remaining politely indifferent. I took off my coat and scarf, trying not to let her fluttering get to me. The fact that she'd picked up a phone and called me for help told me how desperate she was.

Tina's hands shook as she took two cups from the pantry,

filling them from the instant boiling water faucet on her sink. Water sloshed out, raising red welts on her white skin, but she didn't stop. She set down a basket with individual bags of herbal tea, took out two napkins, and folded them into fan shapes.

"Tina."

"Yes, yes. Sorry." She sat, neatly opening a packet of Red Zinger, forcing the tea bag down into the water with her spoon. The water turned the color of thin blood. "Norm hasn't been well."

"I've heard."

"For a long time, now. At first he missed a day's work here, a day there. Started going in later and later."

"Asher never said anything?"

She shrugged. "I . . . I didn't know what to do. Sometimes Norm showered, dressed, then stood at the front door fifteen, twenty minutes, just staring at the knob. It seemed harder and harder for him to force himself out of the house. After Asher retired, Norm gave up trying."

"Have you talked to a doctor?"

"Norm says they can't do any good. Nothing helped his mother, and nothing is going to help him. The others back him up."

"You said they come over every night."

"Y-yes."

"What do they do?"

She looked at me, wild-eyed. "Come upstairs with me. Please. I've got to bring their tray and I can't face them alone anymore."

"Their tray?"

"I'll show you. They're wearing me down. I wouldn't have called and bothered you but I swear to God I don't know what to do."

Tina opened the refrigerator and took out a platter of beautifully arranged smoked fish, herring, cream cheese, three kinds of hard cheese, smoked sturgeon, and two rows of lox labeled "with" and "without."

"Salt," she said. "Norman and Freyla like nova, Pearl and Mookey like regular."

She set the platter on the island counter and began taking assorted rolls out of a bag and cutting them in half.

"What are you doing?"

"They wanted a fish platter tonight. Last night was brisket. It's not that I mind the cooking so much, but all this carrying up and down . . ."

"Why do you bring food upstairs?"

"Norm won't leave his room at all anymore. They come every night to keep him company."

I took the knife and roll from her hands, set them on the counter and led her away.

"But . . ."

"Come with me while I go up and say hello. And then you and I are going to a movie."

"Oh, no, I can't—"

"Can and will. After which we'll have a long talk over dinner." I took her hand, flesh-coated ice, and led her through the perfectly furnished and maintained home. She stopped at the stairs, turning back toward the kitchen.

"The food—"

"Leave it."

"It will spoil."

"Let it." I pulled her along with me. "They are like cats, Tina. You keep feeding them, they'll keep coming around." We walked down the dark hall to the darker bedroom.

Deathwatch. Norm sat enthroned on the king-size bed, flanked by Mookey and Freyla, pillows plumped behind them, stocking feet up on the quilt, transfixed by the drama of a contestant buying an E. Pearl knitted on a nearby chair, working by the light of the television set. A humidifier in the corner shot a steady spray over the group. Mookey glanced up when I came to the door, then looked away, disappointed. I wasn't the food. Tina stayed in the hall, embarrassed to face guests empty-handed.

"Hey, Norm!" I flicked on the light switch and breezed into the room. "Good to see you." He squinted at me, confused, his mind still in the world of the Wheel.

"Sarah?"

"Heard you're a little under the weather. Came to visit for a while. Hi." I nodded to the others and sat at the foot of the bed, effectively cutting off their view of the set. "You're looking great, Norm." Gray skin, large black circles around the eyes, matted hair. "What seems to be the problem?"

If looks could kill I'd be quadruple-dead. In the Rose family, agoraphobia was not one of those human conditions people came right out and asked about, especially not in front of the afflicted. Freyla aimed the remote around me and hit the set's mute control.

"Epstein-Barr syndrome," she said. "He has all the symptoms. Fatigue, slight fever, chills, weakness." And I'm the tooth fairy.

"Sorry to hear," I said. "What does the doctor say to do for it?"

"He hasn't seen a doctor," said Pearl. "Much too sick to go out. Maybe when he's stronger."

"What do you hear from Asher?" Norm's voice rasped from disuse. "When will he be home?"

"Don't know. Said he was thinking of hopping over to France as long as he was in the neighborhood." They all looked mightily surprised. About the way I'd felt when Asher broke the news.

"Why France?" asked Freyla. "He doesn't speak the language."

"What did he say about us?" asked Mookey.

"Nothing." Mookey's cheeks reddened.

"Does he know what the new bosses are trying to do to us?"

"No, he doesn't."

"Haven't you at least told him about Norm?"

"No, I haven't." Martha had. None of their business what Asher did or did not know about them. What did they expect him to do from Europe? I stood, smoothing out the dent I'd made in the coverlet. "In case you hadn't noticed, Asher was a little under the weather before he left. I thought I'd let him work out his problems before heaping yours on him." Mookey rolled himself off the bed, hoisting his pants righteously.

"What do you think we've been waiting for?" he said. "All this time you were supposed to be getting Asher to do something—"

"I never said that."

"And now Norm is out of work, they won't pay him disability, they want to kick in his pension plan, which won't support him and Tina in this style very long, Freyla can't go to Florida without being shifted to part-time, which means she loses her health benefits, Pearl's forced to work on the computer—"

"Actually, I don't mind the—" Pearl stopped, thinking better of turning on her family at this particular moment.

"And they're pressuring me, making me do more than my fair share around the place, trying to make me quit."

No wonder Asher cracked. Forty years of dragging this kind of weight around would do anyone in. Poor Asher, out there struggling for his life while these children in adult bodies watched game

shows and waited to be rescued. How could I have yelled at him?
He should have whipped their sorry asses into shape years ago,
thrown them kicking and screaming into the deep end to survive
or die.

"If you're so unhappy," I said, "then maybe it's time you got
off your backsides and did something about it." I walked to the
door and flicked off the overhead. "Good seeing you all. Oh,
food's in the kitchen. I'm taking Tina to a movie and dinner. I
think she needs a night out."

Tina and I found the silliest movie we could and shared a tub
of buttered popcorn. Every now and then, I'd shudder, and Tina
would offer me her coat, scarf, gloves. But it had nothing to do
with the cold. I was picturing Norm wasting away in bed surrounded by his family. If I hadn't shipped Asher off when I did, he
would have wound up an invalid like Norm.

59

I wandered through the deserted house, through the
heaviness I'd left. No Sarah, no mad vacuumer, no cooking or
cleaning or living or loving. I'd run away to a bright new place and
left my mess behind. I owed Sarah better.

No note. No phone numbers lying around saying where she
was, no Post-It's with smiley faces. Why would there be? She didn't
expect me. Who did she have to answer to? Sarah's production
company would know where she was. I'd take a quick shower,
then go surprise her. Walk in with a dozen roses and champagne
and—

The phone rang. I was too wiped out to talk to anyone. Let the
machine take it. That's what I paid it for. A scarf lay on the kitchen
table. I picked it up, inhaling Sarah's perfume.

"Mrs. Rose. This is Leon Weintraub's daughter. Please call the
instant you get this message." I didn't recognize the name. Weintraub's daughter would have to wait.

A car squealed into the back driveway. I looked through the
curtains. Someone in a taxi. Sarah? I yanked my suitcases away
from the back door, hiding with them around the corner in the

kitchen, holding my breath. Wait till she walked in! Oh, for a camera to catch the surprise on her face.

She flew in the door and up the stairs without ever looking into the kitchen. I closed the door softly, then tiptoed upstairs, excited as a kid playing hide-and-seek. I was going to get Little Miss Sarah for making me miss Paris, grab her and pin her down and tickle her until she screamed for mercy. Been a lotta years since we'd run through the house playing tag. When did we get so stodgy? Here I come, ready or not.

I heard her moving around the bedroom and flattened myself against the hall wall, edging over to the doorway, clamping my teeth to keep from laughing. Easing my head around, I caught a glimpse of her going through her dresser drawers, tossing stuff on the bed. Unmade bed. Not like Sarah. She went into her closet and I raced across the bedroom, hiding behind the closet door. Should I jump out at her? Or go "Psst?" Or "Boo!" or— She came out and I grabbed her from behind.

"Aaaiiiiiii!!!!!" she shrieked, ramming her elbows into my ribs.

"Mumpf!!!"

"Eeeeeeeeaaaaaiiiii!!!" And kicked my shins.

"Yeowww!" I let go, shielding myself from her feet and fists.

"It's me!" I shouted. "It's me! It's me!" Laughing, moving back, trying to get away from her.

"Asher?" She backed off, gasping for air. "What the—" She hauled her arm back and whacked me. "You scared"—whacked me again—"the shit"—and again—"out of me." Then slumped onto the bed, pressing her hands against her chest. "What . . . the hell . . . are you doing here?"

"I'm sorry." I laughed. "I didn't think you'd be that scared."

"I thought it was that taxi driver." I sat next to her, taking her head in my hands, stroking her cheeks, kissing her lips. She threw her arms around my neck and kissed me back. "Why aren't you in Paris?"

"You told me to come home." I couldn't read the look on her face. But it sure wasn't Welcome Home, Asher.

"I did not. I told you to go to Paris."

"The hell you did."

"The last thing I said to you was—"

"You wanted me home. You said I should come home."

"Ohhhh." She flopped back on the bed. "My plane leaves in an hour."

"What plane?"

"Toledo, Ohio. We're going on location."

I couldn't believe it. "I just flew from London to New York to Chicago to be with you."

"I know, I know." She reached up, touching the fading colors around my eye. "Poor baby. Talk about lousy timing."

"You're not still going?" That look again.

"I have to." She rolled off the bed and opened her duffel. "I feel lousy about this. Honest I do. But our ice rink burned down and—"

"I don't want to hear."

"Come on, honey, be fair. This just came up. I thought you were in Paris."

"I would be if you didn't make me feel so damned guilty about going—"

"Yes." She threw the last of her clothes into the bag and zipped the bag shut. "Yes, all right. I wanted you to feel guilty. All those years I begged you to go to Paris with me. But, no, Rosie's needed you."

"That's right."

"Well, fine. Fine. Now my film needs me." She dragged the duffel toward the door.

"Don't go."

"What do you expect me to do?"

"Stay. I expect you to stay."

"This is my work, Asher. I hired on for this movie and I'm going to finish it out." She walked down the stairs, bumping the duffel behind her.

"Bullshit," I said, following her down. "This work is bullshit. I'm your work. Your children are your work. This house is your work." She spun around, staring at me. I might as well have slapped her. I felt her heart closing. She turned away and kept walking. I followed her into the kitchen. "I'm sorry, Sarah. That was stupid. I'm tired. I didn't mean—"

"No, you said exactly what you meant."

"Oh, shit, don't cry."

"You never took my work seriously." She went into the kitchen, dumping the contents of one purse out onto the table, throwing it all into another. Tears rolled down her face. Sarah never cried. "Maybe it's my fault. Always trying to tuck my designing around your schedule." She wiped her nose with her wrist. "You want to know how I survived when the kids were little?"

"Oh, don't start—"

"No, you listen. I never told you this because it sounds Looney Tunes. But while you worked late and the kids were in bed and I had to scrape encrusted oatmeal off high chairs, and clean the bird cage and change the goldfish bowl, and pick up Lego pieces, and Lincoln Logs, and bake brownies for the PTA. . . ." Her body shook. I'd never seen her like this.

"Come on, Sarah, don't—"

"I used to pretend there was this super-secret White Glove Squad, five stone-faced matrons in WAC uniforms and Minnie Mouse gloves who would sneak around the neighborhood at night and ring random doorbells to make surprise inspections. And I'd clean so I'd be ready for them, putting away toys, scrubbing toilets, tubs, floors, walls, dusting tops of picture frames, insides of air vents, places nobody *ever* cleaned, so when they rang our bell, I'd be ready."

"I don't know what you're talking about. I said I was sorry. I'm dragged out from traveling—"

"And I pretended they gave awards, engraved names on huge trophies for the select few who passed inspection. And that's how I stayed sane, Asher. Getting the house ready for the White Glove Squad. Because I needed what I did to matter. The way your work mattered, the way Fanny's work mattered."

"You mattered to us."

"Dust has no romance. Vacuuming no reward. I don't care how much a woman loves her house and her family, unless she has the IQ of a kumquat, housework's not enough to keep her happy once the kids are grown. I was one hell of a good housewife when I needed to be. But it was never my work. This is. And, bullshit or not, I want to find out how good I am before I'm too old to do it anymore. You had your turn, now I want mine." She lifted her bags onto her shoulders. "After all the years I gave you, you have no right doing this to me."

She banged out the back door, threw her stuff into the cab, and climbed in after it. I slammed the door open.

"When will you be back?"

"I don't know."

"Don't expect me to wait for you."

She tapped the driver on the shoulder. "Let's go," she said. The cab took off. She didn't look back.

I gripped the door, watching until I couldn't see the cab anymore. "Don't expect me to wait."

Should never have come home. Stupid, stupid, stupid. I'd go to Paris. No question. I wasn't going to wait around like some . . . like some—what? Like some man whose wife has a job? Shit. I slammed the door and locked it. No need to go right this minute. I carried my bags upstairs. Too tired to unpack. Tomorrow I'd sort out the laundry and dry cleaning, get everything cleaned while I was here. Then I'd go.

First things first. Sleep. Not in our bed. Guest bedroom. Clean sheets, no smell of Sarah on the pillow next to me. Ten, twelve hours to get my head straight. I unplugged all the upstairs phones and shut the door to the bedroom. My brothers and sisters didn't know I was home. With a little luck, I could keep it that way.

How *could* he? My rage went beyond anger into something numb and dead. I didn't remember the flight to Toledo, and barely paid attention to the car rental agent. I'd caught her in mid-manicure, coating three-inch nails with a frosty mauve to match her uniform. She handed me keys for a compact small enough to make fifty circus clowns happy. Marko had warned me Mel Pace had the cheapest money man in the industry. Where was I supposed to stash the costumes I'd be shlepping back and forth across this particular piece of Ohio?

"Have anything bigger?"

"I can upgrade you to a wagon," said the girl.

"Great. And I need directions to the MotOhio."

"Damn!" she said, smudging a thumbnail as she pulled a map out of the drawer. No easy trick to unfold Ohio with the pads of her fingers. Directions on how to get from Here to There were not her strong suit.

"I think this road goes to the MotOhio you want," she said. "One of my nephews, Stevie, no, maybe Ricky, yeah, Ricky, anyways he used to take lessons at that old rink. Might have been Stevie. Saw him skate in the *Nutcracker.*" She rolled her eyes. Guess Stevie/Ricky wasn't good, but I didn't ask. She seemed the chatty type and I was knocked out from my fight with Asher.

"The problem is"—she pointed with the dripping nail polish brush—"you got a river running all alongside this road and you need to find the closest bridge acrost it." I thanked her and left to find my car. The metal gate of the airport's only restaurant clanged shut behind me. Six P.M. The floor vibrated. Probably the sidewalks rolling up. Looked like a long night ahead.

A huge liquor store guarded the road out of town, its flashing neon sign blazing against the night sky. A drink. Of course. Why hadn't I thought of that? A goblet of wine would taste mighty fine tonight, and I sure didn't want to belly up to a motel bar. I swung into the lot, sitting in the car a few minutes, getting up the nerve to go in. I'd bought gallons of liquor in my life, for parties, home, gifts. But I'd never walked into a liquor store and plunked down cold hard cash to buy booze for myself. It wasn't something nice ladies did. Not with any honesty. Fanny's lady friends regularly restocked their supply of Sabbath wine, company schnapps, and brandy for vague ailments. I wasn't about to lie to myself. I was hurting inside beyond anything I'd ever felt before and I wanted a drink to take the edge off, pure and simple.

Pickup trucks with bumper-mounted Christmas wreaths and cars with ornaments dangling from rearview mirrors came and went around me. People called to each other, laughing. Steady, Sarah. This was one of Life's growing-ups and letting-gos that twisted the gut and sweat the palms. Ten years from now, if I remembered the moment at all, I would wonder why it had been such a big deal. Like the first time I drove a car solo, or watched Maxi walk to kindergarten alone, or let Jeff cross the street. Well, I didn't crash the car, Maxi made it to class, and Jeff wasn't killed in the crosswalk. And buying liquor for myself did not mean I was an alcoholic. Luckily, once I made up my mind about something, I never looked back. I wasn't into cleaning up spilt milk.

I selected a chilled bottle of Chardonnay to compliment a tin of pâté and a box of pretzels, a gourmet meal compared to the junk I'd been eating on location.

"Pick yourself a couple." The checkout clerk pushed a wicker Christmas basket of liquor miniatures at me. Why not? I picked out two J&Bs. Maybe a good stiff scotch would knock me out tonight. I pulled out my map, about to double-check the directions to the MotOhio, when two heavily tattooed men in dirty overalls and metal-tipped work boots shuffled into line behind me. Back went the map. No need to broadcast my destination.

Locking the car doors after me, I drove away from the city lights, dropping into the dark at the end of the Earth. I checked my rearview for headlights and took a couple of evasive twists and turns. City survival habits die hard. Didn't want to end up in a back-road car chase, a little cat-and-mouse bumper tag, some sleazebag's idea of Friday night fun.

Half an hour into what should have been a ten-minute ride, I entered a desolate landscape. Not a light, not a signpost. "Always in such a rush, Sarahlah. Always out the door and on your way." Would it have killed me to spend another two minutes at the airport, trying to find someone who could give me better directions? Thick clouds from an approaching storm shut out the moon and stars. Total darkness except for my headlights and faint remnants of Toledo's lights flickering a million miles off in the distance. If the car broke down. If I hit a deer. If I went off the road. If a tire blew. Was I really going eighty? Sweating, I eased my foot off the gas.

No one in the universe knows where I am.

Powerful fear. Deeper into the dark. Heart pounding.

No one knows where I am.

Falling into the dark. Familiar fear. From where? San Francisco. I was fifteen years old, dragged sullen and angry to spend winter vacation with Fanny's old theater friends. My host's children drove at crazy high speeds, flying over city hills, loving how it terrified me. On New Year's Eve, swigging bourbon and ginger ale, they introduced me to grass. At midnight, standing stoned in the middle of the Golden Gate Bridge, I pressed my body against the cool metal railing. Far below me, much too far, the vast expanse of black water moved thick and slow, a great primordial ooze waiting to suck me under. I felt it pulling me toward it and I'd climbed a good way up the railing before the others grabbed me back. Fear didn't come until the next day, when, crossing the bridge sober, I looked down. I curled into a tight little ball on the back seat, hugging myself until my arms ached, terrified at the end I had almost made of my life. That was the fear I was feeling now.

No one knows where I am.

Fanny, snug as a bug at the Wedgewood. Asher, sulking at

home, probably crawling back into bed for the duration, but safe and warm. It's seven o'clock, Sarah Rose. Do you know where your life is? Narrow roads ran along frozen farm tracts, twisting up and down sudden hills. The wagon's headlights punctured the black night, one beam angling up toward gnarled branches of ancient oaks, the other hitting the road three feet in front of the car. No gas stations, no diners, no churches, no place to ask directions. Occasional farmhouse lights tempted me but I couldn't get past dim memories of farmer Gaines stitching women's skins into lamp shades.

No one knows where I am. Does anybody care?

Wind whipped the tree branches. Ice and sleet pelted the car. As soon as I get to the motel—are you listening, God?—I will call the Wedgewood and give them a number where I can be reached. And I'll call Asher. Maybe. All right, all right, I promise. But I can't call if I don't make it. Right, God? Right. So you gotta help me out here.

The Good Thing about killing the opossum was that it helped me find the river. I looked away from the road for a split second to hunt for the rear window defogger, then looked back as my lights hit the startled red eyes on the ugly rat face. I yanked the wheel hard to the left, cringing at the *thunk-ka-thunk* of the body against the fender, under the tire, tangling along the chassis, thudding out from under the rear tire. The wagon skidded onto the gravel shoulder, its headlights bouncing off the ditch, glinting on something beyond. The river. The river I had to find a bridge "acrost." What was it doing over there? How did I get so turned around? Toledo on my right, river on my left. I checked the lavender nail polish dot on my map, got my bearings, and five minutes later pulled into the MotOhio. Never a doubt. What had I been so worried about?

Forty-two dollars a night rented me a ground-floor room at the MotOhio with a breathtaking view of my car. I unloaded my overnight bag and liquor, slogging through the storm toward the motel room, careful not to look at the front bumper. With any luck, the storm would wash away telltale opossum blood and fur.

The airless room reeked of overripe fruit. A gift basket on the heating unit overflowed with banana peels, orange rinds and apple cores. A barely legible note, scrawled on a McDonald's napkin, read: "I am holding the rest of the fruit hostage. Don't mess with me. I have been here two whole days and am on the edge. Ring room 105, or else! Your devoted servant."

Funny guy, this Zachary. What an Asher thing to do. I opened the door and set the basket outside. What I wanted was a hot tub, a good book, and bed. My work started at seven in the morning and could easily go to midnight. I wasn't up for Zack's relentless energy.

While the tub filled, I unpacked my duffel into the cheap wood dresser, putting a little something into every drawer. I didn't have to share. I could spread out all over the place. And I could read without worrying about my light keeping someone up, and watch TV all night if I wanted.

"This calls for a celebration," I said, opening the wine, pouring a hearty dose into the sanitized plastic cup. "To you, Sarah Rose," I toasted myself in the mottled dresser mirror. "A professional woman on her first honest-to-goodness business trip." We took a mighty swig. Ahhhh, yes. Ever so fine. I winked at me and stripped off our clothes.

I meant to linger in the tub like Cleopatra, sipping wine, thinking calm thoughts. No use. My mind churned with things I should have said to Asher, would say when I called, if I called. I know I promised, God, but I'm still a wee bit angry. I would never, ever, in a hundred thousand million years have sent him off on a trip that way. I would have planted a huge kiss on his mouth, told him to have a great time, and stood at the door waving good-bye. Didn't I send him off with his buddies to play golf? Didn't I send him off to England? And that was for fun. This was for work. How could he do this to me?

My mind shifted into all the things that needed doing, calls to make, notes for tomorrow's fittings. I chugged the wine, bathed, shampooed, conditioned, and climbed out of the tub five minutes later.

"You lack the bath personality," I said, briskly rubbing water off my body, slathering on lotion, blow-drying my hair. "You must develop the ability to lounge, the temperament to dawdle. Type A's die young."

Asher used to be the one who centered me, let me be still. He'd always been the one calm place in my universe. Without him, I revved on high. Always had. Not a healthy way to go through life. I toweled off and put on my sweats. It was still too early for the scotch. If I went to sleep at eight I'd be up with the roosters.

I shouldn't have tossed the fruit basket. Its eau de fruity decay had masked the stale odors of unclean habits which, over the years, had become imbedded in the carpet, drapes, bedspread. I'd shop for incense tomorrow. There came a scratching at my door. Some animal, no doubt, eager to come in from the cold.

"Yes?"

"The Marquis de Sade."

"I gave at the office."

Zack blew in with the blizzard, gripping a sodden grocery bag. I could barely close the door against the wind. "Think I've sprung a leak," he said, holding the dripping bag away from his body, heading for the bathroom. He trailed scents of crisp winter air and mouth-watering food. I followed.

"Mmmmmm," I said, "smells good."

"Fresh roadkill."

"Yummy. Opossum?"

"Chicken."

"Why *did* that chicken cross the road?"

He winced. "I set myself up for that, didn't I?"

"Yup."

I leaned against the door frame watching him dump a container of gravy that had split down the side. And how would it be, she wondered, to unbind his braid, working her fingers through his ebon hair until it flowed around him. He turned his head suddenly, catching me staring. We smiled. "Set the table?" he said.

"I'll polish the silver."

I covered the chipped coffee table with a pillowcase, folded a newspaper into place mats, and poured the wine. Zack set out a whole rotisserie chicken, cole slaw, pickles, rolls, and assorted plastic cutlery. He folded his long limbs down to the floor, digging into his Harpo Marx pockets for two candles, melting their bases into ashtrays. My cue to turn out the lights.

"Appetizer?" I asked, unmoving, tearing open the pretzel bag.

"Perfect."

"So, tell me about Napoleon, Ohio."

"Ah, well, to begin with, there's this wonderful old guy, Sean, in charge of the ice rink who . . ."

If you were Asher on the floor next to me, your back braced against the bed, legs straight out, crossed at sockless ankles . . .

If you were Asher next to me electric with stories about your day at work, listening and laughing at my moments . . .

If you were Asher come to be with me in this place, I would hold you with hungry eyes, ripping flesh from the chicken, wiping hot juices from my chin with the back of my hand, growling low animal growls, chewing openmouthed, making knowing laughs in the back of my throat, washing everything down with flagons of wine as I tore and chewed and growled. If you were Asher . . .

". . . half an hour, we'll go skating."

"Come again?"

"Skating. Sean's there until eleven."

"No way, Zack. I'm wiped out."

"You don't have to skate. Just come and see the rink. I have to go over for a few minutes and I'm tired of being alone." He rolled onto his knees. "Please," he said, wrapping empty bones in the comic section. "See? I'll do the dishes."

"I'm exhausted. Drained. Unable to move."

"You'll love it."

"I have tons of odds and ends to take care of for tomorrow." Please haul your beautiful self out of here before I get in trouble. I pushed him toward the door. "Go. I'll see you tomorrow."

I locked the door after him. The danger, for the moment, had passed.

Sarah should have stayed, waited while I slept off the jet lag. The world looked a whole lot brighter after ten hours' sleep. What were we fighting about? She thought I was in Paris, I'd go to Paris. No problem. Let her meet me when she finished her film. If she still wanted to. Of course she'd want to. I'll bet she was under a lot of strain at work. I'd give her a few days to think over what happened, hang around Chicago in case she changed her mind and decided to come home. That was fair. That was more than fair.

A couple of inches of snow covered the front porch. Must have started during the night. Still coming down steady. No morning newspapers. Sarah probably canceled delivery until she got back from Toledo. I opened the refrigerator, empty except for a few miniature Milky Ways and a bag of dried carrot sticks. Just the way I liked to start my day. All right, so Sarah didn't know I'd be home. But it looked like she wasn't taking such good care of herself, either. I grabbed a couple of Milky Ways and a diet Coke. That would hold me until I went out.

I emptied my suitcases on the bed and started tossing clothes in piles on the floor. First I'd take in the dry cleaning, get it ready for Paris. What about the laundry? Sarah probably canceled the cleaning girl, too. Hell, I could do laundry. A machine was a machine, right? What's the big deal?

I unpacked the carry-on filled with maps, guides, Concorde stationery. A paper fell out of the Concorde menu. I unfolded the sketch I'd made on board, plans for my wine cellar. Forgot all about it. Didn't look half-bad. Maybe, if I had to find the Good Thing about this little side trip home, it was that I could start on the cellar, measure the layout, design the shelves, figure out how many bottles I could store before I started buying wine in France.

Jeff's old room still smelled of lumber. It looked like no one had used it since I tore it apart to make a studio for Sarah. I'd been excited about building that, too. What if the wine cellar turned out to be one more thing I wanted that she didn't? One more mess I'd make for her to clean up. Didn't we always used to want the same things? Or did she just make it seem that way? I picked up my tools and went down to the basement.

Freezing. Had to get a space heater if I was going to work down here. I walked through the main room into the back area and pulled the chain on the overhead light. The naked bulb swung shadows along crumbling brick walls, stacks of boxes, piles of junk. Old plaid suitcases mildewed in corners next to pole lamps, Formica tables, vinyl chairs. My collection of old 78s warped on top of needleless record players.

Some of the boxes were marked. "Maxi high school." "Jeff's papers, '83." "Halloween costumes." "Hats." "Accessories." "Books." "Dishes." "Tax info—70–80." "Stuffed animals—Save FOREVER!!!!" "Bar glasses." "Silverware." Other boxes just had names. "Maxi." "Asher." "Mama Rose." "Fanny." "Papa Feldman." "Paul." "Mookey." "Byrd." "Norman." "Freyla." "Pearl." Names of old friends, names of people I didn't know. I started pulling boxes out from the wall and found more behind them, most unmarked, disintegrating.

How could Sarah let this happen? She always said I was the one who couldn't say no to people. This had to be years of accumulation. My brothers and sisters lived in their own homes. And Maxi. And Jeff. Why were they still storing things here? I started pulling boxes off the pile, carrying them into the front part of the basement.

First, I'd clear the area for my wine cellar so I could measure the room. I'd get graph paper, start making blueprints tonight. And I'd call everyone and tell them to come get their stuff. It was all going. All of it. If they didn't pick it up by the time I left for Paris, I'd toss it in the garbage.

It felt good to shlep, move things around, put the place in order. I set aside Maxi and Jeff's stuff to ship. The boxes with names I didn't know went in one corner, people I knew in another. A large box with Pearl's name had almost no weight to it. I cut it open and unfolded the protective blue paper. Like a blow to the gut.

"Oh, Pearly." I ran my fingers over her wedding dress. Sarah worked hours on it, she and Pearl sitting late into the night, stitching on hundreds of tiny pearls, giggling like schoolgirls. Pearl used to laugh. I'd forgotten.

I opened the yellowed newspaper clippings someone had laid on the bodice: Pearl's high school sweetheart when he was captain of the debate team, the announcement of his scholarship to Johns Hopkins, their engagement announcement, and a copy of the death notice from Vietnam. Sarah kept this all these years. How could I send it to Pearl, tear open old wounds? And who was I to throw away parts of other people's lives? I retaped the box and set it aside.

It was better not to open boxes, not to know what was inside. Let the people who owned them deal with their own pasts. I set boxes with my name near the stairs. I'd go through them tonight while I watched TV. Although, if I hadn't needed any of this stuff since God knew when, I should just toss it in the alley. Couldn't. Had to at least look.

Around noon, I started getting a hunger headache. Just a few more boxes then I'd go out, get something to eat, bring in the dry cleaning, buy graph paper. Maybe I'd have lunch at Rosie's. Be fun to see some of the old gang. And I could tell my family to come pick up their stuff. The last five boxes, marked in my handwriting, said simply "Dad's." I pushed them into the front room and cut them open.

Patterns. Arms and legs and torsos of butcher paper scribbled with names and notes and measurements penciled by my father. I traced my fingers over his crude handwriting. I'd forgotten I had these. Remembered the day I got them. The day after the dedication of his gravestone. My uncles called me in to the shop.

"Take these, Asher. You're the oldest. We don't know what to do with them."

"Toss them."

"You do it, we can't. These were your father's old customers. They meant something to him."

I looked through forty-three years of patterns. Why had my father kept these men who had died or moved away or had given up hand-tailored suits for ready-to-wear? Now even the tailor was dead. What could anyone possibly want with them? But I'd taken them home, shutting them away in a corner of my basement because they'd mattered to my father. He'd kept them as proof of who he was, what he'd accomplished in his life. Who was I to destroy that?

"You were wrong," I said, my tears falling onto these pieces of people who never loved my father, never needed him to love them, "*I* am the proof of who you were. Me and Martha and Freyla and Pearl and Mookey and Norm. We're living proof, not these." I grabbed up handfuls of arms and legs, fronts and backs. "Why couldn't you have been as proud of us as you were of these? Why couldn't you have loved us as much?"

I wanted these out of my house, now. These were my father's ghosts, not mine. I shoved the pattern pieces back and hauled the boxes up to the kitchen.

The storm that had been simmering when I went down to the basement now raged full boil. Violent gusts of wind rammed the windows. Tree branches lashed the house. A thick screen of snow unrolled past the windows like lace yanked from a bolt.

Not a day to go out.

The only day to go out.

My father died on a day like this.

I bound the pattern boxes together with heavy twine, then dug my Bears' game gear out of the back closet: down coat, Timberland boots, wool hat with ear flaps, thermal gloves and wool scarf. I slid the boxes, too heavy and awkward to carry, along the snow to my car, cutting them apart again to load them inside. The cemetery was an hour's drive on a good day. I let the car warm up a few minutes then began my long crawl south and west across the city.

This was no day to go.

The only day to go.

"Asher, come," my uncle had said, hanging up before I could ask. As if I needed to. My father's generation used phones only for business or matters of life and death. A call was a command.

I'd bolted from the house, skidding along icy walks, fighting through blocks of knee-high drifts to his shop. Too late to say good-bye. I stood surrounded by my uncles as the funeral home drivers lifted my father onto the cot. The smell of the split-pea soup I'd spent the morning cooking clung to my clothes, a frivolous fragrance in this somber world of cloth and leather and machine oil. The open buckles on the driver's galoshes rattled as the men slipped and struggled up the snowy steps from the basement shop. It was years before I made split-pea soup again. When I did, I smelled the tailor shop, heard the boot buckles, felt the pain of not having said good-bye.

The approach road to the old cemetery, dimly dented from an earlier plowing, was covered over again with fresh snow and deep drifts. No traffic moved in either direction. Snow as dense as spring fog bounced my headlights back at me. Creeping along the tall wrought-iron fence at ten miles an hour, I nearly missed the entrance, fishtailing at the last moment through the gates into the cemetery.

Quiet.

White.

Thick snow mounded over generations of headstones like marshmallows melting on hot chocolate. Poorly marked roads wound around and around and back onto themselves. I hadn't been here since the day before Jeff's bar mitzvah. How did I expect to find my father?

A bench. I remembered a concrete bench and an oak tree near the grave. I sat while Jeff read his Haftorah to his grandfather. If it embarrassed Jeff to read aloud to a dead man, he never said. He chanted the story of Abraham sacrificing Isaac in flawless Hebrew, then laid a stone on the grave. I hugged him, overwhelmed by the love I felt, the pride. And the sorrow, knowing my own father never felt that for me. I never went back. My sisters came once a year to put flowers on the grave and tell their favorite Papa stories. I didn't have time. None of his sons did.

A few times the car's wheels angled up onto graves set too close to the road. Deep snow scraped the underbelly. Traction was a sometimes thing. My eyes strained against the white for familiar landmarks. It took a while, but I found the bench, the oak. I slid to a stop and dragged the boxes out of the car, clutching them as I trudged through the snow. My ankle caught and twisted in a buried rut. I rammed my shin full-force against a drift-buried stone. I fell, got up, fell again. Snow shoved up my pant legs, fell down my gloves, packed into my boots. The wind burned raw against my face.

My father lay waiting where I'd abandoned him all those years ago. I swept the snow off his stone with the arm of my coat, then cleaned the snow-clogged inscription with my fingertips. Beloved husband and father.

"A family does what needs doing," he'd said when I'd complained about having to care for the others. "Those of us blessed by being firstborn are responsible for all those that follow. I did for my brothers. And you'll do for your brothers and sisters."

My hands cramped, the cold froze my fingers into claws. Maybe if I'd had a better father, I'd have learned how to be more of a father to my son. I waited to feel the old anger and hurt. They didn't come. Our time had passed. I would never hear him say he loved me. I would never hear him say he was proud of me. It was time to put him to rest.

"I brought you a present," I said, opening the boxes on his grave. "Old friends to keep you warm."

Layer by layer, I set the butcher paper arms, fronts, backs, pants over the length of his grave. Pieces of a lifetime. He hadn't had a childhood, either. Why should it occur to him that I might want one? The wind stopped suddenly as if someone shut a door. The only sound in the cemetery was the soft tapping of snowfall on paper as I built up the brown blanket.

I took a few pattern pieces back to the car and, twisting them into a rope, held the cigarette lighter to one end, blowing on the small flame until the pieces caught. Shielding the fire with my hand, I returned to the grave. Falling to my knees, I bent over the pattern pieces and held my small fire to the edges. The papers smoldered and I blew life into the embers, coaxing them into flames. The wind started up again as if the door were thrown open, whipping snow across the cemetery.

"Yis-gad-dal v'yis-kad-dash sh'mey rab-bo," I began, chanting the mourner's prayer as the patterns flared.

A great red blaze rose against the storm. I saw Jeff standing in this place, a fragile child wrapped in his prayer shawl, chanting to my father. Abraham did not sacrifice his son. I would not sacrifice mine. Pattern pieces flew flaming into the air. It was too late for me and my father. But I was still here. And my son. There was still time for us. The fire raged, taking on a life of its own, warming me against the storm.

"—o'leynu v'al kol yis-ro-el, v'im'roo O-men." I finished as the last of the fiery pieces burned themselves out and were swept away, their charred remains skipping black tracks across the snow.

The car coughed against the cold, idling hard. I flicked the wipers full speed and shifted into gear. In the near-zero visibility, I could no longer tell where any of the roads ended and graves began. Travel was impossible. My best bet was to aim for the dim halo of light that marked the cemetery office.

62

How could I work when I didn't have half the supplies I needed? Who could fit costumes without threads, needles, pins, and tailor's chalk? I must have dropped my little canvas bag when Asher jumped me coming out of the closet. There it was again, that thunk in my chest every time I thought of him. Dammit, Asher, why aren't you in Paris? Why, after all our years together, did you have to pick this moment to finally listen to me?

The storm that had been moving in when I'd killed my opossum took a real hold on the city overnight. Ice-coated branches bent under the weight and snapped in the wind. The rain froze as it fell, turning sidewalks and streets into rivers of solid ice. I inched my way out to my car only to find it encased in ice, the doors and keyholes glazed shut. No one with any sense was going anywhere. Which, of course, left out Zack, who called at eight in the morning to say he'd hijacked a city snow plow to the rink and would be working there all day if I needed him.

I spent much of the day trying not to think of Asher. The best thing was to keep busy, organizing as much of the costumes as I could by phone, lining up local hockey teams whose uniforms matched the colors of the teams we'd used in Chicago, giving instructions to the casting director on how the extras should be dressed. Working in Chicago had spoiled me; I knew where to find anyone and anything in seconds. Napoleon, Ohio, was short on raw materials, and half the Toledo companies I tried to reach were closed because of the storm. Everything took longer than necessary. Still, wardrobe would be in pretty good shape by the time Mel came with the crew. By then the storm should have let up, the roads would be plowed, and I could get out to buy supplies I'd need.

Ten times during the day I put my hand on the phone to call home, and ten times I took it away. Who would have thought living apart would be this hard? When Fanny toured with her troupe, she always made leaving Daddy and me seem the most natural thing in the world. What had she said to me at the home? "Asher isn't Daddy and you're not me." Maybe they didn't love each other the same way we did. Used to? Still do, please God. Maybe my parents needed distance in their relationship, the same distance that was tearing Asher and me apart. So what happens now?

I picked up the phone and forced myself to dial, not knowing what I'd say. The answering machine clicked on after two rings. Either Asher wasn't home or he wasn't picking up. I punched in the code and collected messages.

"Mrs. Rose, this is Leon Weintraub's daughter again." Again? "I just talked to my father and I want you to call me as soon as you get this message. My number is . . ." Pushy-sounding lady. I jotted the name and number, trying to figure out who she was. Probably a fifteenth cousin thirty times removed who wanted me to make a freebie MOB dress.

"Mrs. Rose. This is Mrs. Lipshultz at the Wedgewood. Your mother left after lunch and did not return for dinner. Please advise us if she is with you." Dinner? This call was from yesterday. Oh, Fanny. Where's Asher?

"Mrs. Rose? This is Mrs. Lipshultz again. Your mother is still not back." What time, Lipshultz? Give me a *time*.

"Mrs. Rose, this is Mrs. Lipshultz. It is now eight o'clock at night. Since we have not heard from you, we are notifying the police that your mother is missing." Why now, Fanny? Couldn't you have been good for just a little while?

"Mrs. Rose, this is Sergeant Webster of the Chicago Police Department. We have a report from the Wedgewood Home that your mother is missing. Could you give me a call when you get this message? I have a few questions."

Yes, said the switchboard girl at the Wedgewood, Fanny was still missing. I called Sergeant Webster. Our conversation was short. I had no answers to his questions, no idea where Fanny might be. When the few dollars she brought to the Wedgewood were stolen from her nightstand, she wouldn't keep any money. Where can you go with no money?

"Do you think your mother might have done harm to herself?" he asked.

"My mother's a survivor, Sergeant. She's not the type to throw herself into Lake Michigan at night."

"Why not?"

"No audience."

Maybe she'd gone back to her apartment. I called Mr. Francosi, asked him to take a look. He called back. The boxes I'd been packing were still in the middle of her living room, and the heat was turned down. He didn't think she'd been there but he promised to call if she showed up. Next I left a call for Dr. Fishman. I doubted she'd called him, but I was desperate. Fanny didn't have all that many people in her life anymore. Lately, not even me. Stop it, Sarah. This is not your fault.

The airport phone lines were busy forever. The storm shut everything down. Normally, they said, the next Chicago flight would be seven-thirty in the morning. *Why go home? Fanny would probably walk back into the Wedgewood any minute now.* I called the Detroit airport. All flights were grounded until further notice. No one was making any predictions or promises. I put my name on every possible waiting list. Then I called Marko.

"Sarah? Hi."

"How's California treating you?"

"So-so." He sounded guarded.

"Is Greg in the room with you?"

"Right."

"Things pretty rough?"

"Yes, that's right. So how's by you?"

"Marko, I hate to lay this on you, but . . ." I told him about being in Toledo, about Fanny disappearing, about needing someone to take over so I could go home and straighten things out.

"Let me make a few calls," he said. "I know some people in Detroit. I'll get back to you."

"You're not angry?"

"Come on, Sarah. You know if I were in your place, I'd make the same decision." Marko hung up, calling back a few minutes later with the name of a Detroit costumer who could start the next morning. "And I'll call Mel, explain what happened. Don't worry about it. Shit hits everyone's fan."

I reached the costumer, making arrangements for him to pick up the script notes and costumes from Zack. Next, I tacked a note on Zack's door telling him to call me when he got in, no matter how late.

I called our house, left a message on the machine for Asher telling him about Fanny. I left my number in case he came home, in case he hadn't followed me right out our kitchen door and flown off to Paris. I was about to hang up, the phone hovering over the cradle, when I brought it slowly back to my ear. "I hated the way we left each other yesterday." And? "I hope you're still home when I get back." And what else? "I love you."

Now all I could do was wait.

I sat in bed with the phone on my stomach, watching it rise and fall with each breath. In my next life I would live where there were no telephones, no answering machines. I would never live farther than a holler from the people I loved. Not my husband, not my children, not my mother. I needed to touch one of them, all of them, right now. Needed to be hugged and loved and—the phone rang.

"Yes?"

"Fanny told you the news?" asked Dr. Fishman.

"What news?"

He paused. "Why did you call?"

"What news?"

"They took routine X rays when Fanny entered the home. There's a spot on one breast. I want it biopsied. Fanny says no. We've been fighting about it. I thought that's why you called."

"Fanny's missing. She left the home and no one knows where she went. I thought you might have some idea."

"I'm sorry, Sarah. If I hear from her, I'll call you. And, when you find her, please try and talk her into the biopsy."

"Got to catch her first."

"No easy trick."

"You got that right."

I called the floor nurse at the home every half hour. Nothing. No word. No idea where she might be.

Oh, Fanny, why are you doing this? To get even with me for putting you into the home? It was your idea, remember? Are you angry I left you to go to Ohio? Well, you win. I'm coming home. Not that I have any idea what I'm going to be able to do in Chicago. But at least I won't feel so far away. And when I find you, we're going to sit down for a real heart-to-heart. This time I promise to listen a little better.

Zack knocked on my door at two in the morning. Big and beautiful and smelling of snow, he opened his parka, letting me wrap myself inside and have a good hard cry.

"There'll always be another movie," he said. "But mothers only come around once."

"Where'd you get so smart so young?"

"I happen to have the world's neatest mother. If she was missing, I'd be walking back to Chicago right now."

"Thanks."

"Come on, I'll help move the costumes to my van."

We worked in the stinging sleet, dragging boxes and bags.

"Can I buy you a drink of thanks?" I said when we finished, not wanting to wait alone. In case the police called. In case they found Fanny . . . somewhere.

"Can't," he said, "I've brought back company." A young girl peeked out the curtains of his room. "Want me to try to stop by later?"

"No. Thanks. I'll be fine. See you back in Chicago." He hugged me long and hard and I hugged back, forcing myself to smile as I let go so he wouldn't think I couldn't manage this small matter of a disappearing mother.

I spent the night lying in bed watching the minutes change on the MotOhio digital clock. Please let the storm stop and roads clear and flights take off by morning. Fanny, Asher, where are you?

Lie still. Press my hands on my belly where a slow hole burns from the inside out. Are you safe? Lie still, pull one end of the night through my life, try to thread these mismatched pieces together. Daughter, wife, mother, artist. Have to mend the holes I've torn in this crazy quilt, keep it from falling apart.

One o'clock two o'clock three o'clock rock, glowing red numbers changing moving marching to morning stomping sleep to smithereens. I can still get six hours' sleep, five and a half, five. Take two aspirin and call me in the morning wash them down with one miniature scotch and water turn on midnight theater *Bamba of the Jungle,* one minute of movie and ten of vanity commercials starring small businessmen clutching platinum-blond models trying to sell me furs and cars and bridal gowns and four and a half hours' sleep and four and the second scotch tastes worse than the first and Fanny oh Fanny you're scaring me. Asher would have an idea. Asher would know something to do and three and a half and my stomach heaves from booze and lack of sleep and lying in a strange room a million miles from everywhere I want to be and my head hurts from bailing out thoughts that won't let me sleep, thoughts pouring through holes I've hacked into my life.

All right. All right. Calm and steady. Lie still. Picture Asher. Clearer. Better. Eyes. Bright, alert, sneaking peeks at me playing dolls with Martha when he thought I wouldn't notice. Eyes for me and only me as far back as I could remember. Even when his mouth said no, I won't marry you, you're too young and immature and you're too blah dee blah dee blah, even then his eyes knew the truth of Us and oh our first night together to be loved like that to be wanted for most of the years of my life by Asher who I'd loved since the beginning.

Three hours. So why am I here, drinking too much, sleeping too little, sidestepping predictable if flattering advances by a young man used to willing women? Truth time, Sarah. This is not about the job. And, as much as it hurts, as much as you wish it, Fanny will never be the Fanny of your youth. She is struggling to live her life one day at a time and you must give her the dignity to do that. So, what is the truth? What is it, Sarah?

I am here because I am afraid to have come and gone and never made a difference. That is the truth. How can people stand to live unnoticed? Does anyone else in the universe worry about this? Maybe it's the curse of growing up Fanny Feldman's daughter, surrounded by stars who would live forever. So where are they now, all those great people? Where are the fans that lined up for hours hoping for a glimpse of their faces? Who can name any of them anymore?

Oh, God, Asher Rose. What have I done to us? The one thing I got right in my life was loving you. That is my greatness. I will find Fanny—please God let her be all right—and I will tell her I am leaving to be with you in France, or England, or Pago Pago. Wherever you want to go. And we will work out a plan for the rest of our lives, however long that may be.

If you will just come home to me.

If you will just.

If you.

63

What an experience. Wait until I tell Sarah. She wasn't going to believe this. She had to. Spending a night in a cemetery was too wild to make up. Playing gin rummy all night with Wenzel Robinson, the cranky old caretaker. Sleeping on a cot in the office. "Keep it for fainters. Women most times. Boss stocks in smellin' salts, but most ladies like a shot o' my whiskey."

Old Wenzel and I swapped stories and worked through a bottle of Black Label while he cleaned me out of every dollar, shilling and ha'penny I had. Then I stretched out on the cot and that's all she wrote. Whether it was the time change or the booze, I didn't wake up until nine the next morning. The plow finally got through to us around noon.

It felt good to come home. I unloaded the car, a couple of bottles of Black Label to send to Wenzel, groceries to fill the empty fridge, graph paper to design my wine cellar, champagne for whenever Sarah came home. Something about spending twenty-four hours in a cemetery put the whole world in perspective. I'd wait for Sarah. We'd work everything out from there.

I heard the phone while I juggled the groceries and my keys. Please let it be Sarah. Please don't hang up. I dropped the keys, picked them up, unlocking the door and bursting into the kitchen as the machine took the call.

"Mrs. Rose. This is Mr. Weintraub's daughter again. I *assume* you got my last message." I remembered her from yesterday. The lady with the attitude. "I really must insist you call me as soon as possible." Right. Sarah *loves* to be told what to do. "I don't approve, don't approve at all of what your mother is doing." Fanny? What was Fanny up to now? I picked up the phone.

"Hello, this is Mr. Rose."

"Thank goodness. I was getting desperate. Not that I want to call the authorities on Mrs. Feldman. But she can't stay in—"

"Hold on, hold on, hold on."

"—my father's apartment. It's hardly the sort of—"

"Hold it!" I yelled. She held. "Now, I just walked in. I've been gone for a while. I don't know what you're talking about." Sarah's scarf was on the table where I'd left it yesterday. I pressed it to my nose, held it against my face.

"Oh?" She didn't believe me. "Well, you *do* know my father, Leon Weintraub." It was an accusation.

"Name's not familiar."

"Your mother-in-law's neighbor?"

"My mother-in-law lives at the Wedgewood Home. I think you must have the wrong—"

"She *used* to live at the Wedgewood Home. Right now she lives with my father."

"Fanny?"

"I will meet you there in one hour."

"Where?"

"Her old apartment building."

"Look, I've had a rough couple of days. I just walked in—"

"One hour, Mr. Rose. Apartment three-fourteen."

I looked under F for Fanny Feldman in Sarah's book. Then under W for the Wedgewood. Then under H for Home. She'd listed the Wedgewood Home under M for Mom. The warm voice answering the Wedgewood phone frosted at the mention of Fanny's name.

"You will kindly come and collect her things as soon as possible. And might I say that this is the first time since I have been with this wonderful organization that I have had to ask someone to leave."

Good old Fanny. Still kicking up her heels. So what if it disrupts Sarah's life and my life and Mr. Weintraub's daughter's life and the lives at the Wedgewood Home?

So why are you smiling?

I should cause so much trouble when I'm seventy-eight.

I wrapped Sarah's scarf around my neck as I left, trying to keep her near me. Like armor. Like love.

64

"Can't you go any faster?"

"Look, lady. I'm already five miles over the limit."

The one time I wanted a Kamikaze cabby I got a milquetoast afraid of blowing his Good Driver's Certificate. I should have driven my car to the airport. Would have if I'd known I'd be coming right home. Fanny, Fanny, Fanny, what are you up to now?

The Detroit costumer Marko put me in contact with was a pro who picked up on everything right away. I'd keep in contact by phone, walk him through the costume changes and script notes. Taking off mid-movie might be professional suicide. Word goes out in movieland, oh yes it does, goes out and out and out. Just pray the next director—if there is a next director, if I'm not blackballed from filmdom, if Asher and I can work my work into our new life together—just pray that director has a mother. Oh, Fanny, what are you doing to my life?

"Why are you pulling over?" Easy, Sarah. Easy.

"Ambulance." It shot past, siren blaring. I'd heard that sound all night, lying awake, staring into the darkness. Fanny, her thin body in a thin dress, freezing to death in some godforsaken alley. Fanny, disoriented, walking in front of a car. Fanny riding the El aimlessly all night, not knowing where she was, or who, or why.

I'd called the home as soon as my flight hit O'Hare. Yes, they said, they'd received word that Fanny was with a Mr. Leon Weintraub. They supplied Weintraub's phone number and address. Fanny's apartment building? Weintraub must be the Leon of the cigar and towel. Fanny was safe. Thank you, God. Thank you. That was, said the home, all the information they had. And would I please come collect Fanny's belongings? Wonder if that included the thousands it had cost to get her in. Probably not. I tried Weintraub's number twice from the airport. Busy. I'd grab a cab and go straight there.

65

The lady on the walker thanked me for holding the lobby door open for her. I was glad for the snail's pace, not at all anxious to go up to Mr. Leon Weintraub's apartment. This wasn't for me to do. Sarah always dealt with Fanny. My mother was easy. I always knew exactly where she was.

How did Sarah grow up with this kind of craziness? Maybe it was because she had a nomadic mother that she thought it was important to stay home with Jeff and Maxi when they were young. Sarah put her career on hold so her children wouldn't walk into an empty house after school. The way she had. The way I would have loved to.

The third-floor elevator doors opened to the smells of cooking: soups, bread, coffee, meat. A person could live on smells this rich. I stepped out into the sound of yelling. That was probably what had brought the natives out of their apartments and into the hall. I passed like a giant through the white-haired receiving line. Not a doubt in my mind which apartment the yelling was coming from. A woman outside number 314 grabbed my arm, pointing a dripping wooden spoon toward the yelling.

"You do something. Yeah, tatalah?"

"I'll try."

"That's a good boy."

The ranks closed behind me. I knocked once. Twice. A small man with steel wool eyebrows opened the door.

"Yes?" He jammed an unlit cigar in the corner of his mouth. Down the hall behind him, a highly agitated woman shouted at Fanny. Mr. Weintraub's daughter, I presumed.

"I am Fanny's son-in-law," I said.

"Good for you." He didn't budge.

"Your daughter called me."

"Good for her."

"May I come in?"

"It's bad enough she's here."

"I don't want to make trouble."

"Then go home."

"I just want to know what's going on."

He shrugged and shuffled away, leaving it up to me whether to enter or leave. I followed him down a hallway into the combat zone wishing I were anywhere else. Sarah was the one who could handle yelling. She'd been raised to it. This particular screaming seemed to center around a pile of shiny black cloth on the sofa.

"You have no right spending his money like this."

"What are you so worried about Leon's money?" asked Fanny. Smaller than I remembered, thinner.

"My father worked hard his whole life for that money. My mother did without for that money. It's not for you to squander."

"Sssssquaaaaahhhhnder?" Fanny stretched the word into seven syllables. "For what is Leon saving? Old age, maybe?"

"Satin sheets?" The woman grabbed the black fabric and shook it in Fanny's face. "You order him satin sheets from an ad in a girlie magazine?"

Fanny smiled at Leon, who poured himself a healthy schnapps. He raised the glass in toast to Fanny and tossed the liquor down. Didn't flinch. Strong man. Maybe strong enough for Fanny. Miracles have come in stranger packages.

"Leon happens to look very sexy on black sheets," said Fanny.

"Don't you talk dirty about my father."

"I'm not talking dirty. I'm telling what is."

Go for it, Fanny. Face flushed, eyes sparkling, Fanny advanced like a warrior in the heat of battle. No complaining old lady here. No dried-up lifeless heap whining for attention, waiting for death. This was the Fanny of my youth, the theatrical woman who laughed and cried, yelled and whispered, loved and hated. This was the passionate mother of my passionate wife, and she had decided to live again. I know what that feels like, Fanny. Go for it! She faced her attacker chin up, shoulders squared, welcoming the daughter's words like kindling to fire. Should I jump in? Should I wait? Fanny was doing fine without me.

"And where," demanded the woman, "is the painting from over the sofa?"

"It was a boring painting."

"My mother and I picked it out. It's a very fine work."

"Ten dollars from a garage sale. The ticket's still on the back." The woman flared her nostrils. A wisp of smoke trailed out. "If you ask me," said Fanny, "you overpaid."

"Those colors are perfect for the sofa."

"Leon's painting a real masterpiece for over the sofa."

"Painting? Daddy?"

"Thursday nights at the Meyer Kaplan JCC. Oil paints and nude models." The woman's jaw unhinged. "He's almost finished. We're having it framed."

"And how much is *that* going to cost?"

"The frame's a gift. From me."

"I don't want your frame. I don't want your gifts. I want my mother's painting back over my father's sofa!"

"You love it so much?" Fanny reached behind the sofa and pulled out an ugly still life. "Here. Take it. A gift from us to you."

Leon sat in his chair, opening the *Wall Street Journal*. If he wasn't going to break this up, why should I?

Both women noticed me at the same time.

"Mr. Rose?" asked the woman.

Fanny rushed to me, grabbing my arm. "Where's Sarah?"

"Mr. Rose, you will please talk to your mother-in-law."

"I've been calling," said Fanny. "Midnight, even, she's not home. I could have died. Who would know?"

Leon leaned back in his La-Z-Boy, popping up the footrest, folding his paper to the stock page.

"Sarah's fine, Fanny. She's on location in Ohio."

"Ohio?" Fanny had forgotten where Sarah was. The forgetting had frightened her. Her face brightened with the dim flicker of memory. "Ohio," she said, tears of relief in her eyes. She blinked them back. She would not show weakness in front of the enemy.

"Mr. Rose, can we *please* talk about this? I have an appointment in half an hour."

"Appointment." Fanny snorted. "By her, a tennis game is an 'appointment.' What is the beauty shop? An 'executive conference'?"

"Fanny," I said, trying to hide my smile, "what's going on here?"

Fanny walked to Leon's chair and sat on the arm, resting her hand on his shoulder. Possession is nine tenths. "Leon asked me to come live with him—"

"My father *never!*"

"—and I have accepted."

Leon ran a finger down the NASDAQ columns, putting checks next to several stocks. He didn't seem inclined to jump in one way or the other. What would Sarah want me to do? What would she do if she were here? I tried turning it around. What if it was my mother moving in with Leon? Impossible to imagine. Where would a woman who couldn't walk out her front door find this kind of courage? Some things, Sarah, just can't be turned around.

"Fanny," I said, "can I talk to you a moment?"

"There's nothing you can say to me you can't say in front of Leon." She kissed his forehead. "We are without secrets."

"Leon?" I said. "Would you mind putting down your paper and getting in on this?"

He sighed, closed the paper, and took off his glasses. "What?" he asked. "What do you want from me?"

"See!" said the daughter.

"See!" said Fanny. I didn't.

"Leon, did you ask Fanny to come live with you?"

"What kind of question?" He patted her hand. "How could I let such a woman stay in such a place? You had no business doing what you did."

"You mean sending her to the Wedgewood? Fanny, tell him, you begged Sarah to get you in there."

"Who knew what it was really like?" Fanny fisted her tiny hand on her chest. Camile. The lace handkerchief pulled from her sleeve added a nice touch. "I begged Sarah to take me home. She wouldn't listen." Maybe because her husband in London, about to receive favors from a nude young lady, yelled at Sarah to leave Fanny in the home. It was easy to be a genius long-distance, to tell everyone how to run their lives. Like Sarah. Like Jeff. "My Leon"—Fanny bent and kissed his forehead—"my Leon listened. He came and rescued me. Just like a white knight."

"My father's too good," said his daughter. "Always has been. A regular soft touch for people he feels sorry for."

"Sorry for!" Fanny jumped up. "Sorry for!"

"Why else would he invite you here?"

"I happen to be de-LIGHT-ful company."

"Company he can get on a park bench. My father needs care. Twice a week I come do his shopping, his cleaning, his cooking, his laundry, his dry cleaning, take him to doctors' appointments, buy his clothes. If he can't take care of himself, how do you expect him to take care of you?"

"I take care of myself," said Fanny.

"Right." The woman started straightening the magazines on the coffee table with a vengeance. "That's why your daughter put you in the Wedgewood."

"I wanted to go—"

"Because you take such good care of yourself. Or maybe your daughter can't be bothered doing for you what I do for my father."

"Now just you hold on one minute," I said. She whirled around, confronting me, hands on hips, eyes blazing.

"I'm not taking care of both of them," she said. "I'll tell you that right now."

"No one expects you to."

"Then just what, Mr. Rose, do you intend that we do about them?" As if "they" weren't right next to us, listening.

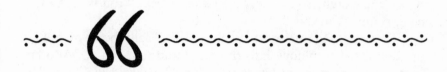

I joined the quiet group clustered in the hall outside Leon's apartment, straining to hear through the partially open door.

"What's happening?" I asked.

"Leon's daughter is trying to tell her father how he should live," said a man.

I reached over their heads and pushed the door all the way open. We peered down the hallway into the living room. Fanny sat on Leon's chair arguing with a woman. That must be Leon's daughter, the one who called and left messages without telling me what she was calling about.

A man walked into view. Asher! Asher was here! Not Paris. Thank you, God. I owe you one. I worked my way closer to the doorway.

"I don't know," he was saying. "I don't know what we are going to do." When had he come? Why? "What I do know is Sarah has done everything for her mother." Oh, Asher. "Like you do for your father, that's how Sarah does for Fanny. The difference is Sarah does it with love and compassion and humor. Never once, in all these years, have I heard her martyr herself the way you just did. She has never once complained how much work Fanny is for her. And believe me there have been plenty of rough times these last few months." Asher walked over to my mother, stood her up, and put his arms around her. He hugged her, rocking her side to side.

I wasn't alone. The thought hit hard and clear. All this time I'd tried to keep Fanny from Asher and Asher from Fanny. Protect them from the needs and demands of the other. I could do it all. I could handle it all. No need to burden you with my problems. The same way Asher had protected me from his family's problems. We were wrong. The weight was too much to carry alone, and it nearly broke us.

"Sarah loves you, Fanny," said Asher. I could stand all day and watch them together. "She put her life on hold for you. For both of us." Oh, Asher, welcome home. Fanny's arms came up around Asher and slowly, so slowly, hugged him back. "You want to stay here, Fanny? You stay."

"I have a thing or two to say about this," said the woman. Part of me wanted to plunge into the room and take her on. Another part, a part so crazy in love with Asher Rose, held me back. The daughter of an actress knows timing. This was Asher's scene.

"Fanny is an adult," said Asher. "She has a few years on me."

"Not so many," said Fanny.

"Your father's been around a while, too. I figure they have a right to decide how they want to live their lives."

"And what if he gets sick? Or your mother-in-law needs care? I have my own life to live."

"Then I suggest you live it," said Asher. "And let them live theirs." Way to go, Champ! Let her have it with both barrels.

"Well"—the woman shoved her arms into her coat—"I can see I'm not wanted around here. Good-bye, Daddy." She kissed Leon's cheek. "I'm not sure when I'll be able to come see you."

"Whenever."

"It might not be until next week." A mild threat.

"Next week is good," said Leon.

"Maybe not until the week after." A clear warning.

"Fine, fine. I'm always happy to see you."

"I'll be sure to call first."

She stormed out of the apartment and we stepped aside to let her pass. This woman was a fighter. An agitator. Good. Fanny liked a formidable foe. She thrived on contests of power and will. They would carry her through her next illness. And there would be a next illness. *If* she let Dr. Fishman biopsy the spot on her breast and *if* it turned out to be benign, something else would come along. But at this moment, she was upright and feisty. And it beat the hell out of sitting in the Wedgewood lobby waiting for her next meal.

Something, I couldn't say what, kept me from going into the apartment. Watching my husband and my mother when they didn't know I was watching, seeing their tenderness and caring for each other, overwhelmed me with love for them both. Asher took out his wallet, slipping Fanny money. She tucked it into her bra, then pulled his head down, planting a kiss on each cheek. I backed out of the doorway down the hall, letting myself into Fanny's apartment. Most of her things were boxed and labeled. "Sell." "Bring to Fanny." "Give to charity." Now I'd have to unpack it all. An independent woman like Fanny should have the freedom of her own place. It was here if she wanted, or she could stay across the hall with Leon. What mattered was she had a choice.

"Pssst." The sound caught me halfway down the hall. All the tenants had gone back into their apartments. There was no one around but me. "Pssst." There it was again.

The door to Fanny's old apartment opened a crack. A hand snaked out, danced a few exotic twists and turns, then crooked a finger at me. I walked to the door. The hand—ring finger broken in a backyard game of peggy-bounce-out, baby finger scarred trying to cut the ends off corn on the cob with a butter knife—was connected to a naked arm—one chicken pox scar at the wrist where she picked even though I warned her not to, the world's cutest freckle just below the elbow.

"Yes?" I said, gathering the fingers in my hand, kissing the tips.

"Excuse me, sir," said the voice behind the door, "but I seem to have misplaced my clothes."

"How very careless of you." I guided one of her fingers around my lips and sucked it into my mouth.

"Yes, well, I seem to have misplaced several precious things, lately."

"Weren't you afraid of losing them forever?"

"Very much afraid."

I walked my fingers up her arm, around behind the door. "You're right," I said. "You have misplaced your clothes."

"I was wondering, if you would be so kind, that is, if you are not awfully terribly horribly busy just now, if you would help me look for them."

"You're in luck," I said, walking into the apartment, gathering Sarah in my arms, "time is the one thing I have plenty of."

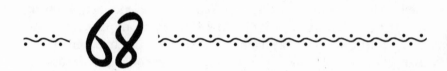

Later, I pulled Fanny's blankets up over us, snuggling into Asher's warmth, my heart pounding as crazy strong as when we were kids. I pressed my ear against his chest, listening to his heartbeat, my head riding on his even sleep-breaths. Nuzzling his chest hairs, I inhaled his special blend of sex and sweat and skin.

I drifted into a dream of climbing the middle girders of a tall bridge, trying to see ahead to the other side. It was shrouded in mist. I felt danger waiting, but couldn't see. Asher stayed behind, afraid.

"Come on," I called, "it's safe," terrified I was wrong, that our bridge would collapse, come crashing down around us. Asher risked one step, then another, reaching out for my hand. The bridge swayed crazily as we crossed, metal plates and fat cables screeching and groaning under our feet. We held on to each other, knowing one wrong step could make any second our last, not daring to breathe until we reached the other side.

Safe. We held each other, couldn't get enough of holding each other. The mist ahead of us lifted and we saw new bridges taking shape on the horizon. Hand in hand, we walked toward them, more curious than afraid. After this crossing, anything was possible. Anything at all.